BOUND BY SECRETS

A.D. DUMAS

BOUND BY SECRETS

A.D. DUMAS

TO THE ONE WHO TAUGHT ME WHAT IT IS TO
BE LOVED BEYOND MEASURE
AND UNBURDEN MYSELF FROM THE WEIGHT
OF MY OWN SECRETS.

CHAPTER 1

"Hey, do you mind?"

"Huh?"

I turn to face a lady who looks more exasperated than those dogs that I've seen online. Ya know, the ones who have to entertain a new puppy and the owner finds the whole situation *so cute*, but you know that their dog's patience has become so thin that the dullest knife could tear away at the last scraps of it. And still, I'm positive that the dog has more patience than this woman standing in front of me.

Still, judging by her gaudy ensemble, I assume she's the type of new money where she's so insecure about herself that she doesn't care how she looks as long as she shows off her wealth. I mean come on, who the hell wears Gucci, Celine, and Dior all in one outfit? And each piece shows the symbols so plainly that you can't even *pretend* it all fits together. Maybe she could get away with the Jimmy Choo's on her feet paired with the Celine clutch, but nothing more.

I, for one, know how to stay *humble* when I walk around. It's not that I'm broke or anything, though that's what people all seem to assume. Just that sweats are way more comfortable and maneuverable than those form-fitting dresses and stuff. I mean, seriously, everyone worries about what will hang out of a dress, but it's not even a thought if you're just in sweats.

And I also eat instant noodles by *choice*. You'd be surprised by the variety of meals you can make by adding different proteins and vegetables. You can never really go wrong.

Anyway, I'm getting sidetracked, and I'm almost certain that the gaudy woman is wondering if I've lost the plot. Maybe I should pretend I did.

I wonder if she'll get scared off if I continue my blank stare. For people like her, they tend to hate things they deem are beneath them.

"I'll pay you."

Pay me? Pay me for what, exactly? Did I miss some part of this conversation?

Instead of a verbal response, I quirk a brow. The meaning should be obvious to anyone who's ever learned the basics of etiquette, right?

"What? Are you dumb? Didn't you hear a word I said?"

She sighs dramatically. I'm talking about the type of dramatic that we like to think is left behind in high school, only to realize that many people peaked there and can't come to terms with it. It's okay, kind stranger. I won't let everyone know your secret.

It's sad though. The woman's love of herself seems to be inhibiting her ability to notice social cues and, you know, be a normal, functioning member of society. It must be really uncomfortable for her with how far up her ass that stick is.

It's okay. As a favor to everyone else here, I suppose that I'll entertain her so that they don't have to go through the same spectacular loss of brain cells that I've incurred during this brief interaction.

Trying not to sound completely disinterested, I ask, "Pay me for what?"

Oof. I hope that didn't come out as robotic as it sounded. I mean, seriously. How can I not when this woman thinks that offering to pay someone without stating the terms is the best idea to get what she wants? I've seen shitty, scammy contracts more thought out than that. At least they understand payment is usually done in an exchange for a product or service. And typically, those are outlined before even offering.

I won't be surprised if one day I see her walking around devoid of all her gaudy clothing and accessories, which would be fantastic for everyone who's forced to witness this eyesore. All because she got scammed out of whatever fortune she found herself bathing in.

She rolls her eyes at me like I did something offensive. If anything, she's the one ruining the peace of my day. My day was going just fine without her. I had literally just broken free from the people who had been following me for *ages*. They thought they were so sneaky.

They should know their stalking skills were shabby at best. This woman just happened to intervene as I was having fun plotting which way would be the most entertaining to ensure that they never bother me again. Maybe I'll—

"We're standing outside of city hall. What do you *think* I'm here for? Obviously, I need you to witness my marriage with my sweetie honey pie."

I have to put serious effort into not gagging. Sweetie honey pie? Who the hell calls someone that? Even worse. Who *enjoys* being called that? With nicknames like that, this marriage has to be doomed, right? There has to be some overcompensation going on.

Apart from that, how am I supposed to know that being by city hall pretty much screams "I'm open to witnessing your marriage for a price" to all the rich snobs? Maybe next time I come, I should wear a shirt exclusively saying "not here to help you get married." I mean, seriously, everyone knows that you need two witnesses to get married.

I hold in my laugh as I try, very seriously, to ask, "So you want to pay me for witnessing your wedding?"

I peer around, looking for a man who might be dumb enough to shackle himself to her. I mean, I should at least do my civil duty and make sure that he's not marrying her against his will. It's not like she's a huge catch.

She's somehow both self-obsessed enough to think that her gaudy attire is appropriate to be worn in public—let *alone* get married in—and dumb enough not to realize that she needs two witnesses to get married. Or maybe he also had an oversight and they're two dumb peas in a pod.

She moves her head, blocking my field of vision and forcing my attention back on her.

"I believe that's what I said."

No need to be rude, lady.

As I glance through the throng of people, my eyes land on someone who seems rich, but in a less gaudy way than her. He's staring in our direction so I can only assume that he must be the groom in question. Maybe *he's* the good fortune that she soaking in. I see now. She's got to marry him to secure her bag, I guess.

The poor lovesick look in his eyes is almost pathetic, but I suppose that there has to be something somewhere deep down inside of me that wants the same things. Something deep, deep, deep, *deep* down, but it's there. I think.

Still, I suppose this could become something entertaining, right? I can always plot on ways of getting rid of annoyances in my life *later*. Those stalkers should consider themselves lucky. For now, this will do. Curiosity always wins out, and I'm curious to see what man wants a woman like her and kind of show their union will be.

In my personal, unsolicited opinion, I'd say it'll be one that starts with s, ends with hit, and rhymes with fit. If you get where I'm going with this.

I shrug. "Sure."

The woman rolls her eyes again and walks toward the man. I was so right about him being her groom. Score one for me and my observation skills! But I am concerned for her eyes. My mom always used to say that one day they'd get stuck inside your head if you kept rolling them. I'm surprised it hasn't happened to this woman yet. (Yes, I'm completely aware that my mom only said that to deter me, but I think it would be hilarious to watch all the rude people walk around with their eyes stuck).

As I follow her, I watch the little lovesick man grin happily as his bride returns with me. It looks like his witness is standing off his shoulder. By the look of it, he actually *is* smart enough to know that witnesses are necessary. Maybe he thought he'd only need to bring one, and his bride would bring the other.

Whatever. Not my gaudy monkey, not my shitshow circus.

"Sweetie honey pie!"

I hold back the cringe as she hops into this man's arms like she's the star of some sappy romance movie. I mean, seriously, do people actually do this in real life? The only time I find these interactions acceptable are when it's military couples. I really do have a heart, I swear. And those couples fight tooth and nail to keep their relationship strong. It's truly admirable.

"Snuggle buggle bear!"

Excuse me? Please tell me that I heard that wrong. They really are pushing my limits right now. I feel like puking. Which would suck considering that my lunch was so delicious.

Listen, spicy noodles with shrimp and homemade kimchi is like the most elite meal one can have. Seriously, try it. The only thing that would have made it better was seaweed. It's the only reason that I left my room today.

My quest for seaweed reminded me that I had an errand to run. It became mildly annoying since it turned out I was being followed, which led me on a journey of ditching my tails and finally ending up here. Honestly, seeing this display of affection, I might have been better off pretending not to notice the tails.

Luckily, I don't have to say anything. It seems that the couple has finally remembered that to get married, they have to *actually* submit the paperwork and do all the other tedious things.

"Let's go, shmuggles."

As soon as this is done, I'm so out of here. I don't know who created the universe or if you're still out there. Please wipe my memory of these terrible nicknames after I leave here. I am *begging* you, universe. People always talk about wanting to bleach their eyes but how can I cleanse my ears?

"Yeah. Let's go, my soon to be lovey dovey hubby bubby."

Knowing that their attention is no longer on me, I clench my forehead in my hand and shake my head. They have absolutely no self-awareness. I mean, weird names like that should stay in the house, and they can benefit the world by knocking the PDA down a notch.

I'm watching them strut around, leaning into each other with his hand very obviously groping her ass and her hand under the back of the dress shirt he'll likely have to tuck in again once it's time for their pictures.

As soon as this is over, I'm having those damn shirts printed.

CHAPTER 2

The paperwork and courthouse wedding part fly by before my eyes. If I'm honest, I don't remember much of it. Was it interesting learning firsthand what these things look like? Sort of, I guess.

But I would be a liar if I said that it was fun. I don't know what I was expecting this to be. Maybe a little drama? Ya know, the type where they start arguing because someone forgot an important document? Or maybe he would learn that she was already with someone else?

But, none of that, unfortunately.

Even if that lady couldn't find a witness, the way those two interact, I doubt he'd even bat an eye at it.

Funnily enough, I remember their names being said at some points but don't remember what they were. I would blame it on me being bad at remembering names but I know that's not true. I'm *fantastic* at remembering names . . . when I care to . . . which isn't often.

Anyway, enough about me and my diverting train of thought. The happy, freshly married couple have left and I'm now a *whopping* $50 richer. I mean, I'm seriously not in it for the money. But someone who wore what she wore and now owns half of her husband's estate couldn't add a zero or two to that?

I know that I dress more relaxed than other people. But in this economy, this doesn't even cover groceries for a week. That's just downright stingy.

I hold in my laugh as I stuff the money in my pocket. I'll probably forget about it by the time that I get home and find it a few odd weeks later when I finally get around to the laundry and inevitably forget to check my pockets.

As the door to the courtroom shuts behind me, I glance both ways. I remember that I came here for some reason other than slipping my tails, but with all the chaos that just happened, I don't exactly remember what it is.

I look around me, hoping that *something* will remind me of why I had specifically chosen the courthouse as my escape route. For as smart as I am, my ADHD has always been my greatest frenemy.

Probably something to do with that shady excuse for an entertainment company, BB Media.

I mean, come on, I could have ditched those guys at the local supermarket if I wanted to. Plenty of people there and more authorities around to apprehend them if they tried anything.

Wait, speaking of authorities, why is this hallway completely empty? I mean, I could excuse the absence of normal people with ongoing meetings, and honestly, I saw that *long* line of people waiting to get married. It would explain the necessity of everyone being behind closed doors.

But there are like no police officers anywhere around here. Maybe something super shady is going on. I mean it's not the bank, but what if someone is robbing the place? At least I don't have a car this time and can't be made into the getaway driver. *Not* to say that it wasn't an interesting experience.

I can't help but chuckle to myself at the memory. I have to admit that it's become a rather fond one in my heart. Like, who can say that they would have wound up in that situation completely by accident and still managed to get off without any real trouble?

I start down the hallway opposite of the way I came. I'm admittedly a little curious about this place, and since I'm so deep in and there are no officers in sight, I feel like I have been offered a free pass to do what I want and explore as I please. I'll play the "I'm lost" card if anyone asks.

I lazily fold my hands behind my neck as I guide myself through the building, boredly drawing a mental map in my head. I do always like to know which way to go if trouble manages to find me.

"Well, where the hell is she then?"

Oh, I think I hear something interesting now. Was some poor sap left at the altar by his fiancée? See, *this* is the type of drama that I was looking for from shmuggles and sweetie honey pie. I can't help the giggle that slips out now that I know they're gone.

I mean, seriously, are they *five?*

"Grandmother, she didn't show up. I suppose this means we should all go home and stop entertaining this outdated custom."

I peer around the corner. For starters, I see where all the police officers disappeared to. Whoever these people are, they're high priority, I guess. They're flanking the arguing man and his grandmother.

For being a grandmother, the woman is *hot*. I mean, it's not the typical "Oh I just have some old skincare secrets" thing. I mean she looks like she could only be *maybe* his mother. And that's heavy on the maybe.

What if they're—*dun dun dun*—vampires?

I slap my hand on my mouth before a true laugh can slip out and give away my position. This drama is way too fun to have to miss out on it.

This has to be a rich family. No poor family looks as good as they do. I wonder how much they've spent on cosmetic procedures. I know I've talked about the grandma, but the man isn't too bad himself. His skin is quite pale and clear. His eyes are sharp as he looks around, and he's pretty tall. Six two, I have to assume. Or somewhere around there. His body is lean—noticeable even through his suit. This family's genetics really are the personification of Asian don't raisin.

Not that I'm envious. As a Japanese African American woman, while we share the Asian genes, I've got the Black don't crack genes swimming through my bloodstream, too. I guess that these are the perks that come with having an African dad and a Japanese mother. I love my beautiful genetics.

"Luke, you'd better get her, and you'd better get her *now*. Everyone is here to see *my* grandson get married and that means they absolutely *will*. I can't believe this. If you had just listened to me and chosen one of those girls I'd set you up with . . ." She sighs. "You know our agreement. While this custom might seem outdated to you, you know as well as I do how necessary it is for our family."

She stalks into the courtroom behind her without waiting for the handsome man.

I watch the man, Luke, pick up his phone and send a text, a look of annoyance on his face. It's almost insulting how hot he still looks with that agitated expression. Not long after, another man leaves the courtroom, bowing his head to Luke. How dare he also be super-hot? Though not as good looking as Mr. Pissed-Off.

He's slightly shorter and lankier with reddish-blond hair with grown out black roots. And his eyes are softer and slightly more playful than Luke's.

"Where the *hell* is Minerva? You were tasked with bringing her here today, Noah."

Oh. He's a man who gets quieter as he gets angrier. That's sexier than any man who raises his voice to make a point, and I'll fight anyone on that. I take a step forward so I can hear the conversation that they're having but still remain out of sight. I hope. My gut has a funny feeling about staying, but my nosiness demands to be satiated.

"She didn't want to leave. Something about being mad about the ring you tried to give her."

Luke's jaw ticks. "It's an *heirloom* ring. If she thinks she's too good for it, then she's telling me that she believes herself better than my family."

"She also said that you told her not to show up if that was the case," Noah adds. "And it seems that she's taken you up on that offer."

I'm barely containing my laughter. He set an ultimatum, and she took him up on his offer. Of course she did. Come on. We all know that there are some women out there who will exert whatever power they have to get what they want, and it seems that this *Minerva* really is no different. Seeing as his grandmother is clearly anxious to see him married, she likely assumed that meant that he would bend to her whims.

"I need another woman."

Noah snorts. "Brother, I can't pull one out of thin air."

"Do you really want me to commit murder in city hall, of all places?"

Noah chuckles but dismissively waves his hand at Luke before walking off. In my direction. Toward me.

I take a few steps away and start "tying my shoes." Can't have them thinking that I've been eavesdropping on their conversation like I definitely was. I am but a lost girl who is tying her shoe in the middle of the hallway. I would *never* eavesdrop on someone's personal conversation or find amusement from someone being left at the altar by a woman who obviously thought the world of herself.

"Hello, miss."

Well, that was faster than I thought. Even with his long legs, I'd expected him to take another five seconds or so. Does that mean that I really lost track of time that quickly? Though, to be fair, I'm always trapped in my own head *and* panic tends to do that.

"Oh, hello," I reply while standing up. "Is something wrong? Do you need any help? If so, I don't exactly work here so . . ."

Noah scans my body, a smirk crossing his lips. Even in my comfort clothes, I'm aware of how beautiful I am. I mean, one time I managed to become part of a luxury photoshoot that I had just happened to be walking by.

My skin resembles the color of caramel and, for some reason, my eyes are some weird shade of emerald. I used to be super insecure about it, but I grew into it. Right now, my usual curly hair is straight, ending at my lower back. My face is devoid of makeup but judging by the looks I pretend to ignore when walking down the street, that doesn't matter.

Noah mutters, "This'll do."

"What'll do?"

"And you smell interesting."

"I'm sorry, I what?" I ball my fist, ready to defend myself if need be. "I don't know if that's the smartest way to greet a stranger."

"I apologize. Do I not smell interesting to you?"

Uh, no! I don't go around smelling people!

I betray my own subconscious to sniff him anyway because my noisiness takes over. I have never done something this weird in my life.

Catching myself before I make it obvious, I say, "Okay, I'm leaving."

"Please wait."

He better not be thinking what I think he's thinking. He was sent on a mission to find a woman, and while I *am* fairly attractive, I did not come here to get married to some random rich guy and his family. Because yes, you never just marry the man. His family is included, too. I don't know him, and I *especially* don't know them. I have enough family issues of my own without someone else's drama.

"Miss, what's your name?"

"You do know that it's rude to ask for someone's name before giving your own? How am I supposed to know you're not some psycho killer or something? Actually, with you talking about smells, it would really check out."

He chuckles. "Fair enough. My name is Noah Moore and I am certainly not a psycho killer. What is your name?"

I hesitate before saying, "I *suppose* I can tell you. Aurelia Smith."

He pulls out his phone, and I quickly realize that he's doing a background check on me. Oh *absolutely not*. He really is thinking that.

Nope, nope, nope.

Before he can finish it, I walk back in the way I came. There's no way that I'm going to sit here and let him con me into a marriage. What if the groom is some weirdo with, like, a murder hobby? Or even worse, a foot fetish.

I hold in the shudder as I call behind me, "Sorry, I actually have to get going. I wasn't supposed to be here this long. Things to do and all that."

Perfect cover. Not too much detail about where I'm going but a polite excuse of myself.

"Wait! Ms. Smith."

I don't wait. Why would I wait when I know why he wants me to? Instead, I walk faster. I've always been one for trying new things but I'm not insane. At least, I don't think that I am.

"Ms. Smith, please! I need to ask a big favor of you."

"Absolutely not," I shout behind me, only to find when I turn around that he's no longer behind me and has managed to match my pace. Damn him and his long legs.

Wait.

Even though he's significantly taller than me, there's no way that he could've caught up to my speedwalk without running. Or maybe I'm just not as fast as I thought?

"So you *were* listening?"

Ripped from my minor shock, I feign innocence because no way would I admit to my eavesdropping.

"Listening to what? I know better than to do random favors for strangers."

He grabs my wrist, which I promptly pull at. But, of course, he's too strong and I can't break his grip. Ugh, people need to learn the meaning of rejection. No is a complete sentence!

"Please, just listen to me for a second," he says as he stops, forcing me to stop with him. "My brother was supposed to get married today, and his bride left him here alone. All of our family is in there, expecting to see him married. He'll really kill me if I don't bring someone back for him to marry."

Noah's facial expression shows nothing but sincerity as he runs a hand through his already perfectly styled hair. I have to admit that I kind of feel bad for the man. He sounds kinda desperate. Not that I'm considering this proposition. I'm not that crazy yet.

I pull out my phone and start typing away as I respond, "He can just tell everyone to go home and fix his relationship issues later."

Noah's response is quick, a bit too quick for someone who seems to be trying to keep his composure. "If he doesn't marry today, he'll be forced to marry someone she chooses who is guaranteed to be . . . less than ideal for my brother. Too traditional, too vain, and likely way too obsessed with him for all the wrong reasons. He wants whatever happens next to be his choice—not someone else's."

"What makes you think that I would have pure intentions? I could be some evil mastermind."

"I sincerely doubt that. How can an evil mastermind get so flustered?"

I scoff. "I'm still failing to see why your brother's failed relationship my problem."

"What if we just call it fate? You being here is no coincidence."

Fate? I doubt such a thing exists. There's too much suffering in the world.

"Don't make me laugh. Fate is a concept that only exists in fictional stories."

"You've never once believed in anything like it? Destiny? Chance meetings with star-crossed lovers? Soulmates?"

"I—"

There was once a time where I was that much of a hopeless romantic. But I was young then and know better now. Marriage is nothing more than a contractual obligation and business transaction. All "love" does is destroy.

I shrug. "Everyone has. We were all children once."

"I'm much older than you and still believe in it. Everyone has that one person who's made for them."

"Then you're foolish."

"I may be foolish, but at least I'm rich. And so is my brother."

"I'm not hurting for money."

"He's handsome."

"Plenty of handsome fish in the sea."

"Okay, fine then. What do you want?"

I smile. "Now we're talking."

Nothin's better than being in a favorable position for negotiation. Now to figure out what I *do* want for doing something so insanely impulsive.

As we have been going back and forth, I've been doing a little background check of my own under the assumption that Noah and Luke have the same family name. What can they offer me that I don't already have? Money? I can make that easily. Power? Who the hell cares about that? There are two things that matter to me: living a life of freedom and finding my sister, Lily, and our best friend, Chiaki.

Whatever happens, that's the line where they have to meet me. And freedom for me isn't like the average person—having fun shopping or skating or reading . . . well, I actually do enjoy that one, but that's beside the point. I'll do something even this crazy if it appeases me.

The Moore family seems to be set for life, but a few curious inconsistencies pop up. Alas, I don't have enough time to look through it all. I suppose this may be something fun to explore.

I'm about to lock my phone when something else catches my eye in his investment portfolio. Everything he invests in is public knowledge, since he's well known for his expertise in business and investments. It's said that anything Luke Moore invests in is sure to appreciate in value and bring a huge payday. But this company . . . safe to say that I'm even more intrigued now.

BB Media, huh.

"I think," I pause, ya know, for dramatic effect, before speaking again, "I think that the most powerful thing that anyone can ask for is a favor to be redeemed at a later date. And not from that brother of yours, but from you."

It's good to have someone who owes me something besides the man I marry. Seriously, if I ever find myself in trouble or needing to get away with something that this Luke character might not exactly approve of then Noah will be my escape.

Before he can answer, I say, "And I'll need that in writing."

Contracts are very important when striking any kind of deal.

I take Noah's number from the background check and send him a text containing a file that I keep for situations just like this . . . except it's usually for the sake of blackmailing people. He doesn't need to know that though.

"How did you—"

"Do you really have time to be asking me that question? Now that I think about it, add a prenup to my list of demands."

People assume that I don't have assets worth protecting, but I do. It doesn't matter how rich or powerful their family is, I won't allow myself to be used.

I clench my jaw—reminded by the people who taught me that lesson firsthand. There's a reason why I haven't seen my mother in years.

Noah chuckles awkwardly. I'm assuming it caught him off guard. "You know we don't need any of your assets. If anything, a prenup is a handicap to you."

"Assumptions are dangerous."

"Fair enough." He sighs. "I don't suppose you just so happen to have a ready-made prenup stored away in your phone already?"

I shake my head, pithy smile on my lips. "You were just talking about your family's resources. I have no doubt that you can have one drafted up quick enough. After that, we'll personalize it a bit. I won't put my name down on a wedding certificate until that's sorted."

"Don't you think you're being presump—"

"Don't you need to stuff me in a dress and have me walk down an aisle? Sign that document, get me a prenup, and I'm your brother's for the marrying."

CHAPTER 3

"Luke, brother. May I introduce you to the *gorgeous* Aurelia Smith."

Noah really does confuse me. I've known him for all of five minutes, yet he shows conflicting personalities. On one hand, he seems to not take anything seriously, but he also jumped when his brother asked him to. I wonder what that's about.

Luke looks me up and down, his lips pressed in a straight line— seemingly unimpressed.

Of course he's vain. Every man wants a pretty woman or whatever. How rude would it be if I rolled my eyes at him or flipped him the bird? I mean, beggars can't be choosers, and I'm not the one begging.

I smile, flipping the switch in my head to turn on my polite voice, "It's a pleasure to meet you. My name is Aurelia Smith, age twenty-five. I hear that you're in search of a bride."

What? I'm capable of being polite. I wasn't raised in a barn, ya know? Though that would actually be so cool. I mean, I love horses and goats.

Oh, and sheep too. Though they aren't always as cuddly as TV likes to make them seem.

Luke turns to Noah, trying to hide his expression. But he can't hide from me. I saw that slight quirk in his eyebrow and twitch of his lips. He's impressed, as he should be. I'm beautiful, polite, and though he doesn't know it yet, smart. Really, really smart. I'm the perfect wife, and any man should be *ecstatic* to have me.

He asks, "Where did you find her on such short notice? What does she want?"

It takes a lot to stifle my laugh. Wasn't he the one who asked his brother to go searching for a bride? I mean, when you give a man a short time period, you should be happy that he didn't bring you back the first hobo he found. That's what I would have done.

Beginning to feel a little offended, I huff as I step closer and use my hand to guide his head back in my direction. I don't care *who* he is because he won't treat me like I'm invisible or less than him. That is something that I consider *not* fun.

"I'm standing right in front of you so talk to me instead of him. For someone who's in this predicament, you've already made three mistakes. One, you haven't even acknowledged my presence except for giving me a once over like I'm some doll that you just brought, which is *super rude* by the way. Two, you've talked about me like I'm invisible, and here's one thing that you'll have to learn about me, Luke. I am *never* invisible. And three, you're the one in this tough situation and you still haven't thanked me *or* your brother who had to put his pride on the line to get *you* a bride."

I tilt my head to the side. If he decides not to marry me, it's his loss, not mine. I only agreed to marry the man because I thought he might have resources I can utilize, but nothing is worth a man who has no respect for me, and I stand by that.

His expression changes at the conclusion of my outburst, his plump lips parting and eyes slightly widening. I'm not easy to deal with and I know that. It's not like I strive to make others happy. Why would I value others' happiness over my own? Especially that of some guy I don't know.

Luke's expression shifts into a smirk before he grabs the hand that's still holding his cheek. Slowly, he brings it to his lips, brushing them against my knuckles. And for some reason, I let him do it.

Well, that was a sudden change in attitude.

I can't help it as my lips part slightly. I mean, what motivated him to do that? He had a stick up his ass only moments ago and now he's being all affectionate with my hand.

Wait, don't tell me that he's one of those guys with a degradation kink. I mean, that's *so* weird. I don't know how I feel about this.

Noah breaks the silence with a clap. "Well, why don't we get our beautiful bride dressed? Lucky for us, she seems to be almost the perfect size for what we already have and grandma had the foresight to make sure there was a seamstress on the scene just in case."

Luke nods his head. "I'd expect no less from the hag."

Wow, okay. Wasn't expecting him to call her that.

I've never necessarily had a relationship with some type of grandparent, but from what I've seen from this guy, I didn't expect that language coming from him or the lack of respect in his tone.

Noah shrugs. "We should really get going."

He grabs my other hand, pulling me away from Luke and deeper into the building.

"Wait."

Noah pauses and Luke targets his attention at me. He's only looking at me because I said something, but it feels like his gaze is piercing through me. His attractiveness is not fair when I'm trying to be assertive.

"You forgot about the matter of the prenup. I made my stance on that pretty clear and it's yet to be mentioned to my groom."

Luke quirks a brow to Noah.

"Oh right, it seems your bride-to-be wants you to sign a prenup, brother."

Luke looks at me and smirks. "Oh really?"

Damn him and those hypnotic eyes! Play it cool, Aurelia.

"Yep," I reply. "And there's no way I'm signing a marriage certificate without one so I suggest you figure it out."

He nods slowly, his eyes swallowing my own. "It won't be a problem. You'll be my wife soon so let this be your first lesson."

My first lesson? Who does he think he is? He should know that—

His lips brush against my cheek. "Anything my wife wants, she will have."

My heart is beating. Hard. I can feel each thud against my chest chasing the last.

What did he just do to me? Is it me or is it getting hot in here?

I quickly turn away from him to hide the flush creeping its way up my cheek. I don't know if I should mention it to him or if it's too late now considering that I'm literally about to be *married*, but I am embarrassingly so, a virgin. And I mean a complete never fooled around, never kissed a boy, virgin. Everything else always seemed to matter so much more back then, ya know?

"If there's nothing else now, I'm pretty sure that I need to get dressed. Ya know, I didn't come here expecting to get married so there's quite a bit of work to be done."

Crud, I need to shut up. I'm rambling now.

Noah pulls at my arm again. This time, I follow him, grateful for the chance to slip away. I even find myself almost tripping over my feet trying to keep up. The man walks way too fast. When I turn back to peek at Luke, he still has that same smirk on his face so I flash him the brightest smile that I can muster before turning around.

It would be *so* embarrassing if I fell on my face.

Noah all but pushed me into a room. I assume it's usually a judge's chamber given its size and the desk that has been converted into a vanity for the purpose of this wedding, I'm assuming. The hum of the air conditioner brings relief to me as I hope that it helps cool down my cheeks that I know must be so red. I really don't want anyone seeing me like this—even Noah.

Before I can unwind, I'm shoved into the office chair in front of the desk and surrounded with women armed with various styling tools.

"He *likes* you," Noah teases.

The man has to be at least a few years older than me, yet he thinks it's fun to tease me like he's a child? Though I'm really not one to talk, either.

Keeping a bored edge to my voice, I reply, "Yeah, what was that whole thing about?"

I mean, I have nothing better to do than talk considering that I have one woman doing my makeup, one doing my hair, and one putting press-on nails onto my fingers. I couldn't even play games on my phone if I wanted to. But hey, this is more efficient than trying to have one person do all of this on their own. Or have them all do it one after the other.

"He realized that you're, and here's the cliche, *not like the other girls*."

I can tell that he's trying not to laugh at his own corny statement with his puffed up cheeks. Like *come on*. Anyone who's ever said that statement has never met the countless different types of girls out there in the world.

I roll my eyes, sarcastically saying, "Brilliant. Haven't heard that one before."

"You know, I watched you do that background check back there. You know who he is and who our family is, don't you?"

I don't even try to hide it. I mean, of course I ran a background check when someone asked me to marry into their family. Again, they're lucky that I find their family fascinating for reasons other than what typically draws other people in.

"Of course. What's the point?"

"You knew that and didn't try to suck up to him or make crazy demands because you were in a position to. As far we know, you don't want anything from him. Of course, everyone will want to know your true intentions for joining our family. Even I have a way of reading people and you're still a mystery to me."

A way of reading people, huh? He's lucky that I'm not a psycho ax killer ready to go after him and his family just for the thrill of it. I mean, seriously. The only *right* way to read people is knowing everything about them down to their dirtiest little secret. I'm good at that one.

"Of course I'm a mystery to you. You just met me." I sigh. "Besides, there's not a single person in this world who completely understands me."

Myself included.

Noah quirks a brow. "Maybe if you tell me what you really want, it'll help us both understand you a little better."

The keen look in his eyes betrays the playful lilt in his voice. He's not completely convinced by my explanation. Smart.

I consider my answer. I'm obviously not going to spill my life story before him in order to make him trust me. It still wouldn't be enough if I'd known him for five years.

"Do you know what the greatest power in this world is?"

He frowns. "What does that have to do with my question."

"Everything," I reply. "It's the reason why I decided to marry your brother. Weren't you the one curious about it?"

His lips relax into an emotionless line. "I'll bite. What is it?"

"Knowledge." I smile, the red lipstick on my lips feeding into my confidence. "What better way to gain knowledge about the upper echelon of society than to be the clueless companion to a man with power?"

"I also did a background check on you. I'm sure you understand plenty what happens up here. The Smiths sure do have their own influence."

"If you've done your research, then you know I haven't taken part in that world for a moment. I was going to stay out of that world for a while longer, but here we are." I sigh. "Besides, there's a certain degree of misguided faith that people put into those who have a higher standing—and their partners."

"That's not a commonly mentioned outlook. You almost sound like my brother. Even without my grandmother's interjection, he always said that people let their guard down more around a man with a wife."

"Well then, he's a very smart man. Interesting mindset, too. I mean, who am I to talk about interesting mindsets though? I'm about to get married to someone pretty much for shits and gigs with a side of people-watching." I laugh. "This will definitely be a trip though, don't you think? You're going to have a cool, more interesting sister rather than having to deal with that grumpy brother of yours all the time. Or maybe that's not always his mood? What do I know? I just met him ten minutes ago."

The memory of the kisses earlier seep into my mind, my hand and cheek tingling with it. That wasn't grumpy in the slightest. To be frank, I don't know *what* that was.

Noah steps closer but still a little out of arm's reach. With all the people surrounding me, he probably doesn't want to get in the way. Especially with the wedding already being behind schedule. That does tend to happen when the bride doesn't show up and then there's a random bride swap.

"Oh, definitely. I've always been saying that a sister would brighten up our worlds."

Before I can say anything else, I'm being pulled from the chair and put in the middle of the room with the seamstress pulling at my clothes. I suppose it's time for me to put on the dress.

Noah clears his throat. "I should probably leave now. Siblings or not. Real love, marriage, or not, my brother would absolutely murder me if I saw his bride naked. See you at the ceremony!"

I don't even have a chance to argue before he excuses himself. Now what am I supposed to do to keep myself entertained while they finish getting me ready? I mean, come on. I've had clothes fitted before, and I know that they won't allow me to move once I'm in the dress.

Except it's not exactly the type of dress that I'm used to.

As soon as the seamstress has moved to the side, I'm able to see what I'm wearing. The reflection in the mirror is still me but with some updo that I'm surprised my hair cooperated with and natural makeup that accentuates my features. It's heavy enough to cover any blemishes and eyebags but light enough to highlight my natural features like my freckles and the mole at the corner of my left eye.

The dress is a traditional Chinese wedding hanfu. I knew they were Asian, but I didn't realize they're Chinese. Still, I've never seen one of these in person, and it's *stunning*. The ornate red and gold features give off such a regal vibe that I can't help but feel a bit of imposter syndrome while wearing it.

Okay, think Aurelia. You need to remember all the reading that you've done on Chinese culture and pleasantries. You'll probably be needing those today when dealing with this family.

I have never been so thankful for my mom's strict enforcement of Asian studies when we were younger. I never thought there'd actually come a day when I'd need it.

It doesn't take long before the seamstress steps away and nods to one of the women behind me. Before I can see it, the traditional headdress—I believe it's called the fengguan—is placed on my head. The beautiful piece matches my dress in its red, ornate beauty, but tonight will be a test of my well trained yet kinda forgotten posture. It's a little more difficult than it should be with the extra ten to fifteen pounds of traditional garb.

Looking around at the women, they seem pleased with themselves. It has occurred to me, though, that they hadn't spoken a word to me since I entered. Maybe it's awkward for them or something.

Still, it's not me to be blatantly disrespectful in the face of their work, so I turn to them and say, "Thank you so much, ladies. You've done a beautiful job."

They smile but say nothing more and guide me to the door on the other side of the room. I hadn't noticed it before but I can only assume that it leads to the courtroom. I will admit that not much gets me nervous, but after being dressed in this gorgeous attire, I realize how real this is. I'm getting married to a stranger today wearing traditional clothes for a culture I've only ever read about.

I try to copy what I think I've seen in C-dramas and history books, placing my hands in front of me in what I hope is a delicate way. As much as I don't take life too seriously, I don't ever want to disrespect someone's culture—even if only by accident.

As I take my first step into the room, I notice the silence as all eyes fall on me. And for the first time since I decided to go through with this crazy idea, I start to question what the hell I've gotten myself into.

CHAPTER 4

Agh! I already knew this was part of the ceremony, but I had *completely* forgotten. If I'm honest, I didn't pay too much attention to the ceremony itself, only absentmindedly doing what was asked and keying in to say my vows. But what comes after vows?

The kiss, of course!

Now we have dozens of pairs of eyes focused on us, waiting for a smooch between me and my new husband. That admittedly feels weirder to say, or think, than I initially imagined.

Okay, focus. It's just a short kiss, isn't it?

While I'm busy trapped in my own thoughts, there's obviously something going on in his head because I'm yanked from my own as he snakes his hand around the back of my neck.

Shocked—because of course I'm still freaking out about needing to kiss the hot guy I literally met like an hour ago—I glance up into his eyes. His eyes, which are completely trained on me the way exactly like I imagine those guys in hot, spicy books do to their women.

This time, it's me whose lips part in shock. I mean, the way that he's looking at me and holding me, it's more intimate than I had imagined. I feel as if he's devouring me with only his eyes, and I'm paralyzed not because I'm scared but because there's a part of me that also wants to kiss him. A part of me that is far more physically attracted than I'd care to admit to even myself.

From this close, I can see his nearly symmetrical facial structure, his sharp jawline that could probably cut through paper like a knife, and of course, those damn plump, kissable lips that are about to be on mine.

Fuck it.

I lift my hands and clasp them around his neck, pulling him in for a kiss before I can think anymore. Sometimes, my thoughts just need to shut up.

And the kiss melts me. As our lips mold together, I realize how soft his are and how perfect they feel against mine.

I understand the hype now. This is why couples can't keep their hands off of each other, isn't it? I always thought it was overrated, but now . . .

Luke's other arm wraps around my lower back, pulling me harder againt him as he works to dominate the kiss. I've never been one to be dominated, but maybe like this . . .

The roar of applause rips me from the sweet, sweet distraction and grounds me in the present. We're standing at an altar in front of many people, and I just lost my first kiss to a man who probably kisses better than most men out there, if I were to take a guess. There's no way that everyone can kiss *that* good.

Rice is flying everywhere. I remember it's another tradition from their culture, but I can't help but concentrate on Luke. While our lips are no longer bonded, neither of us has moved an inch.

The clapping, the murmuring, and the clattering of rice to the floor is all just background noise. Right now, all I can do is stare at this man as he stares back at me with such intensity I feel it in the depths of wherever my soul is.

It's ironic. The rice is supposed to commemorate a sense of togetherness and fertility. And it's supposed to bring us good luck in our future endeavors, too. Maybe it's already working because that kiss . . .

I know that I said I feel a lot of physical attraction, but I now know that I am so fucked.

Or maybe it's all just a natural reaction to someone who's never had any type of intimate touch.

I don't know how long has passed. It could have been several minutes or it could have been only a second, but I finally manage to pull myself away from his gaze. Or rather, my attention is stolen by a bright flash in my face.

Once again, everything resumes at a fast pace as the photographer moves on, and I gently push myself out of Luke's grasp. We're still surrounded by so many people, and I have to remember that I only just met this guy.

While everyone is gathered talking to each other, Noah and the woman who I recognized as their grandmother break away and approach us at the altar. I still can't believe that she's his grandmother.

"It's wonderful to meet you, Aurelia," his grandmother beams at me.

Is it me or is that smile faker than the nails that they just pressed on not too long ago. That type of smile where they're "just trying to be polite" but are secretly looking down on you. What I've come to learn is that people like that have the filthiest secrets hidden up their sleeves.

Still, I can tell from her sharp eyes that she's both very intelligent and can be dangerous when she wants to be. People who are confident usually are. And they *do* say that eyes are the window into one's soul. Maybe *that* explains that whole scene earlier with Luke. But if so, what does that say about his soul?

"It's a pleasure," I say, bowing my head ever so slightly, careful not to bow so low that the fengguan slips off.

At the very least, I'll make sure to be polite, but I won't show weakness either by extending my courtesies too far. I time my bow for two seconds, looking her in her eye with a gentle smile as I straighten.

Her eyes crinkle, but she instead turns her attention back to her grandson. I'm not sure what I see in that gesture, but she'll become a problem for later rather than now. To an extent, social games can also be really fun.

"Before you can back out of this, let's go sign the paperwork to make this official, shall we?"

Once again, she speaks with a sweet voice but I can hear the sharp undertone in it. She's putting on a show for the guests. Judging what I heard earlier, though, she would have preferred he marry someone of her choosing.

Well! Not my problem. If the old woman tries to cause me trouble somewhere down the line, I'll just have to show her that I'm not easy to mess with.

Being the ever-theatrical beauty that I am, I grab Luke's hand and usher him toward where the officiant and judge stand together while

Noah and their grandmother follow behind us.

I look at the paper on the table in front of us. There's something missing from it that I explicitly requested.

"I believe there should be another document here."

The grandmother gives me a dirty look—not even bothering to hide her disdain. For whatever reason, she doesn't like me. And you know what, I am completely okay with that.

As if right on cue, a man in a tailored suit with slicked back hair rushes up to the table with a manila folder in his hands.

"Sorry, I worked as quickly as I can. I hope you find these terms favorable."

I look through the folder, not wanting to hold everything up too much, but also needing to make sure that things are the way that I want them. I make sure to skim through the whole thing before speaking my thoughts.

Pointing at the corresponding parts of the document, I say, "I don't want any premarital assets to become communal property including homes. We can have a joint bank account but must explicitly outline that our personal bank accounts and their balances remain our own. Also, I think you made an error here—maybe just an extra zero or something. In the case of an at-fault divorce on Luke's part, it says that I get everything."

The lawyer starts typing away at his laptop—altering the contract, I assume.

Luke holds a finger out to the lawyer. "Hold on. Don't change that last clause. It is absolutely *not* a typo. It's how confident I am in doing my part as a husband. The other two are perfectly fine."

The lawyer awkwardly chuckles. "I can't believe she wants to change something favorable to her."

I give him a harsh glare. "What makes you think that?"

He doesn't say anything else, putting his head down in embarrassment. People always like to make assumptions without knowing the facts.

Luke nods. "Good choice, Klaud. It will be much appreciated if you don't make any assumptions on my wife's financial and social standing without knowing any of the facts."

I chuckle. "And you do?"

"Oh sweetheart, I think there are probably things I know about you that you don't even know about yourself."

I highly doubt that. You met me like an hour ago.

"Yeah, I seriously doubt that. I know your brother's done a background check on me and everything, but I know for a fact that check doesn't have much."

In fact, I make sure of it. Every time there's something I don't want on it, I make it disappear.

Not long passes before the lawyer gives me a freshly copied prenup along with a pen. I read through it and sign it after confirming it's the way that I want before passing it over to Luke. Only after he signs do I turn my attention back to the table in front of us with our unsigned wedding certificate and a pen.

As I pick up the ornate pen from its place on the paper, I turn to Luke and say, "Seriously, last chance to speak now or forever hold your peace, darling."

Luke smirks, his left eye crinkling slightly with the action. He really is quite handsome, isn't he? Even when he's amused at my blatant teasing. I'm surprised that the cold asshole from before has seemed to retreat into this more relaxed person.

Well, *slightly* more relaxed. He still has that stiff posture and when he's not smirking at me, I notice how tight his jaw is. He must be a teeth grinder or something, which can lead to tooth pains and headaches. Maybe I'll ask later.

He leans down and brushes his lips against my ear. While I try to keep my typical amused expression on, my heart betrays me as it thumps wildly against my chest. I mean, I know that we kissed earlier and everything, but isn't this a bit *too* intimate?

His breath hits my ear as he whispers, "I think that we're a bit past speaking now."

For once, I'm speechless. So stunned that my thoughts barely exist anymore. Well, that never happens.

Nope, nope, nope. Get ahold of yourself and sign the paper, Lia.

Before I register it, my signature is on the certificate in front of me, and I'm handing the pen over to Luke. As our fingers brush, I, no joke, feel a burst of electricity.

How did I end up here?

Have my countless nights of staying up crafting the perfect plan to infiltrate BB Media finally caught up with me and made me delusional?

Oh shit! That's why I was here today. I wasn't supposed to get caught up in two marriages—one quite literally being *my own!* I was *supposed* to catch the talent manager bribing yet another judge to look the other way after there was a very suspicious disappearance of yet another model in the agency.

I mentally facepalm.

Even if I still had time to get there, there's no way that I can break free from this function. Looks like I'll have to wait for another opportunity to get dirt on that agent. There's nowhere on this planet where he can hide from me. Not when he hurt one of the few people left that I care about.

As the judge leaves to file the paperwork, Noah hooks his arm through mine, temporarily distracting me from my thoughts. "Welcome to the family, little sister."

I force a smile even though it betrays how I actually feel. As much as I have genuinely enjoyed this adventure, I still have other things I need to handle. And now I have a few other things to worry about, like making sure my brand new family doesn't try to interfere in my very delicate work.

"Thank you," I say. "It's a pleasure to be here."

CHAPTER 5

I let out a very loud, very unladylike groan as I collapse into the limo and sliding across the seat to allow my new husband in after me. After being forced to socialize for hours and endure dirty looks while I maintained a good face, the privacy of the limo is a welcome and well-deserved treat.

As I toe off my shoes, I ask, "Can we turn up the AC in here? This hanfu isn't exactly the breeziest thing I've ever worn."

I mean, seriously. The garment is *layers* of fabric, and I stood in a room full of people for *so long*. Sweat drips in places where I *hate* sweat dripping—way too uncomfortable for my liking.

A deep chuckle resonates through the car followed by a swift, "Patrick, you heard her."

Yes, Patrick, you heard me. As much as I don't want to be *that* person, I also like the idea of never having to experience a heat stroke.

Luke shuffles a little closer, the atmosphere between us feeling magnetic. The closer he comes, the closer I think we should be. And for that reason, I know that logically, I need to get further away.

"Where to, Aurelia?"

Is it me or is there something special about the way he says my name? I mean I've heard my name called by many people in many tones. My parents usually give me some annoyed tone (which makes no sense since I'm the perfect daughter) and my siblings speak condescendingly (even though I'm unarguably the smartest of the bunch). Hell, I even talk to myself in a variety of tones.

But the way he says it has my pulse racing and gives me the shivers. These types of bodily reactions are usually associated with fear, but why does this feel so good?

Swallowing my confusion, I ask, "What?"

Okay, wait. Why was my voice so soft there? I don't usually soften my voice to anyone unless they're a really cute animal or someone who really needs my comfort (which is almost never).

"Your address, darling. We need to get you packed and moved into my house."

Packed and moved into his house . . . Wait, what? I literally just got over telling myself that the best option is to get space from him and now he's suggesting that we move in together? I mean, I guess we are married and all now, but is that actually necessary?

I mean, technically, my parents *lived* together before my dad left. But my parents weren't exactly the best depiction of a "happy, healthy marriage" either. I remember one time, when I was younger, they used to play this game where my mom would throw knives at my dad and he would have to dodge them. And then I got older and realized that my mother never actually intended for him to dodge them. He was meant to actually get hit.

"I do have my own place though. I should be fine on my own, but thanks for the offer, man," I muse as I pat his shoulder.

"Sweetheart." He sighs as he grabs my wrist. "That wasn't a question. We're married now, and it's my job to keep you safe. I can't do that if you're out of reach."

My eyes land on his hand. There are those little electric shocks again. If this is going to be a common thing, *that's* why this is a bad idea. It doesn't seem like he feels it too, which means that I have to be having some strange moment of insanity.

"I can keep myself safe. I've trained in martial arts since I was a young child. I've managed to hold out for all this time and will continue to do so in the future."

He shifts his hand to hold mine. Should I pull away or just let it happen? Again it's that stupid argument between the logical and impulsive sides of my brain. But, let's be honest, I typically listen to the latter half anyway. I mean, it's kinda how I ended up married, isn't it?

Fine! I'll just let him do it. It's not like I hate it.

"Being my wife is not easy. If we had more time, I would have explained this in full. My brother told me you ran a background check on me," he says, sounding impressed. "Even so, you should know that I have a lot of very rich, very powerful enemies. Enemies who will exploit any weakness they can get their hands on, which could lead to *you* getting hurt."

He's right. If there's one thing about the upper class, there's no completely clean family. Many would do anything to establish themselves in a higher position or bend another family to their will.

And to be fair, I was being chased by some enemies of my own earlier. If I *am* under his protection, I'm protected from both his *and* my enemies. Which means that I can be a little more aggressive with my moves against people without having to worry about being compromised.

This *is* pretty tempting.

Still, I can't just agree without any type of hesitation. It would seem like I actually need him. There are also a few things I need to make clear before we can live together. If that's how we're doing this and our marriage will very likely be public, I feel as if my demands are fair.

"I'll go along with this on several conditions."

"Name them."

Sticking out my index finger, I say, "One, we pick a new house or apartment that we choose together and live there. If I'm living with you, it will be our home and that means that everything will be decided by us."

That allows for me to direct us to where I'd rather be positioned strategically for my own ends. And, admittedly, on a deeper emotional level, home matters to me. It's deeper than somewhere to eat and sleep, not that many people understand that.

I add my middle finger. "We allow each other our own personal space. I'm in a lucrative field of work and that requires privacy. If my privacy is breached, I could end up in serious trouble."

AKA, stay out of my business. I need to make sure my space is protected and I have a place to get my work done. Distractions are also a huge no-no for me, so a private room would work wonders. He'd probably be gobsmacked if he learned what I actually do.

On the surface, I'm a software developer, though my true specialty is cyber security. I tend to have very powerful organizations hire me to protect their systems. Sometimes, they also hire me to attack others to gather information or something like that. Those, I'm more likely to do on a case-by-case basis. There has to be a really good reason for me to use my abilities in that way.

Under the surface, I go after really bad people who have really good resources. Depending on how bad they are, I might just use what I find to get money for myself and those who may have been impacted by their terrible actions. Other times, I'll bring them down and make sure that they can't recover. Those, I guess, are also always on a case-by-case basis. I'm not evil.

I add my ring finger. "As much as I know that we didn't marry for love, I will make it abundantly clear that a public relationship means absolutely no women on the outside. Otherwise, I will very publicly divorce you, and you can marry your grandmother's first choice instead of me. I will also offer you the same gesture of respect."

Because I will not be labeled as the girl who let a man walk all over her. No, sir. Even if there are no real feelings between us.

I add my pinkie. "Considering this is supposed to look real, and you probably keep staff around or have family over, like your grandmother, I don't mind sharing a room or a bed. However, and I'm sure that common sense dictates this one, absolutely nothing happens unless we are both consenting. That means a sober-minded decision made by the both of us."

I actually have to admit that I like the idea of sharing a bed with him. Even when I was younger and used to share a bed with Chiaki and Lily, it used to be super comfortable just having another warm body there. Plus he's attractive.

Unfolding my thumb, I state, "Any major decisions made that affect us both must go through both of us. Understood?"

It's a good thing I've already listed my work as something very lucrative. Even if he manages to get a peek at how much money I make, there won't be much to question. Maybe that will help me keep a thin veil of secrecy.

"Is that all?"

Really? He has no objections or questions whatsoever? I outlined a lot of things and thought he might even argue on my last point.

I nod my head in confirmation.

"Then I have a few requests of my own to ask of you." He gently pushes my thumb back in. "One. In public, I need people to believe we are a madly in love married couple."

My heart rate picks up again at his gentle touch. It's safe to say that he's flirting with me, right? Right?!

He gently lowers my pinkie. "Two. We don't take the idea of real feelings off the table."

I mean, as much as I won't admit it to him, that was the reason for rule number four to begin with. I wouldn't add it if I didn't believe that there was a possibility because physical intimacy comes with the emotional kind. For me, those two things are not mutually exclusive. It's part of why I'm still a virgin.

"What if I don't want you to pursue me?"

"Then ignore me. But you can humor my request, can't you?"

I tilt my head to the side, thinking. I'm not going to pretend there's nothing between us. There's definitely a physical attraction, but there's also something that I'm anxious to explore. Is this what it's like to have a crush on someone?

Whatever. As long as we don't start calling each other "sweetie honey pie" or whatever. Oh, and as long as I don't end up like those lovesick "he loves me, he loves me not" fools. I'd rather do the knife challenge on repeat for hours and risk a few limbs.

And if it gets too much and I get overwhelmed, I can just ignore him and play dumb. I have other things to focus on anyway.

He gently folds down my ring finger. "Three. We go to a jeweler tomorrow and get that ring sized so you can walk around with everyone knowing you are a married woman."

Oh right. He tried to give me an engagement ring during the ceremony but it was a little too big for my finger. Apparently, my love for instant noodles isn't exactly the best way to build my body mass—*especially* when I only eat once a day. Oops.

It's not my fault *really*. Sometimes I forget that eating is a basic human necessity and only remember after a workout when I've burned enough carbs that I can't ignore it anymore.

He pushes down my middle finger. "Four. We look for a house today and either you stay with me or I stay with you tonight so I can be assured of your safety, which leads me to my last rule."

After he gently pushes down my final finger, he kisses my hand before saying, "I need you to allow me to do what I need to in order to keep you safe. I'll try to respect your boundaries, so we'll discuss that part later. But I need to make sure that you're safe, Aurelia."

I find myself nodding before even fully comprehending his words. Something about how he said them makes me feel a sense of worry seeping from him. While his voice is as firm as ever, it feels like he's almost begging me to accept that last request.

"You said you'd respect my boundaries, and I'll hold you to that." I shift my hands in my lap. "Whatever bodyguards you have, I don't want to be able to see them all the time. Make them as scarce as possible. And they shouldn't be my babysitters either. I need my freedom to do as I wish."

"Aside from anything that puts you in serious danger, I'll turn a blind eye. Your bodyguards are only there for when you need it—out of sight until necessary. When you're with me or at home, they'll be much less active. There are times where they won't even be necessary."

"What determines serious danger? Let's say that sometimes I like to go sky diving just for the fun of it. Some people would argue that it's seriously dangerous."

"I mean situations where others pose a threat, sweetheart."

Sweetheart?

I didn't know we were close enough for pet names. How do I respond to that? Actually, I don't know how to so let's just, uh, ignore it.

"Okay," I mutter. "As long as you understand what I've said, I can go along with it."

If he can respect my boundaries, then just *maybe* this can work. But he's in for a shock if we share a room and he finds out just how many of my stuffed children I have. And each of them must have a noticeable position. That's absolutely non-negotiable.

I can't believe I'm married to and will be living with this man. And especially the ways that he flirts with me . . . I can still feel his lips on my hand. Jeez, did Patrick forget to turn up the air conditioning? Why do I feel hotter now than I did before?

I let Patrick know my address, and we're soon on the way to my apartment since it'll be easier to just stay there and pack tomorrow before moving. I hope Luke knows what he's in for. My apartment isn't the biggest and doesn't accurately measure my personal net worth, but it is cozy, and I never needed more than what it provides.

As I glance out the window to see the city passing, it reminds me of the rapidly changing ebb and flow of life. In the limited time we have, everyone makes whatever decision they feel will protect their best interests.

I'd say I'm the same, but I live each day as if it's the last. Because, truly, every day very much might be.

CHAPTER 6

"If I catch even a whiff of judgment from you after I open this door, I'm sending you back to where you came from."

My home is *my* home, and I tolerate no disrespect or negative judgment from outsiders within its walls—no matter who they are. It might be a bit . . . cozy, but that's for me to worry about and others to mind their own business, ya know?

Luke's voice is dry as he replies, "Crystal."

I exaggeratedly shrug my shoulders and enter the code to my front door. As per usual, I type the twenty-five character code in as quickly as I can just in case there's some pesky person trying to find their way in.

Pushing the door in, I throw my arms up in presentation and dramatically exclaim, "Welcome to my humble abode!"

My apartment is just the way I left it with evidence of my many, very busy nights scattered about. Luckily, my work files never left my office so there shouldn't be anything lying around shouting "read me" to the first set of curious set of eyes in here.

The living room table is cluttered with empty instant noodle cups surrounded by countless empty coffee mugs. On the floor are bags of shredded papers I've procrastinated incinerating.

Can't leave anything that leads back to me.

"Take off your shoes," I demand, toeing mine off.

I roll my head, the heavy headdress starting to make my neck hurt. I've lost track of how many hours I've had it on. I don't know if maybe it's the adrenaline wearing off now that I'm home or the time catching up with me, but it feels way heavier than it did before.

Before I'm able to take another step into my apartment, a hand gently grips my shoulder, holding me in place. When I turn to face Luke, his hands are already reaching up to gently work the headdress out of my hair.

Okay, I have to admit that his whole dark and sexy attitude fits him, but the whole seeming to care for me when there's *no one to put on a show for* . . . Now, that's the sexiest part. Like, he doesn't have to pretend to care for me but he still goes the extra mile and that's something that I don't see or hear about much in the world. It's a bit perplexing.

I avoid looking into his eyes, though. Something about what happened earlier is still stuck deep in my mind. I mean, my brain almost completely stopped functioning when we kissed at the wedding so obviously it *has* to be some sort of witchcraft, right? Though hypnosis is probably more likely.

Instead, I look down at his outfit. I hadn't truly taken it in earlier at the reception since there were so many people there, and I didn't want to be caught staring. He's wearing a traditional tang suit that matches mine in color and design—the gold weaving through the red and creating a beautiful pattern.

My eyes rise to his lips, the memory of the kiss that we shared earlier flashing through my mind once again.

Stop thinking about it, Aurelia!

I know it was all for show, but that kiss did something to me. Something I'm not completely sure of and something I don't completely trust either.

It awakened some desire I have never had before. If it's a desire for him or for intimacy in general, I'm not sure. But it feels dangerous. Emotional attachments have always been a doorway for people to start getting sloppy.

"Are you hungry?"

Ripped from my thoughts, I find myself staring down at the hanfu. *My* wedding hanfu now, I guess?

"A little," I mutter.

It has actually been a while since my last meal. It had been around noon before I left and ended up getting dragged into this chaos. And to think, I didn't even get to pick up seaweed. Not only was I unable to secure my evidence but I wasn't even able to have my favorite snack. I'm not sure which is more tragic. The sun is down now, and I'm exhausted.

"Okay, how about this then? You go shower and get changed into something more comfortable while I clean up here? Does that sound alright?"

Alright? It sounds both appealing and mortifying at the same time. I mean, the first time that I have anyone in my apartment and he's cleaning it? But I also can't allow him to stay here while it looks like a pigsty, even if for only one night.

I chew on my thumb nail, contemplating. His offer sounds so kind and genuine that I know he's not trying to look down on me, but still, I hadn't expected that reaction.

A large, warm hand grasps mine, pulling my thumb away from my mouth.

"That's a bad habit, darling."

Coming from his mouth, the pet names he's been calling me have been doing unthinkable things to my biological systems. Heart rate increasing and my face heating up . . . I so need to go cool off.

"Alright, suit yourself," I quickly say. "I'll be in the bathroom, ya know, getting cleaned up. But first, let me get you something to change into, too. It probably won't be the most ideal fit, but I'm sure it will probably be a lot more comfortable than what you're wearing right now."

I know that I can't wait to change. Beautiful as the hanfu is, it's restrictive.

I don't allow him a chance to reply as I practically sprint across the living room and down the hall to my bedroom.

Body, please do me a favor and operate as you normally would. Please and thanks. This whole suddenly feeling things because of a few words or gestures is so not it. Control yourself.

After my silent plea, I rush to my dresser and sort through the clean clothes. I tend to sleep in boxers and an oversized sleep. They *might* be the only thing in this place that would fit him—although they might be a bit snug. Even my longest pants would be capris on his long legs.

I run into my bathroom after throwing his clothes on the bed and search for a towel, washcloth, and bodywash. He will also likely need a shower. While I'm never one to expect guests, I have the bad habit of having extras of everything so I can avoid laundry or trips to the store because I "suddenly ran out of toothpaste" or something like that. It can't only be me who finds that to be the most annoying feeling ever.

Securing everything in my arms, I take a deep breath at the doorway of my room.

Cool off and act normal.

Taking one more breath, I walk over to Luke, who has made his way to the couch, and hand him the items in my hands.

"I don't know if everything will fit, but this is what I have so hopefully it does. I just thought that you might also want to shower and change, too."

I think that sounds nonchalant enough.

He smirks, the sight of his lips once again sending tremors through my legs and invoking backflips in my stomach. Seriously, instead of my body acting normal, it decides to add yet another thing to the list of reactions. I just met the man.

Accepting the items, he rests them on the couch next to him. But before I can move, he takes my hand and leads me to sit on his other side. Of course, I stand my ground and don't let him move me.

Or at least, that's what I wish I would have done. Instead. I'm sitting right next to him, with his warm hand still holding mine.

"I wonder," he mutters, "why you've been avoiding me?"

"I haven't been avoiding you! I mean, I literally just gave you all that stuff to shower with and we had that conversation in the car. I wouldn't call that avoidance."

Hell, we even kissed earlier! He's held my hand on multiple occasions. That's not what I call avoidance. Avoidance would be not letting him into my apartment, sitting as far from him as possible in the limo, and ignoring every word he says.

"You say that," he responds, placing his free hand on my chin. "But you haven't looked me in the eye since after we kissed at the altar."

He tilts my chin so I'm forced to meet his eyes. The dark chasms start to draw me in again, erasing the apartment around us.

He smirks. "Tell me, darling. Are you nervous?"

Nervous would be an understatement. I'm confused about what's happening with me right now, so yeah, that makes me nervous and maybe even a little scared. Nervous and scared are not my emotions. I should not be feeling them.

"I'm not nervous," I lie. "Just exhausted. Ya know, today has been a long day. Sometimes, things like that just happen when you're tired."

I can tell that he doesn't believe me but he drops his hand and says, "Right."

Sir, I don't know if I like your tone. I mean, even if you don't believe me, you can at least do the courtesy of hiding it better than that, ya know?

"But," he adds. "If I catch you avoiding eye contact with me, I'll go with my theory instead, sweetheart. Now, you should go get showered."

I stammer out, "There's a bathroom across from my room. The door's always open so it's a bit hard to miss. Use it."

I can't say that I disagree with his words. Taking the opportunity to escape the embarrassing situation, I retreat to my bedroom and shut the door. Hopefully, a shower will reset me.

•─•─•─•─• 🔒 •─•─•─•─•

I check myself out in the mirror. Just because someone's here doesn't mean I'm going to dress any differently. After washing my body and hair, I went through a nice long hair care routine and pulled it into two cornrows that end halfway down my back.

Next up was my skin care routine, which I always do after wearing makeup. I'm not vain but I also hate having pimples and this ensures that I minimize that risk by a lot.

Now, I have on my long shirt that reads "Big Boobs" with a loading icon under it that's captioned "Estimated Time: This Entire Life" and boxers under them for my typical comfortable loungewear. I put on my glasses—the big frame sitting perfectly on my nose, happy to give my eyes a rest after having worn contacts for so many hours.

Walking out of my room, I feel much more comfortable and am met with a delicious aroma. If my self-control slips even a little, I know I'll start drooling. As if agreeing with my mind, my stomach lets out a loud growl.

Following the smell, I find my living room is almost completely clean. The trash is all gone and the shredded paperwork is neatly placed in a corner more out of the way than I had it before.

Luke's wet hair lets me know that he did shower but my routine was admittedly long, so it's possible he managed to do all of this with time to spare.

On the table in front of him are two bags of takeout, each from the local ramen spot. I doubt that he knows but it's actually my favorite place to order from because the owners are really sweet and make nice, authentic ramen.

"Thank you."

This time, he grins at me. Now that I've seen this, I can say that while his smirk kind of gives a mysterious, dark, sexyish vibe, his grin is still sexy but much more inviting and warm.

"Come eat. I can hear your stomach from down the hall."

While I usually limit myself to one meal a day, it's purely out of laziness—not lack of appetite.

"You must understand," I say as I make my way over. "It takes a lot of calories to keep a personality so vibrant going, alright? If I were you, I'd consider it more worrying if someone doesn't have a large enough appetite. Anyway, what'd you get?"

I make light of the situation because I'd rather see that grin some more. If it goes away, I want to make sure I'll be able to bring it back.

Instead, his face falls and his expression becomes a little unreadable. His eyes, very obviously roam over my body.

I mean, I know that I'm not in designer brands or wearing any makeup, but seriously, staring is rude. Especially when I can tell from his expression that he is *so* judging me right now. I don't look that bad.

Before I can complain and put him in his place, he rips his eyes away from me and concentrates on the food bags. I guess he realized he was being rude. At least he has *some* sense of self awareness.

As he opens the bags, he responds to my earlier question, "Edamame, spicy seafood ramen for you, beef tonkotsu for me, miso soup for both, and a box of salmon rolls for us to share."

"Why'd you pick this place?"

"Well, with the abundant amount of empty instant noodle cups in here, I assumed ramen was a safe bet. I saw your leftovers from earlier had seafood and chili flakes so I went with the closest thing I could find on the menu. I got everything else because I wanted to make sure that there was enough to eat."

But why this specific place?

The level of casualness in his response is mind-blowing. How does he not realize that putting that much consideration into ordering dinner isn't necessary, and it is *way* too thoughtful for a person that he just met? I mean, seriously. Doesn't he think this much effort means something? Am I overthinking it?

"Thanks. This place is actually my favorite."

"Then I'm glad I chose it. Now eat."

His tone leaves no room for arguing, and honestly, neither did the light rumble in my stomach. Like, okay stomach, I get it. Obviously with all the food in front of me, you'll be getting fed tonight. Is it only my stomach that complains after only a few *measly* hours of not eating?

I clap my hands together like how most people say grace. "Itadakimasu."

I pick up the chopsticks, and pretending I eat like a normal person, start digging in. He's my husband, and we're supposed to be living together so, to me at least, it's obvious he'll see this side of me eventually. He better get used to me and all my quirks very quickly.

When I peek at him, he is very composed as he eats. A lot less slurping and broth splattering than how I eat. He reminds me of what I imagine nobility looks like, and I can't help but stare for a few seconds.

Aurelia, eat.

The reminder spurs me into action, and I shovel in more food. For as small as I am, when I choose to, I can put away *a lot* of food. By the time we're finished, nothing remains but the bare plastic container.

Luke pulls out his phone, handing it to me with an open webpage. As I scroll through, I realize that it's a list of houses and apartments.

Right, that was a thing that we're supposed to be doing.

"I've narrowed down the list to places with acceptable security. You pick the one you like best, and we should be able to move in tomorrow."

Okay. I shouldn't act shocked. I already know he's the type of rich that can find somewhere to live in less than twenty-four hours. And somewhere spectacular, at that.

I nod my head as I continue my exploration. One house really stands out for me. It's not exactly city center but it's still pretty accessible. The modern build is gorgeous, both inside and out. And the extensive number of rooms means I'll have plenty of space.

The biggest selling point, though, is the giant pool in the backyard. Swimming has always been my favorite way to work out and clear my mind, so the pool being right there will allow me to do it frequently.

Plus it's close enough to my mother and the high street where all the top businesses are—including BB Media. It's easy access.

"This one."

He nods before taking his phone and typing away. Before I can question what he's doing, a large yawn takes hold of me. I suppose I did have a long day but I'm surprised my usual insomnia is letting me get tired *now*.

Luke puts his phone down and turns to me. "Let's get to bed, sweetheart. We have a long day tomorrow."

And that's when I remember that I will be sharing a bed with this man from now until a very long time. While it's a little nerve wracking, part of me must admit that it's also so very . . . thrilling.

CHAPTER 7

As we walk into the room, I'm hyperaware of every movement either of us makes. I try to keep my breathing in check to hide the nerves. Maybe to even gaslight myself into believing I'm not even nervous in the first place.

But just knowing that he's behind me has my pulse racing faster than a cheetah on the hunt. I mean, seriously, this is so not calm, cool, and collected the way I thought I'd be.

I mean, I couldn't let him sleep on the couch with his long body, and I wasn't going to either. Besides, we're going to be sharing a bed soon anyway, so what's the issue with starting tonight?

"I like to sleep on this side," I say, pointing to the left side of the bed. "You can sleep on the right. I saw what type of phone you have earlier and have hooked up a charger for it on that side already so you can keep it charged."

"Do you mind if we switch sides?"

Switch sides? Now why would we do that? I always prefer to sleep on the side closest to the door just in case anything happens. I even have my bat stored right next to the bed and a knife under the mattress on that side. No matter how confident I am, I'm still a woman who lives alone and can be targeted for any number of reasons.

"Sorry, this is my preferred side," I reply.

Though I don't understand why I apologized. It's my room.

"Aurelia, if anyone were to come in here, you would be the first person they reach. That's not acceptable, especially not when I'm in here with you."

"There's no need for that," I argue. "I *am* capable of defending myself, ya know."

"I really must insist. I won't be able to sleep while knowing that if the attacker had a lethal weapon, my *wife* would be the first in the line of fire. Truly, I have bad enough insomnia as is."

His voice is level but I can hear the annoyance building up. Same here though, buddy.

"Well, *I* must insist because how can I, as a host, willingly put *anybody, especially* my husband, at risk in the very, very, very off chance of an attack? It would be so very discourteous of me."

"Wouldn't it be more discourteous to make your guest, especially your husband, uncomfortable?"

"But it would be more discourteous of me to prioritize comfort over safety."

"But they can also easily breach this window, can they not?"

"After what? Climbing up five stories?"

"Do you think people are incapable of such a feat?"

"I think someone would have to be a bonkers nutzo to ever even *consider* climbing five stories when there are so many floors beneath me. What type of thief would specifically go, '*Oh. Why don't I go climb this wall to specifically rob apartment 515?*' Be for real."

"You never know. You could have a stalker."

"Then, with your logic, shouldn't you stick by the window to neutralize the threat?"

"I'd rather sleep by the most likely threat. Just because I think it's possible someone sneaks in through the window doesn't mean I believe it to be the most likely case."

I stop arguing for a second. Earlier, I *had* been followed through the streets. Maybe he's right about having some type of stalker, or stalkers, around me.

"Fine."

"Thank you."

"What's that tone?"

Luke sighs and pinches the bridge of his nose. "You're the *only* person who can get away with this."

"Well, I'm your *only* wife so . . ." I smile triumphantly at him. If he even thought of speaking to me any ole way, he would learn *very* quickly that I wouldn't stand for it. Though I suppose he learned that earlier, didn't he?

"Please, let's just go to bed," he mutters.

Okay, I guess I'll stop teasing him for now. He's been very restrained in his interactions with me so far, so I shouldn't take advantage of his kindness. But, that all resets tomorrow.

I crawl into bed, scooting across my usual, very comfortable, very favorite side, and onto the side that I've never given the time of day. Or night. That's when normal people are supposed to sleep, right? It's when I sometimes sleep, which means that I'm *totally* normal.

I gaze longingly at my spot. I bet it misses the feeling of my body against it already. As Luke gets settled onto the bed, it dawns on me that it's the last night I might ever use the mattress.

Life really is unpredictable.

When he turns to face me, I can't help but blatantly ogle the man. There's something beautiful about a man who has allowed himself to let go in front of another person. My eyes stroll down his body, and I'm amazed by how my shirt sticks to his broad shoulders, showing off his muscles.

Wow.

Then, my eyes fall on his chest, and I start laughing. I mean a full-belly, not cutesy, huffing and puffing, laugh. I can't believe that I gave him this shirt of *all* shirts. It reads, "Small Tits with Big Dick (energy)."

I suppose it's my fault since I did purposely pick all the craziest jokes for my pajama shirts. I even made some of them myself because obviously other people don't have the same level of creative genius as me.

Luke, likely already knowing why I'm laughing, slowly shakes his head.

"I'm so sorry," I say between giggles. "I had no idea that I was giving you that shirt."

This one is so my bad. But it's such a funny mistake, isn't it? Cheers to our first funny marriage memory. Everyone always talks about their wedding night being memorable, this one is definitely something that I will never forget.

And definitely not because I won't let him live it down. I would *never* do such a thing. Why would I remind someone of something so very funny every time they get on my nerves or I'm bored?

My laugh is interrupted by a yawn that catches me off guard.

"Get to sleep, sweetheart. I'll hit the lights."

I try to tell him where the second light switch is beside the bed, but the exhaustion seems to have caught up with me. The last thing that I remember is the outline of a very muscular, very hot back as he reaches for the light switch.

Guess he already saw it.

A crash shatters the veil of my very nice dream and yanks me to reality. I don't have any cats to be knocking things down and causing crashes at this hour, so that means someone else is here.

On my side, Luke has already sprung out of bed, landing unbelievably lightly on his feet, trying not to let the intruder know we're awake, I presume. I'm a light sleeper and his movement wouldn't have woken me up with how silent it was.

I never knew people could step that light. His brother's freakishly fast and he's freakishly light on his feet. What type of genes are these?

I can barely make out the outline of him bringing his index finger to his lips, warning me to stay quiet. I will. But I also will grab my bat tucked away at the side of the bed.

I stretch my body across the bed and tug the bat into my arms— holding it tightly. Whoever thought they could break into my apartment and interrupt my dream of cuddling a soft baby koala while riding an alpaca through the woods (don't question those logistics) will be feeling a strong level of regret that comes from messing with a girl who obviously has a little crazy in her.

Quietly, I shift out of bed to stand next to Luke, lifting my bat up and at the ready.

In Japanese, a male voice—which I translate with my impeccable language skills—says, "We're supposed to retrieve the girl *without* hurting her. We're supposed to be taking her home, not killing her. Put the knife down, idiot."

I see what this is! Dear old mom wants me home. After all this time, I wonder why she's decided to escalate her methods. I've been refusing her for years, and it's never gotten this far. Maybe she heard about my wedding or something.

Oh, that sure would piss her off.

Another voice, a woman, responds in Japanese, "Alive doesn't mean uninjured. If she fights back, this is the best way to make sure we can still complete our mission."

As the doorknob turns, I lift my bat even higher and move to stand right next to the door. Just because I understand why they're here does *not* mean I'll take it easy on them.

As the door opens, I swing the bat down on the person who enters first. Judging from the height at which the bat hit them, I'm going to assume it's the man. And with my strength, I doubt that he's even still conscious.

"Fuck," the girl mutters. "See I told you that this would come in handy."

She adjusts the knife in her hand, and I raise my bat to swing again but something tugs at my ankle. I'm genuinely impressed the guy on the floor can still move. I'm almost positive I hit him in the head. Luckily, his discombobulation has severely cut his strength, and I didn't budge an inch.

When the woman lashes at me with a knife, her attack is stopped before it can reach me. A hand wraps protectively around my waist and eases me back.

Aw, my sweet husband has come to the rescue. How charming.

As he keeps her distracted, I stomp on the other guy's hand until I hear a crunch. He screams and lets go of my ankle.

I smile up at Luke. "Honey, why don't you let me deal with her?"

He ponders my request then twists the woman's wrist until she lets go of the knife. I think I heard a crack somewhere in there too. Luke lets her go and takes a step back. Without a pause, I roundhouse kick the girl in her head.

What? I never said that I'd give her a fighting chance. Only that I'd deal with her. And that's what I'm doing.

Before she can orient herself, I drop and put her into a chokehold, making sure she's lost consciousness before letting her go and standing up. The other guy, who's still awake, grunts in pain. From the broken hand or the head injury, I'm unsure. What I do know is that the head injury means that I should make this quick before he also passes out.

I switch to Japanese as I say to him, "Tell my mother that if she wants me, she should be a little nicer. Maybe start with a dinner invite that I'll probably turn down, and we'll go from there. If she wants me, she'll have to earn me, and she'll have to figure out that price on their own."

I crouch down, getting especially close to him before I continue, "And tell her if they ever put my husband in danger again, I won't hesitate to make sure that they crash and burn. Okay?"

I don't like people getting hurt because of me.

I hit his pressure point before standing up and stretching out my body.

Hopefully, he remembers my message when he wakes up and delivers it. I'd hate to have to go through the process of sending another one.

I switch back to English as I exclaim, "Now that's all settled! How about we go back to sleep!"

"Aurelia," Luke drawls out. "Go pack what you need to. We're leaving this place tonight."

Is now a bad time to say that the way that he says my name does very pleasant things to my psyche? I mean, bossy isn't usually my type. I prefer to be in control. But, at the same time, his whole bossy attitude can be quite appealing.

"But I'm tired," I complain.

"Then I suggest that you pack fast. And please know that we will be talking about all of this later."

"What happened to Mr. Protective Husband back there?"

"You were in no real danger after I disarmed that girl. And seeing you fight honestly was such an . . . invigorating experience. Very stimulating, my darling."

The depth in his voice has me not wanting to enquire further. Whatever he means likely means disaster for me, and I'm sure of that.

As I inch away, I say, "How about I go pack?"

His voice holds a lot of restraint as he replies, "Good. Idea."

CHAPTER 8

The whole ordeal of packing and leaving to get to this hotel has me completely awake. I have this nagging feeling I won't be sleeping tonight and its name rhymes with "puke."

At least getting a hotel room wasn't too much of a headache. He owns this whole hotel we're in and keeps this suite on the top floor open for whatever person he deems worthy of it, I guess. Too bad I can't sleep. The bed is actually really comfortable.

I barely sit on the edge of the bed when he asks, "What was that?"

"What was what? I mean, I know that my selection of . . . toys . . . is extensive, but it was purely for experimental purposes. I've only ever used a select few more than once or twice."

He switches to Japanese, "Honey, I *do* speak Japanese."

Well damn. So he heard that entire conversation I had with the people who tried to kidnap me. I suppose that means his questions are going to be a lot more specific. Less room for dancing around the question.

"Okay, so you do," I reply, trying to sound a lot less annoyed than I am. "Well, if you know Japanese, then why do you need an explanation from me? You heard what they said the same as I did."

"But *you* have the context."

"But *you* have the power to figure things out."

"But *you* have the responsibility considering that you're my *wife.*"

Touche. He's got me there. And the situation did technically put him in danger. But damn, I don't want to admit to that man that he's right. There's something just so infuriating about losing an argument with him.

I huff. "Fine. That whole situation is my mom's way of demanding I come home."

Which, again, is *so* annoying. She's the one who kicked me out in the first place. Like how does someone throw something away and then want it back badly enough to send people after it but not badly enough to show it some damn respect and come get it themselves?

The slight shift in Luke's eyebrows show intrigue but not shock. It's almost as if he's not surprised that someone's mother would go to these measures to get them back. I suppose it's the whole rich family thing. He knows how these things can get.

"And why would she feel the need to go to such extremes?"

"Because I tell her no any time she asks. Though I really wouldn't consider it *asking* per say. I'd say it's more like . . . demanding and threatening typically. But she never actually takes it this far. She usually tries to do something like threaten to have my landlord kick me out or things like that."

Too bad she can't threaten a landlord who's already under my thumb. That asshole owes me more than his life. I mean seriously, who the hell thinks that getting involved with drug traffickers would mean he was their equal and free to leave whenever? *Of course* they would go after his child. He's lucky I was super pissed off at the whole operation. I mean, seriously, imagine if I didn't have morals.

Not enough morals to not demand payment though. And, if I'm honest, him letting me stay in the apartment isn't that necessary. I could have gotten something somewhere else for free, too. Knowledge, after all, holds power even over the most powerful. It was just convenient to not have my contract uploaded on some system somewhere where my mother could find it.

"Why don't you go back?"

Oh right, we're still having this conversation. Ugh. I'd much rather go run over a computer with a tractor.

"Because she needs to learn that she's not above apologizing. She kicked me out because I didn't want to marry her best friend's son, Shoto. He and I were actually best friends growing up and I thought it would stay that way. That is until our parents got it into their heads that we should be together. He was more than okay with it, which is how I learned of his huge crush on me. I knew that I never could feel that way for him." I sigh. "Even my marriage to you is an act of rebellion in a way."

I remember when Shoto had come to me so excited to tell me the news. I'd pretty much told him that there "wasn't a chance in hell that I would *ever*, at any point, marry him." The poor chap had been so hurt but I saw this kind of possessive anger raging in his eyes. He tried his best to hide it, but I knew his mask of the "sweet kid" was slipping. An actual sweet kid would have let my first no be the only one needed.

I continue, "So I rejected him, and he ran to his mommy who ran to my mother who pretty much forced me to marry the man. No one forces me to do anything. If they didn't already know that, then they were going to have to learn it the hard way."

I almost laugh at the memory. My mom had come into my room and started screaming at me. I laughed in her face. Was it an appropriate reaction? Probably not, but it was the only thing I felt. I had found the whole thing so funny. Then she got out her knives, and I had fun playing the same game she played with dad growing up. After so many years of watching them, I was a pro.

The look on her face was *priceless*. She was both shocked and annoyed that she stopped throwing them and switched to other types of threats. Ya know, freezing my accounts, taking away everything I own, breaking my leg so I couldn't run, having my vocal cords surgically removed. The typical.

I laughed and asked her if she thought that I couldn't expose her if I wanted. I mean, seriously, even if the public doesn't believe what I say to them, it would still look so bad for the family's image.

Oh right, I'm supposed to be telling this story.

"So when she threatened me with these, like, bullshit threats, I mean they were seriously so trivial, I pretty much threatened her back. She cared about the family image, and I didn't care if it crashed and burned. So we were at an impasse."

I cross my right leg over my left and lean forward.

"The next part is pretty fuzzy. I don't really care to remember the boring parts of the conversation. But we came to an agreement that I should never return if I'm not ready to marry the kid. I guess when I left, she thought that I'd come crawling back but that goes to show how much she knows me. Am I right?"

I also don't remember the part that happened before my sister was kicked out either.

I had, indeed, not come back. Nor do I think I ever will. Which *sucks* for her because everyone knows that of my siblings I was her favorite candidate to take over the family empire.

All of my siblings and I interned for one year at the company, and I showed the most noticeable growth. Due to that, I don't think the board would want any of my siblings over me. Sucks that my mom couldn't think *that* far ahead.

Not my problem, either way. I care for that woman about as much as a shark cares for grass.

Luke pinches the bridge of his nose and says, "I see what's going on now."

"Yep! The nag wants me home, probably because of issues with the board of directors cause I'm kinda a prodigy, but she'll have to apologize and beg me first. And let me tell you one thing about her, in my twenty-five years of life, I don't think I've *ever* heard those words leave her lips."

"That's not why she wants you, sweetheart." He shakes his head. "She wants you because you not only defied her wishes for who she wanted you to marry, you married someone else. The news is out there, and her friend would have seen it."

"Oh that makes sense, I guess. Sucks for her though."

"And so you'll just ignore this?"

"For now."

I can't tell him about the schemes I'm cooking up. Not sure about his stance on blackmailing family. Or threatening them. Or doing a hostile takeover because I know I would succeed.

And I definitely can't tell him about my sister. Not yet. Possibly not ever.

"Aurelia, you'll be in danger until this is resolved."

"Weren't you super gung-ho on making sure that I'm secured? I suggest that you make sure that your people are good at defencing me."

"And if your mother reaches out again?"

Oh, I really hope she does. It gives me an excuse to get nasty and show her what will happen if she messes with me. Please, if there are some gods up there, *let me have this.*

I'll respond the same way I would with anyone. Swiftly and without mercy. Luke should consider himself lucky that I actually find him to be . . . whatever he is to me. I still have to figure that out.

Pushing those thoughts aside, I smile and respond to his question, "Then I'll have no choice but to reply."

CHAPTER 9

Luke and I had only slept for the two hours before those nuisances broke into my place. So now, I must admit that I am grumpy. One of the few nights I manage to fall asleep, and it gets ruined?

"It better be done by the time I finish feeding my wife."

I look at Luke, who has been taking and making a series of phone calls all morning while I struggled and failed at falling back to sleep for hours. He asked for some type of update on one thing or another and ended the call after making some demand without waiting for any response. I know if it were me on the other side of the phone, I'd give him an earful for that stunt. It's pretty much been like this since we had that last conversation about my family situation.

When he catches my eye contact, he pockets his phone and gently smiles at me. The man I just watched him be for the last hour is almost nowhere to be found.

"Sweetheart, are you ready to go eat breakfast?"

I shake my head. "Breakfast isn't necessary for me. I typically eat once, maybe twice a day."

He stalks toward me, stopping in front of the bed that I'm comfortably sitting on. He kneels so our eyes are level, his still holding a sense of gentleness but much sterner than before.

"That may have been what you did before me," he says. "But now, you'll be eating three healthy meals per day. It's important for you to remain healthy. You don't have to eat big meals for all of them, but at least one has to be."

While his words, on the surface, sound like a demand, it feels more like he's pleading with me. To do that means that he sees me as an equal and that means more to me than anything. I guess I can meet him in the middle. I'd much rather him be like this than be the asshole he was when I first saw him, no matter how brief that phase was.

I nod in acceptance, no words needed to convey the answer. I have to admit, though, something about him pleading with me to look after myself has me feeling all warm and fuzzy. I don't know why, but Luke means something to me. And while I don't exactly want to close myself off to anything happening with him, I'm also anxious to decide whether I should pursue him or not.

If I do, what does that do to me? I've always been one to leap without being certain of where I'd land. I mean, I always had a good enough estimate and knew that the ride down would be the most fun.

But, with this . . . I'm scared of where I'll land. I'm not good at caring for people. I never really opened myself up to relationships aside from Shoto and my siblings—and those haven't necessarily panned out to be the most positive experiences. I know that there's no way this connection between Luke and I is anything as extreme as love—not that I'd know what it feels like—but if we pursue this relationship seriously, the way that his request seemed to want to, that would be the ultimate goal, right? For us to love each other?

Get a grip girl. You barely know him and even less about love. Can't do a background check on a fleeting emotion. This isn't something you have to worry about right now.

I absentmindedly watch him move around the hotel room as he gets his bearings. I've seen handsome men before, but never any that have broken through the barrier of my mind and pitched a tent in its wilds. Even doing something as basic as getting sorted, he makes my heart skip a beat in a way that's almost nauseatingly pleasant.

I need to figure out what I want to do. A relationship with me, and I mean a *real* one, is going to take a lot more than even *I* know. It means having to eventually spill my secrets about my work. It means giving pieces of myself to someone else without knowing how well they will protect them.

"Aurelia."

I face Luke and cock my head to the side, a silent acknowledgement.

"The car's downstairs. We should get going. Someone will be up for your stuff, okay?"

I hesitate. Some of the stuff I took was just things I liked but could live without. Like my entirely comedic collection of oversized shirts. Or my stuffed animals. Wait, those might be more of a necessity.

But one of my bags holds my computer and all of my work documents. I can't just leave that with any person and risk them snooping or losing it.

"So Luke . . ." I say. "Remember when I told you I work in a lucrative business? Well, I don't feel comfortable leaving those things lying around with anyone who's not me. Is it alright if I bring the bag containing all of that stuff with me?"

"That's fine. Which bag is it?"

I point to the large red suitcase in the corner of the room. I can't believe that one bag contains such an integral part of me. My work is enough to already describe about 75 percent of myself.

Luke stalks over, grabs the handle, and walks toward me while pulling it behind him.

I reach for the bag. "Thank you. I'll . . ."

He uses his other hand to grab mine. "Don't worry about it and let me do my husband duties. It's a great source of pride."

I mutter an okay or thank you or something in between and head to the door. Each time he does something like that, my thoughts navigate back toward the decision I'm not sure what to do about. I mean, I've only known him for a *day*.

I'm not left alone with my thoughts for much longer as Luke quickly catches up and calls the private elevator. Perks of owning the hotel, I guess.

"Thank you," I say. "For, ya know, lugging around that heavy bag so that I don't have to."

"No matter how heavy or light it is, I'll carry any bag for you."

Those words . . . I have to convince myself to hear them for what they are rather than what they can be. He's not saying he'll carry my burdens. Those aren't tangible, material things like bags are. I just need to keep reminding myself of that and everything should be alright.

Changing the subject, I ask, "Where are we going for breakfast?"

"You'll see."

As we sit down at a small table, I look around the quaint cafe. It's filled with greenery that gives it its own unique, lively feeling. Walking past the front counter earlier, I noticed the assortment of muffins, cakes, and tarts. Honestly, it's much sweeter than what I thought would suit Luke's tastes.

"I must admit that I'm shocked you've brought me here," I say, turning to look at him as I do. "Didn't take you for a sweets guy."

"Not in front of everybody. Only those worthy of knowing."

"And I'm worthy?"

"You're my wife."

Before I can stop myself, I bring up something that I've been kind of pushing to the back of my mind.

"But you didn't like me at first."

"Don't take offense to it, darling. I don't like most people at first. But things are different now."

"Different how? We haven't even known each other for twenty-four hours yet."

"That's true, but you haven't tried to take advantage of me even once since we started. When you set boundaries, they were absolute. Your tone told me you would not bend on any of them."

I nod my head. "But that still was after the wedding."

He sighs. "When we first met, I was worried my brother had brought me a fangirl. I wouldn't put it past him to play some *lousy* joke like that on me. But then, you proved me wrong in a very assertive way. From then, I realized that you were the type of person who was true to yourself, which meant that you would always move with integrity."

"That's it? You liked that I . . . told you off?"

"Sweetheart, I have very few people in my life who will do that."

"But the whole 'sweetheart' and 'darling' thing that you keep doing, it's almost like we're in a *real* relationship."

"Is that not what marriage is?"

"I mean it is, but . . ."

How do I explain this to him? We didn't marry because we were in love with each other. We married because I was convenient for him and his family provides a fun opportunity for me. There isn't anything more to it.

"Aurelia. You may be right about our marriage being one of convenience, but to me, you're worth pursuing. You're worth the risk of caring for," he replies. "I may have known you for less than a day, but I know enough to say that I will pursue you the way you deserve to be pursued and learn to love you the way you deserve to be treated."

My heart thumps in my chest as I consider what he's just said. Does it mean what I think it means?

Worth the risk of caring for? The way that I deserve to be treated? Is he . . . ?

"Are you—"

"No, sweetheart. I'm not confessing my love for you. We haven't even known each other for a day yet. I'm declaring my intentions."

Shit.

Shit. Shit. Shit. Shit. *Shit*.

I do *not* know how to handle interactions like this. I haven't even made a *friend* in years.

My heart is pounding even more ferociously now. Something about that feels more real than if he confessed his love to me right now. I could laugh off a love confession as temporary infatuation, but I can't laugh off such a genuine declaration of interest.

"You don't even know me."

He doesn't know what I do, the things that I take pleasure in, the people that I help, the people that I hurt. He doesn't know how I've hurt, how I've healed, how I've hid, how I've decided to live. He doesn't know about my current goal in life. One I'd die fighting for.

He may have noticed my obvious love for ramen and watched as I packed what I considered to be the most important possessions I have, probably picking some things up there too, but that's not *all* of me. I barely know who I am.

"I expect to learn more about you every day. Even years in the future, I hope that remains the case. How could I ever know who you are when you're probably still discovering yourself?"

Speechless. I'm *actually* speechless. What do I even say to that? I can joke it off, but that doesn't feel right. I don't think I can answer with the vulnerability that is required either.

I just find myself absently nodding as I say, "I don't know much about you either though . . ."

"Didn't you run a background check?"

"Background checks only reveal so much."

For instance, any background check run on me will spit out a carefully articulated blend of truths and untruths that I have full control over.

He grins. "How about we get some food?"

Sounds to me like he's changing the subject, but that's fine for me. I actually have a response for that suggestion.

"Fine. Let's do that."

Luke waves down a waitress, who hurries over. I didn't have a chance to look over the menu but I already know what I want. I saw it as I walked in.

When it's my turn, I ask, "May I have a strawberry shortcake and vanilla latte with an extra shot of espresso?"

The woman nods her head and does the usual waitress pleasantries before leaving the table.

"The strawberry shortcake is a good option here."

"Really? It's my favorite, so I can be a little picky with this particular type of cake."

"Well then, you can be the judge of it yourself. How does that sound?"

"We'll see," I reply. "Anyway, how did you find out about this place? It's hard for me to imagine you looking it up on the internet or something."

"My cousin owns it."

I think back to the wedding yesterday. He'd had quite a few cousins and I don't remember a single one of their names. I was kind of on autopilot the entire time. From what I do recall, Noah's his only sibling so his immediate family is quite small. He just has a large extended one.

"Oh, okay."

I'm not shocked since I know his family is super rich. Of course his cousin owns a cafe and had the capital to intricately decorate the place. It's beautiful. Serene.

A bright, cheerful, *very* familiar voice rings out across the cafe, "Lia, is that you?"

My stomach churns—my appetite for cake slowly diminishing.

That voice . . . You have *got* to be kidding me. First, last night, and now this? This has my mom all types of written behind it. Well, talk about a mood killer. Gone are all the good feelings—replaced by frustration.

As the footsteps get closer, I mutter, "Shoto."

Shoto. The man my mom wants me to marry *so badly*. The man who, in fact, tried to use his mom to get my mom to force me. Why the hell would he think it's okay to *ever* show his face again? Now I'm freaking annoyed.

"Lia, I knew that it was you. I've been trying to get in touch with you."

"And I'm sure you know I blocked you."

"Come on, Lia—"

"*Don't* call me that. You lost that privilege long ago."

Luke's expression shifts as he watches the interaction. The gentleness that's there when he interacts with me is completely gone and replaced by coldness. His lips no longer have a grin and instead are pin straight.

His deep voice holds a hint of annoyance as he asks, "What business do you have with my wife?"

Shoto, in an exaggeratedly shocked tone, questions, "*Wife?* How can that be? My Lia's been keeping herself available for me. After all, we're engaged. We're destined to be together *forever*."

At the last word, his tone gets deeper, more menacing. And I feel something at my back that should not be there. Not nearly large enough to be a knife. Maybe a needle? He wouldn't dare actually *drug* me, would he? That would be insane in a public place.

I try to ignore the cold sweat prickling over my skin and subtly move my trembling hand behind me to hopefully intervene before he can do anything crazy. I have to stay calm if I want to get out of this. If I panic, he'll waste no time in injecting me.

Control your breathing, Aurelia.

Trying to distract him from my movements, I say, "I told you to stop calling me that. And I am, in no circumstance yours. I belong to no one but myself. We've never been fiancés, and if you don't leave, I'll show you what happens if you keep pestering me."

Shoto's voice adopts a more confused tone as he says, "Maybe we should be having this conversation in private, Lia. I think there's an awful buzzing going on here, and it's incredibly headache inducing."

As he finishes the sentence, the needle breaks skin. Before he can administer it, though, he's knocked to the floor. Everything happened so fast I don't know what happened. I just know that my husband is pulling me into a hug and the other is taking the needle out.

I let out a breath, blinking away tears that have already started to cloud my vision. Shoto planned to drug me. He planned to take away my control of my own body. How could he? Even as much as he wants me, he knows . . .

My next breath is scarily close to the next. The one after that is even closer. The room closes in around me, suffocating me. When my heart rate increases, this time it's not in the fun way that Luke brings me. It's in the way that makes me want to tear it from my chest so that I never have to feel it again.

Before I can register it, I'm having a full-on panic attack. Shoto knows that my single greatest fear, even more than my fear of inaction, is the fear of losing control.

Losing control is why I can't let this happen. Losing control is exactly why I can't let myself love someone. I know that to love is to give that up.

If I have anything to thank Shoto for, it's that reminder.

But still, as I completely break down, Luke is holding me and whispering sweet nothings as if I'm the most precious thing in the world. His words don't register, but his voice does. His *voice* reels me in. His voice brings my mind back to my body, and his hold keeps it anchored there.

How can something that's supposed to make me lose control also give me back my control at the same time? It could be minutes or only mere seconds that pass by as he anchors me to him, letting everything wash over me, and the world condenses until it's only me and him left. But through it all, I feel my control coming back.

"Thank you," I whisper.

Luke doesn't reply but instead holds me a little tighter. Now that my breathing is under control, I sag into his embrace for a few more seconds—regaining my strength.

When I'm ready, I gently push away and turn to face Shoto. In the midst of my panic attack, I hadn't noticed that he was being restrained by cafe security.

"Why are you *really* here?" I ask. "You don't usually come to spots like this since you hate coffee. And you came prepared to drug me."

He used to endlessly complain when his mother would drag him out on outings to places like this. I know he's not here alone.

"To come see you. Why else do you think I'd come here?"

I frown. I already know who has the resources to have me followed and send him after me. His family is decently influential but everyone knows that mine beats Shoto's ten times out of ten.

"She sent you here," I state.

"No sweetie," a familiar voice says as heels clack closer, beckoning my attention. "I am here. Just letting you know that your little message has been received and thought it best to respond in person with a reminder of your familial duty."

CHAPTER 10

"Oka-san."

I have been in the habit of calling her "mother" in Japanese since I was young. She always wanted to make sure my brothers and I never forget our Japanese. Now, it feels like a curse coming off my tongue.

"Why don't I come sit with you guys?"

"Sorry." I scoff. "As you can see, the table is only for two."

I turn around, showing her my back. If there's one thing she hates, it's being ignored. Especially when it's one of her children doing it.

Her voice lowers to a menacing level as she warns, "Asa."

Oh, she's bringing my *middle* name into this. Is that supposed to scare me? I mean, if she was the type to try what Shoto did, I'd be a little more concerned. That's not something she'd do though. It's way too reckless and impulsive. Besides, my husband is also here so she shouldn't do anything too sudden.

While I'm still a little shaken up from Shoto, I'm at least able to keep my breathing steady and be less concerned about what she'd do.

"My patience is running thin, Mother."

"So is mine, daughter."

"Have you come to apologize?"

She scoffs. That's it. That's her only response. I mean, who does she think she is? For someone who is willing to go through all these extreme measures to get me back when the solution is literally *so simple* .   .

Yeah, the woman's crazy.

Luke's arm snakes around my shoulders and holds me while facing my mother. I guess I can get used to this whole protective thing.

"Well, if not to apologize, then why have you come? You surely know that I'm not coming home with you."

"To talk," she says.

Her footsteps approach and my husband holds me tighter. I can tell that after the Shoto fiasco, it must take a lot of restraint for him to not go any further. Is he restraining himself so that I can handle this?

Now that I've really shifted my attention back to him, his arm is firm around me but it feels like it's trembling and not from fear. It's rage. Rage that he's barely keeping contained. I'm thankful, though, that he is allowing me to handle this on my own.

"Fine. Let's talk. But get that nuisance out of here before I puke."

I don't need to say who I'm talking about. It's obvious to everyone who saw the previous encounter.

"Mother-in-law," Shoto pleads in Japanese. "I should be here, too. You know that she needs her true husband by her side."

And now we've jumped from fiancé to husband. Someone needs to lock this guy up somewhere with padded walls and no sharp edges, if you catch my drift. The social media girls talk about delulu, but even *that* isn't enough to describe him.

"Either he buzzes off or I walk. And you and I both know that I can and will walk, if I want to."

The me ten years ago would never believe that I one day would actually stand up to my mom. Not only defying her but freaking telling her to concede to my demands or, quite frankly, kiss my ass as I walk out the door. Now, she can pick what's more damaging to her precious ego.

To think that there was a time in my life that I was scared of her—and that was still a time in life where I feared very little. I laugh at old me. After going away for school, things had become *so* much clearer, and I realized I also held power.

"Shoto," she says. "Go. We'll talk later."

I add, "Do me a favor and remind him during that talk that I already have a husband, and Shoto will never replace him."

"Lia, you are *mine*."

"Miyagi Shoto!"

"Also," I say as I listen to his retreating footsteps. "Remind him that after today's stunt, he's earned my attention but not in the ways that he thought. It'll only be worse for him if he *ever* shows up again."

"Aurelia, I suggest you stop talking, too."

I laugh. "I'm not the one begging to talk to anyone here. I'm just as fine walking away. You should feel honored that I'm giving you the time of day."

I flip the phrase that she used on me as a child back at her. My mother, as one could imagine, wasn't the most present parent. She showed up when it was time to take credit for our achievements, and rarely any other time. If she took the time to speak to us, even if it was to scold us, she would tell us that we should feel honored that she even gave us the time of day.

How's it feel?

"Honey," I ask, "can you ask someone to bring over another chair so we can talk with my mother? If you don't mind giving up your seat, I'd prefer you be the one in the middle."

I trust that he'll be able to get in the middle if things get out of hand. Considering who my mother is and who I am, there are ample possibilities of things going south, north, east, *or* west. I wouldn't want this beautiful place ruined.

My mother enters my field of vision as she walks over to the very spot where Luke had been sitting minutes ago. A waitress rushes over with a chair, and we all are sat at this two person table with tempers that could account for ten.

My mother folds her hands on the table before she asks, "When did you get married?"

I smile. "Yesterday."

"Why wasn't I informed?"

I can't help but laugh, disbelief making way for amusement. Between what happened last night and today, the answer should be obvious.

"You seem pretty well informed to me."

"You still laugh at improper times," she scolds, shaking her head.

"I mean, you still think that you hold *any* power over me. Don't crack me up, Oka-san." I switch to very informal Japanese. "You really are so cute."

Her eye twitches but she makes no further movement than that. I will admit that, at this point, I'm having fun antagonizing her.

"Come home."

She barely finishes talking before I answer, "No thanks."

"You know that you weren't meant to marry anyone else. This has already been arranged for you, and you should stop fooling around. It's your family duty." She turns to Luke, her back straight and chin held high. "You. Divorce her. I know that it's not serious. You only met yesterday. If you think that I didn't have an eye on my daughter, you're sorely mistaken. What kind of man marries someone who's already spoken for anyway?"

Luke, who now has a way into the conversation, stares deeply into her eyes as he plainly replies, "You're right. We did only just meet yesterday. And she *is* spoken for . . . by *me*. By your logic, that Shoto kid should be the one to back off."

Seeing the two confidently face off, I notice the difference. While I approach situations in a more carefree and relaxed way, these two are a lot more upfront with their fight for dominance. They compose themselves in a way entirely different than I do and it gives their stand-off a ferocity I could never manage. Especially not without laughing.

That's not to say the stand-off isn't respectable. It's to say that it's just not *my* thing. But it does make my husband look intoxicatingly sexy.

"Listen, I don't care that you're from the Moore family—"

"Oh, so you *do* know what family I'm from and who we are." Woah, his voice just got deeper and not in the alluring way that it does when he flirts with me. It's like he's outright challenging her. "Then I suggest you remember your place."

"I do know what family you hail from, young man, and I don't care.

You have no real sway here," she replies. "What I care about is that my daughter cannot be married to you."

"I don't care what you think can or can't happen. My wife has made her decision."

I nod. "I have made my decision, dear husband. Thank you for explaining it in simple terms so that even an idiot can understand. Is that all you're here for, Oka-san?"

I enunciate every syllable in a teasing way. I want her to understand that I'm taking this conversation about as seriously as an orca takes a bull.

My mother sneers. "You will marry the boy. You and I both know that it's the perfect match. And, Asa, it's your familial duty. You know that every member of this family must fulfill theirs, including you. Just get over your temper tantrum already and make up with Shoto. You do remember what happened to Chiaki."

I see red. My blood boils as I jump up from my seat, *barely* stopping myself from lunging across the table at the woman. How dare she bring up Chiaki? After throwing her out and allowing that sham of a company to do what they did because she had no backing . . .

Chiaki, my elder sister. Chiaki, who suffered until the day she disappeared because she tried to protect *me*. Chiaki, in which I wish I could remember what went down the night that started it all. Unfortunately, it's all a blank right now and no one will tell me what happened.

And Lily, our best friend who I have no doubt went missing because she was dragged into this mess.

A large hand grips mine, anchoring me to the present. As angry as I am, I can't let my brain go down that rabbit hole yet. It only leads to despair, and my focus needs to be on the woman in front of me. There's plenty of time for dwelling later, but that time is not now.

My mother wants a reaction from me, and I'm giving it to her.

Thank you, Luke, for reeling me back in. My focus is on the bigger picture now.

I return to my chair, adjusting my composure and taking a deep breath. I won't give her the pleasure of riling me up any further. But I can't stop thinking about what she said. And I *need* to know if it means what I think it does.

"Mother, you didn't . . ."

Did she have a more active role to play in my sister's disappearance? I thought that her negligence was bad enough, but if she personally had anything to do with Chiaki . . .

Now she has my attention. But she doesn't realize that while she may have placed the carrot on the stick, I'm one determined hardass.

"Who knows? And by, the way sweetie," she stands from the table, "you no longer have anything on me. You'd be surprised how much . . . cleaning I can do in two years. Consider my offer."

With that, the maddening sound of her heels clack away, her words still hanging in the air. I'm considering way more than her offer right now.

My mom has *always* been the hunter. Now, I think it's time for her to learn what it is to be the prey.

CHAPTER 11

After a breakfast like that, I don't expect my day to go much better than this. Of course, the queen of narcissism had to come and ruin my mood.

"Sweetheart, are you listening to me?"

I sheepishly turn to face Luke. I mean, I'm obviously not listening but I hope he doesn't take it too personally. I'm just too busy figuring out what my next move will be. I mean, I already was going to bring down BB Media for their role in my sister and our best friend's disappearance. That talent company has been blatantly shady for a long time, and I still wish I cared to do even a modicum of research before they took her. But since my mom has all but shouted from the rooftops that she was involved in sister's disappearance, now I need to take her down, too.

You'd think that I'd be hesitant, but I'm just annoyed. If I had known before, I would have brought her down long ago. If she really has cleaned up her dirty little secrets then I'll likely have to work even harder to uncover her new ones.

"Sorry," I murmur. "It's not that you're boring or anything, but I'm a little pissed off."

Okay, I'll admit. A *little* is an understatement. I think that a bear who has lost their cub is less pissed off than me. If I didn't know that impulsivity can lead to mistakes, I would probably have done something extremely reckless by now.

He gently pulls me into a hug. "I get it sweetheart, I really do. I won't tell you not to worry about it, but we can deal with this later. Together."

I nod against him, not wanting to tell him that I have to do this on my own but feeling peculiarly safe in his arms. He doesn't know what I do, and I'm still not sure when the right time is to tell him. I do know that whatever these feelings are shouldn't blind me from the reality of needing to trust someone before I can even try to let them in on my life's work.

"Okay."

Seriously, I'll let him help but it won't be in some big, extravagant way. Just enough that I'm technically not breaking my word. I hate lying to people that I care about—not that there are many of them out there.

After a few more moments of absorbing his warmth (he's the perfect heater), I gently push myself away and tell Luke to continue talking. Apparently, he had been explaining to me how the security in our new home works along with what all the alarm codes are.

The large house is surrounded with surveillance cameras. Judging by the two different models, I'm assuming that they operate on two different servers—making it harder for a hacker to be able to infiltrate all surveillance at once.

Very smart.

The glass on the windows are tinted, obviously a one way tint so that we can see out but no one else is able to see inside. Considering the precautions already taken, I'm curious to find out if they're also bulletproof.

The modern house, true to the monochrome aesthetic, is a beautiful blend of black and white with some shades of gray in between.

This place is even more beautiful than the pictures we looked at last night. And this place is now my home.

"Let's see inside," I say. "Considering how prepared everything is out here, I have to assume that inside has already been decorated, and I'm curious to see your style."

Luke places his thumb on the scanner attached to the doorknob and a click soon follows. When the door swings open, I'm met with . . . emptiness. Like literally not a single piece of furniture around.

I toe off my shoes in the entryway before stepping in further. For someone who always seems so ultra prepared, this is definitely unexpected to say the least.

"Is the furniture still on the way?"

"I never ordered any."

I turn to face him, and I know that I probably look about as shocked as someone who walks in on their parents doing the devil's tango. Mr. Prepared really didn't order furniture but managed to make sure that surveillance cameras and tinted glass were installed?

"Why not? Was it too much with everything else you had to handle?"

I can smell his approach as he walks closer. He used my body wash yesterday so he smells like me—cherry blossoms and vanilla. I'll admit that there's a sort of mildly possessive part of me that likes that he smells like me. It's like laying a claim.

"Well," he says. "I thought you'd want to decorate it together, the same way we picked out the house. It's *our* home, sweetheart."

Well, he *is* right. At least he errs on the side of caution. I wouldn't have minded if it was already furnished but I can't be mad at the thought of wanting to keep me involved. If anything, I suppose I feel a little touched by this whole thing.

I feign cockiness as I cross my arms across my chest and exclaim, "As long as you know. But we'll be figuring out furniture today. Such a beautiful place shouldn't be so empty on the inside, ya know?"

I glance around the room, already planning out what I'd like to see to liven this place up. A couch here, a loveseat there, a ginormous television on the wall in front . . . I can keep going for hours if he'd let me. But, if I'm honest with myself, there's something else that I need first.

"Hey, when are our bags getting here?"

"Paul dropped them off earlier while we were at the cafe."

Right. The cafe. And the very reason why I need a shower. After that whole showdown with Shoto, I want to scrub my body free of him. I absolutely don't want any remnants of him or his cooties on me. I really will give him a piece of my mind the next time that I see him.

"Okay. I just really need a shower after earlier. I feel . . . dirty."

"Of course," he replies.

He leads the way through the house to the stairs leading to the second story. From the way that he carries himself, I can tell the reminder must not sit right with him either. His movements are very restrained and his muscles sporadically flex and retract as if he's trying to keep his own body in control.

The events of today did affect more than me. And honestly, it would be a lie if I said that I didn't feel kind of warm inside because he also is upset about *my* problems.

When we enter the bedroom, I pause. Although it's bare aside from my boxes and bags scattered around, the view from the balcony is amazing. It's not like the skyline view from some skyscraper, but it faces the backyard with our pool and all the space. I can't help but think up ways to make the scene even more whimsical.

I'm talking fairy lights, foliage, and maybe even a freaking dog. Wait, I hope he's not allergic to animals. If not, I should *really* convince him to get a dog sometime soon.

I break free from my daydream when I hear the door click shut, leaving me alone inside of the room. I guess he's giving me my privacy to handle what I need.

Well, thanks for that, buddy.

I go searching through boxes. I can't believe the people Luke sent to pack up my stuff didn't label every box, only the important ones. So the one that has all my toiletries has managed to blend in with the crowd of unlabeled boxes.

After (finally) getting everything I needed, I am now comfortably in the shower. The water pressure and temperature are perfect, creating a peaceful environment for a shower.

As the quiet consumes me, only broken by the spatter of water against my skin and the shower floor, I have the space to think.

Okay so, here's what I know: my mom and Shoto won't stop coming after me, and the two of them, in my mind, are on completely different levels. That means that my methods are going to have to be different.

In terms of Shoto, he's easy. The man is genuinely delusional, and while I will never be able to forgive him for what happened between us today, I know he's being manipulated too.

To deal with him, I need to absolutely crush his spirits. I can't allow him to, even in his delusional mind, believe there's even a speck of a chance. But considering how convinced he sounded, I'll also need contingency plans in place. If I can't get him convinced that there's no chance, then I'll have to become so undesirable to him that he doesn't want me anymore. If that doesn't work, I'll go to an extreme.

It will crush his family's spirit and reputation, but I will have no choice but to put on a show that will have him forcibly admitted into a psych ward. I'm no psychologist so maybe they can get the crazy out. It's a last resort though. That stigma . . . it follows you forever.

Shoto isn't really much of a problem. My mom on the other hand . . . I had gotten careless and stopped keeping tabs on her while she kept me in her sights. Everything I have on her is likely completely useless by now. People who know they have enemies, especially one as close to home as their own child, always clean up their messes afterwards. My mom is nothing if not thorough.

Not only that, but it's entirely possible that she was part of what happened to Chiaki. No, it's more than just a simple possibility. The woman is guilty of throwing her child to the wolves. And whatever part she played, I *need* to find out. She deserves a punishment to fit the crime, after all.

To destroy my mother, I'll have to figure out her motivations. Why does she want me married to Shoto so bad? Why did she abandon Chiaki while knowing how many enemies she has? One could say that it was to control me but I know that there *has* to be more to the story, though I still can't help the guilt that eats me up because I know I was a part of it.

But this all means I need access to my memories. I don't remember what happened the last time I interacted with Chiaki in person, but I know that the memory has to hold an important key to the puzzle. I just don't understand how I've managed to forget something so important.

And BB Media isn't safe either. I will burn the entire organization. I will make it so that everyone involved in my sister's case wishes that they were dead. Even my own mother.

Especially my own mother.

CHAPTER 12

Three weeks have passed since I've moved in with Luke. We've furnished the entire house and now seem to have settled into a new normal.

Every morning, we wake up on opposite ends of our large bed and have breakfast together before I disappear into my home office and he leaves to go to his corporate building. While he's gone, I feel more comfortable to do my work.

The only slightly unpleasant thing is that he has security all around—though he does order them to stay out of sight as he promised. And there are less in here than when I go outside. I'll admit that they're good at it but just knowing that they're there is enough to have me on edge sometimes.

Back to the positive though, we go on dates every week. As short as the time that we've known each other is, he's good at gauging the things that I like to do. Our living situation is fairly cozy.

Now, I'm sipping on my latte, because *of course* I made sure we got an espresso machine, and I'm lowkey a pro barista. My focus, though, is primarily on the screen in front of me. I've spent the last three days trying to zero in on my first target: Shoto.

According to the information I gathered through some very legal (or not) methods, I now have the whole inside scoop on the marriage thing.

My family, who runs a very successful cybersecurity company, has actually fallen on hard times. They aren't close to bankruptcy, but their competitors have some tech genius on their payroll. Apparently they found this diamond around the first time they tried to push me and Shoto together.

While Shoto's family may not be as prominent as mine, they obviously have something my mother wants. After some deeper digging that may or may not have required hacking into confidential company files in three different companies, I discovered something very interesting.

So, let's simplify this. Let's call my family's company, Company A. Shoto's family company is Company B, and the rival company is Company C.

Company C's tech genius developed a black box that can reportedly strip any security system down to its bare bones and destroy it. Now, any hacker worth their salt can do that, but as this system destroys the security protocol, it also rebuilds a copy of it that lives on the device until it's either exported to be used elsewhere, modified, or completely destroyed by the person who owns it. This opens opportunities to not only destroy competitors, but to also make money off of their research.

So my mother, of course, could not let that type of power stay with her greatest competitor. She was just as likely to become a victim as anyone else—probably even more considering she stood in the way of Company C and full market ownership.

Company B is a "security company." Really, it's just a front for what they really are: mercenaries. They aren't exactly the biggest dogs in town, but they're big enough to have a name for themselves within certain social circles.

My mom, of course, asked her bestie, Shoto's mom and the CEO of Company B, to do her a solid and steal that black box. At least, that's what I'm assuming, considering that not long after the black box became an industry rumor, according to Company C's files, it somehow ceased to be in their possession. Apparently, Company C has been trying to steal it back. But, for some reason, just after my run-in with Shoto and my mother at the cafe, Company B started negotiating on selling the black box back to Company C.

Now, here's *my* theory. Shoto's mom has always given him whatever he wanted. He never really used to be a super snob about it or anything, but I know he never had to earn a thing in his life. I used to think it was something he'd grow out of, but I don't think so anymore. Maybe that's why he's deluded enough to think he can have me.

Anyway, his mom wanted to trade the black box for her son's happiness. In other words, she will only hand the device over to my mom if I marry Shoto.

And to be clear, even with this information, there's not a way in *hell*.

Now that Shoto's mom has seen that I've married someone else, I know she's probably willing to risk her friendship with my mom to back her into a corner. Meaning that now my mom has to take more extreme measures. It probably took me marrying someone else for her narcissistic self to realize I wouldn't come crawling back.

If Company C gets back the black box, it's *extremely* likely they will use it on Company A. After all, recent files from their server say that Company A has reached the top of their suspect list for the theft in the first place.

To confirm my theory, I'm simultaneously digging through the financials *and* the encrypted data that very few people know exist in both Company A and Company B's servers. I'm using the report date from Company C as my starting point and searching three weeks on either side of the date.

I sip my coffee with one hand while typing and scrolling away with the other, humming a tune to one of my absolute favorite K-pop groups. Their music is so cheery and energetic. It's literally perfect for doing some morally gray things, ya know?

I have to admit that getting into the security systems of Companies A and C was a bit difficult. On the other hand, Company B was a cakewalk. They used to be protected by Company A but have been shifting their protections to Company C due to the tensions between Shoto's mom and my mom.

Every hacker knows that a system in transition is the easiest to get into. And really, what is Company C doing? Securing Company B should have been an easy thing—a day, *tops*. There's probably trouble in paradise there.

Aha.

I found something buried really, really deep in the servers. Putting my coffee down, I work to decrypt it. The style looks familiar enough, reminding me of someone I used to go to school with. I forget her name though.

No matter. She always lost to me when it came down to anything. I haven't met a system that can keep *me* out so this will be a breeze.

Unraveling the encryption reminds me of a top speed illegal street fight. Both combatants are fighting with a strong spirit, but for different reasons. In this case, the security system is fighting to protect its system from an intruder: me. In my case, I'm fighting for two reasons. The obvious one is that I want to get to the bottom of this damn marriage thing and the other . . . it's the thrill of the hack.

The deeper into the system I get, the more excited I become. It's almost as if time stops as my jittery fingers fly across the keyboard, and my heart races as if it's trying to keep up with all the action. And by the time I realize I'm actually smiling, I'm already done.

Speaking of, I'm in. And I think I've stumbled across something that dear old Company A probably meant to keep hidden forever. It appears that when Company A was in charge of Company B's cybersecurity, they created a link between the servers so they could hide everything to do with this very illegal scheme. That explains why they weren't too concerned about Company B handing over their security needs to Company C.

The first email, which stems from Company B's side, reads:

Akira,

I have been trying to get in touch with you but you seem to be dodging my calls. Friends or not, I have reconsidered the initial terms of our agreement. I have the product, as you've requested, but there's something else I want.

I've sent you back every dime you paid me to get this job done, and instead, I want your precious little heir to marry mine. There's no changing my mind. Without that, your product will just have to remain safely stored with me.

-Fumiko

I'm surprised that Fumiko, Shoto's mom, would use their real names in the interaction. Maybe she and my mom were overly confident in the abilities of the cybersecurity tool that the company uses.

Anyway, this makes so much sense. According to the timestamp of this email, it's the same day my mother and I had that huge blowout fight that led to me having no choice but to leave.

The reply reads:

Fumiko,

This was not what we agreed upon. You know that I can't give up the only child who's able to succeed me because your son is a little infatuated. Pick something else.

-Akira

Oh, I always knew my dear old mother saw me as her heir apparent. After all, I'm just that gifted. There's no reason to argue what we all know to be a fact.

Anyway, back to the emails. I really wish I had the foresight to make some popcorn before getting to work. I wonder how it would taste with coffee.

Akira,

You're little one will still be able to succeed you. I just need her to make sure she keeps my son happy. I'm not asking you to sign her life away. The two grew up together anyway. Who better to keep her leashed?

-Fumiko

Excuse me? I do *not* need to be leashed. Who the hell do these people think they are? I already knew they didn't see me as much, but I'm way better than a rabid dog. I actually think before I act. And when I hurt people, I never get put down.

Fumiko,

Fine. I'll see what I can do.

-Akira

There's no more on the subject in these files. I suppose they moved it off email. Well, this certainly makes a lot of sense. Of course I was right about why my mother needs me to marry Shoto.

Either way, tough luck.

I save the emails to a flash drive and go searching for the financials. Now that I have a more specific time period, it shouldn't be hard for me to find the money trail, too. I think back to my mom's words about having already cleaned up.

Good thing I know how to fish for new dirt. Especially now that I completely understand the situation.

While Shoto might be delusional and acts dense at times, I also know he's incredibly clever. There's no way he hasn't figured out that I'm being used as currency. I realize now that even *he* sees me as less than human.

A part of me breaks inside. We used to be the best of friends. I remember the times where we'd go out and do stupid stuff just for shits and giggles. Breaking into closed arcades (courtesy of his skills), replacing our teacher's presentations with wildly inappropriate memes (courtesy of mine), and even just being there to hold each other when something went wrong.

Part of me, even through it all, hadn't wanted to let go of the good memories. I never wanted some of the best parts of my childhood to become tainted by the impurity of the real world. The people around me . . . every single one of them is only out for themselves, and I have never truly mattered.

What Shoto feels isn't love. It's not even infatuation. It's a subconscious need to control what he can't have simply because he can't have it. I see that now.

I used to think the foundation of my childhood was like the house made of wood in the old tale about the three pigs. Not as strong as brick, but not as fragile as straw. This has proved me wrong. My house was always made of straw and all the people in my life are akin to the wolf— taking every chance to blow and blow. While it may have been more resistant than the pig in the story, it was only because I used my vigor to keep it together. Alone.

Well, I won't stand for this treatment from anyone else anymore. I'm no longer a child and I've learned how I *can* be treated in this past week—regardless of whether I believe I deserve it or not.

How is it that a man I've known for only three weeks has shown me this? Out of respect for the real respect that he shows me, I won't spare any more sympathy for people like Shoto. Like his mom. Like *my* mom.

Forget all that bullshit I said last week about going easy on Shoto because I know who Fumiko would send on a retrieval mission for something so delicate. Only one person so enmeshed with her that she knows there's no way in *hell* he'd betray her. It's him.

She sent Shoto. And there's no doubt in my mind that he wasn't a part of the deal struck between our moms, too. I was the only one left out. I was the one being traded like merchandise.

Lucky for me, my sleuthing has led me to the next place where all the players will gather together. Even better, I have a way in because I was invited to go last night over dinner with my hubby.

I pull up the website for the event known simply as *The Gala*. No more words are needed because everyone knows that only the richest, most influential people and industry leaders are invited.

And it's just under four months from now. More than enough time to plan.

This gala will be the great downfall of those who have crossed me. They wanted to play chess? It's a good thing that I've been learning to play shogi.

Let the games begin.

CHAPTER 13

Talk about hot.

I admit it. I'm so gaping like a fool. I mean, how can I not? My husband has donned the new suit I chose for him. It's in his typical black, but I made him wear this gorgeous emerald green shirt under it to add a bit more color. In my professional opinion, the ensemble makes his legs look extra-long and luscious, and he looks damn fine in that shade of green.

I mean, damn! I'm married to that?

"Like what you see?"

I nod my head enthusiastically. Ever since his confession of his intentions to properly pursue me, I've been a lot bolder with my stares. Why bother to hide it anymore? I've pretty much decided that my career path is more of a discussion that I'll deal with once we get to that bridge.

It's time for our weekly date night. Every week, Luke has decided he will pick a random day where he comes home from work early and takes me out to somewhere new. Last week, we went ice skating. I'm still shocked at his skill on the ice.

Tonight though, is a bit of business mixed with pleasure. He offered to move our date after he was told there was some event he needed to attend today, but I declined. I would never want to get in the way of his work.

Besides, any work event he brings me to is always going to be an opportunity. A lot of my enemies run in the same circles, and it's the perfect way to dig up dirt on them or to even build rapport without giving myself away.

As we stand in front of the mirror, all I can think is that we are such a power couple.

After I had picked out his outfit, he had also insisted on picking mine out. Partially curious and partially fascinated by the idea, I went along with him. I hadn't expected him to drag me to one of those stores where they only sell one version of each design, but of course he did.

The dress that I'm wearing matches the emerald color of his shirt, it's one elegant strap draping over my right shoulder and wrapping around the rest of my torso leading to a draped skirt with an almost dangerously high slit up my left leg.

To match it, I'm wearing a pair of strappy (very uncomfortable) stilettos and all silver jewelry. My wedding ring and engagement ring sit comfortable on my left ring finger. I have medium hoop earrings in both ears, studs in my other pierced spots (I have quite a few), and a heart shaped pendant that features my birthstone.

My makeup is lightly done, but nothing more is needed. I know I look gorgeous right now. At least my husband isn't overshadowing me.

Luke turns to face me, lifting my hand to his lips and gently kissing it. "Stunning, as always."

I like that about him. He knows better than to walk into blatant traps like those guys who say something like "You look beautiful tonight." As if their girls don't look beautiful 24/7.

I smile, butterflies fluttering in my stomach. Ever since I have learned to accept his intentions to pursue me, I no longer get as flustered as I used to, which is admittedly preferable to the alternative.

I smile. "Thank you. But shouldn't we get going?"

Instead of letting go of his hand, I pull him along as we make our way out of the house. Patrick is already waiting in the driveway standing next to the open backseat door.

As we walk toward him, I say, "Good evening, Pat."

He softly smiles. "Good evening, Mrs. Moore."

We're still working on that. It's a step up from him calling me Young Miss or whatever type title he believed he needed to give me.

As I slide in, I notice Luke nodding to Patrick. It's a huge step up from him only acknowledging the man when it was to tell him to do something. I'd gotten on him about it last week, and we've taken a baby step. It's okay. I'll get him to start using his words with other people one day.

It's not long before we're headed to BB Media HQ for their birthday party. Every year, they have some celebration honoring how far their company has come. Really, it's just them showing off all of their accomplishments.

People only go for the social opportunities. While all the large companies are automatically extended an invitation, small ones have to do much more to prove themselves worthy of the event. In essence, BB Media gets publicity and everyone else gets a chance to build their own rapport with people and knock down their rivals.

I'm actually pretty excited for tonight's event for more than my own personal opportunities. Watching all the scheming people hiding behind their smiling masks and expensive outfits is always comedic.

"Honey," I say. "Why are you going to this event this year? I hear that you typically don't go. What changed?"

It's true. Though I didn't just happen to "hear" about it. In truth, I've managed to sneak into the event every year. For funsies, of course.

"There's a certain business deal I need to close. Tonight gives me an opportunity to get close enough to the only holdout and secure it."

Oh? An actual deal that he'd go out of his way to attend a party that he typically avoids for?

"And," he adds. "This year, I have something rather selfish to do. I want to show off my wife."

When I peek over, he's smirking as he gazes out the window.

Of course the man would want to go because of some deal. This possessive husband of mine wants to show me off. Well, fair enough. Because I definitely also enjoy showing him off too, so I really can't be mad at his reasoning.

Looking out my own window, I let the car fall into a peaceful silence as we make our way into the city.

⚊⚊⚊ 🔒 ⚊⚊⚊

From the moment that we step out of the car, all eyes are on us. The red carpet is always surrounded by the media and some of the lower-ranked attendees. I wrap my hand under his bicep as we take steady steps across the red carpet—eyes forward, completely ignoring the awed gazes and whispers around us.

"I can't believe he actually showed up this year."

"Wow, I can't believe he's actually married."

"So jealous. They look like they were made for each other."

Well, duh. That's because we're both so good looking. I mean, look at us! Now, I'm not saying this to be snobby. I truthfully believe power couples exist. We just happen to be one of them.

With the extra inches my stilettos have allotted me, once we reach the end of the carpet, I pull on Luke's neck, bringing his cheek close enough to kiss. In front of everyone here. Yeah, I'm staking my claim on him right now in front of everyone. Isn't that part of why we got married?

Just keeping up appearances.

From this, I'm met with the gentlest grin before he wraps his arm around my waist and pulls me in close.

So low that only I can hear, he mutters, "I'm going to kiss you right now."

I barely have the chance to grin and nod my head before his lips are on mine—a quick peck that lingers for a second or two and is over far too soon.

Is it wrong to say I'd have liked it to last just a bit longer? I guess it would be weird to do more here, *but still. This is the first time he's kissed me since the wedding.*

When he pulls away, I gaze up into his dark eyes, and he peers back at me as if looking straight into my soul. The smirk that alights his face tells me he knows *exactly* the effect he just had on me, and that he was undeniably proud of it.

He doesn't say another word, instead swiping his thumb at a spot beneath my lip. I guess my lipstick must have smudged after the brief kiss.

Before I can say anything, he offers his arm to me again. I get what he's gesturing. Now is neither the time nor place to talk about the intensity behind that kiss. He better realize we'll still be talking about it later.

Stepping into the building, we follow an usher to a giant ballroom toward the back. The moment we step in, I notice a shift in the atmosphere.

These people aren't like the people outside. They don't stop to stare but the energy of the room has shifted and I've noticed quite a few people make subtle glances at us before returning to their conversations. I guess that this is also the same difference between coming here previously by hacking the system to send myself an invite and coming here on the arm of the most powerful man in town.

How lovely.

As we enter the room, I ask, "So what's the game plan? Do I entertain his wife?"

"Smart, indeed, my wife. Your only job here is to socialize naturally. When the time comes, you'll need to hit it off with Gustavo's wife. I obviously won't just walk up to him."

Interesting. I see what he's saying. I might be able to hurry it along a bit.

"If you insist," I say.

I make my way around the room. I have a few targets of my own tonight.

Target number one: spotted.

Swiping a glass of wine from one of the server's trays, I take a sip and make my way over to a group of women. Included in their ranks: Margaret, the wife of BB Media's CEO himself.

She's not his first or even his second wife. Starting as his personal assistant from the more impoverished side of the city, she came into the picture after his fourth wife. So far, she's managed to last the longest— something over two years now, I believe.

She is gorgeous though. She has short red hair that's styled into a curly bob. Her green eyes accentuated by her peach blush and lip combo. Her body has a smooth hourglass figure that fits perfectly into her deep plum mermaid gown. I don't know if I stylist was involved in the night's look or she chose it herself, but it's incredibly well coordinated for bringing out her natural features.

Inserting myself into their group, I say, "What a wonderful event. It must have taken ages to plan."

Everyone knows Margaret has taken over planning the birthday celebration for the last few years. She takes great joy in selecting the theme and making sure every little detail matches.

The other women in the group look like they want to tell me off for interjecting in their conversation but quickly change their minds. Here's to being married to the most powerful person in the room, I guess.

Margaret briefly replies, "Thank you."

It seems that she's trying to blow me off. She was cordial, but only enough to be polite. Is it boredom? No, it has to be something else. Now that I think about it, she's probably heard some variation of the same thing I said at least a hundred times already.

"I mean seriously, where did you get the idea to import Barolo? I definitely see the idea. Christmas in July is genius."

Her eyes light up and a genuine smile crosses her face.

Score.

"How did you know?" she asks.

"I once went on a European wine tour. You'd be surprised how extensive my palette is."

A half-truth. I just happened to have many different types of wine when picking some of the best hackers in the world's brains. It was a tour through Europe, but the wine was more like a tool to get people to open up.

"You're Mrs. Moore, right? It's a pleasure to meet you," she says, sticking out her hand.

I grasp her hand in mine, shaking it. "Likewise."

"I had no idea that you and your husband would be attending tonight. I must admit it's an honor to have you."

"Why, of course. My husband doesn't make a habit of going out after work, but I think you'll see that's changed. It's what happens when you marry someone who needs a bit more socialization."

I chuckle and sip my wine.

She giggles. "Oh, I get it. Before we got married, my husband would always take these long business trips. Now, he stays around town more to look after us."

"Us?"

"Oh, silly me. I'm not supposed to tell anyone, but we're expecting!"

I want to puke. Like actually. My stomach is twisting and turning like it's trying to escape a maze.

A monster who's involved in many people's children going missing every year is about to have a child of his own? What type of justice is that?

I gasp and cover my mouth, pretending to be excited.

She places a finger to her lips. "Don't tell anyone. He wants to keep it a secret. Especially because he wants to protect our child from being forced to live in the eyes of the public."

Sure, that's why. It's definitely not because your husband is involved in human trafficking or anything like that, and he knows that there are people whose morals are way worse than mine out to get him. Why would that be the case?

"My lips are sealed," I reply. "I can't believe this. I feel so honored to be among the first to know."

"We've tried repeatedly and I kept having miscarriages early on, but this is the first time I made it through the first trimester. I just had to tell someone and . . . I guess it just slipped out."

I smile. "It's fine. We all have those moments, don't we."

Margaret gently rests her hand on her flat stomach and says, "It feels so good to have someone I can talk to. It's just that everyone else here seems so artificial. Would it be too forward of me to ask for your contact information?"

"Of course! My phone is with my husband so how about I give you my number?"

The woman nods and hands me her phone. As I type in my number, I almost feel bad that I'm using her kindness to get closer to my own goals. It's a shame that we could have actually been real friends without sneakiness if she wasn't married to such an awful human.

When I hand back her phone, she smiles and then I notice her eyes widening ever so slightly. I wonder what's—

"I'll be stealing my wife back."

Luke wraps his arm around my waist and walks off with me before

I even have a chance to say goodbye. I'll admit I'm a little confused. It's almost as if he doesn't want me talking to her.

I wonder what that's about.

CHAPTER 14

The boring ceremonial part of the party flashes by. Despite all the gorgeous women and handsome men, I find myself distracted by only one person.

His reaction earlier still has me thinking. I wonder what his reason is for wanting to get me away from Margaret. Maybe he knows about all the dark and dirty things her husband has done. I hope that's it because I actually think that she's pretty nice.

Luke's voice tugs me from my thoughts. "Good evening, Gustavo."

"Good evening, Luke." He turns his attention to me. "And you must be Mrs. Moore. Good evening."

I plaster a smile on my face as a kind old man with gray hair and soft eyes shakes my hand. I'm only here to do what I can in order to help my husband.

Luckily, I happened to do some research on the man and his wife—more her than him, of course. I think I'm prepared for interactions with them as long as I don't let myself get distracted by my very mysterious, very handsome husband.

"Good evening. It's lovely to meet you Mr. Marino," I say.

I've learned that as much as a firm handshake from a woman can hurt a guy's ego, it can also demand respect. That being said, the look of surprise in his eyes before the slight grin has proven my point.

Next to him is a woman who looks to be about my age. No hate to the old man, I mean if they're both happy, then I have nothing to really complain about, right? But damn, I can't help the chills that it gives me.

I swallow my unease and reach my hand out to her. "It's also a pleasure to meet you, Mrs. Marino."

The woman is obviously not as polished as most of the people in attendance. It's not really to be expected considering that, from what I read, she grew up in more humble beginnings. She put herself through college and grew her career to the point where it is now as a marketer for a rather large firm. Similar beginnings to Margaret, yet somehow less put together.

She awkwardly grips my hand in hers and shakes it. The poor girl is nervous.

She replies, "A pleasure, Mrs., uh, Moore?"

I can see the disapproving look in her husband's eyes, but it's only a flash. Of course, someone as old as him is good at keeping up a mask.

Kind, my ass. But two can play it that way.

I smile a bit wider. "What do you say we go grab something to drink and leave the boys to talk business?"

She anxiously looks over to her husband for approval. A small nod is all it takes for her to follow me across the room to the bar. It's not like it carries hard liquor, but it has a variety of wines along with some eggnog.

Maybe a little bit of alcohol will get her to open up a bit more and relax. I don't want to feel like I'm walking on eggshells while I'm keeping her company.

I did *not* expect her to talk so much. I can't even make this stuff up. After barely half a glass of wine, she started blabbing about any and everything.

I now know that her dream has always been to have eight kids, a large house, and three dogs. And, I now have the unfortunate pleasure of knowing that the old man she's married still is very young and vigorous in the ways of the bedroom.

I really need to scrub my brain clean of that.

The second I see our husbands heading over to us, a silent disco goes off in my head. I'm so very excited don't have to tolerate any more of this dreadful conversation. Is it good that I have a new contact who seems to like me a lot? Yes. But I can only take her in increments.

Like those girls in teenage movies, I giggle and whisper to her, "They're back. I guess they finally decided to have time for us."

Her responding giggle makes me think that it was the right call. It's easy to control a conversation when it's obvious her husband is a very important part of her life, ya know?

I jump off the stool and speed walk to Luke, pulling him into a hug the moment I reach him.

Loudly, I exclaim, "I'm glad you're back!" But then I lean into his ear and whisper, "You owe me a book, a bear, and banana pudding. That was *exhausting*."

He doesn't reply but I take the pat on my back as him understanding. I mean, I seriously deserve that and more.

Pulling away from the hug, I turn to face the other couple. "Sorry about that little display. Sometimes the fact that we're newlyweds overpowers my common sense. It's been a pleasure meeting you both."

Both of them grin, and I know they're hooked. It all fell into place once I realized that Gustavo was huge on traditional values and all that. All I have to do is craft a scenario where Luke looks like my protector, and I look like I'm obsessed with him.

After they walk away, I drop my smile. My poor cheeks hurt so much after holding it as long as I have. How do people pretend to be so happy all the time? As much as I already respect models for the discipline it takes for them to craft their image, I have a newfound respect for their ability to smile so much.

I turn to Luke. "It's still date night and that's all you initially came here for. Does that mean we can leave and actually have our date now, Mr. Moore?"

His jaw ticks as he mutters, "Don't call me that. That's not a title meant for my *wife* to call me."

I tease, "Why not, Mr. Moore? I kind of like the sound of it."

"I don't care," he replies. "You're much too important to be calling me that."

Important, huh?

I don't have much else to say about it. I feel like now is one of those moments where I should just change the subject.

"Seriously, what's next for us?"

He grabs my hand and starts walking with me to the exit. "We just have to show our faces to the hosts and then we can leave."

"You always pegged me as the type to show up and leave whenever you wanted."

"I have some tact, my dear wife. If I show up, I always pay my respects."

As we approach the host, I force my smile to stay on my face. Every step closer is a reminder that the man who has this "friendly" smile on his face while he interacts with guests is really a disgusting piece of trash. My skin crawls, and I haven't even been forced to interact with him yet.

His receding brown hair is slicked back in a futile attempt to cover the multiple bald spots. He's wearing some suit jacket and pants that match his wife's dress. It looks fine, but my husband would surely wear it better. Colin's scrawny body betrays the gluttonous image I have of him in my mind. Completely unattractive to me.

"Good evening, Colin."

Ya know, I wish I never had to hear my husband utter that name. It kinda feels like it's been tainted because.

"Oh, Mr. Moore," he greets.

His slim green eyes crinkle as he smiles at my husband and reaches out to shake Luke's hand. I can't help but squeeze his other hand a bit tighter. Controlling my anger really isn't an easy task, alright?

Luke doesn't lift his hand to shake the man's, nor does he smile back at him—his face holds the same neutral expression he gives everyone who isn't me. It's hard to connect this side of him to the side of him I'm uncovering. It's not as if he seems angry, rather indifferent.

"Thank you for inviting us to tonight's event. It has been sublimely planned."

As if just noticing my presence, Colin drops his hand and shifts his gaze to me. It doesn't take long for his grin to shift into an expression of brief shock before returning to the smile he uses to curry favor.

I force a polite smile. "Nice to see you again, Colin."

This time, my husband squeezes my hand. I don't know if he's surprised that I know the CEO of the company or if he's just offering comfort. I return the squeeze in silent recognition of whatever he's feeling.

Colin replies, "And you as well, Ms. Smith."

Before I can say anything, Luke interjects, "It's Mrs. Moore now, actually. As beautiful as her name was before, I find it much more appealing now that it's mine."

Woah. Flirting in front of the other business owners is crazy. I have to admit I wasn't expecting that. I don't even know what to say.

"My apologies," Colin says. "I've known her as Ms. Smith for so long that it slipped my mind."

I laugh. "Apology accepted. I must admit I'm still getting used to it myself."

Colin turns to Luke again. "It's been a pleasure hosting someone of your stature at my event. You usually turn down the invite so I'm glad you were able to make it this year. My wife also gushed over meeting your wife earlier."

"Margaret was wonderful," I reply with a smile. "She also told me about the good news. I believe that congratulations are in order."

His smile wavers but doesn't drop. He knows who I am because I've made it clear that I know the part he played in my sister *and* best friend's disappearance. And I've made it clear that I'll do everything in my power to bring him down. That said, I also know of his huge, new vulnerability, and I can only imagine how much anxiety that brings him.

"Thank you, Mrs. Moore. We're just hoping for a healthy child this time."

This time? Right, she had told me something about other failed pregnancies. It seems like this one must be different though. Margaret seemed so confident about the child that she's carrying. She did say she's through her first trimester.

"My thoughts are with your family. Margaret and I made plans to hang out at a later date so I'll be seeing her again soon. I'll make sure to take good care of her and keep her company."

Okay! I admit it! I'm having fun teasing him with what I know. Of course, I would never allow myself to sink so low that I'd hurt an innocent person or baby. The thing is, because he's someone who would, he automatically assumes everyone else would, too.

"There's no need to stress yourself with that," he responds. "She has plenty of care. I assure you I'd do anything to protect her—even fight the devil and his wife."

That was oddly direct.

I'd like to think it was some type of religious saying, but it's clearly directed at me. It's like a warning that he doesn't care who my husband is in the grand scheme of things. He's willing to fight whoever.

Admirable, if he weren't such a degenerate. Besides, my husband is no devil. People just haven't earned the right to see his sweet side.

"It's no stress. It's what friends do for each other, right?"

Luke gently smiles down at me. "I'm glad that you've made a new friend tonight, sweetheart. You haven't had a chance to make many friends the whole time we've been together."

Like it's been that long. It hasn't even been a month since we got married yet. Though I really don't have friends. I feel like bad things happen to people who get close to me. Like my sister and like Lilianna, the most recent model to mysteriously go missing from Colin's company.

"It's all thanks to you bringing me here," I say, gazing into his eyes and playing along. "Really, I enjoyed myself tonight."

"If you say that, then maybe I should start going to more events then."

I nod my head enthusiastically before turning back to Colin. "Thank you so much. I suppose we'll be seeing you around, right?"

Colin's smile quivers, but it seems he's still trying to save face. He can't outright ban me from seeing his wife or express any ill will toward me. Especially considering I could whisper some things in my husband's ear about shady business practices. That's too easy a punishment for him, though.

Colin stiffly nods. "Of course. I hope to see you around."

"Thank you for tonight. Now, hubby," I say, squeezing his hand and turning to look him in the eye. "We have a date night to finish."

Luke returns my smile and guides me toward the exit without sparing Colin another glance. Once we've weave our way through the crowd and outside to the waiting car, I sense a bit of a shift in atmosphere. It's like the joyous mood has completely vanished and is replaced with something a bit more foreign.

It isn't until the car has started moving and the building is out of sight that Luke asks, "What was that about?"

CHAPTER 15

While I would absolutely *love* to answer his question, I'm struggling to figure out what part of the night that he was talking about. I mean, I've been so polite with everyone I interacted with today, even if my intentions weren't the best. How would he be able to know that though?

"What was what about?"

"Sweetheart, we may have just met, but I've picked up on your typical behaviors. Your behavior with Colin and his wife means you know something."

And what exactly do I know? Other than the fact that Colin is involved in human trafficking and is an absolute piece of filth. Or that he probably has much dirtier things to dig up because there's no way he doesn't have other things hidden. I still don't know what he does with the women he steals away either.

But, ya know, that's *nothing*. At least, nothing that I feel I should have to discuss at length with my husband when he doesn't understand what's really at stake when it comes to me taking down this man.

I have to avenge my sister and my friend and all the other girls out there who were tricked and forced to do whatever the hell they were being forced to do. Whatever it is, all I know is that they never manage to make it back and bodies are never found. Whether they're dead or alive . . . I have no idea.

"I just don't like him."

"I don't believe you. There's more."

"You do know that sometimes people just don't like things or other people?"

"Yet you want to be friends with the wife of someone you're claiming to dislike?"

Okay, so he's capable of being sarcastic, too. I must admit, I never expected that from him. But still, I can't get him involved in my own drama. It's a mess that I doubt anyone would want to get too involved with.

"Why should I allow my dislike of someone else to get in the way of liking their wife?"

"Right, right," he sarcastically says. "Sweetheart, I don't believe you. You're only making it seem as if you really have something to hide."

"Why would you think that? Shouldn't you just be able to trust that I won't hide anything from you that affects our relationship?"

"Answer me this then. Will it affect your safety?"

Okay, that's a maybe. I mean the man does have people out there who are able to make people disappear. I sincerely doubt he handles any of the dirty work himself. Maybe *that* can be a little dangerous considering I don't know who handles his criminal dealings, but it's not like he'd take a huge risk and come after me. Especially considering he now knows who my husband is. No one wants to be on the bad side of Luke Moore, especially when money and power are involved.

Still, I also don't like to lie to people. It's completely possible I could be in danger if I'm considered a threat. But I don't think I'm a high priority at this point.

"Possibly," I reply.

The silence in the car probably only lasts for a few seconds, but it's suffocating. It's the fight between my stubbornness and his protectiveness. I just don't want him to get involved. No matter how rich he is, he's still human and limited by that. I still don't know enough about how deep this goes to believe anyone else getting looped in will be safe.

"Aurelia."

Okay, so he never uses my name. I guess he's really serious. But wouldn't him being angry at me be better than him getting involved and possibly getting hurt as a result of my investigation? It's not fair to drag him into my mess.

Besides, I know things are happening within his own company. It's part of what I saw before we got married. That means he really shouldn't divert his attention to other corruption in the area.

He asks, "You know, don't you?"

Wait, does *he* know? Why hadn't I considered that? Still, let me just make sure we're thinking about the same thing before I give anything away. It would suck if I was talking about all this dark stuff, and he was only talking about some tax evasion or something simple like that.

"Know what?"

"What BB Media does underground?"

I peek at him from the corner of my eye. The lights flash across his face as we move through the city, illuminating his expression. It's not the gentle smile he usually wears nor is it the look of indifference he targets at other people.

It's deadly serious.

"You can't be involved in this," he demands.

Excuse me? There's no way he's going to try to control my actions. Especially when it isn't anything that affects him. I doubt anyone he loves has been roped into this mess.

"Don't tell me what I can and can't do, Luke."

"Aurelia, you don't understand how much trouble you could end up in. I noticed how you provoked Colin when we were talking earlier. You pushed his buttons, and you obviously know what happens to people who push his buttons."

Oh trust me, I know. They tend to go missing. Especially girls who have no one who will miss them when they're gone.

"As I recall, you have a stake in their operations. If you know they do something bad underground, why would you fund it?"

"Aurelia, don't you remember what you said about background checks?"

What is he talking about? Wait . . .

"You faked it?"

"I needed him to trust me. I have my own reasons for getting things done. But my level of resources are vastly different from yours."

I clench my fists—annoyed at his assumptions. "You don't know what resources I have, Luke."

No one knows what resources I have and it's going to stay that way.

"No, I don't. I'm well aware there are things you're hiding from me.

We're both subject to our own secrets. But this whole escapade can lead to you getting hurt or worse."

"It doesn't matter." I turn to look out the window. "It doesn't matter what happens to me as long as I can bring him down."

And that's the truth. Not just for Chiaki and our best friend, Lily, but for all the other girls who don't have a sister or friend who's crazy enough to hunt an entire criminal enterprise and bring them down.

No one deserves to be abandoned like they never existed in the first place. To suffer in silence while knowing that no one will be out there looking for them, and even if they did, by some miracle, have someone looking, they would likely never be found.

These people are obviously very protected, and I need to not only expose their enterprise but break down every barrier to get to them. I will destroy every shield protecting them, even if it requires me using dooming myself in the process.

I don't have anything that's worth the fear of losing it, and no one will miss me when I'm gone. All that matters is making those responsible pay. Maybe, in the end, my instincts will be proven right, and my sister will come back to me. If my life is the price for that, then so be it—at least the one who truly deserves to live is spared. The world won't grieve my loss, but it needs more souls like hers—kind, hopeful, and full of dreams.

"It does matter."

A large, warm hand grips mine, beckoning my attention. I resist the temptation to look into his eyes. I know if I do look, I'll spiral deep into his soul and lose my nerve. I can't afford that.

He continues talking, not caring that I'm ignoring him, I guess. "Sweetheart, you can't let yourself get destroyed for whatever mission you're trying to accomplish. You can't take them down."

"There you go telling me what I can and can't do again."

"Do you even know what you're up against? What you're *truly* up against?"

"I'm still figuring that out. I'm not dumb. I won't charge in guns blazing without intel or a strategy."

"Fine, I won't tell you what to do. I'll tell you what *I* can't do. I can't just watch you run headfirst into what might be a suicide mission. Do you understand that?"

"I need to take them down."

"They need to be taken down, but you don't need to put yourself in danger to do that."

I mutter, "It's personal."

Very personal. I don't even know if I can tell him *how* personal it is. Whether Chiaki and Lily are dead or alive, I have to do what I can. I know that man is responsible for my their disappearances and countless others. No one knows whether they're dead or alive and those who remember them likely don't have the power to do much.

I've heard there are places where you can go to the police no matter who you're accusing—but not here. Here, the rich pull the strings, and most conflicts are settled in the shadows, right under the noses of the people. The police don't serve justice; they only step in once the real power brokers have chosen a victor. In the end, they're nothing more than a PR tool for whoever comes out on top.

"How so?"

I sigh. "Luke, I can't tell you that. Not right now. All I can say for now is that it's extremely personal. There's no way in hell I'm going to stop hunting them. Men like Colin need to learn there will always be someone who can take them down."

And so will my mother. She threw away my sister and had a hand in whatever happened to her. I can't let that slide.

Actions have consequences. You can have all the money and power in the world but all things in the dark will come to light eventually. Then what happens? Why do you think so many nations in history have gone through so many coups in their time?

"Then don't do it alone. You have personal reasons and so do I. It's a mutual thing."

I scoff. "Shouldn't you be able to do it on your own? You were just talking about the differences in our resources."

"Things are a lot more complicated for me. If I personally go after him, there has to be a certain way I go about it."

"What do you mean by that?"

"You have your secrets and I have mine, sweetheart. This is just going to have to be one of them. So what do you say?"

I pause. Help is nice, but he literally just said what I have been worried about. This can get dangerous and then he'd be caught in the crossfire.

But at the same time, he's saying he's got something in it for himself too . . .

"Aurelia. I'm not going to stand by and watch you put yourself in danger that you don't completely understand. Especially if there's something I can do to protect you."

"Why not?"

"Because you're innocent. Because you can get hurt. Because if you get hurt . . ."

I hold my breath. I know the end of that sentence, but I can't speak it into the universe. There's no *if* he gets hurt because I can't allow him to get hurt.

If he gets hurt, I don't think I'll be able to live with myself. Besides, he has no idea. I'm not innocent. Not in the slightest.

I'm cursed, ya know? Everyone who gets close to me will inevitably end up hurt. Not just with this whole situation but also losing jobs, car accidents, things like that. My sister and best friend were the two people closest to me and look at them now. When I was in university, there was this one guy I'd gotten close to, and he'd ended up getting in an accident and was in a coma for three months. Things like that never stopped.

It really is a good thing I don't have friends anymore.

"How can I sit back and watch you get hurt, sweetheart?"

His voice is so gentle that I almost break. It sounds like he's genuinely worried for me and that's not a feeling I'm used to. I have to pick between two poisons here and it's not like I can keep it hidden anymore.

Besides, if I say no, there's no telling if he'll stop trying to do something on the sidelines. Isn't it better to get him involved so I can control how deeply entwined he gets in this whole fiasco?

"Fine," I whisper.

Gosh, why do I sound so weak? Am I really this worried about losing someone who I haven't even known for a month? It's only been like *three weeks* since we got married.

"We have to work together then, darling, I'm serious about this. I know we set our boundaries but I won't sit back and watch something completely preventable happen to you. Okay?"

Jeez. It doesn't help when he says things like that, too. I mean, how am I supposed to react when he's so clear with his affection? Why is it that in a world where men are so shitty at expressing their emotions, I end up with the man who's extremely emotionally available and communicative?

I have to admit, I see why it makes for healthy relationships. I just wish I wasn't such an unhealthy ingredient to the recipe of people's lives.

"Alright," I concede. "We'll work this together. But the same way you want me out of harm's way, I need you out of harm's way, too. This thing has to work both ways. Otherwise, I don't want it."

And I mean it. I will absolutely cut him out of the whole plot if I feel he's taking unnecessary risks. He wants me safe, but I want him safe, too. I won't allow him to get hurt.

A gentle hand grips my chin and guides me to look up into those dangerously deep eyes. "What do you say we seal the deal with a kiss?"

CHAPTER 16

I turn my head and look out the window. Like hell I'll kiss him after he made me negotiate on my own operation. How does one go from *that* to trying to be romantic?

"Fine, no kiss yet. We still have a date night to complete."

Yet? Someone sounds confident. If only he knew the level of pettiness that I have. I once literally sat and watched paint dry because some guy really thought that I was joking when I said that I preferred that to going out with him. People really should take me more seriously.

Not bothering to look at him, I ask, "Where are we going?"

"You'll see."

Safe to say that I'm not surprised by his response. It seems anytime we go out together, unless it's somewhere I've picked, he never lets me know where we're going.

I watch as the city thins, and we cross the bridge into the rural area. I usually spare time to come pumpkin picking in the autumn and apple picking during the summer. I haven't done the latter yet this year but I'm excited for it.

As we pass acres of farmland, the frequency at which we see people's houses and barns lessens as grass spreads out all around us. I don't know how much longer we drive as I watch the outdoors. While I'm not a fan of the bugs that nature brings, I love the sights and the smell.

Patrick's voice grabs my attention. "We're here."

I don't wait for anyone to open the door and instead let myself out. Completely disregarding the formal attire, I ditch my heels next to the car and step peacefully through the grass. Unlike the typical crunchiness that it contains within town, this grass is soft and unbothered by human contraptions.

Luke whispers in my ear, "Look up."

Woah. When did he get behind me? I don't even remember hearing his car door open. I guess I've been too taken by the environment.

Looking up, I smile at the sight of the stars above. To think that each of these beautiful things are giant orbs of pent up gas burning lightyears away. They're so out of reach, but even so, they bless us with their beauty in the dead of night.

Usually, there's too much pollution within the city to be able to see the stars. This has to be the first time in years I've been able to embrace the unburdened beauty of night.

Luke grabs my hand, and I follow his lead without complaint. A few yards away is a large blanket splayed out with four picnic baskets—one at each corner. Once we're settled in the middle, I can't help but be curious about what's in each of the baskets. I can understand one for food and drinks, but not the rest.

Still, a moonlight picnic . . . Did he know that this has always been my dream date?

My heart pounds even faster as I watch him reach into one basket and pull out electric candles—setting them up in front of us. From the same basket, he also grabs large cloth napkins, a small projector, and a scrunchy.

"What's all that for?"

He replies, "Well, I brought the projector so we can watch a movie, the napkins to protect our clothes from the food, and the hairband just in case you happened to wear your hair down tonight."

"I see you covered all the bases." I smile. "Were the electric candles because of the grass?"

"Wouldn't want to risk starting a large fire, now would we?"

I grab the scrunchy from his hand and allow him to place the napkin on my lap. He wants to pamper me, and for my dream date, I'll allow him.

"How did you know? Have you been holding out on me and secretly been using some crazy mind reading technology?"

I mean, seriously. This guy always knows where to take me. There's never been a place he's taken me that I didn't like—and that's insane! It's not like I expressly tell him these things.

"Sweetheart, you're easier to read than you think," he replies as he rests his hand on my thigh. "A few days ago, when you were scrolling through your phone, I peeked over your shoulder and saw you were looking at nature posts. You've also offhandedly mentioned how long it's been since you've been on a picnic."

Okay, I had mentioned that, but it wasn't like I was trying to drop hints. We'd been having a conversation about our favorite activities to do outdoors . . . which I'm now realizing probably stemmed from him seeing what I was looking at on my phone. Oh, he's *good*. I wasn't even onto him.

"Honestly, I don't know what I was expecting you to say but it definitely wasn't that. I can't believe you planned this and I didn't even have an inkling."

His responding smile warms my sends a jolt through my body. I don't think anyone could not feel flattered by the immense amount of thought that has gone into this.

I follow his movements as he unpacks the other baskets. He brought bug spray, wine glasses, wine, chocolate covered strawberries, steak, macaroni and cheese, fries, rice (him having so many options for sides is insane and they're all still warm), salad, an extra blanket, popcorn, and chips.

By the time everything is splayed out in front of us, I notice the projection screen has been set up, likely by Patrick, and Patrick has taken a spot in the car with the engine off.

"Shouldn't we make sure that he eats, too?"

Luke smirks. "I knew that you'd say that. He has his own less elaborate basket in the car."

Woah, he really *is* improving how he treats other people. I must say I feel like a proud parent right now. They really do grow up so fast.

"What do you say we get you some food and then we can watch any movie that you like. Alright?"

Deal! I hope he's ready to see me sob over some sad anime movie. I've been trying to bait this man's empathy for *days*. This is the first time I've got him alone long enough for us to watch a whole movie together.

⌐o─o─o─o─o─o─o 🔒 o─o─o─o─o─o─o⌐

As the closing credits take over the screen, I dab away my tears with my napkin. It's not a full cry but I'm definitely shedding a few tears. This movie always gets me.

With my other hand, I reach for the last chocolate covered strawberry because no matter how sad I am, I can't allow one of my favorite desserts to sit there uneaten. The sweetness on my tongue conflicts with the bittersweet ending of the movie and slowly brings joy back to me.

I rest my head on Luke's shoulder, his stoic expression shifting as he chuckles. I (barely) understand him not crying, but how can he chuckle at something like this?

"You monster," I mutter. "This isn't funny, ya know?"

"I'm not laughing at the movie, darling. What's funny is how you can't decide between eating and crying."

"I'm a very talented woman, okay? I can do both and more if I really put my mind to it."

To prove my point, I dig my hand into a bag of chips and stuff a few in my mouth. Listen, if he can't accept my glorious way of multitasking then he can't accept me.

"Of course, my dear. Still doesn't mean that it's not amusing."

I huff. "Well I'm glad that I amuse you."

It's obvious that I'm not *really* mad considering that I'm even more cuddled up with him than I was a few moments ago but I love to be dramatic. Seriously though, I'm practically in his lap and my head is on his chest. I can even hear the gentle thump of his heart.

Luke gently runs his hand through my hair, massaging my scalp. "I'm glad you do, too. I'm glad that my wife is brilliant, beautiful, and amusing."

"Well *I'm* glad these past few weeks have shown you who your wife is, and you understand that there's no changing her."

Why am I talking about myself in the third person?

"Why would I ever want to alter perfection?"

Perfection. I like the sound of that. At least he understands that I'm a glorious work of art. My beauty on the outside is no match for the beauty on the inside.

"I'm glad you feel that way. Now, I think you've earned your kiss that you tried to scheme out of me earlier through negotiations," I say. "Flattery sure does get you *everywhere* with me."

I barely finish my sentence before his lips are on me. He's rougher than earlier, his lips clashing against mine with an intensity I've never felt before. If earlier he was claiming me in public, I now understand how different being claimed in private can be.

I wrap my arms around his neck, wanting to pull him even closer. Not wanting. I *need* to have him closer to me. He bites my bottom lip, a pleasurable pain erupting from the spot and making waves through my entire body.

I part my lips, welcoming him into my mouth. He relentlessly explores every inch. I melt away with every passing second, enraptured by his touch.

As one of his hands slowly creeps up my arm, my breath quickens as each piece of skin he touches lights aflame. It isn't long before has one of my breasts in his hand, delicately massaging it.

Between his hands, his lips, and his tongue, I can't help the soft whimpers leaving my mouth. Is this how I'll lose my virginity? Under the stars with a man that I've known for less than a month?

If I do, I can't complain. I mean, I've already pretty much decided to accept his feelings. And there's a part of me that hopes to spend the rest of my life with this man, no matter how irritating he can be.

Before it moves any further, Luke pulls away and drops his hand—leaving us both panting for air and absolutely unsatisfied.

"Not like this," he grumbles. "We can't do this like this. You deserve much better."

My heart drops. I get his sentiment, but damn. I was so ready just a few moments ago. It feels almost like he's rejecting me.

Breathe, Aurelia.

I take a few breaths in and out before standing and severing any connection between our bodies. I know I need to get my feelings under control and appreciate his thoughtfulness, but I was too in the moment. I should be fine in a few minutes when the reality of the situation really hits me.

I shouldn't be upset when I've literally spent my entire life avoiding any type of romantic or sexual relations. They're useless and distracting and I can't afford any distractions.

. . . Right?

But I was ready for him. He brought my philosophy into question . . . and then completely shut me down. Like what the hell is that?

Old feelings be damned, this is how I'm feeling right now.

I whisper, "I think I'm feeling a bit tired now."

Luke looks at me and I can tell that he's concerned, but he doesn't come toward me and instead starts packing up. I'd offer to help but I need my space so I make my way to the car and wait there instead.

Later, I'll be fine. For now, I can indulge in a little self-pity.

CHAPTER 17

"Mom, you can't make her do this! She's made it clear she sees the boy as nothing more than a friend!"

Chiaki's yelling at mom like she's never yelled before. For someone who's always so patient with everyone, this is such a huge deal, right? I never expected her to go to war for me.

I try to peer around the corner to see what's going on without getting involved. I had just finished packing my stuff so I could leave after my mom and I finished arguing. After all, she told me to go, and it's not like I'm a kid. I have my DCS and already make more than enough money to live on my own between my two jobs—one official and legal, and one that's a bit more morally ambiguous and on my own time—not that anyone knows about the latter.

My mother's voice rips me from my thoughts, ever calm as she says, "I gave birth to her, so yes, I can make her do whatever the hell I want. If I say jump, her only answer should be 'how high?' Anything else is unacceptable."

Mom is holding a knife and stepping closer and closer to Chiaki. My mom's crazy but not crazy enough to outright stab her own kids. At least, I don't think so.

Chiaki throws her hands up in the air. "So you'll just kick her out instead? Are you insane? You know how many of our family's enemies are just waiting to get their hands on any one of us."

"She's a smart girl. She'll figure it out. Out of all you children, she's the only one with any promise as long as she learns to follow directions. If it has to be the hard way, then so be it."

"How can you say that about your own child? Those people can be dangerous. If one of them gets ahold of her, she'll never make it out alive."

"I won't allow it to get that far."

"How far is too far for you, huh? Is death really where you draw the line?"

"I'm not that cruel. I draw the line at any sort permanent damage. You know she's special."

I take a step forward to get between them but a hand is holding me back. It's my older brother, Jackson. Why is he stopping me? Chiaki shouldn't get in trouble with Mom because of me. I'm not scared of her, but Chiaki . . . Chiaki is usually scared of everything.

Looking back, I see Chiaki shake her head.

"I won't allow this. No matter what you do, I'll make sure that Aurelia never marries that boy. Not unless it's what she truly wants."

My mother takes another step toward Chiaki. The two are standing nose to nose, barely any space between them. I have never seen either ever do this, not even with strangers.

"Child, you can't stop me," she says as she lifts the knife. "It seems that you forget that you're just as expendable as your brothers."

I struggle against Jackson's grip, but he covers my mouth with a trembling *hand and holds my body in place. Even trained in martial arts, I'm no match for his pure strength. But still, I've never seen such a manic look in my mom's eyes, and she might actually do something to Chiaki. I need to stop this.*

"But I have the stubbornness that comes from carrying your blood. No matter what you do, you know I will always protect my sister."

The next part happens so fast. The knife slices down with a wicked hiss and then there's a lot of blood. Chiaki lets out a scream and clutches her left eye. Our mother just cut right through it as casually as when someone's slicing chicken.

A muffled scream leaves my mouth as I lunge toward her again but my brother holds me back. My mother looks in our direction, and I swear I see her smirk before turning back to Chiaki.

"You can leave then, too. I've even left you a little parting gift. Every time you look in the mirror, ask yourself if that little brat was really worth making me your enemy," she says. "And you'd better hope I never see you again."

Mother tosses the knife across the room before casually walking away from my sister. Only then does Jackson let me run to Chiaki. I almost trip over my own feet as I make my mad dash—not caring about anything else around me. Chiaki is all that matters. Why would she fight our mother like this?

Crouching next to her, I cry and try to help her stop the bleeding, but my medical knowledge is very limited. The warm blood stains my skin—something I fear will never wash off. She's talking to me and so is Jackson. They're saying something but I can't hear it.

Wait . . . what was I doing? I can't remember. Why can't I remember?

And then, there's darkness.

My phone startles me from my sleep. I gasp for air as I sit up in bed—my head intensely pulsing. I swear I can still hear Chiaki's screams and feel the blood on my hands as I tried to stop her bleeding.

It appears I've slept in. Luke isn't in bed with me anymore so I can only assume that he must have left for work. It's been about a week and a half since the party and the resulting date. We haven't kissed since then and things have pretty much fallen back into the usual routine. Though we have started to cuddle some nights, which has been pleasant.

Yesterday, he surprised me with a giant koala teddy bear as a one month anniversary gift, and I have to admit that I'd jumped on him in all of the excitement. It really was so thoughtful considering he didn't have to do it. Even if the relationship was real, aren't the important anniversaries supposed to be the years that go by?

Still, it's comfortable. I never thought life could be like this—no matter how short-lived it might be.

My dreaded phone rings again—impossibly more annoying than the first time it rang. With a huff, I roughly grab it and look to see who's calling.

[Unknown Number]

Of course, it's a spam caller. I decline the call. I'm not going to waste my time with one of those annoying calls.

Before I open my phone to check anything else, the same number calls back. I decline again. They call again. And so that cycle continues a few more times until I'm just over it.

I answer the call, "What do you want?"

"Oh man, I thought that I had the wrong number. Lia, it's me."

I hang up. How the hell did he get my number? I haven't given anyone from my past my number, not even my brothers. This is just irritating.

I can't even block the number before it's ringing again.

I answer. "Stop calling me. Leave me the hell alone."

"Not until you hear me out. You haven't talked to me in *a month*."

I weigh my options. If I hang up, he'll probably just keep calling again and again and again until my phone is useless. I could always just turn it off and hope he loses interest. Or I can change my number again and swap the sim cards. But I feel like those last two options will lead to more spam calling later.

"That was because you tried to drug me." I sigh. "You have two minutes."

I walk to my office as he speaks, "Lia, I don't understand why you're being like this. Auntie has spoken to you and so have I. You know we're supposed to be together and that no one understands you the way that I do."

Plugging my phone into the computer, I reply, "A minute and thirty left."

His tone shifts from pleading to scolding. "Lia, stop messing around. Why do you think you should interrupt the union of our two families *and* true love? You've always been stubborn, but this is too much. You can never truly love someone like Luke Moore and he can never love you. Stop kidding yourself. I'm trying to stop you before you end up hurting yourself."

"Our mothers relationship has nothing to do with me. If they let something as simple as this break them, so be it." I add, "And you have about fifty seconds left."

While he's talking, I'm busy blocking any calls from this number and IP address through my computer so even if he tries calling me back, he won't be able to.

"I hope you know I'm not giving up, and since my mom and Auntie are willing to help me, I will rescue you from yourself, okay? You may not understand it right away, but eventually, you'll be thanking me. I'm just calling to give you one more chance."

Well, that sounds like a threat. Maybe I should ask Luke to up the security for the time being. I mean, Shoto's crazy, my mom's psycho. And for the life of me, that dream/memory that I had is massive. I need to deal with that way more than I need to deal with this psycho.

Having finally completed the block, I let out a long, exasperated sigh.

"Goodbye and never call me again," I say before hanging up the phone.

Today hasn't started off very well. First that dream or memory, then manic Shoto. What's next? The delivery driver is going to break in and I have to beat him with my bat? That one actually might be more stress relieving than frustrating, though.

At least the dream had been helpful. I've regained some of my missing memories from that night. I feel like the most important part is what I couldn't hear. Lucky for me, there's someone who was there who can tell me what happened. The only issue is that he's been MIA for a while now.

I will need to find Jackson and get to him without leading anyone else to him. Not only that, but I need to figure out everything with BB Media, how involved Mom was, how to get my hands on the black box so that *nobody* has it, develop a relationship with my husband, and get Shoto off me. I'm probably still missing a few things, too.

Life is definitely more interesting now. I don't know if I'd call it fun yet but it will get there once I take down all of these wretched people and free myself from this crushing guilt.

Once that's done, I can be a lot freer with the love I want to share with my husband. Neither of us deserve any of this extra baggage. Damn it. I never knew that a spontaneous marriage would have me wanting to settle down, but here we are.

CHAPTER 18

I've just finished plating the lasagna when I hear the door thud. Looks like my husband is home from work. I spent so much time making dinner so I could talk to him about what happened earlier. Maybe not all the stuff with Chiaki yet, but at least what happened with Shoto, I can't say with confidence that Shoto won't try to hurt me again in order to get his way.

"Honey," I call out. "After you wash up, come eat, alright?"

He responds with a grunt before his footsteps fade up the steps.

I really have become more domestic these days—eating three meals a day that aren't just instant noodles. I still have them for lunch most days but Luke has been trying to get me to eat healthier, and I can't help but feel charmed by his concern.

I hum the tune of an old '80s song as I bring the plates to the table. While the rectangular glass table is large enough to hold twelve people, we always make sure to sit across from each other toward one end so that we can talk about our days.

I never expected something so simple to always give me a warm feeling inside, but it does. It had only taken one time for my skepticism to melt away, replaced with a craving to do it every day.

Hearing the descent of footsteps, I patiently wait for him at the table.

I smile as he comes into view. "Welcome home. Hope you're hungry."

He grins as he settles into the chair across from me. That grin always makes me feel warm and fuzzy inside—especially considering it's only ever aimed at me. As it should be, of course.

"Thank you, darling. You don't usually go all out like this."

He's right. Usually, he's the one who cooks when he gets home. I always offer, but he knows I tend to skimp if I cook. It's not that I *can't*. Rather, it's more like my attention span doesn't hold up long enough in the kitchen, and I end up having water boil over, things burning. You get the gist.

When I really do give it all of my attention, though, I make some really delicious food.

"Well, I just like to surprise my husband every once in a while after knowing how hard he works all day. Is that such a bad thing?"

He takes my hand, enveloping it in warmth.

"Sweetheart," he replies. "What's wrong?"

How the hell is this guy able to read me so well? Here I am trying to butter him up, and he won't even pretend for a few seconds it's for pure reasons. How rude is that.

Okay, fine. No more buttering him up so that he can stay calm if he's just going to see right through it anyway. Might as well rip the Band-Aid off, right?

"Well, Shoto called me earlier. I think we're going to need to up the security for now. Something he said earlier rubbed me the wrong way, and I think he was threatening me."

"I'll get rid of him," Luke grumbles.

"No, no. Don't do that. I have plans for him," I insist. "Trust me. There are ways to bring any person down, but we all know that there are different levels of effectiveness. Only someone who knows them well, like a person's childhood best friend, knows the most efficient way to handle things."

"I don't need efficient. I need quick."

"Well, I need efficient. I need to make sure that no one is able to bail him out."

"Who would dare bail him out when I'm the one who buried him to begin with? It really wouldn't take any energy." He pauses. "And I can make things much more permanent if the need arises."

The casual tone of his voice mixed with the whole old money thing that he's got going on makes me know he's telling the truth. But still, there's something about solving my own problems that makes me feel a lot more accomplished and surer of myself.

"Let's try it my way first," I negotiate. "For me, solving my own problems is extremely important. I've already extended my hand for us to work together by telling you this to begin with, but I don't think it's fair for you to take over when I already have something in the works. We're supposed to work together, Luke. And in this case, that means me relying on you and your security to keep me safe, and you trusting me to handle this situation."

His eyebrows furrow, and he pinches the bridge of his nose, the typical sign that he's agitated. I don't care how agitated he gets as long as he understands that being in a partnership doesn't mean he can always do things the way he wants.

A beat passes before he mutters, "Fine. But darling, if this isn't handled within the next two weeks, I will personally see to his downfall myself."

I concede. "Fine."

I already know how hard it is for him to not handle this himself. I'm positive he has the resources. It's easy enough for me to speed up the plans that I have for Shoto. I will do what it takes to bring him down and knowing his mother, when his downfall comes, she'll fall while trying to save her son.

"If you need any more of my help though, just come to me."

I smile innocently. "Yes, honey."

His gaze on me darkens as he scans my body even more thoroughly. Under his stare, I can't help but think about our date night two weeks ago. The way he had kissed me. The way that he had *touched* me.

The way my mind and body both craved *more*.

"Sweetheart," he murmurs, and boy, is his voice nice and deep and sexy. "If you call me that once more, you're more likely to become dinner than the lasagna you tried to bribe me with."

Stunned, my lips part, and I can feel the heat racing to my cheeks. Even as I shift my attention to my food, I can still feel him staring at me as if *I'm* on the menu tonight.

"Umm," I stutter before rambling out, "M-maybe we should eat the food before it gets cold. I wouldn't want cold food to upset your stomach."

Before things can go any further, I dig in after quickly muttering, "Itadakimasu."

For the rest of the dinner, I look everywhere *but* at him. As ready as I was to consummate out marriage before, I'm nervous and have become obsessed with figuring out the perfect time, the perfect outfit, the perfect *everything*.

People do say lingerie builds confidence, right?

I feel like I'm ready, but we still haven't known each other for very long so maybe that means that we haven't known each other for long enough.

Ugh. The last thing I need is something else weighing on my mind.

CHAPTER 19

Okay. Operation Take Down Mr. Delulu is a go.

The last few days have led me to understand that if I want to look for my brother who obviously doesn't want to be found, getting rid of my stalker should take precedence for now. Considering the attack on my apartment the night Luke and I got married, my current theory is that my mom sent her goons after me and they were the ones chasing me that day until I ditched them at city hall. Hopefully, the resulting chaos will keep my mom busy enough to forget about me so I can slip away unseen.

I slide my laptop into my bag before stepping out of the house and into the waiting car.

"Good morning, Patrick!"

Patrick grins at me from the mirror. "Good morning, Mrs. Moore."

He's still calling me Mrs. Moore but I'll definitely take the grin over no other progress.

"Patrick, why don't you play your favorite music while we're on the way today?"

"Are you sure?"

"I don't have much of a preference today. I'd love to hear what you like. Don't worry about whether you think I'll like it. I'll pretty much listen to anything but country music."

"Okay, Mrs. Moore. If that's what you want."

"It is," I reassure him.

As I pull out my phone, I'm pleasantly surprised to hear the car swell with love songs. Of all things, I've never thought Patrick to be the type to listen to this type of music. I was thinking maybe something like old school R&B.

Humming along, I scroll through my phone. Based on my research, or internet stalking as people call it, I know where I should be able to find Shoto today.

That's what sucks about being a very public family. No matter what you post, other people will always post about you whether you want them to or not. You could try to have everything removed, but what does that do to your image?

Anyway, that's how I know my mother is meeting with Shoto and his mother today. And of course, it's on neutral grounds considering that Shoto's mom is still holding the black box over my mother's head.

Too bad. I would have loved to see it get violent and watch them take each other out instead of wasting my energy for that. They're too smart to give up the lead that easily.

The posts that I'm scrolling through show them getting closer to the women's favorite cafe where they used to meet at when they were friends.

If they ever really were. I mean seriously, if something like this is enough to tear it apart, it's not exactly the strongest friendship to begin with.

"Patrick, we're not too far out, are we?"

"No, Mrs. Moore. We don't have too much longer."

I send a swift text to Luke telling him I'm planning a confrontation with my mother and Shoto. I know he'll probably want to stay in the loop, considering how last time Shoto tried to drug me.

I won't lie. I'm still a little shaken up about that. Sometimes, when I think about it, I can still feel the cool needle against my back—ready to impede my senses. But, I have to keep reassuring myself that things are different than before.

He doesn't know I'm coming, and I'll have the bodyguards around me. This time will definitely not turn out like it did before. I need to get in and mess with his head just enough to complete phase one of my plan.

Be careful. I'll be there if you need me.

How sweet. But he has too much work he has to do and I would never want to pull him away for something that shouldn't be too much trouble. Paranoia doesn't count as needing him.

I take a deep breath before looking out the window once again. Apparently I've been in my head for five minutes already. Oh well.

Mask on. Total confidence. Unshakeable. Life figured out.

"Thanks, Patrick. Stay here. I shouldn't be too long."

I don't wait for him to let me out of the car, choosing to slide out on my own instead. It's not necessary for him to get out when I can do it on my own.

Shutting the door behind me, I stare at entrance of the old-style cafe. The small structure is very modest but the cafe itself, while looking like a hidden gem, can only be afforded by those in the upper class.

There's actually a prerequisite to entering.

Walking up to the man guarding the door, I notice him eyeing me. I admit that today I made a point to dress in something nicer than my usual. I'm wearing some branded sundress that Luke brought for me a few days ago.

Today, I look like the typical daughter of a rich family.

The man holds out his hand. I grab my wallet from my bag, tugging out my black card. Of course, this is the prerequisite that determines how rich you are. I'm glad I decided to apply for one a few weeks back.

Before I enter, my bodyguards approach, flanking me. They are never far no matter where I go. Even though they follow in their own car per a request I made to Luke, they're always close behind.

Before the security guard enquires, I confirm, "They're with me."

He nods after a short inspection of my black card and opens the door for me and my entourage.

I saunter into the establishment. I know my mother and her party are likely somewhere in the back corner. I won't interject myself just yet. I want whatever conversation they're having to go on for a bit more first before I get involved so I wave off my bodyguards and look for a seat.

Sitting at a small two-person table toward the front of the cafe, I pull out my laptop and pretend to work. I'm surrounded by people who have fans that would gush over them if they were anywhere else. Royals and celebrities all gather here for a peaceful $200 espresso. I mean, people are really willing to pay that much for some privacy.

A message to all people out there: maybe celebrities wouldn't spend so much money to go to all these private places if you respected them enough when they were out and about in public. Seriously, paparazzi are paid stalkers.

I open my custom programming software. I've been working on a Plan B that's slowly becoming my Plan A in case I'm not able to steal the black box. If I can create a software that's able to counter, or even completely contaminate the black box, then there's no need for stealing it to begin with.

There are only two problems with this. For starters, I'm going in blind and unless I completely understand the functions and code of the black box as well as its creator, I can't account for every contingency and create a successful deterrent.

Secondly, if I'm not able to get to the black box before it gets to who knows how many other security systems, then I'm utterly screwed. I'm still not sure who either side would use the device against aside from each other. For all I know, no startup will get going if everything they need to protect is contaminated from the start.

It could actually lead to a total domination by only the person with the black box deems appropriate. Even *if* I steal the thing, who's to say that another one won't pop up? Regardless of whether it's Plan A or not, a countermeasure needs to be put in place to even the odds.

I've already determined some of the necessities based on what I already know. I know that it copies and destroys other systems. While I don't know how, I've been able to drum up a skeleton program. I can only perfect the bones until I find a way to get what's necessary to craft the organs, skin, hair, and senses.

It's a long way from complete, but I intend to finish it as soon as possible just to be safe.

"Akira! I don't care what you have to do! Aurelia will marry my Shoto! You know that's my condition!"

Oh, that sounds like Shoto's mother, Fumiko. It seems that she's not afraid to hash out arguments in public—even if it's surrounded by the nation's elite. They won't snitch or anything because they have way too many skeletons in their own closets, but I can see some people trying to get a look at the drama.

I can hear my mom's voice but can't make out what she's saying. Ever the calm replier, I see.

"Lia loves me, Auntie. We just need to make her see it."

I start packing up my laptop after hearing Shoto's response. I think it's about time I make my presence known.

Fumiko's voice has lowered but it's still loud enough for everyone to hear as she says, "If that's what you have to do, then do it."

Standing with my bag hanging off my shoulder, I take slow steps toward the spectacle. I mean, if they want me to be the main character, I'm more than willing to comply.

"I heard my name," I say as I stand in front of them. "I hope that you're not intending to do anything . . . uncouth."

I wish I could take a picture of this moment! As all three of them look at me, there's very obvious shock in their expressions. Bet they didn't think I would show up at their little meeting.

My mother is the first to speak. "What are you doing here?"

"Well, I thought I should return the favor after you guys surprised me at a cafe a couple weeks ago. How'd I do? Are you shocked?"

Before she can respond, Shoto stands and take several steps toward me. "Lia, I knew you'd come to your senses and come for me."

My bodyguards, who have been hanging back attempting to blend in at different tables, look like they're about to stand up, but I shake my head at them. I don't need their help with Shoto but I will definitely need their help soon.

"Shoto, I recommend you don't come any closer to me. After last time, I'm not willing to even pretend to play nice."

Fumiko shouts, "Don't talk to my son like that! You need to learn your place."

Fumiko looks just like her son, the same jet-black hair that stretches down to her waist and soft features. She's just a little shorter and chubbier than her son. By no means is she ugly on the outside, she's actually very cute. Unfortunately, her interior is much uglier.

"Oh, but Aunt Fumi," I argue, assuming a whiny and innocent tone, "Shoto tried to drug me last time. The way I see it, if he comes in arm's reach I will have to defend myself. How is poor ole me supposed to know he isn't a threat this time?"

She bolts from her seat but is halted by my mother. "How did you get in here? Is that man with you?"

I smile. "Oh you mean my *husband?* No, he's at work. Ya know, he's a *very* important person. He doesn't need to waste his time on little . . . surprises, like this one."

"Did you steal his card?"

"I have my own, *Oka-san*. Did you think that after you kicked me out, I'd struggle to get by?"

My mother's jaw tenses, but she says no more. She doesn't need to. I can tell that fury is enveloping her as she realizes that kicking me out hasn't gone the way she expected. Considering my marriage and my own financial stability, I have no reason to come crawling back.

For my mother, *that's* how to hit her where it hurts.

Shoto tries coming closer as he praises, "I've never seen you wearing clothes like these. Did you come here dressed like that just for me? I bet you did."

I push my arm all the way out with my hand up. He's barely an inch from my hand.

"Shoto, if you come any closer, I will consider you a threat to my safety and have to show you how I deal with those threats."

He should already know, considering how long I've known him. I've taken kickboxing for years, and he knows that I work out every day—even if only for an hour.

Fumiko huffs. "Careful who you're threatening."

"I'd like to advise both you and your son of the same thing." My voice drops a thousand degrees—a trick I picked up from my husband. "You don't know who you're messing with. Careful who you're threatening."

Fumiko and I meet eyes, a battle of wills ensuing. Whoever looks away first admits defeat, and I won't cower to her.

Before we finish our stare-off, I feel as Shoto's chest pushes into my hand and he starts to try to say something. Without any hesitation, I pull back that hand and smack him across the face. Hard. I even feel a smidge of blood on my palm.

When I turn back to Fumiko, I see her hand coming. While I could move, I don't. This is part of the plan, unfortunately. I know she can't slap as hard as any of my opponents when I spar at the kickboxing gym. Still, it doesn't mean that it won't hurt at all.

As the blow lands across my cheek and again across my other, pain spreads throughout my entire face—a bit more than I expected, if I'm honest. Letting the theatrics take over, I throw myself to the ground. Immediately, I'm swarmed by the security guards.

I kind of feel bad. I hope Luke doesn't get mad at them later because this happened. I'll try to explain to him that I let myself get hit on purpose.

One security guard kneels in front of me with his hand held out to help me up. I nod and politely accept it. I can hear the grunting before I see Fumiko fighting against the guards while hurling as many insults at me as she can in both English and Japanese.

I'm sorry Chiaki, I'll have to use your memory a bit.

Thinking about my last memory of Chiaki, I force tears to my eyes and turn to face Shoto. I gently push the guards to the side so that my head is visible but my body is still protected.

"See, Shoto. This is why I can't marry you. How can I when it would lead to me having a mother-in-law like that? All I did was defend myself, and she attacked me."

I admit it. I'm relishing in the confused look on his face as he shifts his stare between me and his mom in horror. I, the "love of his life", hit him. And his mother hit the "love of his life."

My mother speaks up again, her tone dismissive, "Don't act innocent. You hit the boy first."

"Did I or did I not clearly express my boundary? Even if you weren't a part of the conversation, Shoto and I have talked about situations of enforcing boundaries before. Isn't that right, Shoto?"

Shoto and I once had a conversation back when I was too scared to hurt anyone in case I did some real damage. Back then, I had been worried about regretting the damage I could do to the people who hurt me, but I'm years past that point now.

When we had talked about it, he had told me, "If anyone ever steps over a clearly stated boundary, you make sure to teach them it's not okay. It doesn't matter if you hurt them back because they hurt you first. Okay, little sister?"

Yes, I remember what he said word for word. It used to be a very monumental piece of my life, alright? They guy who said it may be a tainted memory but the words still ring true.

I turn to Shoto with the most pitiful look I can muster.

He looks so terrified I wish I could snap a picture. His lips are pale and trembling, and his eyes are as wide as golf balls. Oh my gosh. This poor, naive, little soul.

"Shoto, didn't you also say it's important to keep your word? I followed your advice. Are you upset with me now?"

Fumiko screeches, "Stop playing with his head!"

I shrug. "Shoto, she keeps yelling at me. You know I don't like yelling."

"Lia, don't worry. You're right." Shoto puts his hands up in surrender. "I never expected this situation or anything like it. I'm so sorry. I was wrong."

He's practically begging me to forgive him, but that will never happen.

"You see, Shoto, given these circumstances, I can't even *consider* being involved with you. I'm sorry."

Turning around, I ignore any further argument and walk out of the cafe, surrounded by my posse of guards.

That went better than I thought! Fumiko slapped me not once, but *twice!* I couldn't have hoped for a better outcome. I can only imagine how she felt seeing Shoto take my side. Oh, and I can't imagine how he's feeling right now, *torn* between his mother and the girl he loves so much.

As I slide into the car, I'm met with a very unexpected, and even more *angry* husband.

"Sweetheart," he grumbles. "Who did this to you?"

Well, shit.

CHAPTER 20

I chuckle nervously. "Hi, hubby. Aren't you supposed to be at work?"

He gently touches both of my cheeks. The look of concern on his face makes me a little nervous though I don't exactly understand why.

"It's nothing, really."

This does nothing to appease him. I have a feeling he's going to be much more upset when he learns I provoked these slaps. I know I *should* tell him but I'm not sure if I really want to at this point.

"This isn't nothing."

I grab his hand as he tries to open the car door. I don't need him going in there and making things a bigger mess. Besides, he'll ruin my plan if he reminds Shoto I'm married. His anger over that might eclipse the conflicting feelings I've coaxed out of him.

"I'm sorry, hubby. It had to be done."

Hopefully, the use of this name will calm him down a bit. The atmosphere in the car is a bit suffocating with him like this. His muscles are tight with tension and his jaw set—the quiet between us unsettling.

"You *had* to get hurt? Aurelia, please tell me in what world it's okay for you to get hurt."

"Well, I needed to set the stage and this is what I had to do to do it. Sue me."

I don't understand why he's so upset. I'm not even upset, and it's *my* body that had to go through the pain. Considering that, he should be a bit tamer right now.

"I've expressed to you many times how important your safety is to me. Especially considering those people already pose huge danger to you."

His voice is still low but I can tell that he's warring with himself to keep his composure. Still, it really shouldn't matter what I did. It's over and done with now, and there's no taking anything back.

"Luke," I chide. "You told me you would allow me to do what I needed to do to get rid of Shoto without your interference and within our agreed timeframe. I'm trying to do that so just let me. Why are you even here?"

"When you sent me the message, I couldn't stop worrying so I called Patrick to come get me. I initially only intended to remain close by until you came out. That was until your bodyguards sent me an alert that something had happened."

Those freaking snitches. They don't have to go telling him about every little thing, do they? It was literally like two smacks and that's it. It's not like I got into a whole fist fight or got jumped. Why does everyone think this is some type of big deal? The bodyguards are literally bodyguards. Surely, they've been through worse.

"Dude, I'm fine."

One second I'm sitting in my own seat, and the next, I'm being held tightly in his arms.

"Don't say that," he mutters. "Why do you think getting hurt doesn't matter?"

If I say "because it doesn't," I doubt that would make him much happier. But it really doesn't. I mean if it helps me get closer to taking people down, why should I care much about it? It's not like I broke a bone or something.

"I just . . ." I murmur, "I just don't see this as such a big thing. I mean, I purposely provoked the reaction, and I walked in knowing that it would happen."

"Ari, don't ever do something like that again." He hesitates before almost painfully adding, "Please."

Ari. He's been calling me that for a while now. I'd asked him why, and he said it was because Shoto called me Lia so that nickname was tainted. I have to admit I like the fresh nickname.

I still don't understand why he thinks this was such a horrible event, but I can tell it means a lot to him. What type of person would I be if I take his concerns into consideration? Besides, it's not like I expect anything like to happen again down the line so I'm not really losing anything, right?

I whisper, "Okay."

He holds me tighter and I let him. I guess I'm not used to being important to anyone. Once upon a time, I was a bullied kid, and my mother had pretty much told me not to complain if I wasn't going to do anything about it. When I was younger, my dad had taken the time to show Chiaki, my older brother Jackson, and I some life skills. He also showed up for us. As time went on though and it got closer to the day he'd disappeared, he had started shrugging me off and going about his day.

Wait, I lied. Chiaki always cared about me beyond anything my parents could muster. She would even threaten to go beat up people on my behalf even though she was the most non-confrontational person I knew. And that love never died off because of any outside factors. She never chose to leave me.

Still, I can't believe Luke came just because I sent him a message that I would be here. And he still gave me the freedom to figure things out on my own. But, wait. Is that even true?

I push away from his embrace so that I can look him in his gorgeous eyes. "Luke, how often are these bodyguards updating you?"

We had agreed they would stay out of sight but I never considered how much reporting they actually do on a daily basis. Like do I do anything without him knowing? The only time that they aren't around is when I'm in my home office since I haven't found a need to ditch them yet.

"Every hour at least. Why?"

Every hour? Why would he need an update every hour? I'm not a child who's being babysat while her father is at work. I'm an adult who deserves more privacy than that.

"And why do you need to have an update every hour?"

"To make sure you're safe."

"And you don't think this is an infringement on my privacy?"

The car is silent for a few moments. I can already guess the answer.

"I never thought about it that way. It's how I know you're safe at all times."

"Do you think I'm so *fragile* I'll break in an instant?"

"I think you're anything but that."

"I seriously doubt that. I mean *every hour*. That's insane. You've seen me protect myself. If not me, then you should have faith in your security."

"Do you think I lack faith in you?"

"That's what this whole fiasco makes it seem like. Like you think that at any moment, I'll just crumble. I'm *much* stronger than that, and if you truly believed that, you wouldn't need freaking hourly updates."

I try not to cuss. After all, cussing in arguments makes it seem like you're attacking the person. I'm not attacking him as a whole but rather bringing awareness to a behavior that negatively impacts our relationship.

"I already told you the hourly updates aren't for you."

His casual response is really pissing me off. My annoyance bubbles up. It's charming that he wants me safe but not at this level. Like what if I was planning to surprise him? I bet he already knew that I was cooking for him that other night.

Now that I think about it, *any time* that I cook something small or am feeling hungry, he always manages to swoop in just in time.

"Luke."

"Yes?"

"No more."

"No more what?"

"Unless it pertains directly to my safety, no more updates. You don't need hourly updates on me. Literally, sometimes an hour can consist of me being in the bathroom and I don't think that you need that much unnecessary information on me."

IBS can be a bitch sometimes. But no, seriously. Why would he find any of those things necessary? It's overkill and I'm a woman who loves her privacy.

"Sweetheart . . ."

I get closer to him, keeping my expression deadly serious. Seeing as we've been living together for more than a month, he should understand that serious is nowhere close to my default.

"Don't you dare 'sweetheart' me," I say, mocking his tone. "This isn't negotiable, Luke. Respecting my privacy is the *same* as respecting me, and if you can't do that, we have a serious issue."

This is my boundary, and I'm going to make sure it's respected. I understand that he wants to protect me, but that means nothing if it's because he sees me as less than him. We're equals. I thought he already understood that. It sucks realizing that he didn't.

If he can't promise me and *keep* his promise to me, then there's hardly any future for us, right? And I admit I really hope there's a bright future for us.

His jaw ticks, eyes narrow, and he hesitates for a few seconds. From the way his chest starts to move more rapidly and his Adam's apple bobs, I can tell he's not exactly mad but maybe . . . remorseful?

"I understand," he grumbles. "Only updates necessary for your protection."

"Send the memo now."

He pulls his phone out and sends a quick message before tucking it away. Satisfied, I sit back in my seat. I don't need to see the message to trust that he did what I said. I mean, I know I agreed to accept his protection, but that was a bit extra.

Ya know, seeing this, I don't think I'll ever be able to understand how those other couples I hear about are never able to communicate. It's working pretty well for us, if I'm honest. We both acknowledge our faults, even if we hesitate to understand the reasoning behind it.

I've found that talking to each other also makes it a lot easier to get over all the negative feelings, too. Just his assurance alone has made me feel a lot more at ease and I don't feel angry anymore.

"Hey, don't you still have work left to do today? Everything's fine and you can go back now," I assure him.

He gently cups my cheek.

"Not yet. First, I need to make sure your wounds are taken care of," he replies. "And before you argue, it's not because I think you're incapable. It's because it will help me put my own mind at ease."

I could argue. Honestly, I *want* to argue. But I do understand what he's saying. It's not like it will hurt to let him patch me up, and I must admit that it's one of the book tropes I've always wanted to experience. Now that I think about it, he also hit the "Who hurt you?" trope, too.

Oh, I'm curious how many more I'll be able to get out of him through the course of our marriage. As long as it's not one of those *annoying* ones like miscommunication (which obviously doesn't seem very likely), it's more than welcome.

"Okay," I reply. "As long as you'll make sure to kiss it all better."

Luke's responding chuckle is all I need in confirmation that we're fine. I'm glad we're on the same page of the healing nature of communication.

After a minute, he mutters, "You know I will."

CHAPTER 21

Hi Aurelia. It was really nice meeting you the other day. I know it's been a while, but I was hoping to ask you something. Would you like to go get coffee one of these days?

I stare at the text. I'm surprised that Margaret has reached out. I fully expected Colin to stop his wife from reaching out to me at all—considering he knows I've been on his trail for so long. I just failed to get anything substantial enough to act on. At least, not yet.

I have to admit that it's a good opportunity. It's been a week since my last serving of drama with my mom, Shoto, and Fumiko, so maybe it's about due.

I pick up my phone to send her a response. *Are you free today?*

Yes. I'm free. Colin has me on bedrest these days so I've had nothing to do since the party.

I'm assuming it has to do with the child inside her. I can only imagine it's important to him. Or maybe I'm reading too much into it.

Where do you want to meet?

Meet me at Empire's Diner.

Alright, I'll see you then.

I look at the computer screen in front of me—the screen focused on BB Media's CFO's emails. It had taken me months to finally break through one of the C-suite member's security systems. The encryption wasn't that tough, but there were enough layers that tugging at the right strings was hard.

Luckily, my husband has access to certain systems due to his stakes in the company. I politely asked to use his laptop and he gave it to me. I was a little surprise since I'm pretty sure it has classified documents on it that I shouldn't be privy to, but I wasn't about to complain when it got me another step closer to my goal.

My snooping can wait though. Who would have thought my day would offer up something else? An opportunity to build a relationship with someone close to my enemy. It may all be fruitless, but it also may pan out to give me better direction.

I knew when she directed me to a diner that it would be different than where most upper-class restaurants, but I'll admit that I'm surprised how far down the ranks this place is.

"Mrs. Moore, are you sure we're at the right place?"

I glance out the window at the rundown diner. "I'm pretty sure. It's the only Empire Diner in the city."

Before Patrick can let me out, I open the door and step out of the car. The rundown diner needs a paint job—muck covering most of it. I can see splotches of red and green, but that's about all.

The bodyguards are extra wary as they get out of the car behind me. I'm sure they don't find themselves in areas like this very often, if at all.

I actually find no problem with it. When my mom first kicked me out of the house, this was the first area I ventured. I wanted to explore the parts of the city I had not been allowed to even look at when I was younger. I even made friends . . . until they got jumped and mugged for being associated with me. As much as I'd thought I fit in, apparently I just "had the look."

One time, I went to set up another bank account. As I sat in my car after getting carried away with one of those addictive idle games on my phone, some people came storming in and forced me to be the getaway driver after they robbed the placed. I must admit I wonder what happened to them after I snuck a tracking device into their bags and gave the information to the police.

That's not to say things are all bad in this part of town. There's still lots of good. They have the best treats and even the smartest people somehow manage to stay humble—never forgetting their roots. They are a lot more down to earth. People with money and status refuse to see that and it really is a shame.

Enough sappy memories though. I stroll into the diner without giving it any more thought. All thinking would do is delay the inevitable, I guess.

The interior doesn't betray the exterior. Small booths hug the windows that probably haven't been washed since the establishment opened—spray paint and smudges blemish the glass. Small, round tables with way too many chairs for the space provided are scattered indiscriminately around the floor, leaving very little wiggle room. Soiled menus lay on top of each table waiting for someone to take a seat and read their offerings.

The people lounging around don't surprise me either—the sound of their chatter is the only thing that gives this place life.

I look for Margaret. I assumed she'd do the curtesy of getting here first considering she's the one who asked me to meet her. In a booth in the corner of the far end of the diner, I see her sitting there with her head in her hands—her hair in a high, messy bun. She must be stressed out about something.

I angle my head toward the table—a silent gesture of where I'm going so that my bodyguards can disperse and fight whatever spot to keep their eyes on me from afar. Though, they really do stick out like sore thumbs no matter where they settle.

Claiming my seat in front of Margaret, I smile. "Hi."

Margaret lifts her head from her hands, a smile replacing the tense expression I caught a glimpse of.

"I'm so glad you could make it," she says. "I was worried this place might scare you off or something."

"I told you I'd meet you and so here I am. I'm not so stuck on being wealthy that I'd let somewhere like this scare me off. Why did you choose this place anyway?"

"Honestly, I had to buy myself some time." She skittishly looks out the window. I don't know what she can see through them considering their state, but she seems on guard. "I'm sure Colin has assembled a task force by now to find me. Even though I grew up around here, I'm certain he'll assume I couldn't have gotten here on my own."

"He would go that far? Assembling a task force to find a grown woman is a stretch."

She rubs her hands together. "And further. He was always sweet and caring and protective, but ever since I got pregnant, it's like he's scared of something. He's always trying to keep me close by. If I'm not in my room, I'm wherever he is laying on some type of couch."

"I see."

His unborn child really is important to him then. I'm not cruel enough to use the child against him, but it still is a valuable piece of information.

"So you see, I really needed to get out of there. Thanks again for meeting me."

"So what's up then? I'm assuming you wanted to meet me more than because you needed to get out."

What's her angle? I'm pretty much a stranger, and she's complaining about her husband to me.

"I mean, I did want to meet you in part because I wanted company." She rests her hands flat on the table. "The other part is quite embarrassing. I need advice from someone who's close in age to me and in a similar, yet different situation."

"What do you mean?"

She sighs and starts tapping her fingers on the table. "I mean we're both married to men of great status. Your husband has much greater status than mine, but I think you see my point."

I nod. "I do. No need to explain yourself."

Though I'm almost positive looking at her now that I have a lot more freedom in my marriage. We're more equals than she and Colin are.

"Anyway, I wasn't born into a life of wealth, so to speak. I grew up not far from where we're sitting right now." Her eyes briefly meet mine before settling on her hands. "So I'm not exactly sure what's normal and what's not. He's always treated me well aside from having women on the side. I always turned a blind eye but knew that it was happening. I don't think he was even trying to hide it."

"If you're looking for advice on that front, no woman deserves to be cheated on. I've told my husband I would divorce him without a second thought if it came down to that."

She raises her head—finally meeting my eye for more than a split second. I don't know what she was expecting me to say, but I'd never encourage a woman to stay with someone who doesn't value her. No matter who she is.

"As simple as that?"

I nod my head. "Of course. I know I'd be able to make it on my own without him. And that's not because of the resources at my disposal. It's because I believe in my own self-worth and am too stubborn to back down from fighting for it."

"But you still need resources to be able to run," she argues, "I had nothing before him, and he has so much money and powerful people and . . . he'd never let me take my child. I *know* the type of people he has connections with and I'd never be able to escape."

What type of people does he have connections with?

I'm sure it could be seen as a bit of an asshole thing to do, but I can support her and get some information from her at the same time, right? I do feel bad for her so it shouldn't diminish it.

"What type of people have you so worried?"

She glances around apprehensively, eyes darting from window to window to door—anxious about *something*. What is she about to tell me?

When her eyes finally land on me, her lips tremble. Her voice is barely a whisper as she says, "I don't know if I can tell you. I don't know who's here. Who's watching."

I turn around and pinpoint the people in the room. No one here is anywhere near us except my security, who I trust to keep us safe in the event of an emergency.

"It's okay. I have my people here."

Her lips tremble as she continues, "It started when we were first seeing each other. He would get out of bed in the middle of the night when he thought I was asleep and take some 'meetings.' One time I followed him, and he was meeting with some people. Some freakishly pale people."

What's so scary about pale people?

"I saw them." She gulps. "I saw them with a girl in between them who looked normal but she had scars all over. And they were talking about something like . . . moving more product, I think. They said their supply was running low and they were getting weak and desperate. At the time, I thought they were talking about drugs. But now, I think they were talking about people."

My lips part ever so slightly. She's just confirmed what I already knew. He's been trafficking people. And he's working with others in order to be able to do it.

My blood roars and my head floods with questions. When was this meeting? What did the guys look like? Maybe I can connect them to an organization. What did the girl look like? I can connect with her family for more details and confirm she's missing. Did Margaret witness anything else? I can't seem too interested though.

"What makes you think they were talking about people?"

Yes, that question has enough to do with the conversation to warrant it.

"Well, ever since I got pregnant, he's stopped being so secretive. Stopped hiding these 'guests' he would have over at odd hours. Started showing his true colors." Her gaze shifts out the window and back down to her hands. "Those men have been back—each time with a different woman. I started to notice that every woman looked familiar, and that's when I put it together."

"What did you put together?"

Say it so that I can confirm my suspicions without seeming like I know too much about it already.

"They were all models and small-time actresses that BB Media had signed. Back when I was working for him, I personally sat there as he interviewed her." She looks at me. "I *know* what I saw. That day, she looked so lifeless. Like a robot programmed to take orders, she never disobeyed those two men. In fact, when she saw me, there wasn't a spark of familiarity in her eyes. It was like she'd forgotten."

Woah.

Okay, that's not what I expected. Did they drug her to maybe forget everyone in her past? Maybe they brainwashed her into believing whatever they were doing was meant to be normal? Did they make her believe that whatever they were doing was okay?

What does this mean for my sister?

"And you're positive it was her?"

She nods. "Believe me, I never forget a face. She used to be so gorgeous and I guess she still is, but she just seemed . . . drained. Mentally, physically. I don't know how to explain it."

"I believe you."

Three words. I said three words and her body deflates—tears running down her cheeks.

"I just needed someone who would." She roughly uses her hands to wipe away the tears. "I don't know what to do. How can I give a man like this a *child*? What will he teach it? What will he *do* to it? And I have no one to talk to. My parents passed away last year, and I was an only child. Colin has deleted nearly every contact in my phone—himself included. The only reason I managed to keep yours is because I saved it under my late mother's name and he let me keep my parents' contacts to honor their memory."

Okay, I feel bad for her. I didn't give her my number because I wanted to be friends. I wanted to use her for information. But now she's telling me about her situation, and I don't know what to say. I just know that it's horrible.

"What do you want to do?"

"I don't know. I want to have this child, but not with him. But I don't want my child to grow up fatherless either. I want to leave, but I can't escape. Even now, I know I'm running out of time. He'll find me soon."

I gently place my hand over her trembling one. "To leave, you need resolve. No *maybes* or *I don't knows* or *I can'ts*. It has to be definite."

"How are people able to make decisions like this?"

"I can't tell you. I don't have a child and didn't necessarily have the best childhood either. But when you build that resolve and when you're ready to leave, call me."

The unfortunate truth is I don't know the resources that BB Media has backing it. Even as I go after them, it's dangerous. But what's more dangerous is defying an unknown enemy without complete resolve. Without it, you can hesitate, and hesitation can mean failure. Failure can mean a lot of things.

"I will," she whispers.

"And if you want that option to stay open, do yourself a favor. Write my number down somewhere and hide it. Whether it be checking the phone plan or noticing a call from your late mother in your logs, don't let him take away your only resource." I squeeze her hand. "And even if I'm your only resource, I promise I'm a strong one."

I can't say I care for her in the way I do for Chiaki and Lily, but I feel for her. I understand how scary this all is. And there's a precious, innocent life on the line. As much as I don't believe in *people*, children are different.

"What happens if it's too late?"

I wish I didn't have to be so harsh, but for the child in her stomach, I have to be honest and tell her the truth for both of their sakes.

"Don't let it be too late," I reply. "You have to gain the strength to protect you and your baby. You don't get that from staying trapped in his web. I get that you may be scared and confused and unable to comprehend how things turned out like this. Get your head out of the past, focus on the present, and prepare for the future. You are that child's only advocate."

Memories of my own childhood run through my head. Of my mother never appreciating any of us and always running the house like a dictator. There were times where she'd scream at us for crying—oftentimes hitting us for things children should normally be able to do. The saying really is true. All children deserve parents, but not all parents deserve children.

I grip her hand a little tighter, careful not to hurt her. I grit my teeth in an attempt to keep my frustrations at bay. Knowing another child may suffer the fate of a horrible parent breaks my heart and pisses me off more than I'd ever admit.

The asshole CEO needs to be taken down.

She rests her other hand on top of mine—sandwiching it between hers. They're still trembling, but not as much anymore.

"I wish I was that strong." She tightens her hold. "No. I will. I have to before he's born. Aurelia, I will reach out again."

I nod and gently pat her hand before retrieving both of mine. She looks out the window—her brows gently relaxing. I hope I at least gave her some hope for the future. It must have taken a lot of courage to share this with me. If I were anyone else, there would be a risk of it getting back to Colin.

"Why did you trust me with this? Even if my number was the only one in your phone, I could go and tell him if I wanted to."

"You could." She gently smiles. "I know that. But I saw the way you looked at him that night. I could tell you disliked him. And your husband is richer and more powerful so Colin doesn't have anything that could benefit you. Unlike everyone else there, you were the least likely to have a selfish reason to sell me out."

"Fair. But for your own benefit, make sure not to tell anyone else. The more people who know, the worse things will get."

She nods, her eyes suddenly sharp and jaw tight.

"You should go. There's a back exit to this place that I recommend you take. Since you're my guest, the staff should let you through easily."

I don't need to guess why I'm being shooed off and don't question her coziness with the staff. Instead, I signal my security guards. They come to our table immediately.

"Have Patrick bring the car around back. One of you retrieve yours. We're leaving from there."

The youngest (and snobbiest) of the guards, Joseph, wrinkles his nose. "Are you sure, Mrs. Moore?"

"Yes. Now let's get going."

Bodyguards in tow, I walk through the diner with a promise to come up with ways to help Margaret when she's ready. I *will* keep my promise to her.

CHAPTER 22

Settling into my office, I stare at the emails I left unopened. Whatever information I glean feels like it will be futile in comparison to what Margaret told me today.

I roll through the emails. Maybe I can find some type of connection to expand upon what I know now. How do I filter through it to find something that matters though? Maybe I should be cycling through pay slips or something. But I'd need access to the management side of things in order to cross-reference with resignations or something.

I put the emails on a different monitor and edit one of my favorite programs to filter through the emails for me under several keywords, including: *employee, resignation, pay slip, contract*. It's not as effective as me doing it one by one but it is much more efficient.

After setting that up, I decide it's time to dig somewhere else, too. Maybe I can make more progress in the area that has stumped me the most—Colin's personal correspondence. It'll be encrypted, but I might be able to find something to trace back to whoever he's involved with. Or maybe it will lead me to the next step.

I open the system that had been seeking a direct route into his email. It's been going in circles for weeks without providing me a path. But after finally getting through his CFO's security and my chat with Margaret, I'm feeling more confident than before.

I roll my wrists and stretch my fingers.

I'll just have to break right on through. Neither simple nor elegant and harder to clean up, but it's something, at least.

I take a deep breath—ready for the race ahead. I'll have to keep breaking through firewall after firewall so I don't get stuck in between. I'm risking my computer and everything on it for something that's statistically improbable.

What is wrong with me?

The moment my finger hits the keyboard, I can already feel the firewall bolstering its defenses, and I know it's begun. My eyes zone in on the system, brain working in overdrive as I launch my cyber-attack on the firewall. The entire world outside of my screen simply ceases to exist.

First firewall down.

I don't have time to celebrate as I work through the second, a mental timer playing in my mind. I don't even have a minute to break through the next wall before the previous one will restore itself.

As I break through each wall, I find my brain working overtime to navigate the maze without compromising my speed. I impress myself with how quickly I bust through the firewalls. This shouldn't be possible.

There's a small voice in my head that questions *how* it's possible, but it's quickly snuffed out by the intensity of the chase. Before I know it, I'm through.

Sitting back in the seat with a sigh, I wipe away the sweat that's started running down my temple and check the time. I have to make sure there's still time before Luke gets home. He's making salmon tonight.

What the . . .

According to my phone, less than five minutes have passed. That's literally impossible. It felt like at least twenty. My typing can't be that fast, can it?

Whatever. I should still hurry and look before I'm discovered.

I scroll through his emails using the old fashioned way to sort through them. I don't want to test my luck by using another program until I have everything I need.

Let's see.

A lot of his emails are pretty above-board. That's expected from someone who's likely been doing this for a long time. However, no one is perfect. There's bound to be something incriminating. It's just waiting for me to find it.

Wait. Who is enrichio.mortem@zmail.com?

Anyone in Colin's email should have some type of professional email, given his status. That means a custom domain name and proper first and last name. There's no way someone with this email could be contacting Colin about opportunities for some of his artists as the emails claim.

I skim through the emails. Nearly all of them look and sound legit. Still, the thing with the email is rubbing me the wrong way. There has to be some type of hidden meaning.

I look at the other monitor. My program has finished running, leaving me all of the CFO's emails that have those keywords. Maybe I can try narrowing it down even more. Of the selection, I search for enrichio. mortem@zmail.com along with several of the girls whose names were brought up in the emails.

There are no hits on the email, but several hits on the girls' pay slips. Only one of them seems to still be active—her most recent pay slip being two days ago. The rest stopped receiving theirs at least a month ago, which means either their employment was terminated or they resigned.

Think Aurelia. How do you link this together?

I put the timelines together on the emails. Each of the girls suddenly stopped receiving payment either a week or two after they're brought up in the emails with Enrichio Mortem.

On my third monitor, I do a quick search for him. If there's an Enrichio Mortem here, I can at least try to pin down what happened to them. Maybe he'll know something about Chiaki.

Come on, come on.

A browser page loading has never felt so long before. I wait impatiently for a few more seconds before the results pop up. Nothing. There's not a *single* Enrichio Mortem on the internet. Just this stupid: *Did you mean Enrichio Martin?*

Damn it.

Whoever he is, he's hidden himself well. Maybe I can take his IP address and trace it, but I doubt someone who's managed to completely erase their identity uses one that can easily be traced back to them.

Shifting my attention back to Colin's email, I grab his IP address and move on. There has to be more I can do. I did *not* just beat ridiculous odds and risk exposing myself for naught.

I bite at my thumbnail as I scroll. Maybe I should check for any payments around the times the girls stopped working. Yes, I don't think Colin would risk the money tracing back to his own accounts directly. He can disguise any payment as services rendered—hence the written email log.

Yes, that makes sense!

I further filter the emails and find something else. Every time one of the girls stops getting paid, there's always a large payment coming in from Midicuro Marketing.

Weird name, but I bet that's probably where Enrichio is.

To avoid it being flagged, I take pictures of my screens with my phone so I can hold the information close. I have a new direction to look and feel one step closer to Chiaki.

On my screen where I'd previously searched for Enrichio, I decide to try my luck at their firewall which—has no real security. Did they think because they're a shell that it didn't matter?

I go through their finances and find they get a lump sum of their money from another company. When I look into that company, it receives its funds from another company. And I soon realize that this cycle probably goes on for a *long* time.

I can't do anything to stop them, but what if I try to flush them out?

I feel the idea slink in before my better judgement can advise against it. Going back to the major shell, I drop a virus into their system. They'll be unable to transfer money out. For good measure, I make sure to do the same to the other shells I got into.

That should stop them from being able to do much with Colin's company. The virus will be pretty hard to break through for a while.

There's still one more thing I have to do though. According to the CFO's email, there was already an invoice sent to Midicuro Marketing. There's no telling if it's already been paid yet since those emails can take up to forty-eight hours to process.

What do I do? If they've paid, she's sold and will soon be gone.

I grit my teeth as I consider. I can do something to save their next victim, but I can't tell her everything. And there's no telling what they'll do to track her down.

Fuck it.

I look her up on social media. Considering that she's in the entertainment industry, it's not hard to find her. Morgan Young, about thirteen thousand followers. Enough to be worth money when she enters into the contract but small enough to not be missed if she disappears.

Using my fake account since I actually don't have one myself, I send her a message with a free three-week vacation in the Maldives—all-expenses-paid. It's under the guise of a super fan and the account should look real enough, I hope. I can't do much else for her.

There's a knock on my door followed by my husband's voice. "Darling, I'm home."

With a sigh, I log out of everything and shut down my monitors and laptop. I've done what I can for now, but I'll make sure to follow up later.

CHAPTER 23

"Yuto, come on, you know you can tell me."

"Sorry, sis. I really don't know."

I groan. It's been two days since my conversation with Margaret, and since I have time before initiating stage two of Operation Take Down Mr. Delulu, I've been trying to use it to find Jackson.

No luck.

Wanting to avoid my brothers, I tried easier methods first. I did a scan of social media for any sightings of him, tried to track him through his financial accounts only to discover that if he has any, they're in different names. I even took a few days to track down the people that he used to be closest to. Nothing.

I mean, I even hacked into the personal data of people I know hold a grudge against my family. They always like to have eyes on us so I hoped maybe they'd managed to find something on him. Nothing on Jackson, but I definitely need to warn my elder brother Michael that they're onto his whole secret relationship that he has going on—especially considering that he's married.

I have no idea how he could fall off the grid so completely without slipping up.

"Yuto, if you know anything . . ."

I shouldn't have to beg my older brother for something that can help our sister, but here I am. This is what family means for the Smiths.

"Why do you need to know so bad anyway? It's not like we're some huge, happy family."

"He knows something I need to know."

"Are you *still* trying to find Chiaki? Sis, you know there's no point. You really should drop it."

Here he goes. Just like the rest of them. After Chiaki's disappearance, they all "grieved" in their own ways then told me not to look any further. They told me I should forget about it because there's nothing I can do.

"She's our *sister!*"

"You know she's probably dead. Just mourn and move on."

My heart feels as if someone just drove a screw into it—ragged and painful and wrong. I could never understand why my brothers did nothing. I still can't understand why they assume she's dead. And really, even if she is, does she not deserve some type of justice?

"So because you think she's dead, she doesn't deserve to have anyone out there looking for her? Because you think that she's dead, I should forget that anything happened? Even if she's dead, Yuto, shouldn't we, as her family, avenge her?"

"What's the point in that? You know we're only family in blood and name."

And that screw is yanked out, leaving me to bleed. Our parents weren't there for us but we had our moments as siblings. I always thought there was more to our relationship than genetics only to be proven wrong when Chiaki disappeared. I was the only one who looked for her, and Jackson has fallen off the face of the Earth. I didn't care then, but now I need him. I can only hope I can find him and the conversation goes better than this one. After all, that night he had done his best to protect me.

"I know that's what you believe," I reply. "But there's always been more between us siblings. Do you think I forgot that time Chiaki stayed up all night helping you find an error in your code during your turn at the company? Or when I snuck into school to make sure you weren't caught with weed in your locker? Those aren't things strangers do."

"Aurelia, there's that and then there's having to face the many powerful people who stand in the way of you and the truth. You won't make it out of this unscathed if you don't stop now. *That's* my brotherly advice," he lectures before hanging up.

The way he said "brotherly" is very mocking, but I let it slide. He's of no use to me and he, in one short phone call, has reminded me why I haven't been keen on talking to any of my brothers.

And he was supposed to be the nice one. I don't know if I can handle more conversations like this one. Being constantly broken down and reminded how little I have in life. Being reminded that for me, family might never mean anything.

I hold onto the memory of Chiaki as the only family who treated everyone like family. She was always there for us and would never have us face something alone, if we didn't have to.

I lean back in my chair and slowly let the mental exhaustion take me out. Maybe I'm due for a nap after my insufficient sleep these last few nights.

Everyone around me is in their graduation gowns. I finally push through and will soon walk across the stage to officially claim my new title.

Dr. Aurelia Smith DCS.

There are few things I prioritize over fun, and education is one of them. If anything, it enhances the things you can do by granting insight. Then, you just get creative.

My mother hasn't made it to my prior graduations. She was always "too busy," but this time she promised to come. Considering who she was, I was surprised to get her word on something like this.

"Dr. Aurelia Smith."

I walk across the stage, shaking hands and accepting my degree, before pausing for my final picture with the dean. Taking a moment, I look into the crowd at the seats reserved for my ticket holders. My parents are not amongst them.

I only see Lily and Chiaki standing there, clapping wildly and shouting my name. I smile at them before making my way off the stage. The entire ceremony, I keep looking behind me with the foolish hope that maybe they got caught in traffic or are running late while knowing what the truth probably is.

Before I know it, we're all walking out and I've still yet to see my parents.

"Lia!"

Before I can prepare myself, Chiaki is jumping on me and hugging me tightly.

"Congratulations! I can't believe you really pulled this off!"

I laugh. "I told you I'd do it. Since when have you known me to bluff? I thought you learned that lesson when it came to escargot."

When we had gone to Paris, she had wimped out, and I won the bet we'd made. The massage she had given me after was impeccable.

"Still, you're amazing."

"Not as amazing as some of the people here. Some have high class jobs lined up and honestly, one of the students wrote a dissertation that had professors drooling."

Chiaki smacked my back before letting go of me. "Don't you ever discredit yourself like that again! You're now in the two percent. Even more of a minority now."

I laugh. We always joke about how we're Asian and Black and super rich. All titles that aren't held by the majority population. With a doctorate thrown in the mix, I'm even rarer.

"I won't. I won't." I ask, "Where's Oka-san?"

From the look on her face, I already know the answer. Of course I should have known that mother wouldn't be here. But, as always, Chiaki is. And so is Lily.

Walking around Chiaki, I pull Lily into a hug. The Latina girl is tall and gorgeous and finally following her dream to become a model. I'm honestly so proud of her.

"It's fine that she's not here because you guys are and that means that we can go get some drinks and have some fun."

Chiaki lets out a hoot before closing in behind me—trapping me in this group hug. I can pretend to complain but I know that no matter what, my big sister will always be here to support me and nothing can top that feeling.

⊶⊷⊶⊷⊶ 🔒 ⊶⊷⊶⊷⊶

I'm startled awake by a knock on my door. I don't know how long I've dozed off for, but the knock sounds like my husband's so I have to assume I've been out for at least two hours.

I call out, "Yeah?"

"Dinner's ready, sweetheart. I didn't want to bother you earlier since I know you've been having trouble sleeping."

I didn't realize he noticed. I usually wait for him to fall asleep before going back to my office to get some more work done.

"I'll be right down," I reply.

As I listen to his receding footsteps, my pulse races with excitement as a few things are made clear from that memory.

For starters, I can now relive the feeling I had when both Chiaki and Lily were there to support my every move. No matter how small the achievement, they always *insisted* we had to celebrate. That will never fade away no matter how much time has passed.

Second, the pursuit of knowledge really used to make me happy. I wonder what else I've lost in the past years. After this is all over, I really should reassess who I am.

And lastly, the most mind-boggling one, I think I know who made the black box. That person's whole thesis set the groundwork for it, and I graduated with them.

Overall, I was right. The clues are in my memories and that makes finding Jackson even more imperative.

My phone goes off—a text message from Margaret popping up.

Can we talk later? I think he's on to me. I don't know how much longer before he confiscates my phone.

We have been communicating when we can, but it's not easy. She'll text me then delete it after. I only reply immediately or not at all. Otherwise, she has to call me later and hope that I answer—which I usually do.

"Sweetheart, dinner's getting cold."

I sigh as I respond to her message, *I'm about to have dinner. Try calling me in three hours or so. We'll discuss then.*

Yet another thing added to my list. But I did offer to help her in any way I could. This isn't something that's too difficult for me so I have no issue. I just hope I'm not putting too much on my plate.

This time, Luke's voice is closer. "Darling."

Later. I'll deal with these things later. For now, I have a husband to enjoy dinner with. He told me he was making ramen!

CHAPTER 24

Well, this is a rare opportunity.

In my pajamas and comfortably wrapped in my husband's arms, neither of us have left the bed yet. It's not often that we have the chance to just lounge around without being pulled away for one thing or another.

As he massages my scalp over my bonnet, he coos, "Good morning, darling."

"Morning."

An involuntary yawn escapes as I absentmindedly cuddle closer to him. He's a human heater, and I may have gone overboard last night on how low I set the air conditioner. Oops.

"You didn't toss and turn too much last night."

He's right. I crashed pretty early yesterday and actually woke up today feeling refreshed and ready to continue my hunt. Maybe I really needed to remember some positive feelings like yesterday's memory.

"I didn't." I smile. "That's great for us, right? I feel like I've been keeping you awake, too."

"It's fine, sweetheart. I'm just glad that you were able to sleep. I was getting worried."

"That's sweet, but there's no need. It's just stress."

This is a welcome disruption from my stress. As much as we go out on dates and stuff, this type of comfort at home with him isn't common. I think it's actually the first time since the day after our picnic date.

"Stress I can help alleviate at any time."

Ugh. Reality. He can alleviate it but shouldn't have to, and I have a plan anyway.

"Today, I'll finish dealing with Shoto, okay? Then I'll be free of him, which should soothe my mind."

"No plans of getting attacked, right?"

"Not today."

He holds me closer as if he's trying to keep me safe. I don't complain. He's warm and comfortable and I'd be insane to not relish in that.

He asks, "What's the plan?"

"Well," I reply. "I've already kind of fractured the relationship he has with his mother the last time I saw them. Today, the goal is to build that separation even more. If I put him in a situation where he has to pick her or me, either choice works."

I yawn. I got a lot of sleep last night, but it seems I'm too comfortable now. The environment is coaxing me back to sleep.

"If he chooses her, then I can say good riddance because that means he's made the decision for himself," I drawl out. "If he chooses me then she'll make the decision for him. He's her favorite pawn after all. My plan is—"

Another yawn rudely interrupts me just as I'm about to tell him how I'll pull this off. I hope he realizes that it's so his fault. He really shouldn't be so comfortable.

"It seems like you're still tired. Rest, darling. I'll wake you in two hours."

Sounds lovely.

Not being able to muster a coherent response, I drift back off to sleep.

Dressed in a bold, red gown with straps that drape elegantly off my shoulders and a bodice that wraps around my torso and falls gracefully to the floor. My makeup is done with soft glam. My wedding band and engagement ring, the new teardrop pendant Luke brought me today, and hoop earrings finish the details. My hair is pulled back into an elegant bun secured with an ornate red and black hairpin. Of course, my husband bought it for me to complete the outfit. Tying it all together is my new pair of black heels.

Regardless of everything, no matter what, the best accessory of tonight is my bag, AKA my husband.

Next to me, he looks devilishly handsome in his matching red suit, black shirt, and an exquisitely designed red tie with abstract black designs. His hair has a bit of side part action going on—expertly styled by yours truly. He looks hot.

I've officially decided that dressing him up is one of my favorite hobbies.

I turn to him and smile. "Are you ready?"

"To go anywhere with you? Of course."

The walk to the car is short and silent. I have to admit I'm really feeling myself and putting a little strut into my step. Modeling was never my preferred career path. I dabbled a bit but right now, I feel like I could walk a runway.

Sliding into the car, I exclaim, "Good evening, Patrick."

"Good evening, Mrs. Moore."

I heard a lot of joy in that one. Yes! I love the positivity. Go, Patrick!

Luke nods to Patrick, who responds with a happy, "Good evening, Mr. Moore."

Once we're comfortably tucked away into the car and on the road, I kick off my heels for the time being. There's no point in wearing the things if I'm just in the car with no one but Luke, right?

"So, what's your plan for the night? You said you needed an in for this charity auction, but never exactly elaborated on why."

"Well, Fumiko still has a company to run regardless of whatever is happening here. Tonight, Vanguard Protection Agency has entered the picture and they're looking to set their foundation. I'm sure I don't need to explain the company's reach. It's surprising that they're just deciding to establish themselves here, if I'm honest."

"Yes. Julia has already reached out to ask for advice."

Wait. Let's just pause on my explanation for a bit. Did he just name the CEO of Vanguard Protection Agency by her first name?

"You know Julia Martin?"

"You're shocked? We were actually close childhood friends."

He's right. I really shouldn't be shocked. I know how expansive his business is and their families likely run in the same circles. I hear the Martin family goes back generations, just as the Moores do. Okay, well that's at least a welcome advantage for what's going to happen tonight.

"I guess not," I reply. "Anyway, back to my plan. Fumiko will probably be busy with Julia for a large part of the night. That leaves Shoto alone for me to set the stage for the three acts: jealousy, betrayal, and hatred."

"So you're playing a social game tonight."

"Won't even have to really lift a finger."

"I suppose I'm needed for Act One."

"You're actually needed for all three acts. But you're free to be yourself. You don't need to do anything special at the moment. I trust that you can adapt if it does come to that though."

Luke gently wraps an arm around my shoulders. "You sure are cunning."

"I need to get rid of him."

Not just for my safety and sanity. I need to be able to find and visit Jackson, and I can't do that unless I'm assured that there are no stalkers. Ditching my security team is easy enough, but I can't worry about them *and* others on my tail. It's too many variables to calculate.

I also need to deliver a package to Margaret today. She had told me she should be here tonight, so it'll likely be me only opportunity.

"And you will. Just remember our deal. Anything that happens after tonight, I'll handle him."

I sigh. "Honestly, you'll be more than welcome to. Truthfully, I don't want to deal with it after tonight."

Though I have complete faith in my plan. He isn't the priority, though I really can't say that to Luke. Maybe after this is over, I can explain the whole Chiaki situation to him. But that's a *hard* maybe.

"Then, don't," he responds. "Tonight is your night, and I'm positive you'll shine gloriously."

I'd better. It's also supposed to be a distraction for my mother to get off my tail. I know her well enough to know even if she can't get close, she's definitely keeping tabs on me somehow. The second I break free of my security, she'll swoop in to teach me some lesson since her first one didn't work.

It's not my fault she thought so highly of herself that she thought I wouldn't survive on my own.

I force a chuckle. "Aren't you charming."

He gently kisses my cheek, and I graciously accept it.

Tonight, Mr. Delulu goes down. No more stalking or harassment or just pure craziness coming from him. Sucks that I've lost a friend but there's not much else I can do to save him. Even this plan is a mercy. Plan B involved him having a mental breakdown in front of a crowd of people.

Tonight will be the first real push in the right direction. The chain reaction will likely keep going for weeks, maybe even months. It'll probably be chaotic, but at least I'm not alone. The only family that I ever really knew is gone but I've gained someone precious who will support me through it all.

CHAPTER 25

Stepping into the building, it's obvious we're in a place that only those in the upper-most tax bracket can afford. Everyone is dressed in their designer gowns—covered in jewelry and with makeup caked on.

With my arm wrapped around my husband's, walking through the crowd of people makes me feel powerful.

I pull him closer to me as I scan the room on the hunt for tonight's targets. I know they have to be here. While Luke holds a position high enough to be fashionably late, they're barely high enough to be in the event. That means they have to come early if they don't want to appear as if they're looking down on everybody else.

"Oh, hubby. Tonight should be fun."

Luke doesn't verbally reply but smiles down at me.

When I spot Shoto, his eyes are glued to us. It's obvious enough he finds my outfit gorgeous. Of course he does because I made sure of it.

I flash him a smile before turning to gently kiss Luke on the cheek.

While I would love to see Shoto's expression, I have to play coy to *really* get under his skin.

"Why don't we go explore? We have a great cause to support tonight, and I'd love to be able to do our part."

What the cause is? I forgot. It's probably some disease or "save the animals" campaign. I think those are all the rage right now. Everyone here is only here for the sake of maintaining their good reputations.

Luke stretches out his other arm in the direction as if to guide me to the start of the display's walkthrough.

Stopping at the first item, I feign thought at the hand embroidered blanket. While many will probably pretend it's some gorgeous antiquity, the thing is *so* ugly. Still, I can't do that.

Looking up at Luke, I say, "Maybe we should get this. We've been looking for a new throw recently, right?"

He gently kisses my forehead before replying, "Whatever you want, darling."

The next few displays go the same way. None of them have truly caught my eye yet but these events always have something that is actually extravagant. As much as I despise that everyone uses these events for the wrong reasons, myself included, I do like to support good causes—even the ones I don't remember.

Stopping at a truly gorgeous emerald pendant, I turn to Luke.

"Hubby, I think I've fallen in love."

"Well, darling, I already knew you were in love with me."

I struggle against the urge to roll my eyes. He's flirting with me for the act, but there's something about the tone of his voice that tells me he's intentionally teasing me, too.

I playfully smack his arm with a little extra force so that he knows I'm on to him. "You know what I mean. This pendant is gorgeous. I think it would go so well with the dress you just brought me."

As much as this is a show, it's also true. He's decided he loves seeing me in emerald green and therefore will buy anything in that color with a design he believes will suit me. He occasionally also picks something up in black, red, or white.

Anyway, back on topic. I really will outbid everyone for this necklace if I must. They don't know how extensive my pockets are.

"Then it's my job to complete your ensemble, sweetheart. I'll make sure you have it by the end of the night."

With that, he places his hand on the small of my back and leads me to the next display where a woman clad in red awaits.

The gorgeous woman has elbow-length black hair with springy curls and sharp eyes with bold, but not overstated, makeup. Though she smiles at everyone who says something to her, the intent look in her eyes shows that she's analyzing every person and every interaction.

Julia Martin.

She's already talking to Fumiko as we approach.

"Oh, hello Ms. Martin," I greet, "Aunt Fumi."

When Fumiko turns to look at me, she shoots me a sharp glare. She's obviously trying to hide it from Julia, but I have a feeling that Julia is much smarter than Fumiko is giving her credit for.

"Good evening," she greets. "You must be Luke's new wife. I've been wanting to meet you for a while now but the man has been gatekeeping you."

I laugh. "He can be a bit protective sometimes. He doesn't like when people are unkind to me, ya know? Maybe he's scared your beauty will intimidate me."

Julia responds with a laugh of her own. "Luke would never be so kind to think of me as a beauty. It's more likely he thinks I'll bite your head off or something."

"I do quite like my head attached to my body."

"Of course, I'd never hurt someone as charming as you."

Nice. She and I already have decent rapport. My husband being her close friend, of course, made this whole situation a lot easier to manage than it would have been.

"I'm just glad to meet one of Luke's friends. I don't think I've seen many of those around."

And that's the truth. I haven't seen him communicate with anyone outside of his family, staff, or myself. There has to be something unhealthy about that, right?

Luke tugs me into him. "Okay, okay, enough of that. This is the reason I can't have you people meeting my wife."

His tone is exasperated but I can tell he's teasing.

Julia changes the topic. "I heard you call dear Fumiko here Aunt Fumi. I suppose that means you're family."

"She's my mother's best friend, and I grew up with her son," I reply. "We've been best friends since we were young, and Aunt Fumi always looked out for me. I've always been *so* grateful for their care and support."

Too bad she turned out like this. Caring only as long as her son was happy. The second he wanted more and I didn't, she became this unrecognizable monster I now have to spend energy taking down a notch.

Fumiko takes the opportunity to jump in. "That's right. I watched

Little Lia grow up. You wouldn't believe the cravings I had to satiate for her mother. Do you know how hard it is to get mochi imported from a small family restaurant on the outskirts of Tokyo?"

Julia laughs. "Oh wow, sounds like a journey. It's great you care so much for your family—even if there is no blood relation between you. Family relations say a lot about a person."

I agree. Just wait until you see how Fumiko treats her "family." I mean, at least she treats her son well. It's just at the expense of everyone else.

Fumiko relaxes as she says, "Of course. It's the greatest demonstration of how loyal someone is."

How does she say these things without either laughing or gagging? I mean seriously, it's so hypocritical.

Julia changes the subject. "Onto things more on theme for tonight. Do you guys have your eye on anything so far? I've seen some real beauties out here."

"Actually yeah," I reply. "I have a few things I've got my eye on so far. But, if I'm honest, I really have fallen in love with this emerald pendant. It's gorgeous and Luke just brought me a dress it would pair perfectly with."

Julia replies, "Oh, I saw that one, too. I hope you come prepared because I won't let it go easily."

"I would expect no less," I reply. "It's an auction after all. And we can't forget what really matters is the cause, right? Even if I outbid you, you can say you made me put more money toward it."

"It's never personal. May the best woman win."

We clasp hands with a challenge in our eyes, but I know I'll win. Even if I don't personally have enough money, my dear husband will get it for me because it's part of the plan. And because I've already set my eye on it, of course.

Luke rests his hand on my back as he says, "My wife will always be the best woman."

With that, he leads me to the next exhibit. Fumiko can continue talking to Julia all she wants, but that relationship won't last past this event if I have anything to say about it.

I continue to feign interest in everything and play the happy couple until everyone is called to the auditorium, where the auction is to be held. As we make our way in, I can already feel two sets of eyes on me.

When I peer over my shoulder, I see Shoto with a sullen look on his face as he watches Luke and I. Fumiko, on the other hand, seems to have a bit of a disgusted look. Guess she doesn't like that not only can I stand up to her, I tower over her.

I send them a friendly smile as we continue our walk to our seats, much closer to the front than theirs. As they say, kill them with kindness, right?

And that I'll do. On top of everything else I have to kill them with. Socially, of course. They really have no idea who they have messed with, and I'll admit I'm taking a bit of a perverse pleasure in knowing I'll be the one to take them down.

Anyway, I guess now it's time for Phase 2 to commence.

CHAPTER 26

Sitting toward the front of the auditorium, I'm sure Fumiko and Shoto can't see me from their spot in the back. I rest my right hand on Luke's and hold my numbered paddle in my left. Today, Luke and I have separate paddles since I feel that with this being my personal vendetta, I should take the financial hit—even if Luke *could* technically afford it ten times over.

Lips brush against my ear as Luke whispers, "If you need anything, just let me know."

I smile to him. "Thank you, Luke. But I think I've got this on my own. I'll let you know if there's anything I want though."

I make sure to distinguish between wants and needs. A need tonight is something that goes toward my plans with Shoto and Fumiko. Those are my responsibility to deal with. However, there are a few things I want, and I do know Luke likes to spoil me. It'll probably hurt his pride if I don't let him buy me something.

"I'll be waiting, sweetheart. Just tap my arm when you see something you want, then."

That, I will. Aside from the pendant I saw earlier, which is off limits since I already agreed to compete with Julia toe to toe on that one, I saw this gorgeous diamond hairpin I wouldn't mind having.

I nod. "Thanks, Luke. I'll let you know."

As the lights dim, so does the noise around us. A spotlight hits the stage—highlighting the MC and the box behind her shoulder holding the first item of the night. The MC looks elegant with her simple makeup and black form-fitting gown. She's gorgeous.

"Good evening, ladies and gentlemen. The auction to support all of the animal rescue shelters in the region is soon to start. May I ask that everyone silences their phones and readies their wallets as the event commences?"

Her voice is sweet, but strong. I doubt it's her first rodeo dealing with entitled wealthy people.

A few moments pass as the room sinks into silence. I know it's because the auction is starting, but I have to admit it's the most peaceful part of the night thus far.

"And now, we will start with the first item of the night."

I don't even need to listen to her explanation of the item. I labeled it earlier as something Fumiko would surely bid on and that means I'll need to bid on it myself.

Let the games begin.

⊶⊶⊶⊶⊶ 🔒 ⊶⊶⊶⊶⊶

"Sold to number 849!"

I grin in satisfaction. It probably says something about me that I'm taking so much pleasure from this and don't feel an ounce of guilt.

Once again, another thing Fumiko wanted to purchase has landed into my lap. I have no doubt that she's worked out who's been taking what she wants without her being able to put up much of a fight.

"With that, I think it's time for a break. We'll start our intermission now and reconvene in fifteen minutes. Don't be late or you may miss what I know is to be one of the stars of the auction!"

The lights spring back to life as people move from their seats.

I think I know what star she's talking about. It's probably the pendant that both Julia and I had our eyes on earlier. It will finally be time for our friendly little showdown. I hope she meant what she said earlier about the best woman winning.

I turn to Luke. "I'm going to run to the ladies room. Be right back."

He grins and squeezes my hand before completely letting go. I grin before dropping my number and waltzing out of the room. While I need to use the bathroom, I also really want to take the chance to gloat a bit, too. I just can't make it obvious to the masses.

I don't have to wait long before feeling the heavy glare of Fumiko on me. I turn around with the same friendly smile from earlier plastered on my face and meet her eyes.

Shoto pats his mom's shoulder and mutters something to her before walking over in my direction.

Okay, now I have a quick decision to make. Do I see what he wants to say, which my avid curiosity would prefer, or do I walk away and actually go to the bathroom like I said I would. If I don't, it's possible I won't have time to use it before the auction starts back up and I really must get that pendant.

"Lia, I know what you're doing and you should stop. Mom has been wanting to say sorry for the other day. You don't need to be so petty and hurt anymore."

Oh Shoto, you sweet, terrible liar. I know the last thing your mother wants to do is apologize. She would have done it already if she did, and she definitely wouldn't be so openly glaring at me every time she sees me.

"I'm not being petty, and this isn't about her. It appears Aunt Fumi and I just happen to have the same taste."

"But doesn't it feel bad to take so much of someone else's money, hmm? You really shouldn't use some man's name to steal opportunities from others. You know mom had to build her fortune all on her own and it's not fair for you to use somebody else's old money to take from her."

"One, I'm not taking *anything* from her. An auction is fair game and it really is survival of the fittest," I say with a shrug. "And two, what makes you think I'm using someone else's money?"

"Lia, don't be embarrassed. I know Aunt Akira cut you off. You don't even have enough money to attend an event like this on your own."

Is he talking down to me? His tone isn't too condescending, but his words are unmistakable.

"Shoto, you don't know me. Until recently, we haven't talked in years," I reply. "I have more than enough money to take care of myself *and* outbid a lot of people in there."

Including your mom.

I want to say that, but I can't. I need him to feel as if I agree with him by the end of this conversation. But I can't believe he thinks I'm splurging with someone else's money. I didn't even do that with my family's money when I *did* have access to it.

Shoto sighs. "How would you do that? You've been iced out from your family business, and you have a degree but I know you haven't been working at any company large enough to earn that much money. Lying isn't good Lia."

"Look, Shoto. If you don't *trust* me, that's on you."

"No Lia, I do trust you."

"You trust me but you don't believe me. Explain that."

Shoto hesitates. I assume he's considering how to respond without making me out to be some villain. After all, he still wants me to be with him and believes he still has a chance with me—no matter how much I tell him there's no way in hell.

"Lia, I'm sorry. You're right." He pouts. "I should trust you more. It's just hard considering how much has changed. You really broke my heart. And now mom feels as if you're bullying her for no reason. If you're mad at me then take it out on me. But please Lia, leave my mom out of it. I can handle your anger on my own."

I admit that he looks like a sad little puppy. He's begging me to take it easy on his mom while completely believing I'm mad at only him. How adorable.

I politely respond, "I won't hold any grudges I have for you against your mom, alright? You're two different people, and I'm a very fair person."

Very fair, indeed. I said I wouldn't hold his actions against Fumiko. That doesn't mean I won't hold her accountable for her own mistakes. Afterall, she allowed Shoto to turn out this way. I don't know when it got this bad, but it did, and I was too blind to see it until it was too late.

Now, we're here. No longer the happy best friends or family. I always knew my mom would become a problem for me, but I used to always think Shoto would be on my side.

"Thank you, Lia. There are just so many things mom wants in there, and I'd like for her to get some."

"It will always be the best bidder who wins," I reply. "And that won't always be your mom. It won't even always be me. My wallet has limits."

He probably thinks I can't hear him but I definitely can as he murmurs, "Not with that husband of yours, it doesn't."

"Shoto, you asked for a favor, which I have granted. Don't upset me by assessing my value at the level of my husband. I have my own money to bid with, and therefore, that's what I'll continue to do. Please don't insult me because you're insecure about your own financial ability. We are not the same."

I don't entertain the situation any further and walk away before I can lose my composure. I hate when people think a woman's value only goes as far as her spouse.

Yes, my husband is filthy rich and has unimaginable generational wealth. However, I am my own person who has found a way to earn my own money. Are they the most moral ways to make a buck? No. But I do pay back the community in my own way.

Whatever. I have other things to worry about before I run out of time.

I glance around the hall looking for my target. I'm sure we don't have much time left until the intermission ends so this hand off has to be fast.

I check my phone for Margaret's text. She told me she thinks Colin's getting suspicious—constantly checking her phone to make sure she's *only* using it to watch movies and television shows. She's worried she soon might lose access to it so we talked last night and came up with a plan.

I secured a burner phone for her on my phone plan. He'll be unable to track it or its usage. It will be up to her to keep it effectively hidden, but it will allow us a more stable method of communicating.

I'll try meeting you in the supply closet next to the restrooms. It's never really locked so it should be an okay place to meet considering the crowd.

Heading toward the bathroom, I spot the supply closet tucked away next to it. There are people lounging around it, but no one is really paying it any mind. I act as natural as I can as I weave my way through people and into the closet. I hope that no one noticed.

"Aurelia, is that you?"

It's dark in the room, but I know Margaret's voice well enough.

"Yes," I reply, "But we shouldn't take long. I'll leave the phone here by the door. Wait a few minutes and pick it up on the way out."

"Okay. Thank you for this. You didn't have to do so much."

"I like to keep my word when I can. Have you thought about making the big decision?"

Though I can't force her to make it, I really am hoping she does.

"Not yet. It's just so much to think about. And it hasn't gone too far bad. There's still this glimmer of hope to me that maybe things will go back to normal after I have the baby. Really, he wasn't like this before."

"He still cheated."

"I know that but . . ." She sighs. "I'm just grateful for him."

"I won't mince words Margaret. Your gratitude may be your demise."

I don't stay any longer. I know that the longer I stay, the higher our chances are of getting caught. Part of me wonders how she slipped away from everyone. At least she has that much cunning.

I open the door and let myself out—slipping back into the crowd. Guided by muscle memory, I'm back in my seat in no time, my thoughts return to Shoto's words.

Is that what everyone here thinks about me? Do they all think that I'm bidding using Luke's fortune instead of one earned by my own tediously hard work? I mean, I know people who do only use their partner's resources, and power to them if it works for their own internal moral compass and their relationship, but I couldn't allow myself to do that.

"Sweetheart, are you alright?"

I face Luke. I can feel the concern oozing from him. To be honest, as touching as it is, I've learned that it can end up with me having to hold him back from doing bad things to the people who have done something to me.

I nod. "I'm just thinking." Avoiding bringing Shoto directly into it, I ask, "How many people here think I'm bidding with your money instead of money I earned on my own?"

It's a valid question with all things considered.

"Hmmm." He pauses. "I'd guess, it's most of the people here. That upsets you, doesn't it?"

His question isn't out of curiosity or misunderstanding—more of thoughtfulness.

"A little bit," I admit. "I mean, it irks me how many people assume that, especially in relationships where the man has more money, whoever has less money just leeches off the person who has more. That's even without understanding how much money the other person has."

Like seriously. Absolutely no one in this room knows how much I'm personally worth without familial ties. I've managed to accumulate a small fortune on my own. I have no debts and steady income streams coming from other places.

"Do you want me to say something?"

"No, I'd rather you didn't. They'll likely assume you're BS-ing or something. They'll never say it to your face, but they'll think it regardless so there's really no point. I'll just put my money where my mouth is and prove it myself somehow."

It's not like I could be completely transparent considering that some of my clients really needed to remain anonymous and that not all of the business I conduct is necessarily on the up and up, if you catch my drift.

"The auction will resume in one minute. Everyone, please take your seats and silence your devices once again."

I relax into the chair and listen as the crowd grows louder before getting silent. I tune out most of the noise as the auction starts again—only keeping my eyes on the items as they pop onto the stage.

The first is the emerald pendant from earlier. Of course, it starts with a lot of people going for it, but slowly the numbers thin out as the price goes deeper into the millions.

I realize that the object itself might not actually be worth the amount of money we're bidding on it, but I agreed to a war and already staked my claim on it.

"We're now at 1.3 million. Do I hear 1.4?"

I raise my paddle, continuing my war against who I assume is Julia. I don't bother to turn around to really check though.

"1.4, anyo—"

I raise my paddle.

"1.5!"

And the race goes one until I eventually win at 2.1 million dollars. I mean, of course I do. I wasn't going to back down from this one. Sorry Julia, but I'm too stubborn to let go of something I've already claimed.

Next up on the stage is this *gorgeously* embroidered throw blanket. I know exactly who will bid on it and that's exactly why, I raise my paddle and outbid her.

CHAPTER 27

I grip Luke's bicep as we make our way out of the auditorium. Now that the auction is officially over, I'm supposed to go claim my winnings. Ya know, arrange for payment and delivery to an address of my choosing.

I have quite a few things I have very little use for, so I'll have to figure out what I'm going to do with my new items. Luke also procured some things for both of us that he needs to make arrangements for.

As we exit the auditorium, Julia spots us and approaches.

"Well done," she says. "I suppose the best woman won, didn't she?"

The smile on her face seems genuine. It doesn't look like a bitter feeling of resentment. More like pride.

"I had my eye set on it and said I would get it. I never intended to back down."

Julia nods in what I think is approval. "I also couldn't help but notice that you and Luke were bidding separately. I suppose I've never asked what you do for a living."

"Software engineering and all that boring stuff." A half-truth. "I can't really say much more since a lot of my clients and the specifics of what I do for them are confidential."

Think along the lines of a few world government agencies and some very rich and powerful people internationally. Definitely not people who would like their identities revealed *or* the work I do for them. Confidentiality is a big selling point of mine.

"I see," she says. "At least you stand on your own two feet and stand next to your husband in all aspects—including financial capability. That's something very admirable. I bet not a lot of people here know that."

My heart swells with pride. I have to fight the smug smile that wants to show itself at the acknowledgement.

At least one person cared to not make assumptions.

"They never care to ask," I reply. "It's much more comfortable for them to believe I use my husband's wealth instead of what I have accumulated on my own. Especially when my age is taken into account. Otherwise they would have to face the reality that objectively compares them with me."

Julia laughs. "I understand that. It's the life of being a beautiful, young, successful woman. They will always try to find a way to bring you down or attribute your success to something else. You'd think something like that would change with time."

"History has proven people to be reluctant to change—even if it stunts societal growth." Isn't that why people of different races and genders have had to fight to make themselves heard? "I'll be honest with you though. I'm both pleasantly surprised and happy you saw that easier than most people here."

I mean, seriously. Even my own childhood best friend believes I'm using money doesn't belong to me. Of *course* it belongs to me.

She smiles. "What do you say we go claim our winnings?"

I nod, leading Luke behind me as we walk toward the area. He hasn't said anything since we left the auditorium, but I see the way he's gently grinning down at me. Now I wonder what that's for. I'll ask him later.

Instead, I ask, "So what did you manage to get, Julia?"

"Oh, I mainly focused on the furniture that was here," she responds. "I just moved here and have a penthouse to furnish. I really do prefer having something more unique than you can find at a furniture store."

"I feel like that's ladies' talk for: 'I wanted an excuse to go buy one-of-a-kind things that I would actually never let anyone touch, but no one here knows that.' How's that sound?"

Julia laughs. "Oh, you're blunt, aren't you? Okay, you've caught me. No one's touching any of this. It's for my own personal collection."

I throw my hands up in mock surrender. "I don't judge."

Luke wordlessly grips my hand. I guess he didn't like me letting go, huh? Whatever. This little possessive side of him is kind of cute.

Julia passes me her phone. "If you don't mind."

She doesn't need to finish the sentence. I enter my contact details and save it. I don't want her as a pawn or anything like that. I genuinely think we can be really good friends. She's actually pretty cool compared to a lot of other people floating in these circles.

I send myself a text before handing her back her phone.

"This is my personal phone number," she says. "Not many people have it. Reach out if you need anything or just want to hang out. I'll try to make time for you."

I smile. "Thank you. Same here. I may not be as rich or powerful as you are, but I have my quirks."

"I believe you. Matter of fact, I think there's more to you than meets the eye."

Before I can ask her to expand on what she means by those words, she's called away by an attendant.

Okay, so I'm kind of curious. What part does she mean? I mean, there's a lot that I keep to myself, but the look in her eyes makes it seem like she's confident that she knows something, and I want to know what that something is.

It's my turn to go handle payment and delivery not soon after though, so I guess I'll have to figure that out later then.

I walk away from the counter. Having not used the bathroom since before we left the house, my bladder is hitting me like a truck. Since I dealt with Shoto during the intermission instead of using the bathroom, it takes a degree of self-control I didn't even know I had for me to not do a potty dance in the middle of the hall.

With every step toward the bathroom, I feel a little leprechaun dancing on my bladder.

Realizing the line has died down, I sigh in relief. At least I don't have to wait as long as the people who went there directly after the auction. I slowly make my way to a stall and can't help but eavesdrop as I use the bathroom.

I can't help it. When I hear drama, my ears activate at full power.

A very familiar voice is complaining, "Akira, that girl of yours is absolutely out of control. She knew exactly what I wanted and snatched it up just to spite me."

There's a pause as my mother probably responds to Fumiko. Too bad she isn't on speaker so I can hear more of what's happening.

"We both know she has no plans for them. I can't believe that man would let her spend his money so carelessly like that."

Of course she thinks I'm a gold-digger, too. I swear, some people really won't put their pride aside and admit someone is better than them. It's really kind of sad, if I'm honest.

"You need to get her on a leash! She's just going to keep being a nuisance if she's not put back into her place. After years of friendship, I expect you know what to do."

My place, huh? They want me to start doing things that don't negatively impact them anymore. Sucks for them, but for now, everything I do will be to take them down. My dear Chiaki and Lily will be avenged, and they had an indirect part to play in the whole thing.

"Well, you'd better figure something out then. First Julia and now this bidding war. My patience is at its limit."

Something slams. Maybe it's her phone. I guess there's nothing left for me to hear.

It's laughable though. She wants to "put me in my place" and "keep me on a leash," huh? Not only will that not happen but the exact opposite will. The only people who will be shoved back into their place are her and her son. The place I'm in now is perfectly acceptable.

I step out of the stall after giving it a few seconds. Fumiko hasn't moved yet and I don't enjoy public stalls, even if it is a more upscale establishment like this one.

I innocently ask, "Aunt Fumi, was that my mom that you were

talking to? Or was that another Akira? I'm sorry, I just couldn't help but overhear the conversation."

Fumiko's eyes narrow. While the bathroom isn't full, there are still a few people here. So, what is it she'll do, I wonder. Will she embarrass herself at an event like this or let it go?

"Aurelia, it's not polite to listen to people's private conversations."

"But Aunt Fumi," I argue. "We're in a public bathroom. I'm sure I'm not the only one who heard that conversation."

"Well, it seems you've jumped to conclusions. See that it doesn't happen again. You could really offend someone."

"I'm sorry, Aunt Fumi. Anyway, I need to go meet my husband. He's likely waiting for me after claiming the items he bid on. Some were really quite beautiful."

I can sense the grimace before I see it. She's likely thinking the stuff he's claiming is the everything she wanted. Wait until she learns what actually happened to the stuff that she wanted. It'll be a comedy for the world to see.

"Do you think this is funny?"

"What do you mean?"

"Do you think I don't know what you were doing, Aurelia? Everything I wanted, you and your husband outbid me on. I know you don't even want most of that stuff. Aren't you ashamed?"

"Aunt Fumi, are you accusing me of reading your mind and bidding on things just to get under your skin? Why would I do that?"

"Because you are bitter and petty. You're only doing this because you don't respect your elders and do as we say. You need a lesson in respect."

I inch toward the door and plaster a look of worry and fear on my face. I'm putting on a show for everyone who cares to watch.

"I'm sorry you feel that way, Aunt Fumi. But I have really found my own path in life and apologize that it doesn't align with what you or Mother want."

"You know very well it doesn't align," she says as she follows me out. "You know what we wanted. But forget it. No one would want a daughter like you anyway. You're a disrespectful, insufferable little wench who thinks she can get away with anything. You're not welcome in my family."

"All this over some stuff? Aunt Fumi, I really didn't know," I plead.

Or at least pretend to. Ya know, I have to make it real for our audience. Whether she's realized it or not, I've inched us out of the bathroom and well within the sights of the attendees.

I feel a very familiar, hard body against my back as arms wrap around my front. He's here a little earlier than expected, but enough of a show has been put on, I suppose.

"Is there a problem here?"

Now that he's spoken, I feel every stare turn our way. The drama could be considered a typical family squabble, but with Luke involved, it's anything but typical.

Fumiko is too blinded by rage to stop her verbal assault. "Of course, there's a problem. You let your little wife use your money to settle some petty grudge she holds against her mother and my son through me. She won't admit to it, but it's easy for anyone to see."

"Ignorant."

With one word, I can feel the room go completely silent—not even a single whisper to be heard.

Fumiko sneers. "Excuse me?"

"Anyone who thinks my wife needs my money is ignorant," he states. "Including you."

Oh, I see. He's using this situation to also squash any whispers about me using his money. How thoughtful.

"You know nothing about how—"

"You should watch your next words. I've promised my wife I wouldn't touch anyone who speaks negatively about her, and I would hate to break that promise right now." He holds me a little tighter and I know his words are the truth. "If it happens in front of me, I know my self-control won't hold."

Fumiko opens her mouth to say something but is interrupted as Shoto gently tugs on her arm—giving her a pointed look when she turns to face him. I guess even as delusional as he is, he knows when it's time to give in instead of keep fighting. Always the mama's boy, he'll do what he can to protect her.

"Mom, we can just let it go. Lia is family, and we really don't want to start any trouble."

"Trouble? You think I'm the one who started trouble?"

Shoto faces me. "Lia, you told me that you wouldn't take any of the grudges you hold toward me out on my mom. Was that all just a lie? I can't believe that you'd lie to me. We're supposed to be family."

Fumiko shouts, "She will never be family!"

"And," I interject. "I never lied."

He turns to his mom. "Mom, you don't mean that." He turns to me. "Lia, bid on everything she wanted."

"Not for any malicious reason. I really had no idea. I tried to explain that to her, but she wouldn't listen! I even tried to make things right, ya know?"

"Make things right how? Lia, look at the situation now."

Luke cuts in. "You may not know this, but my wife had a lot of her items sent to your family. She felt bad after the auction and thought carefully about what it was that her Aunt Fumi would have wanted and divided her purchases so that those items would be sent over—even sacrificing some of her own wants."

Fumiko shouts, "Liar!"

"Did you just call me a liar?"

Okay, I'll admit it. Even I have a cold sweat here. I'm so used to the compassionate Luke that I know I completely forgot how he can get when dealing with other people. The unmistakable coldness in his words have me on edge.

"Well, it's true. She only bought those things to flaunt it later. Why else would she spend millions of your—"

"Not my money. And I do not *lie*. Nor will I continue this pointless conversation. I only carried it on since you are family to my wife. But you've said it yourself you aren't family. With that said," he pauses, "I hope to never see your face again."

His words are more than a simple statement. By saying this, Fumiko will be blacklisted from any event that hopes to have Luke's presence. Everyone would prefer him over her. I mean, who wouldn't?

He turns me around with him as we start to walk away.

"I can't believe you would fabricate some story to try to make me look bad for calling you out! You—"

"Mom, please, let's just go."

"Shoto, that woman cannot have you."

"Nor do I want him," I shout. "I'm perfectly happy with my husband, as I've been trying to tell you and my mother for some time now."

I just need to make it clear that he's not on my radar and never has been.

"Mom, let's go."

Their footsteps retreat into the distance. Before they can make it outside though, with impeccable timing if I do say so myself, an attendant reaches them and I can't hear anything but I peek over to see the interaction.

She's hands them an envelope with the greeting card and tracking number for all the items. One final nail in their social coffin.

Fumiko screams something unintelligible before the two are completely gone.

And just like that, I doubt that there will be anymore Mr. Delulu problems in my foreseeable future.

CHAPTER 28

"I'm so proud of me."

I toe off my heels—the fresh air a welcome comfort to my aching feet. As much as I *love* dressing up and showing off once in a blue moon, I will always hate how uncomfortable it is.

"You're satisfied then?"

"More than satisfied. I think I put on a stellar performance tonight. There's no way they'll recover after what I did." I snort. "Actually, I'd love to be there next time they're in public."

I can already imagine the headlines that will be plastered everywhere painting them as an enemy of the Moore family. There are very few people in high society who will even want to be seen with them for the time being. Fumiko may be mad at me, but she'll have to focus her efforts on cleaning this mess up once she calms down. And Shoto will have no choice but to help her as the mama's boy he is.

I sigh and relax into the seat behind me. The ride home is long so I might as well get comfortable, though I'm too ecstatic to sleep.

Luke rubs his thumb over my hand. "You did a good job."

"You think so?"

"Our methods may not be the same, but you've proven yourself to be quite cunning, my wife."

I smile, my chest swelling with pride. Of course I know I'm cunning, but it feels different when he says it. Though I have to admit I'm curious about him more than I'm proud of myself. Like I've come to realize that while I know what I've learned from an early background check and some basic things from seeing how he navigates our home situation, but I don't know anything else.

"What would you have done?"

He turns his attention to the window. "It would have been a lot bloodier than your way. They're lucky you handled it."

My eyebrows inch together, more curious than I'd like to admit.

"That doesn't answer my question."

Luke's eyes meet mine—cold and dark and subtle. Just like how I imagine his rage is.

"If anything were to happen to you, I would handle the threat in the best way to ensure that it won't happen again." It feels like his eyes are peering into my soul as he continues, "I would erase the threat from existence."

My pulse races in my veins. On one hand, it's tantalizing to hear him make such grand promises of protection. On the other hand, there's a part of me that believes he means *exactly* what he said, and that should scare me.

"How so?"

"Sweetheart, if you really want to know the answer, I'll tell you. But something tells me you're not ready to accept who I am completely."

I am. I already want to know who you are. I want you to bare yourself for me and let me feel safe enough to bare myself to you.

"Why would you say that? I mean Luke, I already . . ."

I already what? I just said I barely know him. So what if he's considerate of me and treats me well and is oh so very sexy. I don't know him well enough. But I want to.

"You already what, Aurelia?"

My eyes find his lips—so perfect and *so* tempting. Mine tingle in anticipation, recalling a sensation that shouldn't be as intoxicating as it is.

Focus Aurelia.

"Well." I pause, looking for words that won't completely expose me. "I already married you so I'm kind of stuck with you for a while, aren't I? In that case, I think it's fair to say I'm ready to really get to know you."

He brushes his hand against my collarbone before snaking it around the back of my neck. Held firmly in place, I have no idea what to say or do. Do I move? Do I let this play out? Do I melt into a puddle at his feet the way my body seems to want to?

My mind has no answer, I've forgotten how to breathe, and my whole body is tingling with . . . something.

"Aurelia, sweetheart." He inches closer. "Be careful what you say next. If I let you in, I'll never let you go."

My lips quiver but no words come out. What do I even say to that? My neck is unnaturally warm beneath his hand and I can't help but stare deep into his eyes. His eyes which trap my entire being within their depths.

"Aurelia."

Stop saying my name like that. Hearing my name shouldn't make me as helpless as it is.

His lips brush my ear. "If this is how you're reacting to me now, then how do you expect to handle me in my entirety?"

I don't know.

I can barely hear my own voice as I whisper, "I can handle it."

Since when was I shy?

Luke nibbles my ear before pulling away from me all together—comfortably settling back into his seat as if nothing just happened.

I, on the other hand, can't bring myself to look away from him. My body feels unnaturally warm, trembling lightly as I hold my breath.

Look away.

My body doesn't listen.

"We're here."

Thank you, Patrick.

Whatever had its hold on me has let me go. Before I can get absorbed in Luke again, I turn my head away and open the door on my side. Welcoming the fresh night air, I slide my shoes back on my feet, ready to take a long, hot shower away from Luke.

I'm already a foot outside when I notice that we aren't home.

"Whe—"

A warm hand wraps around my own. I don't even have to check to know that my handsome husband is responsible for it.

"Don't you think you've earned a celebratory meal?"

He doesn't wait for a response as he leads me away from the car and into a gorgeous restaurant. The jagged stone structure sticks out like a sore thumb in the surrounding city landscape, but to me, that enhances its beauty.

The doors are already open as we walk into the restaurant. The marble interior and pillars remind me of a museum. Our shoes echo against the floor—a gentle rhythm ushering us to our destination.

A silver-haired man briefly bows his head to us. "Welcome Mr. and Mrs. Moore."

Luke grins. "Thank you for staying open for us."

Well, I suppose that explains the quiet. It's quiet because this place isn't even supposed to be open. I assume Luke called in some type of favor or something. He even grinned at the man welcoming us. Not many people get to see that sight, especially not aimed at them.

"Where are we?"

Luke moves his hand to the small of my back as we enter. "My favorite restaurant."

Something new to add to the file of things I know about Luke. This place, whatever it's called, is his favorite restaurant.

Only one table is set—and what a beautiful setting it is. The black tablecloth has a bouquet of purple roses on top with small candles on either side. The floor is littered with petals from the beautiful flowers and some gold confetti.

How did he plan this between the auction and here? I mean, he was busy in the car the whole time teasing me.

My face heats up at the reminder so I force myself to think of *anything* else.

"How did you—"

"Darling, I had faith in you before we even got dressed today. This was all planned from the start." He leads me to my seat. "And I'll never miss an opportunity to take you out."

I reach for the flowers at the center of the table. Before Luke, I'd never received flowers before. I mean, people showed interest in me, but I scared them off before they could get the words out. I didn't have time for romance or heartbreak.

But now . . .

"Thank you."

I know my voice was soft, but I'm happy I was able to say anything at all.

He smiles. "Aurelia. Why don't you tell me something about yourself I don't already know. Maybe something from when you were younger."

My heart staggers in my chest. I don't talk much about my past with anyone, even the people who were there. My family is dysfunctional beyond my mother.

"Fine," I reply. "But only if you give something up, too."

He nods so I sigh. I have to think about what story to tell him. Do I tell him a story or just random facts?

"I've never talked about my dad with you. Or anyone, really. My siblings have pretty much forgotten him, and my mom *hates* bringing him up."

I hug the flowers to my chest—a strange comfort emanating from them.

"But I remember him. He was a good man." I gently smile. "My mom was never the type to show affection. She's probably only given me enough compliments to count on one hand. It wasn't *just* high standards. She wanted to command obedience and fear."

Memories flow through my head. Bad memories. Ugly memories. No good memories though.

"But my dad was different. He cared about all of us—including my mom. Even though he left, he toughed out a relationship with my mom for longer than anyone ever should. While my mom didn't consider birthdays important, he would make sure I had a cupcake with a candle, and we would sing together."

That's where the good memories come in. Birthdays and hugs and surprise trips to the beach. I wish I'd been older when he left. Everyone else got him for their entire youth while I was stuck with the scraps. They don't even care enough to bring him up every once in a while. The limited times I do talk to one of my siblings, they act like he never did *anything* for us. Like he barely existed.

"I know he left, and people would probably ask why I still love someone so dearly who didn't love me enough to stay. Or even to take me with him. But he's the source of a lot of my positive childhood memories."

I just can't let go.

"I remember the day he left. He'd kissed my forehead and walked away. That was the last time I saw him. I have no idea where he is today."

I remember him telling my mom I'd forget all about him. I'm glad I didn't though. That I had one parent at some point who truly showed me some sort of care.

Luke reaches his hand across the table and rests it on mine as I grip the flowers tighter.

"Was your childhood truly so miserable?"

"Not all the time," I reply, "My older brother and sister who were closest in age to me got along and were pretty close. Then one day, that got tainted, too."

"What happened?"

I hesitate. "That's not a story for today."

The last thing I can do is talk about either of them. I think I'd actually break down crying and tell him everything the second a single word came out.

He rubs circles with his thumb on my hand. "That's fair."

I crack a small smile, hoping it's convincing enough that I'm alright. "Your turn."

Luke sits back in his chair, his brows scrunched together. I assume he's cycling through memories and deciding what to share.

"My family isn't normal—even by the standards of the peculiar." His features relax slightly. "It's so old that it functions with some long-forgotten traditions."

"Like your need for a wife?"

He nods. "I don't know how much Noah told you about our family and the necessity for marriage, but there are other families with values as archaic as mine. Not many reside in this country, but they're everywhere. And marriage helps establish power."

"Don't you already have a lot of that?"

"More than you know, but not in the way that you think."

He studies my eyes. It's almost as if he's looking for something. Maybe he wants to make sure that I don't have any questions.

"Okay," I pause, "how many generations back does your family go?"

"Many, many lifetimes worth of people," he replies. "And nearly everyone has been raised the same, without bias. That means we're all taught the basic skills of survival in rather extreme conditions. Cooking, cleaning, combat, knowledge. Being thrown in the wild and told to survive for indefinite periods of time was normal for everyone in my family."

"You don't mean . . ."

Even my mom wasn't that crazy.

"I do. There were times where I've been blindfolded and transported to somewhere in the middle of the wild with nothing but the clothes on my back. There were also times when I was forced to play Go against masters of the game and was mercilessly punished at every misstep."

"How can you talk about this all so casually?"

I can't even *think* about my sister without feeling pain rush through me. What he went through sounds so traumatizing yet he's able to sit here with a straight face as if it happened a lifetime ago.

"Sweetheart, it all happened so long ago. As much pain as it caused back then, there's no use dwelling on it."

I guess it's fine if he says so, but his grandmother is on my shitlist now. There's no way she had no idea what was going on.

"And Noah also went through this? No one helped you guys?"

"It was tradition. No one cared to stop it. In fact, things still are this way across the family."

"Really?"

"That's what I've been told. I have a very big extended family, I only keep tabs on the ones closest to me. The rest of us aren't exactly on good terms."

I want to ask why, but at the same time, I don't want to pry. As someone who isn't prepared to talk about my entire family dynamic yet, I don't think it's fair for me to dig without being prepared to reciprocate.

I consider my words before saying, "I get it. We don't have to talk about it any further."

Selfishly, it's for me more than you.

"Let's eat then."

CHAPTER 29

Two days have passed since the auction, and I'm feeling much lighter now than I did before. I'll admit it. That whole Shoto situation bothered me a lot more than I let on, and I'm just happy that I don't have to worry about it for the time being.

Still, I don't know how long my peace will last. As it stands, my mom, Fumiko, and Shoto are likely trying to pick up pieces, which will keep them busy for a while. That means I have a limited amount of time to find my brother without them trying to look for me.

The thing is, I've exhausted so many routes and still can't seem to find him.

I lean back in my office chair and sigh deeply.

I never thought he could fall of the face of the Earth like this. If only there was just some clue that could point me in the right direction.

Wait! There might be a way.

Back when we were younger, Jackson, Chiaki, and I ran this blog. It seemed like a normal nature and adventure blog to the outside world, but we would use it to send messages to each other. Usually gossiping about something we didn't want to risk anyone overhearing.

I don't know if he still uses it, but maybe I can get a message out to him through it. That might be my best bet.

I find the old email and hack into it. It's much easier than trying to remember a password that I have long since forgotten.

Glancing behind the scenes of the blog, I see something I hadn't expected. There are so many new posts since the last time that I entered, ending only a few months ago.

Looks like I have a lot of reading to do.

I peacefully sip my iced latte as I scroll through the posts. It seems they start up again a few weeks after Chiaki's disappearance. It appears I have some decoding to do.

The first one has an easy enough code to crack. It's in the first letter of each word in the post. Put together, it reads:

Ari, I don't know if you'll see this but I have to let you know. What happened to Chi was not an accident, it was a warning. And I think that I'm next.

The next one is almost a few days later.

I need to disappear. I can't let them find me. It'll be a fate worse than death.

A fate worse than death? Does he know what happened to Chiaki and Lily? What does he know that I need to know?

Nearly two months later, another post with an even harder to decrypt code is there. I realize it's one that we came up with as kids. Luckily, I remember it and am able to read what he wants to tell me.

They got Lily. I didn't think that they would go after her, but they did. I can't risk coming out. Not ever. Ari, please be careful.

Another one from three weeks later.

They found me. I need to leave before the same thing happens to me. Ari, there's a world you don't know about, and I can't even tell you the half of it.

I squeeze my free hand into a tight fist. It's all I can do stop myself from hitting my monitor. It's not just Lily and Chiaki. These people tried going after Jackson, too. And I was right, he's a wealth of information that I need. But, why do I have this bad feeling in the pit of my stomach? Like finding out might lead to a whole lot more trouble than good.

Still, I can't stop reading. My brother left these because he needed to reach me and I didn't even think about this blog until now. I have to keep reading. I owe that to him.

Ari, I'm okay now. I think that I've found somewhere they can't reach me. I don't know how much more I can reach out to you though. I can't leave a trace behind.

I don't know who he's running from, but he's scared. Jackson needs my help. I can't let him be the next victim. Not after Chiaki and Lily. Jackson and I weren't as close as I was to them, but he was always there when I needed it, and we really did have a few years when we were younger that we were close. It broke after he took his turn at the company, but he was still there that night to protect me.

Maybe there was something that kept him away. Am I reading too much into things?

Ari, it's been a few months since my last post. I'm okay. They haven't found me yet and I haven't seen signs of them being close. Please, you must look out for yourself. If you need me, you know where to find me.

And that was the last message he left. He tried to reach me, and he couldn't. Even as he disappeared, he reached out to keep me safe. From who, I kind of understand. It has to be my mother and BB Media, right? But I feel even more confused than ever about what they did.

What happened to my sister and my best friend?

I hide a message of my own in a post.

Jackson. I'm here and I need you. Please reach out if you can.

I put my computer to sleep and rest my head in my hands. I can't believe I missed so much.

⊶⊶⊶⊶⊶ 🔒 ⊶⊶⊶⊶⊶

"If we're ever in trouble, we can always use this website to communicate. Isn't that right, Ari?"

I nod my head. "I programmed it myself. We know all the same codes and stuff so we should easily be able to sneak them into posts."

Chiaki pushes her face in front of mine. "You'd better make sure not to turn off your notifications. You're infamous for doing that, ya know? It's how you missed the news that we were throwing Anna a surprise party."

I awkwardly laugh. The red head had been so angry I wasn't there. I just was tired of all the notifications coming from the social media app. It got exhausting.

"Fine," I reply. "But you'd better make sure not to overuse it."

"I'll try, but I always have a lot of important things to say."

Jackson interjects, "Yeah right. Like you need us to come kill a little spider for you?"

I add, "Or you can't tell if your eyebrows are symmetrical after sitting in front of a mirror for an ungodly amount of time."

"Hey! I knew you saw that message! You just ignored it."

I shrug. Of course I ignored it. If I got pulled into that, I'd be there for twenty minutes with her asking me the same thing and how sure I was about my answer. It's just way too much of a pain in my rear, if ya know what I mean.

I ask, "Didn't Lily come to your rescue anyway?"

"As she always does," Jackson adds.

Chiaki huffs. "That doesn't matter. You guys are my siblings and should always have my back."

"Fine then." I sigh. "You're right. I'll keep the notifications on and never turn them off."

"Me, too," Jackson agrees.

Chiaki excitedly shouts, "Me, three."

As timid as she is around everyone, she's the biggest extrovert around her close friends and family. Always super comfortable and just free to be herself.

Jackson rolls his eyes. "And you'd all better make sure to reach out if you need help, alright?"

"I'm never in trouble," I reply.

"One day, you will be. Or maybe Chiaki will. Seriously." He sighs.

The serious look on his face makes me feel a little concerned, but I nod anyway. I don't know why he's suddenly so big on safety. We always end up in conversations like this these days—ever since he started college. Maybe it's something I'll understand when I get there.

"Okay," Chiaki and I reply together.

Chiaki roughly pats his arm. "I know I can always count on you. And our dear little sister can always count on us."

"I can be counted on too, ya know?"

The two look at me and laugh.

I wasn't joking though. I can be relied on, and I don't want them to forget that.

Chiaki, I guess trying to make me feel included, says, "We know we can count on you too, silly. Now come join this hug."

I don't have a choice but to be pulled in by my pushy older sister. In that moment, though, while I know they don't believe I can help, I silently vow to be there whenever they need me.

I awaken with tears streaming down my face and an ache in my chest. I wasn't able to protect either of them the way we had promised. I didn't keep my promise. At one point, I'd turned off the notifications and soon after completely forgotten about the account, which is probably even worse than the first offense.

Jackson had reached out to try to protect me, and I hadn't seen any of it. I might have even been able to help him if I had just been more aware.

A sob rips free from my throat, and I pull my knees to my chest.

I really let them down. Chiaki's who knows where dealing with who knows what, and Jackson is in hiding because he might be the next target. And I'm not even completely sure he hasn't been caught yet.

My body trembles as I cry harder, tears soaking through my sweatpants and onto my knees.

What type of sister am I?

And then, I hear a notification ring through the room. Jackson has replied. I don't know whether to keep crying or read it now, but I know whatever it says is probably the most important message I've ever received.

CHAPTER 30

It takes me a few minutes to pull myself together, but staring at his response, I feel a fresh wave of tears slowly seep from my eyes.

Ari, it's really you. Listen, I have a lot I need to explain to you, but I can't do it here. You're going to have to meet me, and I need you to make sure you aren't followed by anyone.

This is what I was waiting for. I just need to ditch my bodyguards, and I can see him again. I can get answers to the growing list of questions plaguing me.

I send a message back.

How do I find you?

It doesn't take long for his response to come through.

You have always known where to find me. Just think. I need to log off now. I'll be expecting you soon.

I don't respond for fear that someone will find out what we're up to. Especially since this account has been out of use for so long and suddenly has four new posts that honestly aren't as put together as the rest since we're more focused on getting our messages across than making sure each post makes sense to any viewers.

I'd honestly be surprised if we still had people who followed the blog to begin with.

That said, what does he mean that I've always known where to find him? I hope it's not part of the night I've forgotten. If it is, I'll never be able to find him. Should I ask for a hint?

No. I don't want him to take a risk. Someone else could break the codes. I have to find out what he means on my own.

Okay, Aurelia, think. Where would he hide that only you would know about? And possibly Chiaki. We had quite a few places growing up where we'd sneak off to. Could it be one of them?

There was that old, abandoned house a few miles away from our house that we used to sneak inside, but I think I heard it was torn down. There was a treehouse in the little forest-like area on the edge of town, but I doubt that's a sustainable living situation—especially when it rains.

For Jackson to be able to live somewhere, it needs to have access to internet and electricity, which means it can't be too far out in the middle of nowhere. He needs to be able to bathe, and most importantly, get his medicine. He can easily get it from less than legal sources, but that would still requires him to be close enough to civilization.

That crosses a few places off my list.

Could he be staying with someone?

No. If he was, it would be a loose end that could cost him his hiding spot. All it would take is one slip up to become compromised.

Think, Aurelia.

Wait! When we were younger, Dad had taken me, Chiaki, and Jackson into the woods one day because he wanted to teach us a very important skill. He had shown our brothers before us, but I guess we were the newer batch of kids. Mom had no idea where we were or what we were doing—not that she even cared.

According to Dad, we were given a separate site. There, we learned basic survival skills in the wild. Hunting, foraging, *building*. I remember us building something, now that I think about it.

I spring from the chair and rush out of the office, almost tripping over my feet as I run to the bedroom. I know I put it here somewhere.

I tear apart the one suitcase that remains unpacked, searching for what I need. A map. I need a paper one so I can narrow down where he may be.

Spreading it out, I try to remember everything about where we went.

I remember we left at dawn and were headed in the direction of the sun. East. That already eliminates a large portion of the map.

What else do I remember?

Foxes, I think. They would roam around at night but weren't particularly aggressive. If I'm correct, that means that the area isn't too far outside of town—considering we manage to spot foxes in town a lot, too.

What else? I need to narrow down the search area a bit more. I remember berries, but I don't remember what kinds. Just that dad had warned us to never, ever touch them. They were extremely poisonous.

Wait. I remember there was also a small, natural waterfall that fed a lake. Not a lot of people knew about it and Dad said that it wasn't on any map, but we'd always be able to find it again because . . .

I've got it. I know where Jackson is. Or at least, I kind of, sort of, have a general idea of the two places where he could be and am lucky enough that the two places aren't too far apart.

There's no time to waste. He's waiting for me, and if I don't make my way out tonight, it will be hard for me to get away until Luke goes to work tomorrow. I know he wants to protect me, but I can't risk Jackson's location getting out to anyone. He's already taken a big risk by giving me the clues to find him. It's not that I don't trust my husband, just that there's always an entourage of guards and stuff that follow.

I don't think that's ideal. I've been playing on my mom's patience, and I know that no matter how qualified I am to succeed her, I will reach her limit soon. When that happens, I'll be just like Chiaki, thrown out to the wolves on my own.

Actually, I guess that isn't so true.

Images of Luke flash through my mind. Of the dates we've gone on, the time we've spent together, and the conversations we've had. I really wouldn't be totally alone, now would I? And I have faith he can protect me.

Speaking of him, I should probably leave something behind so he doesn't think that I've been kidnapped. I wouldn't want him to believe that and send out an army to find me.

I walk around the room, looking for a pen and some paper. I know I don't have much need for it, but Luke seems to love the stuff. Such an old soul in that young body.

I write him a quick note that will hopefully help alleviate some of his worries. I know he'll likely be upset when he learns I've taken off without letting him know.

Hey so, sorry I had to do this. There's a lead I have to follow, but I have to do it on my own. Worry not, though! It's with family that actually likes me. I should be back by tomorrow afternoon, I hope. Don't forget to eat dinner!

Seriously, I hear the man forgets to eat dinner if he's not worried that I'll skip meals. I remember hearing from Patrick that Luke's day-to-day used to involve his close team of staff playing rock-paper-scissors or some other game to determine who would have to tell him to eat. Apparently, that changed when he didn't only have himself to feed. So it's probably the most important part of the whole note.

I grab a backpack and pack it with things I'll likely need. Judging by the time, there's enough sunlight for me to reach Jackson without stopping. But, I will bring a cozy blanket and a change of clothes.

Leaving the bedroom, I grab a large bottle of water and stuff it in along with some canned food. Of course, I need to make sure I can keep my energy up.

Now that I think about it, I might need another outfit change. I'm not sure which route I'll take to ditch the guards, but it might be helpful.

After zipping up my bag, I grab a bottle of bug spray from my suitcase, just in case. I love nature, but I freaking hate bugs. Okay, honestly, anything that creeps, crawls, or slithers is *not* my friend. I don't make the rules, I just follow them.

Now, time to leave and ditch the guards.

Prancing down the steps, I send a message to Patrick: *I need to get to Atom's Café. Can you get me there asap?*

The response is quick: *Of course, Mrs. Moore.*

I know by the time I'm outside, the man will be pulling up. Sometimes, I think he sleeps in the car with the speed he responds.

The plan is simple. Get to Atom's, change clothes in the bathroom, take the bus from outside, ditch at the next stop, and start my journey. It's foolproof!

It was not foolproof.

I curse myself as I start the walk. The guards seemed to have caught on just a bit too early, so I had to jump in a random taxi and ditch it at the first red light before the guards caught up.

Still, I have this eerie feeling as the buildings fade into trees. The sun is still high but it feels like something's watching me. I'm positive the guards shouldn't be on to me yet and by the time they are, I should be long gone.

My skin's crawling. Maybe I should go back. I'm not sure it's the guards, and I know I've gotten under a few people's skin, so that's the smart thing to do, right?

Just as I decide to turn around, I feel a prick in my neck. And then, complete darkness.

CHAPTER 31

Opening my eyes feels like fighting against a heavy weight, and inside my head is a 24-hour construction site. Whatever they used to knock me out must be some serious stuff. What do they think I am? An elephant?

A few minutes pass and I'm barely able to pry open one eyelid. Let me tell you something, the assault of light hitting that one eye is worse than *any* migraine I've ever encountered. And you may not know it, but that means a lot.

I squint hard, trying not to shut my eye again. I don't know if I'll have the willpower to open it again. I'll admit I'm not a huge fan of pain, if ya know what I mean. Fighting through it once was hard enough.

At least it does one thing for me. It tamps down the level of fear I'm actively feeling. Pain is a good distraction. Honestly, a welcome one right now.

Slowly, I work open my other eye. I hope that will help me adjust to the light in the room. The pain isn't as severe this time. Adrenaline, maybe? I guess I'm awake enough for that to kick in.

I'll admit my ability to tell time is off. It could be a few seconds or a few minutes, but I'm finally able to get it open.

I turn my head, and I *swear* I can hear my neck creaking like an old, rusty hinge. There's a bit of a strain with each movement, but I need to get a read on my surroundings. It doesn't feel like a moldy, dusty, insect-infected cellar or anything like that, but that doesn't mean escape will be any easier.

Through spotty vision, I make out a white vanity and tall white lamp. The walls are a dark blue which, while I love the color blue, seems a bit dusty and ugly.

Slowly turning my head the other way, I see some clothes hanging on the back of a door. I squint, trying to get a better. Maybe it will help me identify who my captor is.

The clothes are a bit more civilian than I expected and . . . wait . . . those are the clothes I changed into when I tried to ditch the bodyguards.

Okay, forget pain outweighing fear. The fear is definitely starting to sink in now.

My heart races faster than I imagine a cheetah hunting its prey, and my breathing soon follows. Quick and shallow breaths take over my body, the gravity of the situation sinks in. I'm not in control of this situation.

I've been drugged and, judging by the weight of whatever I'm wearing, redressed without knowing any of it. I don't even know *who* got their hands on me.

I dip my chin, trying to see what I'm wearing and whether I'm restrained, but blood rushes to my head and I'm so nauseous and can't breathe.

I can't do this. I really, really can't do this.

I raise my head in an attempt to let more oxygen seep in, but all it does is force me to hyperventilate even more than I had before.

I think I'm having a panic attack. Oh no. Oh no, no, no, no, no. That's not good. I need to be alert. Just barely managing to drag in enough oxygen to keep my body functioning.

Breathe, Aurelia. Breathe.

Okay, positive self-talk isn't helping. I can feel my consciousness rapidly slipping away, and I can't keep up.

Before darkness takes over, I hear the only voice I want to echo through my head.

"Stay put, sweetheart. I'll be there soon."

I guess the lack of oxygen is making me delirious, huh?

This time, opening my eyes is a little easier. My eyes, while still heavy, feel a bit lighter. More like a two-pound weight weighing them down instead of twenty. And thankfully the construction in my head has quieted down a bit. Now it's more of a pulse than an active ramming.

I look down at my legs—white entering my field of vision. Not because of pain or consciousness slipping, but because I'm in a silky and lacy, long, white dress with white pumps on my feet.

Am I in a wedding dress?

I try to move my legs, but they're stuck. They're being held by something, maybe manacles.

Okay. So I'm chained to a bed in a wedding dress. At the very least, it clears up *who* has me and why they have me here.

I was wrong. I haven't handled Mr. Delulu. I haven't handled anything. Even if Fumiko doesn't want me anymore, the kid is so convinced he's so in love with me that he really broke through his whole mama's boy thing and went to the extremes. I really didn't expect that. If I wasn't so scared, I think I'd even be impressed.

I take a deep breath and remind myself at least I know who's taken me and that's a step. A long breath out reminds me I'm still helpless. A deep breath in brings the hope that comes with at least knowing my captor and maybe being able to appeal to his sense of empathy. A long breath out reminds me he's also got a screw loose and the possibilities of his reactions are endless.

In and out, hope clashes with the reality of my situation. Still, that's good. It means I'm aware, and my brain is at least functioning better. I'm no longer stuck in the throes of a panic attack.

I need to find out who he hired to help him. There's no way he could pull this off without his mom's help, and I know for a fact that after the auction, she's probably been trying to convince him to forget about me. It's safe to say that it's someone else.

I take another deep breath in and out. It's only a matter of time before he comes in here. He didn't go through all this trouble just to leave me in here alone to starve to death.

I remind myself not to think about the fact that *someone* had to redress me, and I was violated in that way. To try not to think about the drug coursing through my system that left me defenseless against the attack. To try not to think about the chains holding my body to the bed.

"Sweetheart, stay calm. I'll be there soon."

Okay, I'm definitely going crazy. Ya know, hearing Luke's voice in my head and all. I mean, I admit that it's definitely a bit reassuring, and I really hope that he's on his way. Still, I know that I can't just rely on a hope and a dream.

A knock echoes on the door. "Lia, I'm coming in."

Why even pretend to give the semblance of choice? Something about that just feels cruel. But who really knows what's going through this psycho's head?

My blood cools until it feels like ice water flowing through my body as he enters the room and moves close to the bed.

He touches my cheek. "Are you alright? I told them to be easy on the drug but they said better safe than sorry." He smiles—manically, if you ask me. "But Lia, I finally saved you from that man."

I flinch away from his touch—his hand feels like the most disgusting piece of garbage that I've ever been near.

Saved me? He had to *drug me* and he thinks that's *saving* me? Does he really believe his own delusions?

"Don't touch me."

He's not Luke. He doesn't deserve to touch me. He hasn't earned any bit of my respect or love. We may have been friends once, but he's ruined that with his own actions. Luke would never do something like this to me. He would never force me to do something I don't want to.

"Lia, you don't have to act like that anymore." He raises his hand to grab the other side of my face. "He's not here anymore. I know he was keeping you under his control, but he won't be a problem anymore."

He's not my problem. He's who I want to be with.

"I said don't touch me!"

I'm surprised by the intensity of my own voice as I jolt back. Hot pain shoots through my head as it hits the wall behind me.

Shoto, still not getting the hint, anxiously reaches for me. I guess he's trying to help or whatever, but I don't want *his* help. I'd rather let myself be concussed and in pain than let *him* touch me.

Nausea settles deep in the pit of my stomach, but I force it down. I can't let him see that. I can't allow myself to do anything that can be perceived as vulnerable in front of this man.

"If you want to help, go get me some water!"

He stops short of grabbing me again and almost robotically turns to leave the room without another word. Weird, but at least I can have a few more minutes of peace.

I clench my eyes shut—the light not doing much for my throbbing head. I really yanked myself back hard, huh? I mean it kinda worked, but it hurts like a mothertrucker.

I open my eyes as his steps approach the room again. I guess he didn't have to go far for water. I mentally prepare myself for him to walk through the door. I have to try to ignore the pain to at least stay aware.

"I got you some water, Lia," he says as he answers the room.

As he approaches the bed, he looks like a dog excitedly bringing back a bone to his owner. Actually, maybe a dog is a bit too cute of an analogy for him or this situation. He's more like that one psycho kid who brings home a dead bird. Yeah . . . I'd say that's more like it.

He hands me the bottle, completely oblivious to the one glaring issue with the situation.

I dramatically pull against the shackle. "Do you mind . . . ya know, *unchaining* my hands so that I can actually drink the water."

He opens the bottle. "Oh, right! I can just hold it for you, then."

"Shoto, you know me better than that. Remember the last time that you tried doing that?"

The last time that Shoto tried, it had been years ago, and I'd been so sick. I ended up choking on the water and the brief moment of feeling like I was drowning really freaked me out. I don't know if I could ever try it again.

But maybe with *him*, if he really wanted to, I could give it a try. He knows a thing or two about patience and being gentle. Not Shoto, of course. We all know which "*him*" I'm talking about.

Shoto clutches the bottle, panic washing across his face before he puts the cap back on and rests it on my legs.

"I have to go ask for the key. Just give me a few seconds, Lia."

Ask for the key? Why would he need to ask for the key if . . . ?

No, no, no, no, no. You have got to be *kidding* me. I knew he couldn't be alone, but if he's not the one running this thing, the odds of me talking my way out of this have just severely dropped.

I know we're all thinking the same thing right now. Who would offer to "help" Shoto get me even after all the chaos that has happened? Who would be able to seize control and still work as the puppet master behind the scenes? Who wants *so badly* to "put me in my place" that they would go to this extreme without any regret?

The answer is obvious, isn't it?

CHAPTER 32

By the time I hear the clacking of heels in addition to the sound of Shoto's footsteps, I've already solved the mystery. I've, at least, solved it enough to know my life itself isn't truly in danger. Of course, the line is drawn around the point of trauma that no one should ever have to experience. But I should be alive right?

Right?

I consider everything that she'd be willing to do. The ways I can be hurt without disfigurement, the ways my psychological safety defenses can be crushed, the way my emotions can be tarnished.

To hell with being positive. Who cares about life or death when this can lead to something worse than death? I might as well start saying goodbye to my dignity. Adieu to my sanity. See you never to any positive emotion I can have.

As they enter the room, I'm immediately proven right. Of course my guess is right.

I turn my head to look at Shoto—ignoring the throbbing that has taken root. "You couldn't get your own mother to help you with your fantasies so you had to steal mine, huh?"

It's a bad attempt at a joke in an even worse situation. My mother, no, *Akira* has never been my mother. She's been the person who forced us into the world to fit her image of what we were meant to be. She had our whole lives planned out before we were even born.

Hell, her will is so strong she bends the universe to it. She wanted seven children—five older boys and two younger girls. The only thing she couldn't control was aptitude. And let me tell you, she *really* tried.

"Lia, don't be like that. She'll be *our* mother soon enough. She even went through all this effort with me to save you so that we can get married. Seriously Lia, she's even willing to bear witness. Isn't that great?"

Oh, poor, *naive* Shoto. You really don't know a thing about life. Or my mother. Definitely not a thing about my mother. She's only using you.

Akira has an all-too-familiar expression of annoyance by the time Shoto ends his spiel.

"Shoto," she says. "Why don't you go get us something to eat? I think your Lia might like some pizza tonight, don't you?"

"Yes, of course!"

His eyes widen, and he scurries out of the room muttering something about how dumb he is for forgetting that his "precious Lia" needs to eat. It's cool, Shoto. It's not your fault that you're so scatterbrained in the reality of your delusions.

"I suppose it's just us now, huh?"

Akira walks to the side of the room, pulling the stool from the vanity and taking a seat. She sits with her back straight and posture proud—not a trace of discomfort showing though I know that there must be some.

"You should have listened."

She looks me in my eye—challenging me. The me five years ago would have looked away. Defiant but not foolish. Loving my mother but scared of her at the same time. The me before Chiaki was thrown away would have considered, even if only for a second, giving in and marrying Shoto.

That me is gone. That me left when she realized just who her mother was. Who she always had been.

I match her vision. Headache and lingering drugs be damned, I won't back down from her power play.

"I wouldn't do anything differently," I reply.

I wonder how I look. Does my gaze look as fierce as it feels? Am I matching hers? Am I beating it? Whatever, I can't let her see I'm worried about it. I'm chill as an ice cube.

"You must think you're bold now. That you're *something*."

"Something? No, I don't think I'm something. I'm *someone*. I've just had the space away from you to find out exactly who that is."

"You've learned nothing from me. You don't get to be someone until you do something worthy of it. What have you done?" She mocks, "Get your doctorate? Do a little time at the company? Please. Don't fool yourself."

I always knew she didn't think much of me, but she's never outright said it. Probably because we rarely see each other in private settings. I'm no longer the blind girl who thought she'd come to my graduation and got my heart broken when she didn't. Her words are a few years too late to truly phase me.

"You still think that I care what you think about me?" I scoff. "You don't *know* me and you never did. My siblings and I were born and given to nannies. Dad spent time with us when he was around but you were only there to scold. Don't kid yourself with this mother act. You're not fooling me."

I turn her words against her—a very fun method of pissing her off.

"Who do you think you are now? You're stuck in *my* possession with no one to help you. Where's that husband of yours now? He can't even protect you when it matters the most."

"Are you trying to taunt me? Make me believe that this is because he doesn't care enough about me? Me getting caught is utterly on me. I ditched my bodyguards and I ended up in this situation. You sat and waited patiently until that happened and that's when you got me. No pride in cowardice."

Though, I kind of feel bad, now that I think about it. My bodyguards are probably going to get scolded for something that really wasn't their fault. Especially considering something *actually* happened to me this time.

I should really buy those guys some cake or something when I get out of here. Judging by their builds, it's probably way outside of their diet, but everyone deserves a cheat day.

Akira sighs slowly. Calculatingly. "You really think I wouldn't be able to get my hands on you otherwise? You have no idea the connections I have. The people and *things* I have at my disposal."

"Guns, knives, yada," I reply. "I know the things you can use to get me. I'm not saying that I can outrun a bullet or anything, but I have bodyguards trained well enough to live through a gun and knife fight."

"But not trained enough to contain you, huh?"

"That's because I'm not an object. To contain me, you have to chain me. But you know that already, don't you. That you simply *aren't enough* to keep me on your own."

I attack her ego. Everyone knows the woman has an inferiority complex beyond anything many of us have ever seen. If she doesn't have the power, then she'll fight tooth and nail until she gets it. But she's not as powerful as she likes to portray herself. She can't even handle her own youngest child.

"Well, you don't get to decide what you are. Look at you. Thinking that you're married and there's nothing I can do about it." She scoffs. "You can't marry unless I say so. *That* is how this family works. I won't allow you to go off and defy me to this degree."

"You were the one who kicked me out," I remind her. "Besides, what are you going to do now? Everyone knows who I've married, and I doubt you can manipulate anyone into doing what you please."

"No one has to see you," she replies. "And I know of a few places where we'll be able to marry you two kids off. No one ever has to see you again. I'm sure with time I can also fabricate something to tear you and that Moore boy apart."

Oh, it seems she's joining the delulu club.

"You think you can get away with that?"

"Easily."

Oh, scratch that. She's the freaking founder of the club. How long has it been since she was actually down to Earth? Definitely longer than my lifetime. That's for sure.

I let my gaze linger on her for just a second before I turn away and break the eye contact—annoyance rooted in every fabric of my expression. I want her to know her mind games don't work. There isn't only one way to win a battle.

"You do know that no matter what you do, Fumiko isn't going to accept me into the family, right? I know you're well informed enough to know what happened between us. She said herself that she'll *never* accept me as part of her family anymore."

Seriously. I doubt the whole black box thing is pending my acceptance anymore. If anything, Akira should be *thanking* me for probably opening negotiations up to something else. I'm sure the new terms are probably more reasonable.

"It's not about that anymore, sweetheart."

I cringe. I don't like that name coming from her mouth. She always uses it in such a patronizing way. Not in the respectful, caring way Luke always uses it. In fact, there's no one else I'll like hearing that name from again. It's his. He claimed it.

She continues, "It's about showing you that your defiance has consequences. That you will *never* be able to defy me and actually get away with it. I always get what I want, Aurelia."

"Now, that's not exactly true," I reply. "You want to make it seem that way. *Especially* to your children."

I recall all the times growing up that I used to see my mom manipulate situations to her favor. I went through the phases of thinking it was the coolest thing ever to learning how to do it myself to realizing how truly cruel her methods could be.

"But there has always been one thing you can't control. Human nature. You can use it to bend people to your will, but those with more brains than you or who are simply more stubborn, can't be so easily bent. I've seen it."

It all just dawned on me during this conversation. She tries so hard to bend me because she hasn't succeeded in bending Fumiko. She *needed* me to marry Shoto because her own best friend became the one person she couldn't bend to her side. And the situation had been a first.

I had seen it growing up. Watched the two women do things together and as Akira made Fumiko do stupid things without making it seem like she was controlling the situation.

She's trying to save her pride. The thing that cares about most in the world.

"Oh really? When?"

"My own situation aside." I chuckle. "Fumiko. I've seen how you two interact now. You no longer have control of her, do you?"

I meet her gaze again, wanting to see her expression. Challenging her on my own terms. I may not have the physical power right now, but I will gain that psychological power. Bury doubts in her head like little parasitic insects who will continue to eat away at whatever's left of her sanity.

Her left eye twitches—her subconscious way of showing irritation. I don't know if she's just never noticed or if she just doesn't care to work on it. Maybe she secretly wants people to know when they're testing her nerve just a bit too much.

"You always were the smartest of the batch. The most promising, too. Too bad your stubbornness has led to stupidity. You're right. I need to get Fumiko back in her place too, but that's not my number one problem. She may be my best friend, but you're my child," she explains. "You being disobedient is much worse than her."

I hesitate. I'm not sure where her mind is going. I understand her plan, but not really. It's more in the way that a dog understands a cat. You eventually reach an unspoken understanding, but you never truly know what's going through their head.

"You could always have just seen one of your children as somewhat of an equal. Ruling with fear only can incite defiance."

It's why things like rebellions, civil wars, and betrayals happen. All it takes is enough people without fear and your reign of terror ends. Seriously, has she never taken a history class in her life?

"Defiance is easily squashed by more fear. Besides, I don't need fear to control you. Look at you now."

Actually, even fear isn't *enough* to control me. I am actually really scared. I put up a front to act like I'm not. Like an iceberg whose depth betrays what you see above water. But my heart is pounding in my chest and blood is racing through my body. Even so, I can still hold a conversation and feign more confidence than I feel.

Why?

Because for me to bend at the threats of a dictator would be a disservice to my sister who stood by me, even when a blade mutilated her face. Even when she was always the most non-confrontational person I knew. Even when she knew that not being protected by Akira meant she would be the number one target for those who hate her.

I will never dishonor Chiaki's memory like that, and that's why I have to keep fighting.

CHAPTER 33

A few hours have passed since my conversation with Akira. I refuse to refer to that woman as my mother anymore—even in a mocking tone. Of course, I've had no water in Shoto's absence. I have to assume that wherever we are, we must be a decent distance away from the city in order for him to be gone for so long getting pizza.

"Lia!"

A voice calls my name from the hall as hurried steps approach the room. Shoto, ever the worrier, has an anxious look on his face as he plops the two pizzas on the bed.

"I got you one of those pepperoni pizzas with basil from that place that you like. Aunt Akira says I can't let you go yet, but I should be fine to feed you."

"Shoto, you can't believe this is for the best, right? Like you can't honestly think all of this is the right thing to do. I'm *married*, and I will never love you."

"Of course it is! Especially considering this so-called marriage of yours," he replies, "It's the only way to save you from that other man. I know he'll never be able to treat you the way you deserve. The way I can treat you."

"Shoto, even if it wasn't for him, I would *never* marry you. You have to know that. You have to let me go."

All I can do is convince him to take my side. If he still has doubts in our ability to have a future together, he really will go through with this. Why is it that nothing I say seems to get through to him? Why is he so smart every other time but so dense when it comes to matters revolving around me?

Actually . . .

"Lia, I don't understand what you mean."

Now that I think about it, his act is a bit *too* convincing. I don't know if it's the lingering drugs in my system or the fact that I haven't eaten or drunken anything in a while. I can feel the hunger and thirst gnawing at my stomach, my chest, and my mouth—the smell of pizza further perpetuating the feelings.

Still, his brows are furrowed just perfectly. Confused but not able to be mistaken for anger. His mouth pulled down slight enough to show sadness but not deep enough to show anger or despair. His eyes always linger on my face but never betray his "feelings" to roam anywhere else.

"Shoto," I say slowly. "I think that you *do* know what I mean."

"What do you mean Lia?"

He opens the box of pizza and frees a slice as I observe his actions. I compare them to when we were kids and to the things I know he does for his mom. Someone ignorant can't get away with that. Matter of fact, someone ignorant doesn't let their mom blackmail her best friend into marrying off her daughter.

Shoto has to be more manipulative than I thought, right?

And that thing he did with the drug. At the time, I thought my mom had put him up to it, but she wouldn't be reckless enough to let him do something like that in public if she had prior knowledge about it.

My eyes are opening again. I think, for the first time in my life, I understand Shoto for who he is rather than who he pretends to be.

And I am petrified.

For him to be able to get one over on me for so long. To be *blinded* by a past that's likely filled with carefully manicured lies. He has to be more formidable than I thought. My mother has always been an obvious threat, but he . . .

"For once in your life, be honest with me." I enunciate every word, "Is. It. All. An. Act?"

My world view fractures once again. Before he even responds, I see the light in his eyes slowly fade. I notice the slight frown transform into a straight face. I see the softness fade, replaced by the hardened face of a man in control.

Then slowly, his lips slip into a smirk. Not the sexy kind my husband uses when he really wants to flirt, but the scary kind all those villains in movies use when they've lured the hero into their trap.

And then he laughs. Seconds bleed together while my brain tries to keep up—trying to register which parts of my life have never been true.

"You finally caught on, huh?"

My lips part but no words come out. I have thoughts though, many thoughts. I want to know if it's all been a lie. How many people know the real him? Did he ever have good intentions toward me? How I could be so *stupid* that I never saw him for who he truly was?

He only showed up where he'd otherwise be missed, but never anything more. When I graduated, Chiaki and Lily were there, but he wasn't. He gave some excuse I can't bother to remember, and I willingly accepted it without question.

I think thoroughly before saying, "I guess I did."

"I can't believe how long I was able to keep you thinking I was this sweet, naive man. I mean, *come on*, you should have put the pieces together ages ago." He sits on the bed next to me as if we're old pals. "Tell me, what finally gave it away?"

Wow. So this is the real him. The real Shoto sure is different from his old persona.

"I guess being drugged, dehydrated, and hungry helped put things in perspective. No one could really be that dense. I shouldn't have let it slip by me for so long."

How could I allow him to jerk me around for so many years? I used to think I had a keen enough sense of who people are, but I guess I was wrong.

He laughs again, impossibly harder than before, patting my shoulder as he struggles to breathe. I flinch away, but this time, he grabs me harder. I flinch as his grip digs deeper, and pain shoots down my arm.

"You're a hoot, you know that? I have to admit, it was kind of amusing seeing how long I could string you along. Very . . . invigorating."

"Were you always going to hide this part of yourself?"

"Maybe." He chuckles. "Honestly, it really depended. I think it would have eventually gotten old, and I would have gotten bored. Of course, I was willing to wait until after we were married. But, what the hell? You won't marry by choice anyway, and we've already done me that little favor of taking that little pesky thing away from you."

He called choice a "little pesky thing"? Wow. He really is someone completely different than who he pretended to be.

"Why do you really want to marry me so badly?"

"Oh my. Don't tell me that your mother *still* hasn't told you. I even stayed away a bit longer so I could give her plenty of time to break your world apart so I can super glue it back together. Nothing better than a trauma bond."

What hasn't she told me? Is he talking about the thing with the black box? I mean that explains her motives, not *his*. But I still don't want them to know how much I know about the stakes.

"What are you talking about?"

He laughs again. "Oh wow. All your siblings know. Hell, they even married for the same reasons that you should be *wanting* to marry. Considering you're the only one worth anything of the bunch, it's a little surprising that you're the only one left in the dark."

"Then explain it to me."

Explain why marrying me is worth so much. Explain why marrying me is something that you absolutely need to do. Why you can't let go of the idea. Why you even teamed up with my mother to do it this way.

"I don't know if I really want to." He wraps his arms around my shoulders. "It's actually more entertaining with you not knowing what's going on in the world around you. I'd rather you be paranoid and stuck on the words I've said. We both know how much it'll bother you. Especially when it has something to do with that precious sister of yours."

Chiaki?

He's right though. Once my mind is stuck on something, I'll keep thinking about it until I figure it out—especially considering it involves Chiaki.

"What do you know about Chiaki?"

He laughs. "Way more than you. To think that—"

"That's enough, Shoto."

I was so sucked into the thrall of this conversation that I didn't even notice Akira entering the room.

Shoto switches back to his innocent voice. "Oh Aunt Akira, I had no idea you were coming back in." In his more menacing voice, he says, "Come, have a seat. I was just explaining things to poor little Lia."

I look at her. "You knew?"

How does she already know who Shoto really is and I'm just now finding out?

I really want to know how she could know who he was and still try to make me marry him. She cares so little about me that she would set me up to marry someone who's like this. Who truly is a terror. It's not surprising, but it makes her ten times worse in my mind.

"I had suspicions," she replies. "The kid is a bit stingy with that persona of his, but it was plenty obvious that there was a lot more to him."

Wow. So there's the truth. She didn't even try to marry me off to the sweet kid, not that it would make it much better. She tried marrying me off to an unknown variable without a second thought to achieve her own victory.

She's *still* trying to marry me off to him actually. What the hell is going on? I think I've been transported to another universe.

And how did she know his true nature before I did? I spent so much time with him.

"Now Aunt Akira, why haven't you told Lia the truth about this world?"

What is he going on about? They keep saying this, but I have no clue what they're talking about. I think I've lived enough life to see the truth behind people, but I have to admit that I'm doubting myself *a lot* right now.

Akira scoffs. "She doesn't deserve to know. Not when she doesn't understand who her allegiance should lie with. Until she understands, she'll never know."

He sing-songs, "Oh but there's a certain truth to her husband I feel she deserves to know."

What does he know about Luke? I mean I know that he has some dangerous connections and stuff. I mean, he has quite a bit of money and power and that usually comes accompanied by some . . . underworld dealings.

"I'm almost there. Just hang on a bit longer."

And of course I'm imagining his voice in my head again. Seriously, *what* is going on with that? I get that I have all these things working against my body, but I do not want to join Club Delulu.

"What are you guys talking about?" I ask.

Shoto puts his finger to his lips. "Oh, I won't be the one to say anything and Aunt Akira already says she won't be saying anything about it. Plus," he pauses, "it's pretty fun watching you squirm in realization of your own ignorance. You're not always the smartest person in the room, Lia."

I swallow any retort. I know that I'm not the smartest person in the room, but I'm plenty smart. I want to say that when I get out of here, I'll find out what they're talking about on my own. Instead, I say nothing.

I don't know if it's because I feel like the crazed look in Shoto's eye could mean tragedy for me or if it's because I'm so confused by this whole situation that words are evading me.

Akira laughs. "Nothing to say now?"

I have to say something. I don't know what, but I can't appear weak at this moment. "I always have something to say. You may just not be ready to hear it."

"Lia, you're the one who isn't ready to hear what we have to say."

"Bite me."

And then this mothertrucker actually bites me. On my neck. Hard.

I clamp down on my inner cheek to stop myself from crying out. It freaking hurts. It hurts so bad that I'm sure I'll bruise and I'm sure that it's on purpose.

A few seconds pass before he pulls away with a smirk. "Don't threaten me with a good time."

I'm still biting down on the inside of my cheek and fighting away tears for a few minutes while my mom and Shoto eat pizza in front of me. It's a cruel punishment for not going along with their whims. Watching them eat while I'm hungry enough to eat both pies on my own.

Shoto has finished yet another slice before he says, "We should be leaving soon. We have a wedding to get to! I do adore that dress on you, Lia. Can't wait to see you walk down the aisle to me in it."

I want to puke. If they get me out of the country, there really may be no hope for me. I really may never get back here. I may actually lose my life. I may actually lose Luke.

Luke.

"I'm here."

My poor brain has literally convinced itself it can hear Luke. I mean, at least I can hear his voice in some capacity before I'm taken away from him forever. It sucks that the last thing I said to him was through a note. And I never even got to tell him how I was starting to feel.

And then. BOOM!

CHAPTER 34

Debris is everywhere. On the ground. In the air. Trapped in my throat—forcing me into the nastiest coughing fit I've ever had. And through that, I only have one hopeful thought that has consumed my entire consciousness.

Is he really here to save me?

There's a lot of movement around me, but I can't see. The debris has settled into my eyes. I clamp them shut and try to wipe the torment from my eyes.

While I can't see, I can hear. Grunts. Hand to hand combat commences. The hiss of knives through the air. Many footsteps that I can't distinguish between friend and foe. I involuntarily flinch every time a set gets too close, fearing this will be my end. Unintelligible words are exchanged amongst men trying to communicate in the chaos.

And then I can hear him, and his voice drowns out the rest of the noise.

"Sweetheart, I'm so sorry I was late."

Late? He's right on time. I want to tell him, but the debris in my throat elicits a cough from me instead.

The shackles holding my wrists and ankles stop weighing me down only seconds before I'm lifted into his arms. Into my very own safe place.

I'm safe. I'm where I know no one will ever be able to hurt me.

He walks with me, and it's as if the chaos parts to make way for us. It sees the situation and knows that anything that gets between us and safety would be met with a swift ending and that feeling . . . means the world right now. In a world where no one I know is who they say they are, *this* is what I need.

"It's alright, sweetheart. We'll be home soon. I promise."

We transition into the car, and he shifts me so I'm sitting on his lap. His arms tremble with pent up emotion—though I'm unsure which feelings. I know he holds me like loosening his grip will allow the wind to whip me away. Tears that had been suppressed for far too long dribble down my face—helping clear the debris from my eyes but making my heart ache in ways that I've never known.

As I gently press my lips to his, it's a silent declaration of how I feel for him. Something that I should have already told him, but this is all I can manage. For now.

⚬—⚬—⚬—⚬—🔒—⚬—⚬—⚬—⚬

My eyes flutter open. A feeling of relief washes over me as I snuggle into the familiar arms of the man that I've come to care for in our home.

I don't remember anything after the kiss, but I guess he brought me home after everything and not bothered waking me up. I feel clean and not so weighed down anymore. I guess he cleaned me up and put me in one of my pajama shirts.

"You should sleep more."

I look up—feeling his eyes more than I see them in the dark of night. I don't need to see him to know that he's looking at me with concern. That it's not a mask or facade that only seeks to make use of me in one selfish way or another.

"How long have I been out?"

"Not long enough."

His tone isn't harsh, but I can tell there's probably something pent up. And to be honest, I'd be an idiot if I don't know why he's mad. I broke one of the core agreements we started out with and he doesn't even know why. I hope he doesn't think I was just trying to run away from him.

"Look, this whole—"

"We'll talk about it in the morning," he replies. "For now, we both need to get some sleep."

Right. I probably wasn't the only one scared. I can only imagine how he felt when he realized that I was missing and that he couldn't find me. For him to have found me, I can only imagine the stress, the worry, the skipped meals, and the exhaustion he put himself through. For the sake of me.

"Okay," I whisper.

I relax into his embrace but sleep doesn't find me easily. My mind is too cluttered with the events of the last few days. I grieve the last bit of the Shoto I knew at one point in my heart. The Shoto who was a sweet kid who would never do anything to hurt me. Whether it was a lie or not, I still treasure those days. For him and only him do I grieve.

The Shoto that I met during this whole . . . ordeal is not someone I ever knew. Is it wrong to want to separate that monster from the Shoto I once knew, even if they really were the same person?

It shouldn't hurt, but it does. A deep part of me aches at the loss.

And all the strange stuff they were saying . . .

"Sleep, sweetheart. I can still hear your mind racing."

Luke's hand creeps up to my hair and starts massaging my scalp. Gentle, purposeful movements that are meant to help me calm down, and they admittedly do.

I yawn. "Okay."

My voice is barely recognizable to me—soft and meek. A vulnerable voice I can only show to him. A vulnerable voice I didn't even realize I still have.

I let the gentle movements of his hand lull me back to sleep. In the safety of his arms, I feel untouchable.

CHAPTER 35

The vibe is off. Really, the vibe has been off since we got back three days ago. Luke is still being attentive to me and trying to make sure I'm alright—even put salve and a bandage on the bite mark that Shoto so graciously left behind. The sting of his lie will fade with time, just as this physical wound he inflicted will disappear without a trace.

Regardless, Luke is acting strange. Colder. It's like after confirming I'm okay, he's locked himself away to work more at the home office he barely uses. I'm assuming he wants to keep me close but still needs distance.

His assistant, Marvin, has been floating around the house all day—making trips to the kitchen to get things along and checking on me from time to time. It's like I've been passed on to be his responsibility.

And I really have to admit, it hurts.

I make my way from the living room couch to the kitchen. Luke had Patrick and Marvin refill the fridge and pantry earlier so I'll be able to eat.

You'd think me not eating for a day was the end of the world with how overboard he went.

At least it provides me with the materials to make dinner. Usually, it helps us wind down after a long, heavy day. And judging from what his assistant has been bringing from the kitchen, the man is surviving on croissants, water, and coffee.

As I gain my momentum in the kitchen, I feel eyes lingering on me. All day, the bodyguards have remained in sight with wary eyes on me as if they're waiting for me to bolt. It almost feels like I've become a prisoner in our house. They haven't made a move, but I'm positive they will if I do.

I swallow my discomfort and irritation though. I understand I've caused a state of anxiety to flow through the house, and it's indeed my fault. Things will probably go back to normal soon.

I hope.

Dinner is quick to make considering I've only made him steak with a homemade béarnaise sauce and a few of his favorite side dishes.

I hop up the steps as the steaks rest and knock on his door, hopefully just as cheery as I usually do. I don't want him to worry about me and there's this possibility that maybe if I act normal, things will go back to normal a lot faster.

Well, it's more of a hope than a *real* possibility.

"Hubby, I made dinner. Do you think you can take a break to eat now? You haven't had more than a croissant since this morning, and it's already well into the evening."

He's silent for a few seconds. I debate whether I should knock again or walk away. Whether it's better to continue to be a thorn in his butt or give him space. Though it's selfish, I want to be able to have our normal talks and dinners.

Just as I raise my hand to knock again, his voice is gravely as he replies, "Marvin is bringing me something. I'll be fine."

I sigh. If anything, *this* confirms he doesn't want to see me. He's never rejected an invitation to a dinner I have cooked for him before. It's all new territory for me. I'm actually lost on what I should do next.

"Hubby, it's steak. I even made the béarnaise just the way you like it. Please come eat with me. I haven't seen you since this morning."

Another hesitation. Another stint of time where I'm wondering where this whole fiasco puts us. Whether he has deemed me too much trouble to handle anymore. Whether he's secretly figuring out ways to be rid of me in the near future.

"I have some work to get done."

He always has work to get done. But at least I used to be worth putting it on hold temporarily so we could have a normal dinner and conversation like normal couples do. Like normal *families* make time to do. Maybe it's my bloodline's curse to never experience family.

By the time I feel it, a tear has already escaped and slid down my cheek as I grieve the family that I was only starting to have. It's gone already because of my actions.

"Okay." My voice is barely a whisper, and I'm almost positive that he can't hear it. "I understand."

Walking away from the door is difficult. The bodyguards still haven't let me out of their sight and now there's this humiliating show of me not being able to contain my emotions. I go to the only place where I can be alone.

Our bedroom. The bedroom? His bedroom.

If he's just thinking of ways to kick me out anyway, then I should just leave on my own. It's much less humiliating that way, and it saves me the pain that the conversation will likely bring. Really, it's better for everyone. I doubt the bodyguards will keep me here when it's obvious their boss doesn't want me around anymore, right?

I feel like a robot. Almost mechanically, I walk toward my suitcase and start randomly throwing clothes in it. None of the gorgeous pieces that came as a result of our union. Anything he paid for is probably too much of a reminder of what used to be.

Ya know, this whole process would go a lot faster if my heart didn't feel like it was being squeezed by a bodybuilder and these tears would stop freefalling down my face like a freaking waterfall.

Time is quite the conundrum right now. All I know is that it passes, and I don't know what to do as emotions continue to pour out in ways I'm not familiar with.

Who knows how long has passed. A few seconds? Five minutes? Ten or fifteen? All I know is that the familiar scent of apple spice has invaded my senses and a large hand has covered my trembling one as I sit on the floor entombed in my own grief.

"Why are you packing?"

Now he wants to talk to me, huh? He's asking why I'm packing when it's obvious he doesn't want me here anymore. I should be the one asking questions. Why wasn't he talking to me before? Why is he so repulsed by me that he won't even eat with me?

Instead of saying any of that, another sob rips from my throat instead. How do people talk when they have so many emotions rushing through them? I guess I'm starting to understand where some of those issues with communication come from in other relationships.

I barely register his arms under me before I'm up in the air being carried across the room. By instinct, I wrap my arms around his neck, desperate not to fall yet feeling pathetic at the acknowledgement of how intimate the position is. I probably look so desperate hanging on to a man who no longer wants me but just won't bite the bullet and say it.

As he settles me onto his lap as he sits on the bed, I unwrap my arms and push on his chest, trying to create some distance. Being so close inspires feelings I'd rather avoid.

"I'm leaving," I finally manage to say. "I'm going so that you don't have to kick me out the way that you want to."

"Who told you that I want you to leave?"

"You all but said so yourself. You haven't bothered with me beyond the necessities. It's like I'm some chore for you. I don't want to be your chore, and I don't want to live somewhere I'm unwanted."

He sighs. "I don't want you to leave. I just needed some space to get my emotions back in line, sweetheart. I don't think you understand what this last forty-eight hours has been like for me. You're in no state to have that conversation right now so I've taken some space."

"What do you mean?"

"When I found out that you were missing, I thought I had lost you. That I had scared you away. Why else would you slip away from the bodyguards? You must have thought that I wasn't enough and that *crushed* me," he replies.

This is the most vulnerable I've ever seen him. Wiping my tears, I see the tenseness in his jaw and how his eyes look straight ahead, avoiding mine even though I'm right in his lap.

He continues, "And when my bodyguards tracked you, they found a discarded syringe not far from the city, and I knew that something was wrong. I had never been so scared in my life."

Scared? My actions caused this man to fear?

"And then when I got home and saw that note, there was this anger at the situation. All consuming. And once I had you back, it came back. I just don't understand why you wouldn't tell me first or why you would ditch the bodyguards who are here to protect you. Why would you put yourself in danger like that? You know that even if you had gotten Fumiko off your back, there are still people who would want to have you. Just why?"

And there it is. The crushing weight of his emotions. The realizations of my own selfishness and its effects on other people. And what can I really say to him? *Nothing* is okay. I can't expect normal when all sense of normality has flown out of the room.

Luke holds me tighter—his arms sparing no strength in holding me. It's not painful, not in the way that it probably should be. It's a reminder that he's here and he cares *so much* that he also needed time to digest.

I realize how self-centered and single-minded I am.

"I'm sorry," I whisper.

I just wanted to see my brother. I wanted to learn what I was missing. I wanted to color in the blanks of my memory with the help of the only person left to help me. And now, I have even more questions from how Akira and Shoto talked during the whole kidnapping.

"You didn't *think*, Aurelia." Hearing someone say my name has never stung so much. "If you really sat down to consider things, you would have realized that even if it weren't them, I have enemies. Your *mother* has enemies. And quite frankly, I'm sure you have other enemies of your own."

His tone doesn't get louder as if he's talking down to me. It does carry a hint of emotion though. Not exactly anger, but concern? Care? I'm not completely sure.

"I know," I whisper. "I really know. I had plenty of time to think about it."

"Then please help me understand why you would go out and ditch your bodyguards like that. Why would you put yourself in so much danger for a lead that might not have panned out? A lead isn't always concrete."

"This one was. But I couldn't risk anyone knowing where Jackson was."

Jackson is the last sibling who cared for me. If something happened to him because I accidentally led people to him, then I would carry the guilt of his demise with me the same way I carry guilt about Chiaki and Lily.

To risk the safety of someone I care about is unthinkable to me now. But the only way to make him understand is to tell him my story and lay myself bare without a way to ever cover myself back up.

But I understand now. To protect the people I care about isn't as simple as making sure they are physically protected. There's a mental and emotional aspect I have tried to remain blissfully ignorant to and no longer can.

Because Luke. I hurt him. And I would do anything to make it right, and I will never allow myself to do it again.

"Sweetheart, now is the time to be honest with me."

He's right. I know he's right. But suddenly my tongue feels like sandpaper in my mouth, and I have that uncomfortable feeling in my throat.

It's now or never. I know what I have to do to preserve this relationship and to keep myself safe. I know that I have to tell him everything. I will have to become so vulnerable that I'm practically transparent and part of me is scared, but part of me has an impending feeling of . . . relief?

CHAPTER 36

It feels like we've been talking forever, but I've just barely started the story. I start from the beginning. From the night in which it all happened. The way my siblings defended me like their lives depended on it. The words that I can't remember.

I tell him how soon after being kicked out from the house, my sister managed to find work with BB Media, where our best friend Lily was already employed. I remember seeing her go in and out and watching her wear her new scar with pride—even as it stabbed me in the heart every time that I saw it because I knew it was all my fault. It had to be our mother's work. How I hadn't even known at the time I actually witnessed it happening.

I tell him how it wasn't long before Lily started telling me that something strange was going on within the company, and she couldn't put her finger on it, but girls were going missing. I knew she was holding something back.

I tell him how she tried to warn Lily to run away, but instead she and Chiaki became victims, too. And how the last time I interacted my sister in person was the night of terror and even as we sent messages to each other, it was never of much substance. That when she went missing, I at least knew where to start digging and so I did.

I tell him how it's not long after she went missing that Lily also disappeared. It was as if she never existed by the time BB Media was done. I had lost my sister and best friend in such a short timeframe that I thought that my own sanity was on the brink of breaking down. The desire for revenge consumed me.

I tell him how I've spent the last few years trying to find out what's happening and who's involved and what I learned recently. How Akira was likely a key player in Chiaki going missing. How I'm still trying to learn more and more. How for some reason my memory seems to be failing me.

I tell him about the black box and how it can affect everyone. I tell him the part that it played in Shoto and my relationship. I tell him about Shoto's true nature and what he and Akira had planned for me.

And then, I tell him about Jackson. The last remaining person from my past who has actually cared for me. Who I have to protect because I couldn't protect anyone else and if he's gone, then I've really failed. And who can fill in those gaps in my memory to bring me closer to the truth.

And when I finally finish telling him, his arms hold me tight as I allow myself to cry the tears that I've needed to cry for years. To sob away the pain and fear and guilt and feeling of worthlessness I have carried with me for far too long. To express the emotions I have been ignoring since my life gradually started to fall apart until I couldn't even recognize it anymore.

For once, I'm confronting these feelings without hiding behind crude humor or fake smiles. I'm not watching my words for fear of confrontation with their hidden truths. I've let loose a part of me that should have been free long ago.

And it's a good thing.

Minutes blend together and before I know it, hours have passed. I've stripped myself bare and there's no going back to the me who existed before I did. And I can say I'm content with it.

As my tears die down and breathing evens, Luke holds me with the same protective nature as always. Still kissing the top of my head and plumpness of my cheeks every few minutes and allowing me to calm down before he says anything.

Later, I'll thank him for the time he's given me to compose myself when there's so much composing to be done. Now, I think it's time we continue our conversation for fear I'll sink into my shell if I don't get it all out now.

"I'm sorry. I'm so sorry I couldn't bring myself to tell you this before." And I mean it so much. "This is a part of me I intended to keep hidden forever. In some ways, it's embarrassing, and in others, I feel it shows my incapability."

And that's the truth. To confront the reality of me not being able to protect the people who always stood by me has always been difficult. I felt that at least getting revenge would redeem me in some way, and I guess somewhere deep down, that meant I had to do it on my own.

I knew revenge was not the right reason so I convinced myself I was doing it for the other girls who had been affected, too. I realize I fought this fight for the wrong reasons, but doing it on my own is an injustice to the battle.

I admit it to myself now.

I do want revenge. I want the type of revenge that makes people wish they were dead but keeping them alive all the same because death is entirely too easy a punishment.

I do want to help others. Even if it's not as strong as my craving for revenge, all those other girls were someone else's best friend or daughter or sister or mother. Even if they didn't have much, they all had something.

And I want to satisfy my own perverse desire to punish those who have done wrong. Who have used what they have accumulated in life to harm others instead of do right. I mean, even if you don't want to do right by people, you can mind your own business and not harm others either. It's that easy.

Luke gently rubs my back. "It's alright, sweetheart. I understand now. I just need you to keep me in the loop. I understand everything, and you should know you don't have to hide anything from me. *You* don't have to hide from me."

"I won't. Not anymore," I reply. "I know now what my limits are and I completely understand them. No more secrets or trying to do it alone."

"That's good. Better. I'll support you in a more active role from now on, if you'll let me."

"Yes, I think I'd like that."

Shoto's words echo in my head. *"You're not always the smartest person in the room, Lia."* He's right. I've tried things my way, but it's time for a change. It's time for me to accept help from other people.

"Thank you," I mutter. "Thank you so much for everything. I never really understood how much I have while I'm with you." *Until it was almost too late.*

He's worth so much more than I've ever imagined. He's someone I have faith will never betray me. Someone who will be honest with me. And for that faith, I can lean on him.

"I will always look out for your best interests and help when you need it. Only you hold that power over me, sweetheart."

He massages my scalp and pulls me impossibly closer to him. The smell of apple spice overwhelms my senses, filling me with a feeling of safety. I never realized safety could be so incredibly important. So *incredibly* fulfilling.

Our eyes meet like the sun meeting the moon—intense enough for the world to want to watch.

The feelings running through me are hard to explain, and I can't contain it anymore. We never talked about the kiss I gave him last night when he'd saved me. The first time I had truly initiated anything intimate without anyone around to put on a show for.

Conversation be damned, I reach pull his head down to mine, crashing our lips together like a door to its frame—perfectly cut to hold its keeper.

I may have started this, but it's very clear that Luke intends to finish it. His grip in my hair becomes rougher as he pulls me closer to him. His teeth nip at my bottom lip—demanding access. His tongue wars with mine, claiming victory before the fray has even started.

And I'm nothing but a puddle of unspoken feelings in his arms. Not knowing what I can do or say aside from this. Giving him this very important part of me without holding anything back. Luke Moore isn't the kind of person who will accept bits and pieces. I have to give him all of me, and he'll take it.

He'll take it and leave me a completely helpless heap of lovesick innards. Bare to him and only him. And it's at that moment that I finally come to terms with how I feel. It crashes into me like a typhoon—drenching me with the answer that I now know.

I've fallen in love with him. I love him.

I love Luke Moore.

CHAPTER 37

Waking up the next morning is the most revitalizing reset I've ever had. I know there's still so much going on, but I feel lighter. Like there isn't a boulder weighing me down with every little thing that I do.

With this newfound feeling, I know it's best to start my pursuit back up while I feel refreshed. Time waits for no one and I have a brother who I still need to visit.

"Good morning."

I kiss Luke's cheek. "Good morning."

His grin melts me. "Feeling better?"

I nod. "Way better. Thank you."

He cups my chin and pulls me in for a quick peck on the lips. I definitely think I can get used to a good morning kiss.

After yesterday, it's safe to say our relationship transformed. Something about it feels a lot more real. The barriers that were once up have collapsed and left space for everything between us to finally evolve and unite. Everything is just so real now.

"I finished enough work yesterday to take today off. It was supposed to be to talk but we did a lot of that yesterday. Yesterday you brought up needing to see a brother of yours."

He leaves the question unasked but I know what he means. And the answer is yes. I need to go see my brother and now is as good a time as any. The wound on my neck hasn't even healed yet, and here I am welcoming another adventure. I really must be insane.

"We should. I know where he is and he was expecting me a few days ago. I hope he's not too worried."

I consider reaching out, but I know that we've probably overused that form of communication in the last few days. I don't want to put any unnecessary risk on him if it can be avoided.

"When do we leave?"

"I'd say as soon as possible. I just need to shower and pack then we can get going."

As much as lazing around all day sounds appealing, I also know we have things to do and people to see. It'll be great seeing my brother again and perhaps finally getting all the answers that have been evading me to no end.

I also have to admit there's still anxiety that harshly clenches my chest. Last time I left the house, I ended up kidnapped by my psycho mother and arguably more psycho ex-best friend. There's comfort in knowing that this time Luke will be with me.

Actually, now that I think about it . . .

"Hey, Luke."

He groggily plants a kiss on my forehead. I guess he's going to rest while I take a shower.

"What happened to them?"

He doesn't need me to clarify. He knows exactly who I'm asking about. It's not like we're exactly far removed from that nightmare.

His eyes snap open, fury fuming like an inferno. There's no doubt in my mind his anger stems from the whole ordeal. Even if he's forgiven me, I doubt he'll ever forgive them. Personally, I'm more exhausted than anything and just want to put the whole thing behind me. It's just that my inkling of curiosity wants to know how it ended. The finale to this torturous chapter.

"They won't *ever* be bothering you again."

Well that doesn't sound creepy or like he did anything illegal.

"Luke, what did you do?"

He doesn't say anything, but his gaze has gone slightly unfocused. He's staring into whatever hell he sent them to. Otherwise, there's no explanation for his reaction.

"I'm not mad." I reassure him, "I have no pity for them anymore. What they did crossed a line that was an entire dimension too far. Whatever's happened to them, they deserve it."

Should I feel worse? Should I feel worse for losing my mother and childhood best friend? Should something terrible happening to them outweigh the lies, the betrayal, and the way they dehumanized me?

"I don't think it's something you really want to hear, darling. Sometimes, ignorance really is bliss. Sometimes, not knowing is the greatest gift that can be received."

"It's that bad, huh?"

The silent resignation in his expression gives me the answer his mouth won't. I can kind of guess what's happened. I can make assumptions all day, but at least these guesses aren't confirmed harsh truths. What do I actually want to know?

"Are they dead?"

He shakes his head.

"Are they hurting?"

Silence. And then, "In a way."

"In what way?"

"Nothing as meaningless as physical pain. At least not *too* much."

I never bothered to ask because it didn't concern me, but he has money so there's the possibility that he's involved with some type of underground activity, isn't there? Wouldn't their go-to be physical pain though?

Unless I'm wrong. But do I really want to know?

"Will they recover?"

He shakes his head again.

I don't know what I was expecting him to say. I don't even know what I wanted to hear. But it's fine.

"Okay."

He says that I don't want to know, but I'm getting the feeling that he doesn't really want to tell me either. And I have enough information to quell my curiosities. Besides, confronting what he's done means confronting the lengths he'll go to for me. What he'll do to someone who hurts me. I don't know exactly how far it is, and I'm still unsure of what that would mean. Now isn't the time to discover it.

"I'm going to go freshen up and get ready to go. You should probably dress for the outdoors. As much as I *love* seeing you walk around all dressed up and sexy, it might be a little inconvenient for our trip."

He grins and nods. It's not that he's a chatterbox or anything, but he hasn't spoken much today. I have to admit that I find myself curious why. I've seen him wake up a lot earlier than this before. Maybe I'm just reading a bit too much into this.

I gently lift his arms from around me and slip out of bed. He consumes my thoughts as I get ready. Not my kidnapping or Jackson or Chiaki or Lily or any of the numerous other things that should be haunting my thoughts

But damn if he isn't a better distraction.

CHAPTER 38

I reapply bug spray for what must be the hundredth time as we draw closer to the location. We've already trekked for about two hours, which isn't really that long, but I am an absolute *hater* of bugs, and I will forever stand by that.

I can't help the sigh in relief as I see the waterfall ahead of us. It's just as beautiful as I remember it. The trees and shrubbery are almost perfectly placed, as if someone spent weeks making sure that it would be absolutely meticulous.

When I was younger, watching the reflection of the moon and stars on the water always made our father's teachings feel so much less tedious.

I turn around to face my husband, who is dressed in sweatpants and a tight tee shirt. I have to admit I find the ensemble very, very pleasing to the eye. Maybe I should be dragging him on more excursions like this just for the excuse to keep seeing him like this. It really does things to a girl.

Pretending I'm looking back for any reason other than checking him out, I ask, "Are you alright?"

He smirks so I'm sure he has realized why I was actually staring at him. Damn him and his intelligence and arrogance and hotness.

"Doing just fine, sweetheart," he replies, very obviously playing along with my little ruse even though he knows that's all it is.

"Okay, I admit it, I'm checking you out." I huff. "At least you tried playing along, I guess."

He grins but says no more. I turn around and head to the waterfall. So, there are one of two places Jackson can be. We built a little cabin near the waterfall with our father and Chiaki. Chiaki, Jackson, and I came back once and transformed the little natural cave behind the waterfall into a little getaway of our own. We always used it when we needed to escape one of Akira's many tirades.

My first bet is on the waterfall. It's got better cover and a good vantage point to see if anyone is approaching. A cabin is a bit too conspicuous in comparison.

At the very least, we've reached the flatter leg of our journey so there's no more tripping over fat tree roots (and obviously having to expertly play it off so that Luke would have no idea), going uphill, or Luke's constant pestering about whether I'm alright.

"We're almost there," I call out.

Apparently, my voice carries a lot further than I thought and beyond even the noise of the waterfall because in less than a minute, I see one foot followed by the rest of a body as my brother exits the little cave.

He wears his jet-black hair longer—stopping at his shoulders. He always wanted to grow it out but Akira never gave him the chance to. She said she wouldn't "allow the world to think that you're some sissy-boy" every time that he brought the subject up. His face is as clean as ever. He was never able to grow facial hair there no matter how much he wanted a goatee. And he's still the same tall, lanky man who could never buff up.

"Lia, you're here! I got worried after it took you so long to get here."

I run to him, Luke completely forgotten, as I throw my arms around him. When I was younger, I never thought that a time would come where I would seek comfort from him. Back then, I never would have thought that I'd lose my best friend or older sister either. Life really is unpredictable.

He holds me in his arms, and I can feel in his grip how worried he must have been in these last few weeks. Hell, in the last few *years* that we've been out of touch.

Once he releases me, I proudly show off my left hand and the ring on it. "I'm married now."

His face falls. "Please tell me you didn't give in. Not after everything they put us through."

"No, I married someone else. I actually brought him here with me."

He looks up behind me, suddenly very tense with concern as Luke approaches behind me at the same steady pace he's been at all day.

Jackson softly says, "Lia, I told you to come alone."

"Well, about that." I pretty much word vomit the rest, "I was on my way a few days ago, slipped my guards and everything, and then mom and Shoto kidnapped me but then my very protective husband rescued me and has dealt with them. After all that, he insisted on coming with me because after that scare, there's no way that he can let me out of his sight. I should have told you before but I didn't because I didn't want to expose our only form of communication to anymore danger, and I'm sorry about that so please forgive me. I love you."

If I was less stressed, I'm sure I'd find the transformation of his expression a lot more amusing. Going from concern to anxiety to relief to concern to understanding, the emotional rollercoaster of the last few weeks speeds through him faster than light.

Same, bro.

I can smell Luke before I hear him—apple spice wrapping me in the warmth of a campfire in the fall. His arm around my shoulders weighs heavily on me as he gently pulls me into his embrace.

Jackson's still skeptical as he sizes Luke up. "So *you* saved my sister? The fearsome heir of the Moore's."

"She's my wife."

Luke's curt response doesn't aim to please, just stating the fact of the matter. He rarely uses more words than necessary when he's talking to someone who isn't me. And when he's upset, he can even slip into that habit when he speaks with me. I hope Jackson doesn't take it personally.

Jackson sighs, scratching the back of his neck awkwardly. He looks at me with concern in his gaze before returning it to Luke. It's like maybe he's trying to consider me in his response.

"Fine. Family's family and all that," he mutters.

I inwardly sigh but we know that statement's not true in our family. Our family uses each other to control one people in the name of "helping" or "protecting" the family. It's ludicrous and so very wrong—so very damaging. At the very least, it leads to kidnapping someone because they dare to defy someone who's deigned superior.

"Shouldn't we be getting inside? I have to admit I miss my big brother's cooking."

Jackson's always been a good cook. The only reason mom allowed him to indulge in the hobby was the hope of it making a prospective wife happy.

I push by him, welcoming myself into the little haven we created behind the waterfall. What used to be a sweet escape has become a necessity, but I'm more than proud of the fact it's provided my brother shelter when he needed it most.

There's a new large wall with a door at the entrance of the cave. Opening it, my eyes are blessed as I enter. He's added more structures for shelving and is using fairy lights to make the place look magical.

It actually looks like a normal home. The entryway has a carpet and small loveseats on either side of the little foyer with a table in the center. I'm curious how he managed to get furniture in here without exposing his location to anyone.

I follow the fairy lights into the tunnels branching off from the main entrance. He must have explored deeper in to make this place a true home. Makes sense. I doubt he'd want to sleep right at the entrance.

"You've fixed this place up."

"Added the wall to limit the sound coming in from the falls," he replies.

I nod in acknowledgement, curious about the rest of the place, but also wanting to get to talking. We have a lot to discuss and I'm not sure how long it will take.

"That's great," I respond a little half-hearted now that I remember what I need to do. "But don't you think we should talk? Ya know, about everything."

It's probably rude to cut to the chase. I completely, wholeheartedly, acknowledge that. But it's necessary considering everything that's happened and the fact that I'm still not close enough to getting answers to do *anything*.

While I appreciate Luke's help, I can't rely on him to handle everything. I can't rely on him to claim the sweet, deserving revenge that may either darken or brighten my soul. I can't either save or put my sister and best friend to rest without being the one to lead the charge in this battle.

It's selfish. It's probably stupid. But that's how I think about it and that's who I am.

He sighs and gestures toward one of the loveseats—his expression tense with what I can only assume is hesitation or worry. Maybe it's even both.

I take a seat and am joined by Luke seconds later. Knowing what I need, the man places his large hand on my thigh and squeezes it comfortingly.

Jackson pulls the opposite loveseat closer so we're sitting only three feet apart. Whatever is about to happen, whatever he has to say, I can tell from his expression it's something heavy. It was something that would change my life in ways that I've never imagined.

I don't care though. I don't care what happens as a result. What I care about is the truth and what happens once it's revealed. What I *care* about are the people who deserve to have their stories heard.

What I care about is trying to fix the things that are so very wrong in this world without having to offer anyone else up as sacrifice. No more girls going missing and family's worrying about a sister or daughter or niece or whoever.

"Jackson." I sigh. "I know you're probably wondering where to start or how much to tell me. And I'm telling you right now that I want you to start from the beginning and tell me everything. I'm ready."

He nods and finally gives me what I've been seeking for what feels like an eternity. Answers. The truth.

CHAPTER 39

"How much of that night do you remember?"

I stare at him for a moment. Two. "Just tell me it all from the beginning as if I remember nothing."

I don't want him to pry for what I know so he can try to do that annoying thing that brothers do to protect their sisters. Ya know, half-truths to conceal a truth that can be hurtful. Now isn't the time for him to be trying to protect my feelings.

He stares at me before ultimately giving up—a sigh slides through his lips. "Fine. From the beginning."

If it were any other conversation, I'd smile at my small victory. But to smile is pointless when there's so much tension in the room. Cave? Whatever, I know what I mean.

"I wasn't there for all of it. I only got there around the time I held you back, but I do have information you were likely not privy to at the time. I'm just unsure of where to start," he says. "For starters, while

Chiaki was defending you, her injury was not your fault."

My lips feel like glue are holding them shut. I have no way to reply to that. How could it not be my fault? She was standing there arguing with mom because she was defending *me*. She was trying to make sure I was not forced to marry someone.

Everything was my fault. I don't understand how he doesn't see it.

My body trembles. With what, I can't say. Trepidation? Guilt? Anger?

Before I can spiral, a warm hand envelopes mine, grounding me in the present. A reminder I'm here for a reason. That if I collapse before I hear the answers I so hope for, then I may not survive the entire story.

Luke speaks to me in the most serious tone I've ever heard from him. "If you want to be the solution, you need to understand the problem."

He's right. That's why I'm here. To understand the problem. To paint a picture no matter how dreary the colors.

"Continue," I say. "I need to know."

Jackson nods. "You know how all our siblings are married. None have married someone that they love. They married who they were told to marry for what our blood carries. Something I doubt you'll even believe. I barely believed it when I was first told."

Luke stiffens before squeezing my hand again. I guess maybe he's shocked that *everyone* was forcibly married off by our mother. I mean, I'm not really surprised she'd use us to achieve some greater purpose for herself. Or maybe it's this idea of special blood that my brother brought up. Being married to some sort of mutant would impact his life.

"Our world, Aurelia, isn't what you think it is. It's filled with things you can't even imagine. Things that will do *anything* to gain power in similar and worse ways than our mother. Things that want *us* because we carry latent genes in us that, even the slim *possibility* of our offspring presenting it in a dominant way makes us extraordinarily valuable." He pauses as if he's thinking very intensely. "Aurelia, I know you used to read all those fantasy books with the vampires and faeries and demons and all. The creatures from those stories actually exist. Well, at least most do."

He sounds serious. He actually believes what he's saying. But how am I supposed to believe what he's saying? What he says sounds entirely too improbable. Maybe all this isolation is finally getting to his head. Still, I agreed to listen, not accept everything that he says at face value.

"Our parents both carry the genes of very powerful races. Our mother is the daughter of a devil. She's a demon and our father is an actual god."

I can't help it. I know it's rude, and I know that I'm supposed to be sitting and listening like a good little puppy, but what the actual hell? I come here looking for answers and my brother tries to feed me crap like this.

"Lia, I'm serious."

I mean his face is serious. His voice is serious. But the words coming out of his mouth are so *un*serious that I'm not exactly sure how I'm supposed to react. Gods and devils and demons? Seriously?

I quickly raise my hand to cover my mouth, but it's already too late. I snicker. I guess it's a bit too ridiculous to maintain my self-control.

It takes all of my will to compose myself again.

"Sorry, sorry. I'm supposed to be listening, so listen I shall."

He takes a few seconds before continuing, "All of our siblings have been married off to different creatures for our dear mother's benefit. Yuto is the most recent of her victims. She married him off to some changeling on the other side of the country. Chiaki was supposed to marry some vampire who really made an impression on our mother. Mom probably expected Chiaki, of all her children, to obey without complaint. Instead, our dear sister refused to meet the man and defied our mother. Mom arranged for me to marry something, but I didn't stick around to find out what."

"So we're all just here to help our mother gain more influence through marrying whatever supernatural creature then?"

Influence from creatures that quite literally only exist in books and television shows might I add.

Can you sense the sarcasm—even in my own thoughts?

"Yes."

I slowly nod my head—not wanting to outwardly doubt him, but also not wanting to feed into what he's saying.

Anyway, the whole marrying us off for power thing is not very surprising with what I know about my mother. She's someone who will do whatever it takes to get what she wants. No pawn is off the table for her. There's really no deed that's too dirty. It's a shame.

"You have to believe me," he replies. "Mom's always only been after one thing, and our father has been out of the picture for years. I suppose that makes sense if he's a god, right?"

Jackson's hands are shaky as he rubs them through his hair. He even chuckles at his own joke, but it's so ragged and dry I can tell he finds no humor in what he says—probably only trying to for my sake. A for effort at least.

"You were different though, Lia. You were the child who showed the most prowess. You've always had the intelligence that's to be expected of a child of a god and a demon. You've always been athletic and tough. You never let anyone keep you down, even when it was the toughest decision. I know you've cried, but I've never been there to see it. Even that night, you wanted to scream and tried putting yourself in between them, but I didn't see a single tear until you got to Chiaki."

He's right. Even in my memory, I didn't truly start sobbing until I really saw the damage. Those tears had been so filled with sorrow and rage that my memory of everything after is still blacked out.

Doesn't mean that I'm some supernatural being.

And regardless, Chiaki didn't deserve anything that happened to her. I don't care if she didn't do as she was told. I don't care if she was trying to protect me. No one deserves to be put down and abandoned over something material and petty.

"What does me crying have to do with anything?"

"It's typical of supernatural beings to lead with logic—emotion an afterthought. Haven't you seen that with our mother? That night was traumatizing and you somehow managed to keep it together for so long."

"Jackson, that's just how some people are. Not everyone has some grandiose meltdown every time something like that happens." I pause. "And don't compare me to that woman."

He sighs. "How about this? Have you ever considered that your technological prowess and ability to hack are something extraordinary? I've watched you work. Seen you do things like hack into the school system to change Chiaki and I's grades. I couldn't even follow along with what you were doing. Consider this, maybe you have unnatural speed like our mom. Or you can manipulate time like I hear gods are able to."

"My skills are extraordinary, but that doesn't mean I'm using some crazy ability to pull it off."

"Then why do you think you were mom's favorite?"

"Because I was smart."

"You may have been the smartest, but that doesn't mean much. You weren't around for it, and I barely was, but you should have seen how she treated our other siblings. Michael was clever, but she didn't put so much effort into him. And that was *before* you even existed."

I don't want to keep going on and on in this back and forth. We can go on forever and it wouldn't lead to any of the answers that I'm *actually* after. Maybe I should guide the conversation a little bit.

"It's insane to think that others live under the assumption that our mother loves us so much. If only they knew the truth about how she sees her own children as little more than pawns."

Jackson shakes his head. "I wish it were as easy as exposing her. Let me finish the story before you make any rash decisions or plans without understanding the full truth of the situation."

I nod, gently squeezing Luke's hand. His presence alone is comforting, but his touch will always be my anchor.

Jackson says, "So that night, when that all happened, our mother was already mad at Chiaki, but when she stood up for you, she was even more angry. She was angry that both of her daughters *dared* to stand against her. She was angry that Chiaki not only defied her but also defended you when you defied her. To her, everything was a personal attack. While you were the most promising one, her most valuable pawn, Chiaki, wasn't."

He's right. Chiaki and I weren't the same person. I've always known how different we were but didn't actually think it was a big deal. Chiaki brought home decent grades, but mine were perfect. I've always been an extrovert and good at communicating, but she was always in her shell. I always took risks, but she'd rather take the safest path.

Akira never really showed any of us attention, but I always got the closest thing to positive feedback from her. While I at least got compliments occasionally, I can't recall a time when Chiaki got any.

"I know," I reply. "I think I understand what you mean. I don't think I realized it up until now because I always loved who Chiaki was and wished I could be kinder the way that she was. I always wanted to be able to understand and empathize the way that she did."

I never voiced it. We all knew it. Chiaki's always been such a good person. I guess that means I see myself as kind of a bad person in some sense then, right?

"I won't mince words, Lia. Chiaki was always mom's greatest disappointment. I remember once hearing mom complain that Chiaki was only good for being someone's pet. But when the time came where Chiaki would finally 'fulfill her purpose,' she declined. You know how mom is."

We all know how mom is. Mom is always looking for the next best thing. I truly wonder if there was ever a time in her life where she was actually happy. How can someone be happy in the present when their mind is trapped in the future?

It does still hurt my heart though. Knowing that Chiaki never did or even could have held a positive standing in Akira's mind. Even if she married the way she was supposed to, Akira would have still only looked at Chiaki as a pet. As an obedient being who was good for nothing else. Who even thinks of their children like that?

Luke draws small circles on the back of my hand with his thumb, and I have to admit that I'm grateful for the silent offer of comfort. It at least helps cool my head off so that I can listen to what my brother is saying without interrupting him too much.

Jackson continued, "That night, after everything went down . . ."

This time, I can see the pain in his expression as he remembers what happened. The horror in his eyes as if he were reliving the memory again in his head. Trapped in the despair of regret. I can tell he wonders the same thing that I do.

What if . . .

I look to my side at Luke, whose presence alone has a calming effect on me—even if it's not one hundred percent. It gives me the confidence to look Jackson in the eye and say something warm that I mean from deep within me.

"It's okay," I reply. "I know it's hard. But we can't stay trapped in the web of possibilities. It's too late to change anything about that night, Jackson."

His eyebrows drop in defeat and he releases a breath he must have been holding for an impossibly long time. Even with Luke here, this feels like a moment between siblings who grieve the same memory and same feeling of inaction.

"After you ran to her, I followed you. You thought mom was gone, but she wasn't. She came back with a warning. She told Chiaki that her disobedience, above everyone else's, would never be tolerated. That she could leave, but she'd better hide. That if she was found, she would be married off one way or another," he replies. "So we tried to tell you everything once she was really and truly gone."

Jackson sucks in a deep breath. "We tried to tell you about the marriages and the things that may come after us. We tried to tell you there was more to that childhood friend of yours than met the eye. We tried to tell you how to hide from these *things*—to cover your scent."

I stare at him. I don't remember any of this. I remember their lips moving. I remember them trying to get me to pay attention. But I couldn't focus on anything but the deep gash and the blood and the guilt. That *suffocating* guilt.

His eyes scan mine and I can see his expression drop. "You don't remember?"

I shake my head. "I only remember you guys trying to tell me something. I couldn't hear a word though."

Shock isn't hidden from his voice as he asks, "Then how do you know how to cover your scent?"

"What do you mean?

"I can smell manna root mixed into whatever lotion or body wash you use. It's what covers our scent so that we can't be sniffed out," he replies. "That's something we had told you that night."

Maybe I subconsciously remembered a few things and it got ingrained into my actions? I don't know. I just use whatever smells good.

Wait, he's talking about the way that I smell. Didn't Noah say something about it back on that fateful day?

I can't help but glance briefly at Luke for a few seconds before shifting my attention back to my brother.

I have to be reading too much into this. There's no way.

"Anyway," he says. "After that night, we all split up. I made myself scarce when I heard Mom had a woman she was trying to get into business with who had a daughter. I already knew where she'd go with it, and I wanted no part. I already saw how open defiance to her face went and decided to be a bit quieter."

"So then what happened to Chiaki? Do you know?"

He sighs. "I don't know, but I have a few guesses on what went down. And if it happened the way it did, then Lily's disappearance will probably also start to make sense."

Okay, finally, I'm getting answers not to only one, but both mysteries. Even if it's only guesses on top of guesses, an educated guess is better than an uneducated one.

"What happened, Jackson?"

CHAPTER 40

Jackson stands, pacing in front of the loveseat. From what I remember, it's what he does when he's thinking seriously about something.

"Chiaki was taken because the bloodsuckers were involved—the ones that she was supposed to marry. She was taken by someone who had to have connections with mother and sold off to them. That's what I think," he replies. "And I think that Lily was taken to pacify Chiaki."

This is all still so hard to believe. Bloodsuckers? I'm trying to remain open-minded and remember that it makes sense that there are things out there that I don't know of. Things beyond my comprehension. I mean, we haven't even explored half of our ocean and all that so it should be possible right?

Deciding that I should at least hear him out in full, I ask, "What do you mean?"

"Well, from what I hear about vampiric rituals, they all have to be agreed upon—marriage included. If Chiaki continued being stubborn, they would never be able to marry. And they couldn't physically harm her in any way to get her to agree either. Family is off the table because of blood relations and all that. However, the same protections don't extend to friends. No matter how strong the ties, they share no blood. No blood means no protection."

"Would they really threaten Chiaki with Lily?"

"Sister, they'd do a lot more than that."

I stay quiet after that, my mind swirling with thoughts. If what he says is true, Chiaki is alive but in a loveless marriage and Lily might still be alive because I'm almost one hundred percent sure Chiaki would never allow her best friend to suffer for her own stubbornness.

I'm relieved but scared and worried and want to find my sister. I'm thankful to have answers but still need to know what BB Media has to do with these "vampires."

And then it clicks.

Every story I know about vampires paint them as pale creatures. When I spoke to Margaret, she told me the men who would come around were extremely pale—and the women seemed sickly. I can only assume that the "vampires" in his story are the pale men that he works with. Though they could always just have one of the much more likely answers: vitamin deficiency, albinism, or even anemia.

This "Enrichio" person Colin is working with doesn't have any online presence *at all*. There's only one person aside from myself whom I know that would be able to completely erase someone's identity from the internet in such a way that it's like they don't exist.

That person gave birth to me.

That would be Akira's connection to them. I mean, yes, she's had business with Colin before. Yes, they've done business. But if she were to have an interest with the "vampires" who apparently were supposed to marry Chiaki, and they had a close relationship with BB Media, then all parties would have worked together to bring Chiaki in.

"What do you think happened to them now? Do you think that they're okay? Are they alive?"

"*If* they were taken by the bloodsuckers, at the very least, Chiaki should be alive. Likely trapped in a marriage and Lily would be kept alive for the purpose of keeping Chiaki in check. That's all I can think of," he replies. "Unfortunately, there's no way to know for sure."

AKA, we're just guessing. I know that we're only guessing. I know that we won't know for sure what's happening unless we find her.

"How do we get them back?"

Jackson is silent as he looks down at the floor. I know that look all too well. He doesn't think there's any hope in finding them.

"Jackson, we have to—"

"We can't," he cuts me off. "We can't and even if found her, there's no way we'd be able to make it out with her."

"But we're her family. They can't—"

"There are many things that they can't do, but it doesn't mean that they can't do anything to us, Lia. When she married them, if that's what we're assuming, they would have become her primary family, which opens doors for what they can do to us if we threaten them. Our families are allies until they're not."

I sigh. "We can't just leave her and Lily to suffer."

"What do you expect us to do?"

I think. I'm supposed to be smart so plans should come easy to me, right? I mean, there's no way Chiaki and Lily are lost to us forever. There's at least hope they're alive. If they're alive, they can be saved, right?

Blood rushes through my body. Full of vigor and hope and a new sense of determination. I can't believe Jackson seems to believe there's nothing we can do. Where there's a will, there's a way, right?

"Something," I snap. "Quite literally anything that's not giving up. We don't just give up on people that we care about."

"Lia, without knowing who or what they are, where they are, the extent of their power and, oh yeah, how to fight them without literally *dying*, what do you expect us to do?" He stops pacing to loom over me. "Riddle me this. Say we go in guns a blazing and die trying to save her, what will Chiaki have to live for? Huh? What's left for us? Or even if we were to get her out, they will *never* stop hunting us. Neither will our mother. And there are more than just demons and gods and vampires out there."

Thing is, I still am struggling to believe that there are even demons and gods and devils out there. I mean his confidence makes me think that maybe there is that possibility that there is something else out there. But if that's the case, how have we never seen any? I can't figure out how I wouldn't have picked up on it.

What he talks about is supposed to be fictional. The object of books and movies and the oddly dark tv shows that get so popular. There's no evidence or peculiar sightings that have been proven to be anything more than some prank. How can he expect me to believe something that's obviously so . . . implausible?

"Jackson—"

"No, Ari. I need you to listen to me and believe me. I know I can't shove proof of what I've been saying in your face, but you can't tell me that odd things didn't happen around us growing up. Open your eyes!"

I clench my fist, frustration washing over my like a tidal wave. I know what I want to believe and what I should believe, but both come with hard truths to swallow.

"My eyes are open," I argue. "I don't know what you're talking about, Jackson. I'm trying to believe you in everything that you say. Believing you means that I get to believe that my sister and best friend are still alive somewhere out there. But it also means that I've been living in this crazy, hidden world for my entire life without even knowing it and that vampires and gods and demons and who the hell knows what else is out there. Jackson, what do you expect me to feel?"

"I expect you to feel all the feelings, but I don't expect you to do anything rash. You're supposed to be the smart one."

I open my mouth, but nothing comes out. I *am* supposed to be smart. I'm supposed to make rational, well thought out decisions. I'm not supposed to be so thoughtless, right?

Luke interjects, "She's supposed to be who she is. I'm her balance."

I turn to look at him with wide eyes and my mouth slightly agape, his words echoing through my head. He's my balance, huh? I guess that may actually be the case. How utterly like him to speak only in my defense. Gosh, it makes him that much more attractive.

"Thanks," I mutter, unsure of how else to respond.

Luke smiles gently at me, his eyes softening into a caring gleam. He wraps his arm against my waist instead, pulling me closer.

"Continue," he says.

Jackson looks between the two of us, shocked. I assume he never thought he would ever see me so . . . comfortable with a man. To be honest, I never would have expected this either. I grew up with the idea of marriage being nothing but a contract where two people use each other for their own gains. Emotions were never mandatory. I don't think I've ever actually seen my parents be loving toward each other. That was the foundation of it.

I should give my dad some credit though. He showed some care toward us growing up. Ya know, until one day he disappeared without saying goodbye or even looking back. He just left us with our mother, even though he knew who she was.

"Lia, we can't face them. Not so easily," he replies. "And honestly, I'm not sure if I should allow myself to leave yet either. I don't know what *thing* mother has set up for me to marry. I don't know what abilities it has or the lengths that it will go to in order to reach me. I'm not sure I can risk it."

This time, I see fear in his eyes. Not pain or worry or caring. Fear. I believe someone is after him and there's no way that I can allow him to put himself at risk when that risk exists. Hell, he had to throw away his life and isolate himself.

"If this is how you choose to *exist*," I pause. "Then I'll let you. But this isn't a way to live, Jackson. It's gorgeous in here and you seem to be getting by, but not only is this temporary, it doesn't solve anything. You'll be running and hiding for your entire life."

That's not living. Not even close. What he's doing will never be fruitful. He would never have any other relationship of any kind with another person again. How can he want that?

"Ari, it's this or whatever they do to get to me. For all I know, they'll kill me for making a fool of them for so long. You're the only non-expendable child to mother. Don't you see that?"

"That woman is not our mother! She never has been!" For the first time in a very long time, I'm shouting my feelings, "She carried us and delivered us and that's it. A surrogate at best. We've never been nothing but a trophy and a pawn. No mother treats her children like that."

Jackson replies, "Lia, you know that's not what I mean."

"Then what *do* you mean?"

Jackson sighs. "Listen, she's been bad and everything, but she's still the only mother we've got. Wouldn't you feel guilty abandoning her in the end? Besides, what can we really do about it? She's a *demon.*"

I scoff. "Would *you* feel guilty? You're on the run because she thinks she has the right to play the puppet master of our lives. She thinks she has the right to force us to marry people or things or whatever the hell for reasons that benefit *her*. Not *us*, her. That's the truth. She's a selfish woman who will only *ever* consider herself. I shouldn't be the only one standing up to her."

"Lia, she's not a woman either. She's a demon. Regardless of our supernatural blood, we're still too human to ever hold a candle to her."

Right. A demon. That's what he's been saying, right? To be fair, she is crueler than anyone that I've ever met. You'd think that only something inhuman could be so inhumane. Call me crazy but I'm starting to think he's not just off his rocker.

"Fine. She's not human, but we can still stick up for ourselves, and she's also not our mom. Just a plain old devil."

"Demon," he corrects. "Devils are much worse than our mo—Akira can ever be. Demons are all the mutts of devils, but devils can only be born if one parent is a demon or devil and the other is either also a devil or a god. If and only *if* that child's devil nature beats out the other genetics can they be a devil."

"Okay," I respond, kind of confused.

"All of us are born from the union of a god and demon, meaning that each of us had the chance to become full devils," he explains. "Which is the *initial* reason we were all born. Now, our blood is the only of use to our mother. Even if we're not devils, we still carry the blood of a god and a demon who is a direct descendant of a devil."

"So her being the daughter of a devil means *nothing?*"

"I don't know. Believe it or not, both of her parents are devils. She was their only child and she never ascended to being a devil. That's at least what I know. I wouldn't be surprised if there was more to being a devil than I thought there was. What I've gathered is only from books I managed to steal from Mom—Akira—before I left."

"Do you mind if I borrow those?"

Jackson nods. "But first, while we're on this subject, *run* if you ever see a devil. They're easy to spot in their true forms with their crimson wings and eyes, sharp teeth, and their large curved horns. You'll understand once you read the books but . . . They are the most dangerous creature to us."

He doesn't wait for me to reply before standing and walking away. He disappears into the system of caves not long after. I'm pretty curious how he's organized this place for himself anyway.

Oookay. Well, that was . . . strange.

"Luke . . ."

He hums in response.

"Do you believe what he's saying? Ya know about gods and devils and stuff?"

He sighs. "What do you think about it?"

I'm quiet for a moment. I'm starting to believe Jackson. Not just because he sounds confident but because something inside me believes it. Something inside me believes that even my own intelligence might be the result of something inhuman. It would make so many things make sense. So many things that I've overlooked in the past.

"I think he might be telling me the truth." I hesitate. "I mean, it makes everything make sense. It makes the mystery behind Akira's enemies make sense. And what Shoto said before . . ."

"Now Aunt Akira, why haven't you told Lia the truth about this world?"

This has to be what he was talking about. Shoto knew this entire time. So did my siblings and so did my parents. Then that obviously means that I've been the only one left in the dark this entire time.

"What did he say?"

"Something about Akira not telling me the truth about the world. I thought he was just being patronizing or something, but that's not the case. He was trying to hint at everything I don't know about."

I had thought he was just being arrogant before, but he was serious.

"What do you want to do with this?"

That's a good question. I still want to save my sister, but this complicates things immensely. Maybe, if these *things* are with BB Media, I'll be able to negotiate, or blackmail, them into giving my sister back. I refuse to leave her with them. Especially if these "pale men" are *vampires*. What if they're using her to drink blood?

I can't let that keep going on.

"I want to keep moving forward. I can be smarter now that I know what's happening. Nothing is invincible. There has to be a way to get my sister back, and I will find it."

I will make sure that she never has to suffer something like this again. She deserves to live a life of happiness, not suffering.

"Not alone," he says.

"Not alone," I confirm.

With perfect timing, Jackson returns to the room with a tote bag full of books. He hands it to me with a look of worry.

"Be careful," he says. "Knowledge is power and power can be burdensome. You can't unlearn anything after you have. Once you know, there's really no going back. Once you truly believe, Lia, that's when life will seem to restart for you."

Restart, huh? Maybe that's what I need. My life has been pretty stagnant up until now. I can't consider what was before truly understanding anything that I thought I understood. I won't make this mistake again.

"Thank you." I take the bag from him. "I'll come back to visit."

I stand from the couch and pull him in for a hug. I hope to get another one someday soon and I hope that Chiaki can be a part of it. She always enjoyed group hugs, ya know?

"Don't be a stranger," he mutters, and I can hear the longing in his voice.

His voice is so shaky and emotional, as if he's about to cry. I know I can't understand what he's gone through handling this alone, but I can try to create a world where he can come out of hiding and live again. And until then, I can remind him as often as I'm able that he's not alone.

"I really will be back," I promise.

We hold each other tighter for a few minutes more, enjoying the warmth of our embrace for as long as we can. But it's getting dark and apparently, the dark is more dangerous than I thought.

CHAPTER 41

The walk back to the city was a comfortable quiet, completely different from the awkward silence that now surrounds the car that's taking us home. I think Luke is giving me space to sit with my own thoughts, and I have to admit that I'm thankful for the consideration.

"Luke."

"Yes?"

"I think I believe him. I hope that doesn't make you want to send me off to some loony bin somewhere."

"First," he replies, placing his arm around my shoulder, "I would *never* send you to a looney bin, even if I thought you were crazy."

Aw, that's sweet. That means he'll put up with me when my other personalities come out to play. No loony bin for me.

"Second," he continues. "I would think it's smart to be skeptical but open to even the most improbable possibilities. I don't blame you."

"And what do you think?"

He's silent for a moment. I look up to find his eyes staring out the window, his mind deep in thought. As much as it makes me wonder, I can only imagine the effect that it has on him. Especially considering that he's considered someone so powerful in this city. There might be people who can get to him due to supernatural abilities.

I've never felt so thankful for the obsessive amount of security he has. It keeps him safe for all those who might want to hurt him. If vampires are as portrayed in most books and movies, he'll never be able to outrun them or fight them off.

"I think anything is possible. I never shut myself down from the possibility of the improbable," he replies, looking down at me. "I took a chance at the possibility of our relationship, and I think it's paying off."

I turn away from him, cheeks ablaze. I haven't been so caught off guard and flustered by him in a while. I thought I'd gotten used to him already.

Still, what I know is that I can rely on him and trust him. He hasn't lied to me and always genuinely listens to what I say. He supports me no matter how crazy the idea. Regardless of how he's used to treating others, he tries to be kinder when I'm around.

I really, really like him. I think I love him. But, I don't know how to express that. Not when I've never experienced any care like this or have all these things weighing me down. But he knows what's happening and hasn't left me yet. That has to mean something, right?

Ugh, this is so confusing. I'd rather chase a chicken around a pen than think about what to do or not to do. Confess or not confess my feelings. He's already made his position clear and has never sent any mixed signals about it. I'm the problem.

I sigh. "Luke."

"Yes?"

Let's see. How do I say this? Maybe I should have decided that before saying anything. Like I can't just say, "Hey Luke, I love you," can I? We haven't known each other long enough.

But something like "I have a crush on you" feels so incredibly awkward and childish. Like those playground confessions in elementary school. Ugh, I'm cringing already just thinking about it.

"I just, uh, wanted to say something."

"Go on."

How am I supposed to follow up such a blasé response with what I need to say? I'm thinking: abort mission. But if I abort now, I also know I'll probably never get the courage to say anything again. What do I say?

"I know this is probably weird timing, considering how our last few days have been. Maybe it can wait . . ."

I'm such a wimp. I can't believe after tearing my mind apart, I don't have the guts to actually say anything to him. *"It can wait."* Really? What was I *thinking*? All I had to do was say the word, but now it's way too late to backtrack.

Luke's warm hand cups my cheek as he raises my head until my eyes meet his. It doesn't take an expert to tell that he knows what I want to say. I just know he's waiting for me to *say* the words.

"If you can't admit it out loud, then your feelings aren't strong enough, sweetheart."

My feelings are plenty strong, I'll have you know.

I take a deep breath in, count to five, and slowly exhale. Once. Twice. Thrice. And then I open my mouth and hope that this time the right words come out.

"Luke," I say. "I think . . . I mean, I *know*, I have feelings for you. I think it's love but I have to admit that I don't have much experience in that area."

I try to turn away, embarrassment fueling my shame. I've found something with someone that some people spend their whole lives searching for, but I'm unable to say it.

His hand holds me in place, trapping me in the deep abyss of his eyes. I'm sucked deeper by the second and filled me with more complex feelings than I can decipher. I question whether they're true love or just basic lust fueled by emotional attraction. It feels stronger than the latter, but how do I know?

"I'm sorry," I mutter. "I'm not good at this."

I feel like my confession should be a straighter answer than this. He at least deserves that.

"It's okay," he murmurs. "I get it. Rather than trying to rationalize everything, why don't you do me a favor and just start *feeling*? Everything will become clearer then."

The hairs on my arms stand at attention as his hand wanders down my cheek to my neck, down my arm. My tee shirt offers very little protection from the intoxicating nature of his touch as his other hand slowly follows the same path up my other side.

Am I breathing anymore? My heart rate picks up, racing faster than a mouse trying to outrun a cat. And my essence becomes buries deep into his soul because it has to be true, the eyes have to be windows to the soul.

Once his other hand reaches my neck, he roughly pulls me against him, his lips striking mine with all of his emotions channeled into a single action. I feel myself melt away as he takes advantage of my enraptured state and starts the battle of my tongue against his. Battle isn't the right word though. It's straight domination.

Slowly, I lift my own arms to wrap around his neck and pull him in closer to me. If he can use a kiss to channel the extent of his feelings, I can do the same thing. Who cares whether I know if what I feel is love or not? I know what I feel is way beyond what I've ever felt for anyone, and it's real and it means something to me.

I *hope* that he knows how much it does.

Ignited by the reciprocation of my feelings, he gets more intense. His hands slip under the hem of my tee shirt, touching the bare skin of my back as he pulls me closer and slowly lays me down on the back seat.

Is this how it happens? Is this how I become his once and for all? Body and heart and soul joined together? We're already husband and wife, and both have deep feelings for each other. This is the next likely step, and I am in no way opposed to it.

Slowly, painstakingly slowly, he pushes up my shirt, cold air brushing against my bare skin.

The heat of arousal blends with the cold of nature. My navel is exposed now, only a few more inches until—

He stops.

I'm sorry, what? He stopped? Why did he stop? Is he not as into me as I thought?

"Luke . . ."

His breathing is heavy, his jaw clenched shut. It looks like it's taking every ounce of self-control for him to stop. The warmth of his hands leave me first, pulling my shirt down as he gently lifts me back to a seated position.

"Why did you . . . ?"

Why did you pull away?

I know I shouldn't try to guess at his feelings—especially if my assumptions will only hurt my feelings more than his actual answer. But things were going *so* smoothly. I confessed and he reciprocated, and I did everything right . . . unless I was wrong?

"Not now," he responds, voice tight with restraint. "Not like this. This isn't the time. Soon but not yet."

Gobsmacked. Confuzzled. Perplexed. Each of these words describe the feelings that are swirling around inside of me. But really, the one that's leading the charge and making my heart throb is hurt. Hurt that he can reject me like this. Hurt that this all hurts so damn much at all.

"Why not?"

Did my voice crack? I hope not. I hope I at least sound confident or even defiant, but not hurt or sad or dejected.

"Sweetheart, please don't overthink this. I promise there's nothing wrong. There are just some things that I need to figure out."

His vague answer only sounds like an excuse to me.

Before I can stop myself, I reply, "Yeah, right."

I push myself to the other side of the seat and stare out the window. The hot sting of tears gathers in my eyes but I try to ignore it. I try to blink them away. In no way should I cry. Not right now.

Maybe this really is love. I've always been warned about how much it hurts.

CHAPTER 42

The next week is awkward. Luke has been trying to talk to me, but I've been avoiding him like the plague. As much as I care for him, I can't stop hurting. I still feel so dejected.

I can't tell you how awkward it is sleeping next to him every night. Most nights, I try to create some excuse to stay in the office, and I am more than a little sleep deprived. By the time I get back to the room, Luke's gone, too. Maybe he can't sleep either.

I spin in my chair in my office, a loud groan escaping. I have a never-ending headache that I keep taking ibuprofen trying to quell. The annoying thing just makes this whole situation so much worse.

I've been unable to concentrate on anything. I even hoped that Margaret would reach out so that I at least have someone to talk to. It's a little concerning, but I can't bring myself to dwell on it for long.

I groan. "Why can't I talk to him?"

Gosh, I sound like a whiny baby right now.

I know he's in his home office today, can almost *feel* it. He hasn't gone back to the office since the kidnapping. I can sense his eyes on me, likely relaying messages to my husband so he knows I'm okay.

I'm okay, I guess. At least physically, perfectly fine. Peachy, even.

Maybe I should go talk to him though. Ya know, if he's not sleeping either, he might have stopped eating, and we don't want that, right? It's my wifely duty, regardless of how awkward things are between us. Right?

I spring from the chair with newfound determination pumping through my veins. I've got this. And I mean it this time. It won't be like yesterday or the day before that or the day before that when I wimped out after standing in front of his office door for minutes at a time.

Confidently, I strut toward my office door and throw it open. Walking out, I instantly feel my confidence drop from my chest to my stomach.

Oh no.

Before it can drop any further, I half speed walk, half run to his home office door and lift my fist to knock. How should I go about knocking though? Do I bang on the door like I deserve to be in there or knock like a normal person? Or maybe like that one princess from that one movie when she was singing to her sister.

My fist hovers a few inches from the door, and I consider different knocks. I had no idea there were so many different ways before this.

Actually, why don't I go make food or something so I have a reason to bother him? That should work. Way better than walking in to go, "Hey, so I know that things are awkward, and I *may* have been ignoring you but I just came to make sure you've been eating and sleeping and taking care of yourself."

Yes, that's the route to go. I should go make some food. Oh and it'll take time if I need to order some groceries. Looks like this will have to wait.

I turn to walk away, my mind made up to procrasti—I obviously mean to, uh, be more strategic in my approach. Yes, that. Always come bearing gifts, that's what I say.

It looks like my luck has run drier than the freaking Sahara. The office door swings open before I can even take a single step away. My husband stands in front of me looking very . . . nervous?

"You're here," he says, sounding almost shocked to see me.

"Uh, I . . ." I start thinking of excuses. "I'm here but like not because of anything crazy. I just was making dinner cause ya know, I feel like it, and wondered if you'd also like some."

Smooth. I said something that sounds totally plausible, doesn't come across as worried. I'm just a solo girl doing some solo things for my own enjoyment and kind enough to offer my food to others.

Luke nods. "I'd like that. I was actually just on my way to find you. What do you say we cook together?"

Cook together? Have we ever done that before? I've made dinner for him and he's made dinner for me, but we never made dinner together.

Images instantly flood my mind of all those cheesy rom coms that have couples doing cutesy things in the kitchen. Like those hugs from behind or when they start feeding each other samples of the food or splashing water on each other all cute-like.

That's definitely *not* happening tonight. I don't think. I mean, my feelings are still kind of hurt from the other night and stuff, so things can't suddenly become so cutesy and comfortable. Actually, scratch that, I think I'd puke if things ever got like that.

My body betrays my thoughts with a smile and a, "Sure."

It seems that my mind and body don't want to be on the same page. Why is it so frustrating? My goal today was to talk to him and make up, so at least the kitchen should hopefully offer us a kind of distraction that makes it less awkward.

Okay body, maybe it's a good thing you decided to disobey me.

Before I can make any more mistakes, I take off down the hall in what I hope is a very brisk, very confident walk. Though I'm assuming I look like a giraffe trying to strut on a runway. That could be freaking *awesome*. It just might look a bit . . . ya know.

Before I know it, both of us are in the kitchen wearing aprons with a mountain of groceries in front of us. Apparently, Luke was planning on making food anyway and already had stuff delivered to the house. Though, with as much is here, I have to say he's definitely gone a bit overboard.

I see about five different sources of protein, vegetables I've never heard of, and way too many types of cheese. Was he planning on fattening me so he could eat me like that witch in the old children's tale?

"So." I ask, "What should we make?"

It's still a bit awkward with us maintaining a friendly distance as we stare at the groceries instead of glancing in each other's general direction. And by friendly distance, I mean we are socially distanced at opposite ends of the kitchen bar.

He shrugs, a casual gesture that is not common for him. "I was going to make all of your favorite dishes as an apology, but I seem to have gotten myself caught while on the way out of my office."

His casual tone doesn't even shock me regardless of how sweet the words are. I can't believe that he intended to make everything I liked in order to get me to forgive him. For some reason, I still can't even look at him though, and that reason is not the same as five minutes ago.

But, if we're confessing . . .

"I was also going to make your favorite food," I admit. "I wasn't sure how else to approach you."

Silence descends upon us, and we're drowning in an awkwardness that doesn't even feel right anymore. I mean, I'm always preaching communication, but I'm also failing at it. I've been avoiding him like crazy because I don't know how to express my feelings.

"Why don't we do something together? A stew and some sides. Whatever we come up with is whatever we eat," I suggest.

I'll admit that it's something I always wanted to do. Make a stew with random additives and hope that it comes out edible. I mean, stews are literally made for the purpose of using leftovers, I think.

"Let's do that then," he agrees.

We both start grabbing random ingredients and chopping them. I've made a bid for carrot and beef as my first additions. I wonder what he's picked. Considering that we've somehow ended up on opposite sides of the kitchen, it's a bit difficult for me to see what he's doing.

Not wanting things to go back to awkward, I shout, "How's everything going over there?"

He chuckles, the sound refreshing after having gone a week without hearing it. That's at least one step back to normal then.

"Sweetheart, you don't have to yell. The kitchen isn't that big," he replies.

"Don't you know that all chefs have people yelling across kitchens? Haven't you watched TV? It's always 'I said dice the onions, not chop them like a discombobulated chicken' and 'Yes, Chef.' Obviously, I'm head chef around here."

I turn to face him, knife in hand as I gesture up and down at myself. I made sure to grab the apron that said Kitchen Master on purpose. I'm always in charge.

He turns to face me. His apron says "I put my FOOT in it" with this hairy foot picture. You can guess who brought which apron.

"You and I both know who the Kitchen Master is, sweetheart."

"Yeah," I agree. "The one wearing this apron. He who wears the crown is the king just as she who wears the apron is the Kitchen Master. I don't make the rules, I just follow them."

Luke grins, shaking his head before turning around to finish his prep work. I laugh then focus on what I was doing, too. As head chef, I obviously can't have him beat me. Wait till he sees these epic knife skills.

The kitchen is filled with the sounds of chopping which I find oddly therapeutic as we continue prepping the ingredients for our stew and sides. My father used to make the best mac and cheese, and I'll also be showing that off today, too.

I peek over my shoulder, trying to see what Luke is preparing, but his large frame blocks the view. So rude.

Slowly and quietly, I take a few small steps closer, hoping to peek around. When that doesn't work, I try again. And that's how things go until I, the beautiful, gorgeous, nimble klutz, trip over my own feet and into Luke's back.

"Well." I chuckle. "How did you get over here?"

I look at him. He looks over his shoulder at me. And we both descend into a pit of laughter so deep that it feels as if we're children again. I mean, for him, it's a lot more reserved. For me, it's more like red-faced, gasps in between, teary-eyed, not pretty *at all* laughter.

Now I'm wondering why I let this whole thing get between us. I mean, I didn't even give the guy a chance to explain himself. He wants to apologize for something he really shouldn't have to apologize for.

Feeling just so foolish, I pull myself together with a few gaspy breaths as I try to regulate my breathing. It would be weird for me to apologize while I'm still laughing. Might make it seem a little inauthentic.

But I'm unable to wipe the smile off my face as I say, "I'm sorry, Luke."

"You don't need to apologize," he replies. "I'm the one who—"

I cut him off. "You didn't do anything wrong. I was the one who started jumping to conclusions and avoiding you. I didn't communicate with you and left no room for you to communicate with me either. Nothing can be fixed like that."

As I say the words, they hit my own heart. Everything I'm saying is true. I confessed to the guy and literally shut down ten minutes later. Maybe things like this are why people tend to get therapy after not-so-normal childhoods.

Before he can reply, I continue, "I won't do something like that again—ignoring you instead of talking it out. Sometimes, I need space, but a week is overkill. And I have to admit there were many times that I realized it but was too embarrassed to say anything to fix the situation."

He pulls me in for a hug and I have to admit that I really needed one after all this time. His smell and touch calm me, completely dissipating the awkwardness that I had still been feeling. This. This is what I like. This is the normal that I want.

He murmurs, "I should have also made myself clearer. There are reasons why we can't go any further than we already have. It's not permanent, it's just that I can't right now."

Not anger this time, but confusion takes over. What changes between now and later? We already live together and have these feelings. It's not like he has another woman on the side or anything, and we're quite literally already married. There can't be any beliefs in that regard that hold him back.

Instead of venting every thought, I simply ask, "Why?"

He sighs. "With everything going on, there are parts of me you still don't know, and I'm not ready to tell you about."

Ouch. That kinda stings. I've confided in him about everything, even the things I've never even really been comfortable admitting out loud. And there are things that he feels like he can't tell me?

I can't help the ache in my chest at his words.

"When all of this is settled, or at least not so chaotic, and there's room for us to truly explore each other, maybe then I can tell you," he continues. "But in good conscience, I cannot consummate this marriage that I've come to love and respect so much. In that, I would be disrespecting you, darling."

What can be so big that he can't tell me now? I mean, I guess I'm happy he wants me to have all the facts before we move further, but now I'm going to be anxious everyday what his secret might be. But what we have right now, it should be enough. I never even dared to wish for this level of closeness before.

"That's not a proper answer."

"In the kitchen, in the car, none of those were right. And the time still isn't right with your mind still trapped in what's happened with your family. Would you rather I take you when your mind and heart are both distracted?"

I guess he has a point. Besides, we just made up. I don't want to start problems again.

I push away from him and look at the kitchen around us. The chaos that has ensued since we decided to make dinner together deserves some serious appreciation. I mean we have chopped ingredients in bowls everywhere. A few discarded knives because it seems we both have the habit of switching knives as we go for sanitary reasons.

Even across counters, we have half-prepped side dishes and, from what I can see, it looks like Luke was also preparing dessert. There's some banana pudding in a glass bowl that likely still needs to go in the fridge.

Not wanting to succumb to awkwardness or any more pain, I lean over and swipe my finger through the pudding, wiping it on his cheek.

The shock on his face quickly shifts—a playful gleam in his eye being the only warning before I have an egg cracked all over my, or technically *his* apron.

"Oh, it's so *on!*"

CHAPTER 43

Last night was fun. By the time we finished our little food fight, I had been covered in all the ingredients to bake a cake, and Luke was soaked in water from when he'd asked me to "help clean up." We ended up taking showers before finishing the interesting mix of foods we'd blended together.

Waking up next to him today was the most refreshing experience—even compared to all the other times. Maybe it's the relief from us finally dealing with the tension.

It still bothers me that he won't confide in me. Knowing there's something he doesn't want to tell me because of "everything going on" makes me feel weird and like he doesn't trust me, even against my better judgment.

Luke pulls me closer to him, my back meeting his chest. Part of me wishes we didn't have the barrier of clothes between us. That I could feel the comforting warmth of his skin against mine every morning, knowing that it's a feeling that I, and only I, will be feeling for the rest of our lives.

Does that make me weird? Selfish? Whatever it is, it's how I feel. I also know I can't force him to tell me what he doesn't want to. Even if I don't really understand it and am not the most okay with it, I have to respect it and respect him. I have to trust that whatever is holding him back isn't something that will tear us apart.

"Good morning," I mumble.

He responds by nuzzling his nose into my hair. I can feel him smelling me without needing to see anything. The slow rise and fall of his chest tells me how relaxed he is in this position, not a thought on his mind.

While contrary to my racing thoughts, I should accept it as how he tells me his feelings. I'll wait for him to be ready to tell me whatever it is he can't say yet.

"You slept in pretty late today," I note. It's already 9:30 a.m. "Is everything alright?"

He lazily throws an arm across my stomach. "I haven't been sleeping well lately. Marvin probably already canceled my morning meetings."

Marvin and I don't speak too much, but I have noticed that he takes his boss's wellbeing into consideration. He always rearranges Luke's schedule whenever it's necessary for his basic needs and health. He once had a migraine, and Marvin cleared most of his afternoon schedule to make sure he wouldn't try to work through it.

He and I don't really speak much, but we're always on the same side as far as Luke's wellbeing goes. The man tends to neglect himself. That's why he has us.

"That's good. Why don't you stay in bed then? I'll go make us some breakfast."

He hesitates before grumbling something incomprehensible under his breath and letting me go. Something tells me he was perfectly happy staying here for the rest of the day. But he still has to work, and I want him to start his day on a good note.

I make my way to the kitchen, stretching my arms and neck on the way. Really good sleeps always leads to even better stretches.

The kitchen is the complete opposite of how we left it. I'm assuming someone called in some cleaning service after seeing last night's catastrophe. I must admit I'm thankful because the *last* thing that I wanted was to clean up that mess.

I hop over to the fridge, curious about what ingredients we have left. Hopefully, we have some eggs.

What greets me is nothing. Absolutely nothing. Not even a jug of milk. I have to admit, I didn't realize we used literally *everything* yesterday. I'm feeling a lot less appreciative of the cleaning service because we should have had leftovers for days once everything was put away.

Even the banana pudding is gone and I was really excited to be unhealthy and eat that for breakfast while giving Luke something proper to eat. Just because I have the energy to take care of him does *not* mean I have the energy to take care of myself.

Sighing, I look down at my cozy oversized shirt and shorts. I mean, I don't want to go back there empty-handed after promising him breakfast. We have a store a few minutes' walk away. I can just pop over and get some basic ingredients from.

Okay, yep. That's the plan.

I make my way to the shoe rack that's filled with all the basic, everyday shoes we wear. I take my warmest, fluffiest pair of boots in hopes it makes up for me not wearing any socks, and slip out the door, leaving it unlocked behind me since I don't intend to be gone for long.

Outside, clouds cover the sky—obscuring the sun from view. I have to admit it sucks. When I had checked the weather yesterday, it said today was supposed to be sunny. Of course they had no idea what they were talking about.

I complain to myself as I walk, "Why, oh why, does mother nature despise me so?"

Nothing but a dry breeze answers that question. I mean, at least it's not raining, right? I guess that would have made this situation worse. I'll keep that thought to myself. I don't want to jinx or tempt anything.

Something does feel a bit odd though. It's not like I expect there to be other people walking the streets right now. Our neighborhood doesn't encourage that type of behavior. Matter of fact, I'm pretty sure this store I'm headed to only exists to help all the employees at each of the houses get something quickly when needed. They'll sure be shocked when I show up there in my pj's.

But, even with that considered, it feels a bit quiet. Like that type of foreboding quiet that says something bad is about to happen.

I look up at the sky, hoping mother nature didn't actually hear my thoughts and decide to let it start pouring anyway. I don't have an umbrella or even a jacket. I am in way too good a mood to get myself sick.

It's cloudy, but not dark enough to signify rain. Still, this nagging feeling is familiar. Actually, it's *very* familiar. Very familiar in the sense that it reminds me of a really bad experience that I recently had and know can't happen again because my husband dealt with those people, right?

I turn around just to make sure that my invisible bodyguards are there but am met instead with a familiar sense of deja vu as an arm wraps around my neck. I grasp at their arms, but they've already got too strong a hold.

The fight leaves me as I lose consciousness. A single thought echoes through my head.

Not this shit again.

CHAPTER 44

I'm greeted with the same familiar pulsing in my head this time, but not the comfort of a proper bedroom. Instead, I'm chained to one of those rusty old chairs they only use in thrillers in a dimly lit room.

Who wants to kidnap me now? I swear if it's somehow my mother and Shoto at it again, I'm going to freak. Considering the conditions though, I'm not exactly sure what that would look like.

"It smells like she's awake."

A strange voice that's definitely *not* familiar seems to be alerting someone that I'm awake right now. Pro: I now know that it's likely not Shoto or my mother. Con: It's not Shoto or my mother who have me.

The large, reinforced door swings open on creaky hinges that make me want to flinch away to ignore the assault on my ears.

In step two men. The first is the owner of the voice. He has the build of an average man except there are black crow's wings on his back, and his eyes are solidly black—not a speck of white in sight.

I think back to what Jackson says, bewilderment capturing my breath as I try and fail to fight the tremble in my arms.

Those aren't costumes.

The person who really shocks me though is none other than the CEO of BB Media. Apparently, we've reached a point in our rivalry where I'm deemed enough of a threat to be taken by him. If it weren't a life and death situation, I'd feel honored. Instead, dread and terror gnaw away at the remnants of my composure

Part of his usually very human looking face has scales on it, and I'm sure it probably extends beneath his clothes—not that I can say that I'm particularly curious about that.

"Why am I here?"

I might as well make conversation. Pretend to be confident even though the reality of my situation is sinking in. The horrid stench of urine makes me want to puke. Only the knowledge that I'd have to live with the smell and sight of it for the next however long is stopping me.

CEO Scaleface looks down at me with a sneer. "You've been getting too close to things you shouldn't. Did you think I wouldn't learn you've met my wife? Or that you were getting in the way of my business dealings? They're still trying to debug our systems. You were really getting to be a pain in my ass until, and then your mother lifted her protection off you. Meaning you and that special blood of yours is free for the taking."

He paces in front of me. I'm not sure if he's trying to be intimidating or just has attention span issues. It doesn't matter what the answer is. It's already intimidating enough that he has me here, ya know, bound against my will without knowing whether I'll ever be able to escape. Luke finding me last time was some happy luck, but who's to say that Lady Luck will favor me again?

"You really don't understand," he continues, "how valuable that blood of yours is. How much people would pay to even have a *taste*. How much people would pay to breed offspring with it. What should I do with you? I can't waste such a rare, valuable resource."

My blood? Offspring? Is this guy going to try to sell me to whatever other mythical creatures I would be a fool to doubt any further considering the evidence in front of me? Is that his plan?

My heart rate increases, the familiar feeling of an anxiety attack taking root. The same heavy breaths I try to hide from my captor but fail to because there's self-control when I'm kidnapped by people who wish to hurt me.

"Ah, I see you're still being affected by pitiful human affairs like *anxiety*." He says that last word like it's the most disgusting thing he's ever said. "Your sister was the same way. All tears and sadness and anger and fear. *Pitiful*."

For just a moment, anxiety is forgotten and a deep anger rises from the pit of my stomach. How *dare* this man speak of my sister in such a way? *Pitiful?* No matter how timid she may have been, she was a fighter.

"Don't speak about her like that." Rage has almost consumed every ounce of rationality and self-preservation in my body, "Just because you'll never be able to understand the things that make us tick, doesn't make them pitiful."

"Oh really? Then tell me, did your dear sister ever make it back to you? Did your friend, Lily?" He stops in front of me and lifts my chin until I look at him. "I already know the answer to that. Eventually your sister learned her place and, well you'd be surprised what she did to that dear friend of yours."

"Liar."

I refuse to believe it. There's no way that Chiaki would ever do anything to Lily.

"You have no idea." His smirk shows no hint of emotion other than complete sadism. "Your sister has become truly a new creature. Something quite exquisite, if I do say so myself."

I nearly puke. I know he's probably just trying to get a reaction out of me and it's working. I can't help but react when he's using my sister as a weapon against me.

"You actually have quite a few brothers-in-law." He cackles. Yes, actually cackles. "A devious bunch, I must admit. I wonder how much they've *drained* her. I must admit I'm curious how she's fared with those royals."

A few brothers-in-law? The hell does he mean? How can they force her into marriage with multiple men? How is that possible? What do they see her as?

"My sister is a better person than you'll ever be. No matter what you do or say has happened, I won't believe you. It's clear you think our humanity weak, but it's what makes us who we are. We've always been fighters."

We never had a choice in the matter.

The CEO laughs again, throwing his head back like he just heard the best joke in the last decade. Nothing I've said is funny.

"You really think she's still the *person* you remember?" He chuckles. "Dear, I sincerely doubt she even resembles a human anymore. I'm positive one of them has already turned her. How else are they supposed to make sure that she can carry their kin?"

"One of what?"

"The vampires, of course. Those noble houses never could get along. That is until *she* came into the picture, and they *all* wanted their chance with her."

I turn away repulsed by the clear amusement he finds with the whole situation. He wants to see my reaction. He wants to see me give up and cry and beg to see my sister. I won't give him that pleasure. But he still holds my chin in place, his grip painfully tightening as his expression contorts into something rage filled.

"Did I give you permission to look away from me?" His voice is deeper, darker. Sinister. "Listen, I'm not your mother or your husband or anyone who will tolerate your disobedience. In my world, vermin are *punished*."

Vermin, huh? I've sunk so low that I exist in the realm of the rats who scour the city looking for scraps. Perhaps even lower. At least rats have the chance to run and fight when they need to. I can't fight or flight, and freezing means giving in, and I can't afford to do that either.

"Lucky for you, I've decided you would get one free warning. I'll be back tomorrow though." He drops his hand and turns to face the door. "You won't be getting out of here. So throw all hope away and let despair guide you."

He walks out of the room soon after without even a semblance of hesitation. All I can see are his shoulders shaking with what I assume is silent laughter. He's amused by this whole thing.

I release a deep breath after he leaves, sinking into the chair, not wanting to fight the restraints anymore. It's exhausting trying to appear confident or unfazed or somewhat strong. I can't do it. I don't even know what happens to me next.

"Sweetheart, I'll find you. I'm coming."

Once again, the comfort of Luke's voice comes into my head when I'm in a situation like this. Whether it's me losing my mind or my defense mechanism, I'm grateful and hopeful that maybe it will end the same way as last time. But the pessimistic snake deep inside whispers to me that things aren't going to end the same way as before.

CHAPTER 45

A sliver of sunshine peeking in from a crack in the wall is the only indication that morning has come. The night wasn't peaceful or easy. Sleep didn't come to rejuvenate, only collecting a few minutes here or there—too scared to actually stay under for any longer than that.

No one else had entered my room. "Cell" actually probably fits the bill better. But I could still hear voices outside. They weren't trying to be quiet at any point. Instead, I think they were intentionally being loud—intentionally trying to make sure I hear every word they say and delve deeper into fear.

And it's working. The sweatiness of my palm spreads to the rest of my body even though the room itself is cold and even had my teeth chattering at one point in the middle of the night. My heart rate has risen to a permanent state of anxiety beats per minute, and I keep trying to keep a conversation going with myself and cracking jokes to keep myself somewhat present.

"When do we get our chance with her?"

"The boss says we have to wait until he's done. He might even be auctioning her off and unless you have some secret stash, I doubt you'll ever be able to even *see* her."

Another voice chimes in, "Can't we at least have a *taste*? I hear her kind has very tasty blood. Not only that, but there's this rumor that it can awaken latent abilities within our kin. Haven't you heard about what happened with her sister and her husbands?"

Goosebumps fan out across my skin. The possibility that my sister's blood can be used to empower beings who are cruel and powerful is quite frankly more than a little nauseating. My body tries to reject the idea, warring with my mind which believes what they're saying might actually be true.

"Come on, you know those are just rumors," a voice argues back. "We haven't seen them since they came to collect their bride in the first place. I can't believe you guys are idiotic enough to believe a tale like that."

"But there's no evidence to prove it otherwise! We already know that both bloodlines are really strong. We also know she's the better sister."

"You know there are consequences for people who disobey what the master says. He says she's off limits so she's off limits. Complaining does nothing for you."

"Can't I grieve an opportunity? We all know we'll never have another one. Their family is the only one who's succeeded in reproducing, not once, but *seven* times." It sighs. "Not only are there only two girls, only *this one* and one of the other boys remain unwed. And I wouldn't risk the fury of a siren legion or the changelings or whoever the hell else they've married for a *taste*."

So it's true then. My brothers have all married other *things*, too. Things I enjoyed reading about because they were oh so hot and sexy and mysterious. These things now have me captured and at their mercy.

Remind me to get rid of my entire collection of dark romances and romantasy books if I ever get out of here.

"There's nothing to grieve because you never had her. It's none of your concern."

There's a grunt, but eventually they walk away. Conversations like that are commonplace around here, apparently. All night, there were similar interactions outside, never really talking about my siblings but *always* talking about me.

How they couldn't *believe* that such a valuable resource was married off to some human rather than to someone who could *use* me to the fullest. They couldn't believe I've caused so much stress to beings who are better than me and much more deserving of respect.

There were talks of what happens to me next. Whether I'll be brought by someone who wants to eat me (I'm not sure if they mean my blood or my actual body) or someone who wants to use me as a surrogate of sorts (a nicer way of phrasing the things they'd said).

Some even stood outside of the door teasing me. Saying how they were sure I would taste good. Saying they were sure that I could learn to please their kind no matter how long I've "paraded around as human." Saying that maybe, just *maybe* they'll disregard the rules to have their way with me first.

No wonder I've been stuck in this state of anxiety. No wonder I anxiously turn my head every time I hear the slightest noise that's out of place. Most of the time, they turn out to be creatures that kind of remind me of rats but are a bit too cute and shy.

"Is she awake?"

I know that voice. I guess he's back again to torment me or whatever it is that he's doing. Doesn't he have more important things to do? Hell, he has a pregnant wife. I would *love* to know what her position on this whole thing. Is she also being used? Does she not know anything about what's happening here?

"Yes, sir. She hasn't slept much."

"Good. Open the door for me."

The door creaks open, that same feeling streaking through my body and making me feel a lot more on edge. It means that the lion is once again entering the den. And I, unfortunately, get to play the part of the prey.

As the same crow-winged man shuts the door behind him, the CEO stalks toward me, a horrid grin on his face. It's like he has already formulated something in his head and is excited to do whatever it is.

My heart rate doesn't slow, but it skips a beat as he circles the chair once, then twice, stopping behind me in a blind spot. Anxiety grabs me by the throat only seconds before his hand does.

I can't breathe nor can I lift my hand to try to defend myself. To try to make it stop. Tears have started their desperate descent down my face as my lungs try to grasp at any bit of fresh air.

"Listen well," he murmurs. "I've been doing some thinking and thought that auctioning you off is probably the *best* idea that I've ever had. But there's something else I want to do. For your arrogance in thinking that you, a little *half-breed*, could take me down and trying to turn my *wife* against me, I think you deserve some sort of punishment."

I see dark spots and bright stars in my vision and wonder if I'd go to heaven or hell if I died. As a half-demon am I judged the way other people are? I mean, I lived my whole life as a human. Even if I didn't believe in organized religions and stuff, that doesn't mean I'm damned, does it?

Before I can find my answer, he lets go, leaving me a gasping mess. I can't even grab my throat the way my instincts demand. My heart's racing uncontrollably, and I can't do anything but blink away the tears that won't stop streaming down.

"You see, I think I deserve that for myself. If I schedule that auction, say, a month from now, we'll still have time to play and leave you enough time to heal." His hand wraps around the back of my neck—not suffocating me, but causing pain in the tender area. "Aren't I *genius*?"

I have nothing to say. No snarky remark or even a serious response. I can barely breathe, so how can I reply to this psycho?

His grip tightens as his voice deepens. "That wasn't a rhetorical question."

I cringe, a yelp escaping from the pain in my body. How can he expect me to speak after that?

I wish that I could say sorry to Luke. He warned me that unless I knew everything, I shouldn't be declaring war on *anybody*. Now I'm stuck here with these *things* who want nothing more than to hurt and use me.

He lets go of my neck a few minutes later, a sigh of relief slipping past my lips. "Fine. I forget how fragile you are. Maybe I should change that."

Change that? Like how? He can't mean changing *me* like what I heard was done to Chiaki. I am perfectly content being me and staying that way.

He paces around me. "I suppose I can start with stripping away those basic necessities that you seem to need. Let me think. Food, water, sleep. The others should come to me eventually, but at least I know where to start."

He stops in front of me, wearing a cruel grin as he looks down at me. His eyes are calculating, almost proud as they drink in what must be the very pathetic sight of me.

"This time isn't like last time with that sister of yours. There's no need to be careful. I can do what I want and experiment how I want to," he explains. "Maybe I can figure out how to make one of those sides of you dominate the others. But first, we need to defeat your body's pesky desperation to remain as human as the creatures you've surrounded yourself with your entire life."

I don't see the point of this whole thing. If he wants money, sell me. If he feels offended at how I've impeded him, kill me.

"Anyway," he teases. "I think it'll be best if we don't see each other for a few days. It's not me, it's you." He cackles at his own morbid joke. "I need you to be a little less—you, the next time we meet. Understood?" He doesn't wait for a reply. "Wonderful."

The other guy walks across the room, opening the door, the same old screech from the hinges making me cringe even more than usual. I wonder if it's possible that the hinges cry for all those who have passed through here. And I wonder if I will be another addition to their wails.

Only after they're gone and I'm alone in this creepy, dark cell, do I roll my neck, trying to get the ache out of it. Then I allow myself to cry even harder than before—restraint a foreign concept to me.

Do I allow myself to hope and pray and wish that someone comes to save me? Isn't my dad supposed to be a god? Shouldn't he be able to see this? Shouldn't someone, *anyone*, be able to rescue me?

CHAPTER 46

Days pass by with no CEO or no *anything* really. My whole body has completely cramped up and stiffened—only my neck has semblance of feeling left. I used to feel the bite of the chains digging into my skin, but now it just feels like they're one with my body.

My clothes are warn and dirty—my sweats drenched with urine and feces. Being a prisoner, I guess, means no bathroom and it stinks. Both literally and figuratively.

And my body is weak from the lack of food and water. At least I haven't had to poop in a while. I can barely hold my head up anymore with the lack of sleep. I can barely even think.

Since these *things* have such a good sense of hearing, every time they can tell that I've started to drift off, they start banging or the door, keeping me awake. No food. No water. No sleep. How long can I survive like this? Most humans can't stay alive for long without water, so I guess I'm not human.

Every day, I hear Luke's voice in my head, trying to keep me going and cheer me up. He keeps cheering me on and saying that he's getting closer but there's a lot of ground to cover. At one point, I even started talking back. In my head, at least. I'm too parched to open my lips at all right now.

I've had plenty of time to think. What's next? Wouldn't I be better off dead at this point? Dead would be better than this Hell on Earth.

I roll my neck, trying to maintain its movement, but each shift is harder than the last. It doesn't help that I'm sure it's still bruised from Colin's last visit.

The memory is enough to suffocate me all over again. My throat grows impossibly drier as my breathing ties to keep up. I gasp as if his hands are still there, but only the memory and trauma remain. Unfortunately, those two things are enough.

I'm still gasping for air when stars and blobs enter my orbit until I finally am rendered unconscious.

○-○-○-○-○-○-○ 🔒 ○-○-○-○-○-○-○

"Where am I?"

The words reverberate across the open expanse of my surroundings even though I swore I only thought them.

The environment is so blissfully contrary to my reality. A blend of whites and golds and blues paint the flowers and a sky that I've never seen before. Since when was there white and gold grass and flowers?

A gentle sea breeze brushes my hair out of my eyes and sweeps at the hem of my ankle-length dress. I definitely didn't have this on in that cell. I have to assume this is a dream, right? I've never had a dream like this before.

"A gift for you," an oddly familiar voice says. "A vision of my home."

I turn around quickly, looking for him. It's Luke. Even if only in a dream, I have to see him. I have to fall into his arms while he tells me that everything is okay and that he's coming to get me just like he did before. I don't care how he does it as long as it happens.

"Where are you?"

"I'm here." A gentle hand rests right above my heart, but he's nowhere to be seen. "I can't show myself to you now. This is all I can do until I reach you. Sweetheart, please stay strong."

His voice is more strained than I've ever heard it. Gruff and gravely and so filled with pent up emotions.

"I can't." Tears start streaming down my face as I shout, "I just want to die! Why do I have to keep putting up with all of this? Why does he want to keep me alive and punish me and sell me when killing me would be so much easier? I don't belong to this world!"

Luke sighs and invisible arms wrap around me as I collapse beneath my own weight. Beneath the burden of all the fear and anxiety and hopelessness.

"You have to. You do belong in this world," he soothes. "I'll be there. You've been much more help than you know. Now that I've reached you here, I'll find you out there. When you awaken, I'll be there. You may not know it right away, but I'll be there."

He lays my body on the foliage and holds me tight. "To get to you there, that means that I must leave you here. This is my gift to you. Now sleep darling, you need it."

My eyes close again, and this time, darkness answers.

CHAPTER 47

It's dark. I can't open my eyes. I'm in some half-lucid state where I'm aware of what's happening around me, but not present. It's as if my body won't allow me to wake up. I'm really thankful for that.

Especially when CEO Shitface walks into the room. Wait, how do I know he's in the room? He hasn't even said anything yet. It's like I'm sensing the room. It's like how I know the other guy doesn't follow him in.

"Why isn't she awake yet?" His voice grows louder as he continues his rant. "She was supposed to be kept awake until I came back. Why was she asleep to begin with?"

He paces the room, an aura of contempt and deep-rooted hatred hanging around him. I'm starting to doubt I'm the only thing upsetting him right now. There's probably so much more to this story than I'm aware of.

I can sense it as he strikes me in my back but I feel nothing. I sense water as it's splashed onto my unconscious body, yet don't feel that either.

"I swear, I'm going to *kill* him for letting this happen."

He stomps around the room for a few more minutes, reminding me of a child who just got their favorite toy taken away. Maybe he had, considering I'm not awake for him to torment.

He turns to the other guy, *thing*, in the corner and demands, "Do what you have to do to *get her up*."

He storms out of the room leaving me with the other guy. Wait no, now that he's gone, I think that it's not a guy. Wait, I'm wrong again. There is a guy but it's a guy within a girl?

"I'm so sorry, Aurelia," the familiar voice apologizes. "I really did like you. You were the only one who spoke to me like a person rather than as his wife. You offered to help me."

Margaret approaches me, gently rubbing my back.

The guy within a girl, it must be her. She's having a son.

"After our talk, things got so much worse. He found out I met you that day."

She pauses and I have time to consider. We'd only talked a couple of times and she considered us to be friends. I guess we were, weren't we?

"Then bad things started happening in his business, and he blamed it on that night we met. He asked if I was working to bring him down, too," she whispers. "He never went back to the nice man I knew. I knew that he was a bad man, but raising out child together and with good resources was important to me."

But I was supposed to just be using you. That was my initial plan. But I remembered how I felt when we talked at that dingey diner and I left with empathy for her. I made her a promise that I'm not even sure I'm able to keep anymore.

"As time went on, I started to see you weren't the monster. *He was.* And then I tried leaving him and . . ."

Somehow, I'm seeing her memories like I'm a detached being watching her memories like some kind of movie.

"You think you can run away from me?"

Margaret turns around, taking desperate breaths and trying not to trip over her own feet. She hadn't even bothered to pack anything more than a simple backpack, but her bump slowed her down.

He grabs her by her hair, and she yelps in pain. "Listen, woman. With my son inside of you, you have no hope of escaping. And you will die in service to me."

The color drains from her face when she realizes she was never supposed to survive giving birth and that the child would be subject to a life of living with a father like him.

"Why do you want me?" she screams. "You can have a child with anyone so why me?"

"Because you were stupid enough to want to do anything for me. Easy enough for me to get my hands on without having to sweat." He yanks her hair again. "And disposable enough that no one would miss you when you were gone."

He knocks her to the ground. Only after he can see that she's given up fighting does he pick her up and carry her back inside.

"Besides," he mutters. "You're the only one who's lasted this long. I will have my son, and you will give him to me. When he takes your lifeforce in exchange, you will then die like you were made to."

I inwardly flinch at the memory. I'm the reason why she can't live an easy life until the day she gives birth and . . .

But how the hell did those thoughts get into *my* head? Is this some type of ability that comes from having supernatural parents? I didn't do anything special. I just . . . I don't know.

"He dragged me back," she continues. "And since, I've become nothing more than a trophy to show the public and a servant behind closed doors. Even now, if I can't wake you, he'll likely take something away. He never takes away what the baby needs, but he will always make my life even more difficult."

My heart hurts for her. Truly. She's like me. Dragged into a world where she doesn't belong by circumstances she could have never imagined. Except she's least human.

I don't belong in this world.

Not in this world where it seems only pain exists. Where it's used or be used. I don't even have the power to defend myself.

"You do belong here, sweetheart. I'll show you. It won't be long now. But you'll have to do something for me. Awaken."

But I don't want to wake up.

"I know, but all supernatural creatures must eventually awaken their souls—who they're meant to be. Your time is here."

His voice brings comfort but I can't bring myself to agree with him. I know I'm not human myself. But I don't know if I want to wake up to become one of them. Look what this world has brought me. If not me, then look at *her*. It's nothing but pain and hopelessness and humiliation.

Still, something stirs within me. Anger and frustration and heartache rip at the very core of my being.

"He even cursed me," she adds. "I can't raise a hand against myself. Can't end my suffering or prevent the suffering of my son. I'll die bringing him into this world and can't do anything more to protect him."

I sense the tears streaming down her face as emotion clogs her voice, "I know you're asleep, but I thought with our friendship . . . Can I ask you one favor?"

Anything. She could literally ask me anything right now, and if I make it out of this, I will make sure it's fulfilled.

"Please save him. Save my baby when he comes. This is stupid, I know, but they say you have a very slight potential to be powerful, and if that means you'd be able to, you're the only person I can ask."

Wake up, Aurelia.

I wish more than anything that I could wrap my arms around her. That I could tell her everything would be okay and her child would be fine. But I know it's not true and it's not like I can move anyway.

But if I can, I'll make sure her child doesn't turn out like his father and that he has a chance at a life full of love and cherished memories.

Anger fills me to the brink and it's almost like invisible staples rip free from my lips as I manage to mutter, "I promise."

I'm unsure if she even heard me at first, but her shocked pause before she collapses to the ground in tears says it all. I've just added another vow to the list, but I will try. I can't promise results, but I can promise to try. Somehow. Maybe once I read those books that Jackson gave me.

"Thank you, thank you, thank you," she sobs over and over.

I can't say anything more as the darkness shifts into something else.

CHAPTER 48

It's like that other dream with Luke, except somehow different at the same time. I'm surrounded by water and I can stand on top of it. I'm literally somehow *standing* on water.

"Where am I?"

I thought the words were inside my head, but I seem to have said them out loud. It even echoed from an unknown source.

"Turn around."

That voice sounds familiar. Actually, it sounds like *my* voice. But I know I didn't say anything. I didn't even *think* anything.

"Turn around," the voice repeats.

I turn around and face me, but not me. I mean, it's me, but different.

She looks like me but has giant black wings that branch into red feathers. They're dark and gorgeous. Her ears have pointy tips, she has one red and one gold eye, and she has half a horn on her head.

"Who are you?"

She replies, "I'm you. The true you."

"The true me?"

Oh, I hate this place. I hate the way it messes with my head. My thoughts shouldn't be announced like this.

I look around. "Where are we?"

"Inside your soul."

Part of me is shocked, but after everything that's happened, I one hundred percent believe this is real. I'm not human, and I never was.

"Why are we here?"

"Because you need me."

Her simple answers are a bit frustrating, but I guess it's better than nothing.

Actually, I think I'm a little pissed off at her answer. *Now* she decides to make herself known? If she had made herself known *before*, then we wouldn't be in this situation. I could have saved Chiaki back then and none of this would have every needed to happen.

A bitter laugh slips past my lips. "I think I've needed you before now. Matter of fact, I wouldn't need you now if you came to me before."

"Do you only come when it's convenient to you?"

She blinks. "I am you."

"Why now? Just answer me that."

"You wouldn't have wanted me before. You wouldn't have believed me."

"It's not up to you to decide that."

"You're right. It's up to you."

She places her hand on my shoulder, the touch cold and soft. I don't get the chance to question her before memories rush into my mind.

Memories I don't remember. At least, not in the same way.

I hacked things that should have been impossible. Time *actually* slowed down for me. It was never a race because I was controlling time itself.

My parents gave us weird tests while we were growing up. Like racing dogs bred for racing, or lifting things twice our weight, or dodging things that were entirely too fast to dodge.

"Wait, is that why Dad always managed to avoid getting hit by Mom's knives?"

"I have shown up for you time and time again. You may not have succeeded at the highest level, but you were better than your siblings."

I always did pick things up faster than Chiaki and Jackson. I never thought twice about it, but things that came naturally to me had to be studied intently for them to pick up. I skipped quite a few years in school while they excelled but stayed on track.

I've always been extremely athletic—able to run, lift, fight better than any of my siblings—including the eldest.

"But your intellect comes with a drawback. You dismiss whatever you cannot explain. And you were never given the tools to understand what you truly are."

I see Colin's face and those of the beings in his employ. I see my mom throwing knives at a speed that can barely be seen, and my dad *catching* them. I see my elder brother Yuto accidentally breaking a thick wine bottle by squeezing it with his bare hand and calling it an accident when he was a teenager.

"You all have power, Aurelia. But yours is different. Unlike your siblings, you inherited the power of both races."

"How do you know that?"

"You never watched, but I always did. Your brothers inherited abilities from your mom. Your sister inherited your dad's abilities. And you . . . you inherited both of your parents' abilities."

I shake my head. "This makes no sense."

"Yes, it does."

I snap, "This still doesn't explain why you've never revealed yourself to me."

"Would you have believed me to be more than a dream? A figment of your imagination? Personification of the books that you like to read?"

"She's right."

I would have probably just written it off as one of those things. I never would have believed it was true without proof—proof I didn't get until this whole ordeal. But still, I feel like things could have been made clear.

"You could have tried!"

"Aurelia, you're too smart to argue with me like this. You have bigger things to worry about."

I sigh. "I don't know what to do. You're showing yourself to me, but . . ."

This place doesn't allow my sentence to remain unfinished. *"But what do I do with this?"*

I've been kidnapped for the second time in like a month, and this time, it's not as simple as the first. Luke said he's coming in that dream, but things are bad. He might not make it in time. I don't know what he can do against creatures like this. What if he ends up hurt? It'd be all my fault.

I clench my eyes shut, hugging myself as I try to control my breathing that's getting more and more erratic by the second.

"If anything happens to him because of the situation I put myself in, I'll never forgive myself."

"Then don't put yourself in that situation."

I look up at the embodiment of who I really am. Her forward words take my breath away as my trembling arms hug myself even tighter.

"Stop fooling around and accept it. Accept who you are. And I don't just mean acknowledging that you're not human. *Accept it, Aurelia.* That is the only way you can reach down and access the core of your being. The only way you become the you that you were always meant to be."

I clutch my chest as my heart starts rapidly pounding—a feeling of a hand squeezing it with all its might ripping a groan from my throat.

"Wake up, Aurelia."

I crumble to the knees as my head joins my heart in this very new, *very unwelcome* sensation. I can't help the tears that build up in my eyes, ready to spill over.

"Stop fighting it."

The rest of my body is overtaken by a raging heat followed by an icy cold and back to a raging heat over and over and over again. Tears freefall down my face as I curl up, trying to soothe the pain.

"What," I bite out. "What are you doing to me?"

"Awaken your abilities or suffer the consequences of fighting your nature."

Another voice pries itself into my mind. Its familiar warmth pulses with a sense of urgency. "Darling, awaken."

And then, I let go.

My body trembles from the pain of whatever is happening to me.

My head, heart, and even the blood in my veins foreign. I cry and scream and just when I feel like I can't take it anymore, it all stops.

I take a deep breath, wary of everything. Slowly, I move my limbs. First, I clench my fingers, then my toes, then my arms and legs until I regain control over my body. Then I pry myself off the floor, my body sore from the effort, but not in a truly painful way.

The woman is no longer in front of me. I turn around to find that she's not behind me either.

"Where'd you go?"

"Inside of you. Now go. Wake up and show them who you really are."

My body sways, falling into the ocean beneath my feet. On the way down, I get the barest glimpse of myself—of who I *am*. Just like the version of myself who stood in front of me earlier, I'm beautiful.

CHAPTER 49

My eyes snap open, but this time my body feels different and the world *looks* different. It's the same room and I'm stuck in the same chair, but I'm freshly energized and *pissed*.

I roll my neck—tension slipping away—and do the same with my shoulders, wrists, and other joints. The tension turns into excited jitters. It's like my body is ready to break free of the restraints forced upon it. My body feels unfamiliar yet like it belongs.

"Aurelia, your eyes, your back."

I remember the glimpse I got at myself. The wings on my back are an unexpected added weight. My gold eye sees the world almost in slow motion, and the red eye works like a magnifying glass when I move my head. My pointed ears hear more than I thought possible. I can hear conversations of people or creatures or whatever I should call them all over. My slightly sharpened canines seem bred to tear things apart. And with the single curly horn on the right side of my head . . .

I'm as inhuman on the outside as I am on the inside now.

"I know." I rest my eyes on her. "This is me. Who I really am."

Margaret smiles. "You're beautiful. Not like those others around here."

"Shouldn't you be a bit more scared of me?"

She shakes her head. "I think I know who you are. You've already helped me with the phone and advice. You had enough opportunity to harm me rather than help and you didn't. Maybe it's because I foolishly want to believe in some sort of good that can help me, but I trust you."

"That's an . . . interesting take."

I look around the room again, trying to get used to my new heightened senses. I have to stop myself from cringing away from the smell of my own filth as it penetrates my nose twice as much as before. Still, there has to be a way to stabilize this disorienting power in my eyes.

"Margaret, do you happen to know the way out of here?"

She nods. "They let me outside at least once a day for the baby's wellbeing."

I look at the door, an enormous surge of energy flows through me as I yank at the chains. Under the pressure of my newfound strength, the links pop—releasing me from this seat at last.

I don't know if it's this new body or adrenaline, but the malnourishment and exhaustion aren't impeding my movements at all. In fact, I'm doing better than before this whole ordeal.

Margaret's lips part—shocked by my strength, I'm assuming.

"That's amazing."

My ears twitch at an approaching voice. Colin's voice.

"Let's go see if that bitch is awake. There's an auction soon, and I need them to see that she still works."

If I'm strong enough to break those chains, then there's a likelihood I'm strong enough to get out of here with Margaret.

I look over my shoulder at my wings. The large beauties arch high, but I've never had flying training, so they'll likely be useless in this escape. If anything, my inability to fold them may prove to be a problem.

Aurelia, figure that part out later. You have to use your incoming opportunity to escape.

"Come here, Margaret."

Margaret shuffles over to me, and I kneel in front of her—beckoning for her to get on my back. I can't have her running alongside me or she'll never make it. Especially not with her baby bump. The strain probably wouldn't be good for the baby either.

"You asked for my help," I say, "You're getting it."

She carefully tries getting on, muttering, "So sorry, this probably isn't the most comfortable thing."

"It's fine. I just need you to be able to keep up and this is probably the only way."

It's a bit uncomfortable, but she manages to wrap her arms over my shoulders and her legs under my wings.

As if on cue, Colin slams open the door. I barely have the time to react as he points some type of gun at me.

I mentally face-palm at the thing I overlooked.

Of course he could hear me. I was able to hear him.

"You'll make me even more money now. You really are quite the catch." He tilts his head. "Do me a favor and drop my wife before I have to get rough."

"You'd risk hurting her?"

He scoffs. "It won't hurt her too badly. She's human. This is specially modified to only damage creatures from our world."

"Your child is of both."

"There are enough barriers to protect him."

"You're willing to take that ri—"

The shot shocks me followed by Margaret's scream, but not for long. It's as if the ability from my gold eye has completely taken over—slowing everything down for me. The shot has barely left the barrel of the gun, not even an inch from Colin.

I won't waste this opportunity. Especially considering that I don't know how long this ability lasts.

I close the gap between myself and Colin in about a second.

Okay, so my natural speed has been enhanced, too. Good to know.

I pull back my fist and use all my strength to punch Colin right in the nose. For extra added effect, I kick him in his most sensitive area. I don't know how much time I have, but it was necessary for my own petty revenge.

I push Colin out of the way and head into the hallway. There are guards of all species up and down the hallway.

Shit, Margaret's caught in my ability, too. She can't guide me. I have to think up a way out of here and fast.

I sniff the air—trying to find any scent that leads to outside. Water or trees or snow. Anything.

Very faintly, I pick up on the scent of pine. I don't think twice and run in that direction. With my nose as my guide, I run for about two minutes before I notice people around me are starting to move a bit faster. There can't be much time left before my power completely wears off.

I don't know how to use any of my abilities—whatever they may be. That said, once this wears off, I'll have to fight my way through a crowd with a pregnant lady on my back.

There has to be a better option.

Margaret's weight shifts on my back. "How did we get here?"

And that's the signal my time is up.

Shit. I think I'm getting tired.

"Hey, isn't that the prisoner and the boss's wife?"

"Margaret," I warn, "This is about to get a bit more bumpy."

I don't wait for her response. She has no choice but to be ready. As we keep running, the men block our path. Using only my arms, I push, punch, and slap my way through.

"Turn left!"

At least with her awake, I'm not just guessing our escape route based off some smell.

Something holds me back as I run past the next intersection— someone grabs hold of my arm.

"Hold on," I yell as I tuck my arms under Margaret's butt so I can roundhouse kick our attacker before he can react to me. I bet he thought my legs were out of commission with someone on my back, but with this new strength, he was sorely mistaken.

We're on the run again without a second wasted. But I can feel everything wearing on me. My limbs are starting to ache and the exhaustion from earlier is weighing my legs down.

We have to make it.

I run faster and dodge as we keep charging through. Attacks are taking too much energy, and I need to get us far enough away to hide. I don't even know what environment I'm looking at when we do manage to get outside.

"Next right and straight ahead. We're almost there Aurelia."

I heed her instruction—hoping I don't collapse before we make it.

Then I see it. The door. It's bulky, made from some type of metal, and I have to assume that there are layers of it. And I bet it's locked.

"Hold on tighter, Margaret. I'll have to bust through."

I feel her grip tighten as I speed up. It will probably take most of the energy that I have left, but I'd rather fight out there than in here.

As we approach the door, I prepare myself before ramming my knee right into the door handle. Luckily, this sends the door flying right off of its hinges. Unluckily, it saps so much energy that I stumble as I step into the snow outside.

The men standing guard advance with freaking *spears* pointed at us.

I'm already breathing heavily but try to get away. Margaret's fallen off my back into the cold snow, and even if I save myself, there's no way I can save her.

One of the guards taunts, "What are you guys doing out here? You're meant to be inside resting and ensuring the baby is born healthily." He points at me. "And *you're* meant to be human."

Margarets visibly shivering as she glares at them. "You guys know you can't touch me. Colin will—"

"The boss won't care what happens as long as the baby survives. Surely, you know that."

Unfortunately, she does.

Instead, while they talk, I'm fighting my exhausted body. I need that ability from earlier *urgently*.

Come on. Activate. Please activate!

I probably look freaking weird—closing and reopening my red eye like that will make my gold eye's ability work.

"Come on, let's get them. The boss will reward us for our hard work."

I shakily push myself off the ground—scraping my bicep against the tip of his spear. "Get away from us."

The other guard laughs. "You think that because you aren't human that you can boss us around? You're nothing special."

I'm trembling. From the cold. From the exhaustion. From the mental mindfuck this torrent of self-discovery has been.

"Nothing special?"

My blood rushes through my body. I'm tired of being helpless and resigning myself to the fate of death anytime it seems that I have no choice. I *have* a freaking choice.

I feel something deep inside of me fighting—*clawing* its way to the surface. Whatever it is, it's powerful. And it will probably take what's left of my energy.

And then the whole world fades away.

⸻⸻ 🔒 ⸻⸻

"It's dangerous, you know. And once you use this ability, your life will never go back to normal."

"I don't care."

"Your mom and your dad—both of their people will hunt you down. The first full-powered Nephilim to grace this world in centuries."

"So be it. I will do whatever it takes to survive."

"Just a few days ago, you were willing to throw your life away at the pettiest inconveniences."

I don't argue that they weren't petty, because with what I know now, it was. Giving up when my mom and Shoto captured me was weak. Even in saving Chiaki and Lily, I was willing to throw my life away if it provided a path forward because nothing else mattered.

But things are different now.

I wasn't choosing to sacrifice myself because it was necessary, I was doing it because it was easy. Because I thought I deserved it and I could use it to do some good. But I can do what I need to and live at the same time because I'm not a damn quitter.

"I've found my true self now."

"Is that so?"

An almost mocking laugh echoes across the waters, rippling the currents.

"Then unleash the power of the Gods on them. And don't regret it later, Aurelia."

⬤–⬤–⬤–⬤–⬤ 🔒 ⬤–⬤–⬤–⬤–⬤

With a barely human roar ripping from my throat, I'm nearly blinded by the gold light emanating from my own body as I collapse into the snow.

Everything around me is still. Not slowed down, completely still.

I stopped time.

Next to me, Margaret is also mesmerized. For some reason, she wasn't impacted by the spell. Maybe it's my own subconscious realizing that it's my turn to need her.

"Margaret." My voice is weak. "I can't move very well right now."

My whole body is pretty numb. I can probably move my legs once I get up, but I can't do much else. I can't even handle picking myself up.

Margaret trips over herself as she clumsily forces herself to stand.

She's shivering, which is to be expected considering she's only wearing a dingy sweatsuit.

I reach my hand out to her and she pulls me up. I use some of my remaining energy to help her when she struggles. My wings definitely make me heavy.

"I don't know how long this will last, so let's just try to get as far away as possible."

She nods and we slowly put distance between ourselves and the facility. I just hope I don't collapse before we can make it somewhere safe.

CHAPTER 50

"You're different."

I try to smile at Luke, but it feels more like a grimace. Even in this dream state, I'm exhausted.

"I know."

The beautiful environment we're in hasn't changed much. Still just as surreal as the first time that I came.

"You escaped."

"I did."

"You aren't questioning this dream?"

"I am."

"Even after everything you've been through."

I sigh, too exhausted to feel angry. "I'm not questioning its validity. I know I'm really talking to you somewhere in between our two consciousnesses. I don't know why we're able to do it though. Most importantly, I don't know what you are."

The sting of betrayal pricks at my heart. He had so many opportunities to tell me but he never said anything. It's clear he's not human and neither is his family.

"I'm your husband." He gestures to the world around us. "Ana this world is a subspace in between our two souls, if you were wondering."

I scoff. "Husbands are meant to tell their wives everything about themselves. Like what they are. And why we're able to communicate in a subspace between our souls of all places."

"We should discuss this in person."

"Then hurry up and come get me."

As frustrated as I am, I have no idea where Margaret and I are. Hell, I apparently lost consciousness at some point in our journey, which is how I ended up back here talking to my supposed husband.

At the very least, I'm confident he has the resources to find me.

"I'm on my way."

"You said that when I was still stuck in that place. And here I am having to rescue myself."

"It was harder this time. His people were a lot harder to break than your mother's people."

"I don't want excuses."

Though it does explain how he was able to find me last time. I'd say it's a shame he had to hurt others to get to me, but they weren't exactly innocent. Any person who helps wicked people are just as wicked.

I think back to the taunting words and vile threats that were targeted at me in that place. I know if they had the opportunity, they would have followed through. They would have tried to break me just for the fun of it.

"I know where the facility is, but not where you are now that you've escaped. We're connected, darling. When you wake up, you need to focus on that connection so that I can find you."

"Don't know if you noticed, but I'm kind of new to this whole thing." I scoff. "And don't call me darling."

As much as I thought I knew about him, I didn't know enough. How can we be as close as I imagined when I didn't know the most important thing?

"You're smart, sweetheart. You'll figure it out."

"Don't call me sweetheart, either."

"I've let you in, my love. There will be no more secrets between us anymore. I promise. Don't you remember what I said about what happens when I'm let you in?"

My heart rate picks up at the memory. He had said that is he let me in, he'd never let me go.

"Don't you think it's a bit late to let me in."

"My other half, now that I've found you, I'm still not letting you go."

CHAPTER 51

My head is *pounding*. I guess I overextended myself.

Next to me, Margaret is curled up and asleep—clearly exhausted. As she should be. She's pregnant, been stressed and pretty much held captive, and she had to help carry me to wherever we are.

I look around. We're inside some cabin under a stack of blankets. I'm grateful for the warmth they provide, but who's cabin are we in? The woodwork is well done.

I doubt Margaret could have taken me far in her state. We're still close to Colin. In fact, I'd wager this is his cabin. Which means we probably don't have long. I know Margaret's sleeping, but we don't have the luxury of time to rest.

I gently pat her arm. She groggily swats my hand away and mumbles something that I can't hear.

Okay then.

I shake her. "Margaret, you have to wake up if you want to really make it out of here."

She mumbles, "Aurelia, what are you doing here? And why are you waking me up?"

"Margaret, remember we broke out."

She shoots up to a sitting position, darting her attention around everywhere for a few moments before understanding settles on her face.

"Right. I brought us here because I didn't want us to freeze," she mutters, "I even had to keep the fireplace off so the smoke didn't signal anyone."

"You did well. But we need to figure out our next steps. Snow makes it easy to track people—and I'm sure Colin will assume that you ran to this cabin."

She rubs her stomach gently. "He has quite a few out here. I thought it might be safer to run to one at random."

"He has enough people to check all of them. I'm still too tired to fight—even without using some ability. We have to be strategic if we want to survive."

When we were outside, I remember it wasn't snowing. That means our footsteps are likely visible unless the weather changed in however long we were asleep. What bought us time is the fact that he likely had to organize units.

"What are we going to do?"

I never thought the survival skills my dad taught us would come in handy. If I ever see him again, I'll have to thank him . . . right after smacking the sense into him for not letting me know about my heritage.

"I need to try to reach my husband. He said something about us having some sort of connection that I think is like a GPS beacon that will lead him right to us."

"How did he tell you that?" Her brows perk up. "Do you have your phone?"

"I wish. He came to me in a dream."

Her expression deflates, but I see determination in her eyes.

"What do we do until then?"

"Staying in here is probably our safest bet. While I try to meditate or . . . something, you should look for whatever can be used as a weapon. If they find us first, we benefit more from worrying about them entering through the front door and having walls to protect our other sides. Out there, we'd get surrounded easily with little to no options for cover."

Margaret nods her head, stumbling out of bed and walking past me.

I guess it's my turn.

I climb on the bed and sit in a comfortable position. I've never necessarily tried meditating before, but I heard it requires being comfortable and emptying the mind, so here goes.

I close my eyes and try to relax my body. I take a deep breath in and push it out through my teeth a few times—forcing myself to forget the anxiety of being sitting ducks in enemy territory and the fact that I smell *atrocious*.

In and out. I ignore the sting of betrayal from my husband who, though we haven't known each other for long, should have told me he wasn't human. I still don't know what exactly he is.

In and out. I let it go—even if only momentarily.

In and out. I ignore the memories of my days in captivity under Colin.

In and out. I remember the feeling of connecting with myself. Becoming whole with the person I was always meant to be.

In and out, I somehow enter the space that usually only grips me in a state of unconsciousness.

"You're here."

"I am."

"And your awake."

"I am."

"I'm glad you're still safe."

"So am I." I sigh. "And I'd like to keep it that way, so do me a favor and hurry up, alright? This is what you needed to get to me, right?"

"Yes."

"I don't get how this works though. How is it that it works differently entering this state while conscious rather than unconscious?"

"It's complicated, and I can't stay in this state and come for you. So I'll explain it later."

"Right."

I hope I sounded as sarcastic as I meant to.

"We will talk later. But I have to go now. Stay safe until I get there."

Margaret dumps weapons on the bed. "We should probably prepare now."

"What's wrong? Did you see something?"

I look down at the weapons. Some kitchen knives, a fireplace poker, and a gun similar to the one Colin pointed at me earlier.

"I saw something in the trees. It has to be them. They keep these areas hunted clean."

Looking down at the weapons, I collect the knives. Kitchen knives of varying sizes—all heavier than throwing knives—but still more useful in my hands than hers.

"Grab that gun," I say, "It'll help you defend yourself better than any of these other things. Stay back as much as possible and only show yourself when you need to shoot. And remember, your bullets are limited."

"What are you going to do with those knives?"

"I've got myself covered."

As someone who used to watch her mother chuck knives of all types at her dad, I picked up a thing or two. I even used to practice for shits and giggles because I thought it was a cool skill to have. I never had the guts to try my hand at dodging them for the same reasons though.

I drop down and slink toward the window. "Stay low."

I stick my head up to see what's happening. There are about a dozen men in front of the door armed with spears, swords, and guns.

I drop down and take cover again before they can see me.

"We have to take out those gunmen first."

Their range will be a huge issue for me. Luckily, there's only two of them. But that means I'll have to take them out at the same time—or at least as close enough to each other that they can't get a shot off in between.

But there's only one way for me to be able to do that.

"On my signal, I need you to stand up and open the door. They might kill me, but there's no way they've been ordered to kill you, Margaret. I need their attention to be on you." I look her in the eye. "Can you do that?"

I can see the glimmer of fear in her eyes, but her mouth is set in a straight line of determination as she nods her head and shifts closer to the door.

I close my gold eye, testing the red eye's zoom capability. I can't control it very well. It zooms in, but I can't force it to stop without blinking. That seems to reset it. I'll have to be quick.

I peek my head up and focus on the gunmen with my red eye—a knife in either hand. Slowly, I push the window open and prep the two smallest knives.

It's been a while since I've had to throw a knife, but I'm sure I can do it.

Taking advantage of the fact that no one has spotted the open window yet, I turn my head to Margaret, nodding ever so slightly. She nods back at me, her hands shaky as she pulls the door open.

"So you found me," she announces.

"Come back with us. You know better than running. You have a duty to fulfill."

Whether its fake or not doesn't matter because her voice is strong as she replies. "I'm not going anywhere. Even if I don't live to hold my child, Colin will never have it."

The man laughs. "You don't have a choice. Now hurry before we have to rough you up. And bring your friend while you're at it."

The two gunmen scan their surroundings, seemingly looking for me. "She's not here."

The man steps forward toward her. "We saw two sets of tracks."

I did tell her the snow would give her away. Moot point now. I have a better shot now that he's moved up and out of my way. Before anyone notices me, I fling the blades straight toward the men. The speed at which they whizz through the air shocks me.

Both knives hit their marks in each of the men's temples.

Please be as fatal as it is for humans.

Both men point their guns at me before bright purple veins creep up their faces. They collapse.

I was scared there for a moment.

It's definitely adrenaline running me right now—my body trembling with pent up vitality. But I need this. I need the reminder that I'm alive and the instinct that leads me to wanting to survive.

The man who was talking before lifts his spear and launches it through the window. I drop as low as I can—my horn grazed as it passes. It doesn't feel like a cut, rather a blunt force impact that knocks my head back a little. The glass around me shatters. Luckily, it doesn't pierce my skin.

"Fine, we'll take you by force."

"Margaret, close the door and get down!"

She slams the door and dives to the floor on her side, just in time for all the windows to shatter. I guess that means at least one of them has some special ability like I do. Considering that they're not human, I guess that tracks.

"Aurelia, do you think you can do that thing you did earlier again?"

I shake my head. "All I can do is fight with what I have."

I peek my head up just enough to see through the window, flinging a knife at one of the men the first chance I get. He manages to dodge the blade's direct trajectory—it digs into his arm instead of his chest.

Damn.

I hunch below the windowsill look at the knives I have left. One small one and two larger ones remain. I need the larger ones for in case they get in but—

Boots land in the glass beside me.

Aurelia, you are not allowed to freeze.

I brace my hands on the floor as I launch a full force kick at his most precious region. People call that move dirty, but I say that nothing's considered dirty when your life is on the line.

He stumbles back but stabs a sword at me.

Shit. I have no space to move.

A loud bang goes off, and the man falls to the ground.

Margaret's voice is shaky as she asks, "Are . . . are you alright Aurelia?"

I don't look back, but I can tell she must be shocked at what she's done. I doubt she's ever needed to fight—much less kill anybody. I never thought I'd have to kill anybody either.

I ignore the pounding in my head and the shakiness in my arms. I force myself to stand and face the window just in time for another man to come in and tackle me to the ground.

Shit.

Another shot is fired, but the man on top of me still has control. And then there's another crack followed by Margaret groaning.

Double shit.

"You've been a pain in my ass, ya know?"

I look at the guy on top of me. His skin is the color of the weeds in my garden, a yellowish green. His black eyes are filled with hatred.

I cry out as he slashes me across the face just under my eye. "You killed Henry."

Another slash across my neck, though not deep enough to kill me. And I scream.

"Stop! Leave her alone!"

Bless Margaret's loyalty, but there's nothing she can do. There's nothing more I can do either.

"Shut up, you."

There's a thud, a whimper, and then Margaret's silent.

"Margaret," I pause, my voice raspy from the strain on my body and the man weighing me down, "are you okay?"

No response.

No.

The man pinning me snarls, "Worry about yourself!"

I feel the pain before I see the blade lodged in my wing. Fresh nausea fills my stomach—my wing feeling as if it's trapped in an inferno. And I scream louder than I've ever screamed before.

Another thud hits the floor close to us.

I'm dead.

I squeeze my eyes shut, breathing heavily as I call for *any* remaining power. Nothing listens to me. Nothing comes to me but agony.

The weight of the man fades as the pain start to morphs into a harsh throb.

Am I dying?

Then it hits me. A scent. One whiff of something out of place in this fight.

It's something familiar. Something apple spice and big and safe. Something strong and vivid and here for me.

Slowly, I pry eyes open knowing for sure I'm not dead. And there standing before me, is my husband. Except instead of his typical stature, he has crimson wings and eyes, two full horns, and sharp upper and lower canines. He's impossibly bigger with muscles more pronounced but that doesn't stop his stride from being . . . regal?

Jackson's words echo through me. He warned me about the single most fearsome species amongst us all. The species that half our bloodline is derived of. I know the truth.

And yet tears of relief stream down my face. Later, I can deal with the lies and whatever the hell this all means. Later, I can worry about my injuries. But for now, I just want to go home.

His arms are around me in no time and I feel a comfortable sleep coming, but before I slip away, I murmur his truth, "You're a devil."

EPILOGUE

"It's done, my love."

The princess glances up into the mirror in front of her. Her deep red eyes had once been green and filled with the naive glow of ignorance. Sometimes, she misses those days.

So many things have changed since then. She'd been put through the ringer, reunited with her best friend, and found love. But it wasn't easy.

It isn't easy.

"She knows?"

Her handsome husband steps up behind her, wrapping his arms around her stomach as he gazes lovingly at their reflection.

"She does."

"Does that mean that we can reach her now? Can we really bring her in?"

"That part is . . . a bit more complicated."

"Why?"

"Well, your sister seems to have found herself a rather powerful husband. One who has a rather tumultuous relationship with our house."

The princess rests her hands atop her husband's, her stomach roiling. "Are you saying I still can't see her? Are you saying that I never will be able to?"

"Not never, sweetheart." Her second husband joins them in their embrace, one arm wrapped around the first husband's shoulders and the other joining the stack of hands already on her stomach.

"Then when?"

"For starters, it seems our partner here has forgotten to mention a very important piece of information—the biggest reason why they'll be so on guard."

The princess sighs, anxious to hear everything. "And why's that?"

In the mirror, she watches her first husband glare at the second, but the second pays him no mind. If she wasn't so caught up on figuring out how to get to her sister, she'd find the interaction charming. In this case, she's grateful for the second husband's propensity to tell her everything—even when he's told not to.

"Your sister awakened."

The princess's lips part, eyes widening. "What did she awaken as?"

She had hoped that would never happen. *Knew* that if she did, her life would become exponentially more dangerous. But she'd been told that by vampire law, she was unable to bring in anyone who could contribute to their growing list of political rivals.

She wishes her sister was there so she could properly understand the situation and have their protection.

"What has she awakened as?"

Her third husband walks in, arms crossed as he steps in front of the mirror. "A Nephilim."

And the princess's heart drops. Of everything their genetics had the chance to become, that was the least likely and the most dangerous.

Her sister just became the single most desired and feared thing of every supernatural out there.

"We need to get to her."

"Princess, that—"

"I don't care how possible it is. No one's going to stop me from protecting my little sister."

She roughly pulls away from her husbands and strolls toward the door. She needs to find her best friend. She doesn't have to go far. The vampire woman leans against the wall just outside the room with a dagger in hand.

One look between them says everything. They both know, and they both had the same thought.

The princess can already hear her husbands hurrying to catch up with her, but she has no intention of letting them convince her otherwise. To hell with vampire laws. She would be their queen one day. She might as well start breaking the laws before she's responsible for making them.

"Let's go save her."